Under

THE

BUS

LORI BERHON

Copyright © 2015 Lori Berhon

All rights reserved.

ISBN: 0985384042
ISBN-13: 978-0-9853840-4-3

This book is affectionately dedicated to the termites, especially any
with whom I've been privileged to share a cubicle mound

CONTENTS

The CEO was already standing on the windowsill with Mr. Microphone, when we started trickling in. It was a great and perpetual puzzlement, how he always managed to be up there before anyone arrived.

The monthly address was held in the Sales Pit, of course. While few would disagree that a good sales force is essential to having a good business, there is some school of thought that equal value might reside in those who ensure you have a product to sell, and possibly even in those who keep the engine running smoothly. At Pinnacle, not so much. To Kippy, as he democratically insisted on being called by everyone from the President down to the woman who brought his tuna sandwich, Sales *was* the company. Under Scott Bell's leadership, this crack team operated on the premise that "if the client asks for it, we have it; and if we don't, then someone will have to make it happen." The result of this strategy was a robust flow of commissions for Sales and a hefty Sisyphean boulder for everyone else. Kippy often touted the company's 94 percent retention rate, a figure that never made sense to those of us who were apparently achieving it. Word of defections regularly leaked from the Front (as Client Care's section of the floor was sympathetically known). Even so, in light of broken promises and the fumbles of the over-burdened, under-staffed Fulfillment teams, retention was greater than any of us thought reasonable. Someone suggested that it was like changing banks or phone companies: once a company commits to a service and embeds it in their systems, switching is just too much of a pain in the ass.

Sales packed a bench of healthy young men with polished hair, polished shoes and brass-section voices. They pitched their game in white shirts and ties, suit jackets neatly smoothed over the backs of chairs or draped on hangers that were suspended from wire thingies that hooked over cubicle walls. Glenn Levine paced his cube like a caged tiger, swatting the air with a tot-sized souvenir Yankees bat whenever he hit a brick wall. When Roger Didilian was on a call, he always sat on the edge of his desk, squeezing a stress ball in one hand, addressing his chair as if the prospect sat there. Lesser stars remained anchored to their desks, headphones blocking out their neighbors' trumpeted claims, oblivious to anything other than making that sale. We liked to say that if a tornado blew a house out of the sky and landed it smack in the middle of the Pit, no one would even hit "hold." Sales only noticed the quarterly fire drills because the bells were too loud to talk through. Otherwise, it took something as major as a World Series closer to disturb their focus. However, the team was all rapt attention now.

The minute Kippy called out his first "move down!", any sales guy (or, on two memorable occasions, gal) who wasn't already working the line with a hot prospect, took off his headset and stood to face the sun. Some of us tried to stand near their cubes; these were good hiding places. Kippy spent so much time with the team that he tended to look past them at the monthly

1

assemblies. It wasn't healthy to have too much exposure at these events; you wanted to stay as invisible as possible. You'd be standing for at least half an hour, during which time you were likely to have to shift your weight from leg to leg or feel compelled to fidget or, most dangerous of all, feel an expression slap across your face too quickly to rein it back. There was an art to finding your spot for the monthlies. Those who lingered at the edges of the Pit would find Kippy corralling them in, calling out their names like a manic game-show host. You didn't want Kippy to call out your name; there was a very real danger he'd remember it later, when he was trying to coax questions from the audience, and then you'd really be on the spot. Sales cubes were prime locations for hiding in plain sight. For those adept at keeping a blank face, the big bank of file cabinets made a reasonable leaning post. The very best spots were by the cement columns, which were left over from the office's first incarnation as a light industry space and will likely be the only architectural note to remain in the building's next incarnation as a residential condo (floor plans available online). Their protective shadows supplied just enough visibility to debunk the idea that you were hiding. If you couldn't score any of these desirable spots, you stood as still as possible in the aisles, hoping to blend in with the other prairie dogs.

"So when the car picked me up at the airport, I couldn't believe this weather!" Kippy showed a third-grader's enthusiasm for a snow day. Those of us who'd lost an hour's sleep to shovel out the drive or trudged through hip-deep snowplow banks to get to stuttering mass transit were less chipper. "Yesterday it was summer and today this! I don't know if you knew this, but I just spent the last two weeks in..." He took what was, for a man who discharged words like machine-gun fire, a long dramatic pause. "...Africa!!" Any other speaker would have waited for a reaction from his audience, but Kippy always took the expected as given and rattled on to his next point.

"We went as chaperones with a group from my son Alex's school. They were building a library for this village. What a place! Didn't even have running water. This was for the Senior Class Humanitarianism Project, a terrific program they have, to give back to the community. It's so important for kids to be exposed to another culture, especially a disadvantaged one."

Those of us taking seven or eight years to finish school at night, while scrounging to cover the cost of anything beyond rent and food, were interested that one had to go to Africa to do this. Those of us who were African-American and would probably never have the money to set foot on that continent had other thoughts.

"You can't imagine how poor. Dirt floors. Our kids left their all their work clothes behind and you shoulda seen how excited these people got about a buncha t-shirts. Here we are with so much, taking everything for granted. And the people there, I'm telling you, they had absolutely nothing. But the spirit there! We could learn something from these people about how to be happy with what we have. They were so happy! With nothing! The last day we were in the village, they had this big party in our honor. You should hear the kinds of music they can make with just drums and singing. Okay, I know I'm not the most musical guy, but to me it sounded just as good as *The Lion King*. And they had all the paint on their faces and the animal teeth bracelets and all of that. Ha! They put on some show. Well, our boys wanted to do something in return. Someone had packed a basketball, so he pulled it out and we helped rig up a hoop. Who knows if they'd ever seen a basketball before in their lives, these village kids, and most of them didn't have more than a word or two of English, but our kids showed them how and they played a game....Let me tell you that was something to see. All these kids, African and American, playing together like that. I was really moved. I mean, that's what it's all about, right? So the next day, after we saw the class off to the airport with the teacher, Marcy and I and the other couple who'd chaperoned, we took our kids and went to a game park for the weekend. Because how can you go all the way to Africa and not see the animals, right? I tell you, this is a trip all of you should take some day. They were terrific! Magnificent! Seeing them in their natural habitat? Ha! Nothing like the Bronx Zoo! One morning I tripped, almost fell into what looked like a pothole. Turned out to be a hippo's footprint. Who knew they were that big? Enormous! But that's not what really impressed me. Here's what really knocked me out. They had us walking down this trail to get to where they'd parked the Land Rovers and, standing there, in the middle of nowhere, I see this....how can I describe it? This tower. I mean, it was taller than Walt."

Everyone laughed politely. This was an old joke. Walt Sacco wasn't outrageously tall, but he was taller than his boss of twenty years. Kippy used the laugh to take a breath. His round blue eyes were glittering now.

"Seriously, this thing was maybe twelve, fourteen feet tall. I thought it was some sort of sculpture, like those carved poles we saw up in Alaska? Only in clay or something. I asked the guide and...you're never going to believe this, because I couldn't. It was a termite mound. A nest. That's right! And not even a big one. The guide said they can go as high as 30 feet, easy. A termite nest, can you imagine? Think how small a termite is. In human terms, this would be like what? Anybody know? Gotta be like building a skyscraper a coupla hundred stories tall. Out of spit and dirt. Ha! That's what they build them out of, all these tiny insects, thousands of them, working together. It takes generations to build to that height. One generation dies, the next just keeps building right on top of them. Their skeletons or whatever become part of the place. They spend their whole lives building this thing, and they never see how it comes out. But the nest or hive or whatever wouldn't have succeeded if all those generations hadn't banded together and sacrificed to do all that work. I looked at this termite tower, and I couldn't help thinking about what we're trying to achieve here. How the goals we have as a business are so much bigger than any one of us. It's only by working together that we can build this powerful structure, this great company we're all trying to build. And if little insects can get this done, imagine what amazing things we can do if we all work together and don't give up. None of our competitors are growing as fast as we are. We will win this race! So give yourselves a round of applause, for the greatest managed office services company in the world!"

MONDAY

1 MISFITS AND BROKEN TOYS

The elevator doors slide open, a blink, a temporary iris through which we spy an office that isn't our own.

We don't usually think about it, but every place in the city is someone's place of work. Pass the open kitchen on the way to the restaurant toilets; stand on the escalator and catch the department store sales assistant running down with a stack of shoe boxes; wander onto the subway stairwell and spot a fluorescent-lit room full of battered desks. It's oddly unsettling, this peep behind the scenes. The places where we work are as familiar as home to us, but these...

These are exotic, unknowable, maybe even a little creepy. In that fleeting glimpse through the elevator doors, the alien space looms hollow, like an after-hours mall. Any strangers we see have no substance, they're mannequins whose only purpose is to illustrate that this place is meant for human use. The doors shut and the impression ends with a whiff of impossibly unused air, surely an olfactory hallucination whipped up by the trigger in our brains that signals fiercely "this is Other. This is not Us."

We get off the elevator on our own floor. This is what a door ought to look like. Our shoulders relax at the normalcy of everything here. Our coworkers are real people, each face associated with a name and a packet of stories and shared experiences. It's hard to remember the time when they were strangers, too and this place was as alien as Mars.

Δ

Judy Schreiber sat outside the glass doors of Pinnacle Management Services, staring a white stencil of what appeared to be an iceberg, trying not to giggle at the unfortunate monogram at its center. She couldn't afford hysterics, not today. This was her first interview in the 37 weeks since Trowbridge Wardell and Benedetto went belly up, taking with it not only her job but her 401K and the modest portfolio she'd scrimped to acquire. Thanks to Trowbridge's blithe assurances and employee statutes, she'd been left with nothing except the few grand that she'd prudently hidden in her old credit union for dire emergencies.

After 37 weeks, it couldn't get much more dire. The Unemployment checks, which hadn't even covered rent, had stopped after 26. Her precious safety net was evaporating at a frightening rate. COBRA alone sucked off almost five hundred every month, but you couldn't not have health insurance; at least not until it became a choice between insurance and food or rent, at which point, if it came to that, you gambled on staying healthy enough to not need doctors. This was a gamble she would soon have to take.

Since Trowbridge folded, she'd knocked on every door; she'd reached out to everyone she knew, multiple times; she'd posted on every online job board she could find and filed with every recruiter who didn't flatly turn her down. It seemed impossible that there were absolutely no jobs out there for which she qualified. She knew she had a solid resume. Thing was, no one was hiring for any of the things on it. Or so they said. Maybe people thought failure was contagious, that having Trowbridge on her resume made her some kind of business Typhoid Mary.

Then why was Arthur Russo so brave? And where had he found her? One of the online boards, probably. Not that it mattered. She'd be grateful to take anything anyone might offer, as long as it came with a steady paycheck. And whatever this Pinnacle place actually did, at least they weren't an investment bank.

Judy reminded herself to breathe. Russo's phone call was a lifesaver. She was going to survive.

She'd arrived a careful five minutes before the appointed time and handed her resume to the skinny young woman who met her at Reception. It was handed right back, along with a clipboard that held a job application asking for much the same information. Ushered outside the door to fill it in, Judy was tempted to scrawl "see resume." Instead, she copied out dates, names, "key deliverables" and "special skills" in the best handwriting she could muster and tucked the rejected sheet of fine cream bond away in her bag. No one could say she wasn't cooperative.

And then she waited. She couldn't tell how long she waited. She didn't wear a watch and there was no discreet way to check her phone. There had been one other person waiting with her, a very young man in a suit he'd either borrowed or never grown into. Was there such a thing in the world as a job for which you didn't need an interview suit? They'd nodded encouragement to one another. It felt like ages now since the skinny young woman, Chris, had come to claim him. He was still inside somewhere. Judy didn't know what that meant. It was hard not to look for meaning.

Wishing it were a more absorbent fabric, she pressed her hands against the hem of her summer skirt; a clammy handshake could be the kiss of death. She was going to nail this interview and get this job, whatever it was. She had to.

"Judy?"

She blinked, flustered. How could she be staring at a door and not see it open? She handed over the clipboard, and followed the girl inside.

Someone had neatly lettered "Testing Room" on the back of an index card and tacked it to the door, but Judy could tell that the space had been intended for storage. Under a glaring fluorescent light, it housed a double stack of cardboard file boxes and a single computer station. "I hope you don't mind," Chris apologized, with an oversized grin. "It's just a few tests. Everyone has to do them. I'll set you up."

Forcing her own fake smile, Judy hung her bag over the back of the chair and sat in front of the monitor.

Chris placed a few rumpled pages on the desk and reached over her shoulder to log in. "They're self-guided," she explained brightly; "but each has a time limit. You'll see in the instructions. I'll be back when you're finished."

The door closed behind her.

The tiny space was claustrophobic in the sudden silence. Judy tried clearing her throat to break the tension. It didn't work. She picked up the first page: some kind of confidentiality agreement. She hated signing anything without having a lawyer friend review it, but there wasn't any choice. Anyway, as Tom had told her time and again, these things were mostly boilerplate and didn't mean much. There was no pen on the desk. It was a good thing she always carried one. Was that part of the test, or was she being paranoid? She signed and moved on.

The next sheet held the instructions. Following step two (step one being a reminder to read and sign the confidentiality agreement), she loaded up the first exercise. It was a vocabulary test. Humiliating. Once upon a time, Judy had gotten a nearly-perfect score on the English SATs. Only a year ago, she'd been putting words in the mouth of a billion-dollar investment bank. "I need this job," she reminded herself, and plowed ahead. For nearly a third of the questions, none of the multiple choices were correct. Had anyone tested the linguistic competence of whoever'd written this test? Gritting her teeth, she pushed the thought aside and made the best guesses she could under the circumstances. Hardly surprising, the next test turned out to be math skills. Was she being considered for a job that would require her to calculate percentages and area? And if so, wouldn't they use a calculator for that kind of thing? When the test program timed out, three questions remained unread. She didn't know whether to laugh or cry. The final part was some sort of ethics test. There were about a dozen brief scenarios to read, each with two or three questions along the lines of "what would you do?" Only an idiot, a sociopath or someone actively trying to avoid employment would get these wrong. She breezed through, logged off the computer, and completed the assignment by sending a message to Chris on the internal email system.

Judy waited again. She sat, hands folded in her lap, considering what she was going to do when she didn't get this job. Teach English-as-a-Second-Language at the sleazy school from the subway posters? She'd jump at the chance, only the waiting list was already overflowing with downsized journalists and copy editors.

The closet door finally opened. "Sorry to keep you waiting like this," Chris said, with another meaningless smile. "Arthur wanted you to meet our VP of New Product Development, but he got pulled into a conference call. He's ready for you now."

Weaving through the maze of cubicles, Chris walked as quickly as she talked. "We're a growing company," she said, dipping her head over her shoulder. Almost running to keep up, Judy didn't see much of anything except that everyone seemed to be on the phone. "We've grown 20 percent every one of the last five quarters and we plan to keep growing."

"Wow!" You didn't spend a decade working for the overly-privileged without learning when a conspicuous reaction was called for. "That's so impressive!"

"It's a great time to come onboard," Chris burbled. "People start in one position and a few months later, boom!, they have a whole team working under them."

Judy felt a little confidence seeping into her spine. The girl would surely only say such things to a serious candidate, right? If Judy could make a good impression on this Vice President, maybe she'd land a job after all.

Nick Andreas, an affable man in shirtsleeves, rose only long enough to shake her hand across the desk. "Hi! Sorry for the wait. It was a conference call with our CEO. Not something you can easily get out of. Have a seat." His desk chair bent back almost to the wall. Judy recognized the posture as a favorite of all the golden boys at her old firm. Something about being a master of the universe seemed to oblige you to stress furniture to the breaking point.

"So, I've been looking at your resume..." He waved a printout, probably whichever version Arthur Russo had downloaded from whatever job site. Her application lay on his blotter, ignored. "Trowbridge Wardell," he sounded regretful. "What a mess, huh? I had a friend on the floor there, Brad Cushing. Know him?"

Judy shook her head. "It was a big place. I didn't have much to do with the guys on the floor. I was Communications and Corporate Events."

"That's why I wanted to meet you. It's an interesting skill set, especially with that theater background. Playwrighting?"

"Writing is writing," she shrugged, skilled at this feint. It had broken her heart to transition from starving playwright to respectable office worker, but she'd gritted her teeth and done it. She'd done it well. "Know your material, know your audience. The rest is organization. Whether it's a play or a consumer event, you're organizing deadlines, people..."

"Exactly." When he grinned, Andreas had a way of arching his eyebrows that made it seem he was letting you in on a secret. "I notice you did a newsletter for Trowbridge."

It was such a minor "accomplishment" that she'd almost left it off the resume. "Communications ran several. Mine was HR-to-employee. Promotions, benefits, holiday schedules, that kind of thing. What I really enjoyed were the Employee of the Month interviews."

He nodded appreciatively. "So how did you get from Broadway to Wall Street?"

"Broadway. I wish!" Judy decided it was okay to give a little laugh. "Never closer than Off-Off. It's a tough business. I had a few small productions, and won a couple of awards, but I was barely scraping by. I was temping, to make ends meet. One night, I was on a shift at Knickerbocker and ran into a friend from college. She was a junior partner there and passed along my resume. One thing led to another."

"Well, I'm not really sure where this might lead," Andreas admitted. "We're in a period of explosive growth at Pinnacle, which is why we're actively seeking people with experience at larger companies. I've only been here about ten months myself. Part of my role is conceptualizing what we need to do across the board to support this kind of growth. It's a whole new ballgame. We don't really know yet what skill sets we need; only what we don't already have. From where I sit, one thing we're missing is a Communications team. Right now our Client Care people are making stuff up as they need it, which is taking them away from what they do best. Also, we have custom software we use for practically everything, but nothing for training our new employees on how to use it. At the very least, someone has to put together this kind of stuff and organize some of the marketing events I'm planning. I see this. So does Art Russo. We're still trying to convince the others. I think your resume can help me sell it upward. That newsletter for example; Kippy's got a thing about addressing the troops and all that. So let me tell you a little more about the company and then you can ask me any questions that come to mind."

"Okay." Still trying to convince the others? Judy carefully pretended she hadn't just heard a door slam.

Andreas kept her for half an hour. She smiled politely and said things she immediately forgot because she would never need to remember them. There was no job at Pinnacle; it was a snark hunt. She shook Andreas' hand and he walked her to the door. She kept walking. She walked all the way home, a long way in heels. It was lucky her traffic radar was working, because she never noticed the intersections. She just kept walking and thinking.

Art Russo called sometime around noon the next day. At least he had the grace to sound apologetic. "I'm sorry," he said. "Nick and I have been trying to get this position in the budget and I thought we finally had everyone on board. We're going to keep trying to push it through. We only hope you're still available by then. Nick liked you a lot."

Judy took a cold shower, hoping it would clear her head enough to face yet another day of unemployment as productively as possible. She found six focus groups on Craig's List and signed up for all of them. If she booked one, at least she'd have grocery money for that week. What else could she try? Who hadn't she called? There had to be something out there for her, something to save her before her money completely ran out. She felt a mortifying nostalgia for the survival jobs of her theater days. She'd be pathetically grateful for any of them now, except they didn't exist. Digital Age lawyers could do their own typing and receptionists had to be young and cute. Maybe a private medical practice would consider maturity reassuring. She'd been told she had a pleasant voice. There were plenty of phone sex opportunities on Craig's List, if only she could manage not to laugh. Otherwise, grim as the prospect was, she might have to sign on for telemarketing.

She was stunned when Russo called again on Friday. "Can you come in today?" he asked, sounding breathless. "Around 3, 3:30? Nick's been selling you like crazy. We want you to meet the COO and the head of IT. If they all agree they can use you, share you, we have a chance."

A little before 3:00, Judy Schreiber sat outside the doors of Pinnacle Management Services for the second time that week, staring at the iceberg on the glass. A pinnacle, she corrected herself. Maybe an Alp. Or Kilimanjaro? If this manic about-face meant she might actually have a job here, there'd be plenty of time to find out.

Δ

Well, you know what it's like. You've been there. Maybe not at Pinnacle, but somewhere like it.

Mondays. You scrape yourself out of bed, exhausted from all you tried to do over the weekend, from trying to waste not so much as a quarter of an hour of the two days allotted for your real life. The life you were supposed to have is lived in tiny slices of time between each night's dinner and sleep, and in those two precious days you pay for by working the other five for someone else's dreams. Mondays, you jump out of bed the second the alarm goes off, afraid that if you lie there listening to the morning news you might accidentally slip back into sleep; and you promise yourself that next week, for certain, you won't screw with your biorhythms on the weekend by staying up all hours and sleeping in.

And you stand at the sink brushing your teeth and you pluck out that one witchy hair that keeps growing out of the mole on your cheekbone; and your stomach falls like you're in an old elevator, because today is your first day and, after ten months without a job, you're not sure you still know how do it.

You shave, which you don't technically need, not being a hairy kind of Red Irish, because you want to look extra neat for the first day; and you pull on the same pants you wore for the interview, the ones you bought to wear for those catering gigs that never really paid off, because they're all you own that aren't jeans and there's no point in shelling out another dollar until you've had a few paychecks to prove that this job is going to stick.

You shower in the basement, because Phil can't do the handyman thing anymore and you never learned about pipes; so until you can spare a few bucks for the plumber, the rattle from the upstairs bathroom will wake Phil and he needs his sleep.

You're late again because the nanny is late, as always, because she's young and it's Monday for her, too; which you understand, and that would be okay if only Angela could sometimes cover the gap, so the team would stop ragging on you for being such a doofus; but Angie's job has a career path and comes with perks that make yours look like a joke, so it always has to be you. On Monday.

A whole weekend wasted catching up on all the paperwork you never had time for last week, with eyes boring into your bowed head and chiding about missed drives out to the beach or up to Storm King; which would be easier to shrug off if you felt all that work was making a difference, but every single thing turns into such a battle that you wonder why they ever hired you if they didn't want to use what you had to offer.

You wonder if it would be any easier if you were going into the shop with Dad; they'd call you a VP there, but really it would only be the same kind of grunt work for as long as Uncle Ray was hanging on and you'd be in Minnesota while here, if nothing else, when you get out of work, you're in New York City.

You kiss Cathy on the cheek and she straightens your tie, looking proud but worried; and you tell her not to worry because this time you know you've found a place where your gifts will be appreciated, and things are going to be great from here on out.

Monday, with a long week looming ahead. But at least there are the others, your team, your friends: that guy in Compliance who can explain all the footnotes to *Infinite Jest*; the woman in IT whose ensemble played a gig at

Carnegie Hall on a bunch of Russian instruments you never even heard of before; the former pastry-chef who taught you a trick for pie crust; the comedian who's funnier than most of *Saturday Night Live*; the only other Capoeira practitioner you'd met, outside the Center, in your five years in NYC.

Still, you wonder how many more years you'll have to do this, week in week out, until your real life finally begins. Or you wonder how many more years you'll be able to do this, without losing your mind from boredom or frustration, without having a heart attack from the stress. Or you wonder how many more years you'll be lucky enough to find a place that will hire you, because you'll never be able to afford to retire, not when it costs almost as much to live as you take home and each time you put together a few bucks for your IRA, you break a tooth or your car breaks down, or your computer dies, or your sister is getting married and you need a gown and a shower gift and a wedding gift and a flight out for the wedding.

Or you wake up to the first week of utter terror, because only today does it sink in that they laid you off on Friday, and as awful as the job was, there was a paycheck coming in, and even the worst job is better than this horrible uncertainty that only makes you want to creep back under the covers.

#effingmonday

Δ

You would think, wouldn't you, that to get to work an hour earlier you only had to leave the house an hour earlier. Not if you usually take the 7:25 from East Norwalk. You see, there's no such train as a 6:25. The 6:36, getting in at 7:44, would work if the office were five minutes closer to Grand Central or if Kippy weren't such a stickler for punctuality. But with the office where it is, and Kippy seeing no reason why mass transportation should interfere with the pattern of his day, on Mondays Edie Brewer left for the station 90 minutes earlier to catch the 6:06.

All of Kippy's Senior Management meetings started at 8 a.m. Promptly. An early-to-bed-early-to-rise kind of guy, he was up every day at 5 on the dot, no alarm necessary. He jumped out of bed, gulped down his protein shake, burned off his daily 5K, showered, and hit the road. There was even time enough to skim *The Wall Street Journal* while breakfasting at his desk. By 8, having put in a solid morning, he was bursting with energy and at the top of his game. That was why he saw his key people then, to give them the benefit of Kippy at his best.

Edie's days also began early. Things were simpler now that Russell was away at college, but she still couldn't jump out of bed into the car. The aide wouldn't arrive until nearly noon, so Phil's breakfast, with a thermos of coffee, had to be set out on the bedside table for later. Millie, the service dog, needed to be walked and fed, and have an interlude of doggie playtime before starting her own working day. In winter, Edie often had to factor in an additional hour for shoveling out the drive; the rest of the year, she found some warped consolation in pondering this.

She used the commute to check the messages on her Blackberry and catch up on paperwork, tasks she would repeat on the ride home in an effort to clear her mind for the evening. 8 p.m. was late for Phil to eat dinner, but as long as he took his afternoon nap, he had enough strength to stay coherent and sit with her. For a couple of hours, it was almost like old times. If she had work left over, she waited until he nodded off at 10.

Not only did Mondays start earlier for Edie, but they came on the heels of a weekend's worth of cleaning, cooking and attending to all the householder jobs Phil couldn't do since the stroke. She woke up exhausted and dragged through her morning routine. It was all she could do to keep awake on the train; nursing her travel mug of coffee, she was often snapped alert by a splash down her wrist.

She made her way down from Grand Central on auto-pilot. It would be another hour before Megan arrived at the front desk, so she used her key to let herself into the dim office. Only her early crew, and one of Renee's, were bent over their work. If it were a pay week, Gene Siriano would also be at his desk, tackling the extra mountain of paperwork. It was so quiet that she could hear the keyboards clicking. Edie always had to resist the urge to tiptoe to the corner cube that served as her office. If anyone looked up, she'd manage a smile and a wave.

She locked her shoulder bag in the bottom desk drawer, and unpacked her laptop from its case. Booting up was faster since Conrad found her the new dock. Minutes later, her leather portfolio tucked under one arm, Edie picked her way towards the break room, looking away from the spooky cavern that was the darkened Pit. The empty room was clinically bright and sterile, but her nose was comforted by the smell of coffee. One of the early crew, probably Noble, bless him, always got a pot going before she arrived. She topped off her mug and fortified herself with a sip. The Monday polish on the refrigerator was enough for her to give her hair a pat and smooth her skirt before striding briskly towards Kippy's office. Once her weekly session of listening and nodding was done, she'd be safely propelled from crisis to crisis through the rest of her day. All she needed was to make it through the next half hour.

She hoped Kippy wasn't going to complain about Renee again. Renee Ochs was doing a superb job of building a professional Client Care department, but if she refused to play it soft and slow she was eventually going to cut her own throat. As much as Kippy liked the idea of hiring bright, driven people, he hated having anyone rattle his applecart. He somehow believed that he would become the next Michael Bloomberg or Warren Buffet by doing the same things he'd always done.

Unlike the Director of Client Care, who was the closest thing she had to a friend in this place, Edie understood this. Right from the start, Phil had observed that Kippy had never worked for a company as large as the one he hoped to build; that in fact, other than his father, he'd never worked for anyone at all. They weren't crazy about her being in such a delicate position but there was no other option: the chain that was taking over the inn, The Seven Maids, had their own management team; Phil's disability claim was still in review; and there weren't a lot of opportunities on the horizon. At least this Pinnacle business seemed solid. If Edie could make a place for herself while it was growing, it might even see them out until she could reasonably retire.

Edie knocked on the door and waited for Kippy's cheery "Come!" It troubled her conscience, but there was a limit to what she could say on Renee's behalf without putting her own job at risk. She must open by thanking him for this new assistant that he'd insisted she hire. She needed one. She only wished that she could have promoted one of her own kids to the spot. With a determined smile on her face, she turned the knob and pushed. If he raised the issue, all she could do was express her honest admiration for the rapidly rising professionalism of the Client Care team and remind him that Renee was from Texas.

Δ

Martha Moon stood five-feet-nothing in the flat sandals that barely clung to her feet as she raced to catch the E train. The shoes, she thought ruefully for the thousandth time since May, had been a mistake. They'd felt comfortable enough walking across the carpet at Macy*s; more than comfortable, in the glow of take-40-percent-off. On the streets, however, every bit of gravel jabbed through the thin layer of latex; and the fashionable ankle straps turned into ankle nooses, jerking the shoes in opposition to the rhythm of the flexing soles of her feet. They stabbed, like walking barefoot across sands that were littered with broken shells. Martha was stuck. Even on sale, they'd blown her shoe budget for the season. Too bad her toes couldn't hold flip-flops like everyone else's. There was nothing for it but to stick it out. Next spring she'd get a pair of Boothbays at the Bean factory store when she went home for her sister's birthday.

So much for wanting to look like a city girl! Even after all these years, you can take the girl out of Maine... Not true! Between her cute little apartment (about the size of Dad's boat shed) and the subway, she counted two giant drug stores, four cell phone places, and take-out food from five different countries. Her door had two locks and a chain, her shoulder bag was all zippered compartments, and she always carried a book to read while waiting. Shoes aside, she felt like a real New Yorker. She was a million years away from the silly git who'd jumped when Neil Dagget handed her a bus ticket all done up in gift wrap. Funny how it had been Neil's dream, but she'd been the one to stay. It took no time at all for Neil to see that, when there were seven million people to choose from, he was no one special. He ran back to Freeport. Sometimes when she went home she passed him on the street. He was Assistant Town Engineer now, married with two kids, strutting around like a cartoon king. She didn't regret losing him, not one bit, though she sometimes got wistful about the kids. She was 31 now and starting to wonder if she'd ever have any of her own.

Other than that, Martha's life was pretty good. It wasn't glamorous, but she was proud of what she'd accomplished. She'd gone to City College and night and finished her degree. The place she worked wasn't bad. It wasn't great either, but it wasn't bad. She was comfortable there, like being at home. She knew people. At one of those giant corporations, she'd just be another tick on the body of the beast. Here, Kippy said "hello" to her every morning. And with all the recent growth, her job might even turn into a career. Renee had made some amazing changes. If nothing else, she was teaching them how the big boys did things. Change was scary but someday, when Martha was ready, she'd have what she needed to move on.

The train pulled in as she was flying down the stairs. It was the good train. The next one, always twice as crowded, would come in five minutes and get her to work 15 minutes later. That made no sense, but the subways never did. She wiggled into the space by the connecting doors and pulled out her book. Marla had loaned it to her: *The Time Traveller's Wife*. Everyone was reading it; very romantic, they said, and a little different, just what you need on a Monday.

Δ

Dave Broussard was the only techie anyone had ever met who spoke fluent Sales. Then again, Dave could speak anything to anybody. "His gift of gab," his Papaw used to call it. When he wasn't much more than knee high, it helped set him up as one of those kid evangelists on the circuit, the only one of Papaw's crazy schemes that ever brought them any joy. The seventies were tough for jazz musicians; passing the hat made all the difference to the family, so long as it lasted. After his voice cracked, Dave was Daddy's unofficial roadie, learning pretty much all there was to know about how to kluge an antique sound system. He became "the Buzzard," a friendly guy who picked up a lot of free beers years before he should have been allowed to drink them. Through folks he ran into, he got enough work in the galleys of rich people's yachts to pay his own way through LSU. With so much proof of his own appeal, Dave briefly harbored a fantasy of hosting a TV game show or maybe something like traffic reporting. A stint at the college station taught him he didn't read well on camera. Luckily, what he'd learned helping his dad with sound systems was enough to make him a welcome addition to the station's crew, where he met some computer science students who introduced him to a new world.

In Dave's experience, life was like that. One thing led to another. You kept your nose clean, did your best and kept an open mind, and you never knew what might happen next. The charming young college graduate parlayed his shipboard contacts into some major partying and, thanks to his nature-plus-nurture knack with sound systems, a good run with a hip South Beach club. Miami loved Dave. When the club failed, former patrons were happy to throw him some work wiring their home audio, video and computer systems. One of these clients recommended him to someone who was putting together an internet startup in New York. Dave leaped at the chance to see The Big Apple. For a couple of years it was an absolute blast. Then, just when Angela got pregnant, the startup folded and he found himself without a job. But again, one thing led to another. Avie Ganz, who'd done some consulting for the startup, called him with an offer.

Ganz's business card described him as an Application Designer and Architect. He knew someone who knew someone who played golf with Kippy Melcher, someone who put that card into Kippy's hands on the 19th hole on a day when several entrepreneurs were congratulating themselves on their foresight in jumping onto the technology bandwagon.

Kippy's own small boast in that area quickly depreciated by comparison. Years ago, a lucky index card on a campus job board had brought him together with a clever young Russian. Leon Shnapik turned a handful of Kippy's tenuous ideas into software Pinnacle could use to compile client orders, track fulfillment progress, and generate billing: Bridge, Kippy's crown jewel. When Leon eventually decided he needed an assistant, his mumbled request was approved without hesitation. He brought in Ina, an older woman from the class he taught to new immigrants at the Brighton Beach JCC. The two Russians worked in quiet harmony, steadily strengthening Bridge and adding minor improvements.

Leon did a solid job of work. Bridge was more than seven years old and going strong. It came as a shock to Kippy to learn that this was considered a generation in technology years. He was the kind of man who bought a new car every other year, like clockwork, but thought anything computer should last forever. Until that day at the golf course, it never occurred to him that Bridge might be considered quaint. He made an immediate decision to ramp up his efforts. He got Avie Ganz on the phone the very next day.

Once he had a handle on what Pinnacle actually did, Ganz pitched big ideas for growing the business by automating many of the services they provided. With fewer people needed to perform the same tasks, costs would come down; sales, driving work load, could increase exponentially without ever adding to payroll. "Cutting edge," Ganz said.

"The wave of the future," Kippy echoed gladly, envisioning himself as the office services equivalent of Henry Ford. His only stipulation was that anything new be recognizably built around the only technology he trusted, Bridge. In a flash of inspiration, he dubbed the project "Bridge, Mark II."

Ganz was installed in an office three weeks later.

Used to the taciturn Leon, Kippy hadn't known that a computer expert could be an energetic go-getter, with a robust network of other go-getters. He was dazzled. His new VP brought in a team of code-slingers: application developers who kept their radar out for the latest thing, tried it, and discarded it before it even became a trend. They were bright and talented and, contrary to Pinnacle's usual employee pool, didn't hesitate to declare the value of their own gifts. The young men (for they were, like Sales, universally young and male) gave the impression that they would only hang around as long as they found the work entertaining.

At their regular meetings, Ganz lolled easily in the guest chair, hands clasped behind his head, staring at the light fixture as if the team's progress report was written there. Did the impressive string of jargon pouring from his lips make any sense? It didn't have to. Kippy loved the idea of technology but found the actuality as unfathomable as ballet. He sat in a temporary beatific trance, contemplating a glowing future just within his reach.

Ganz was never clear about exactly what he expected his assistant to do and he made Dave feel stupid for asking. "Just keep an eye on things," he shrugged that first day. "I'll be in Seattle the next few days."

It was left to Dave to make a place for himself. His coding skills were nothing compared with Avie's cowboys', and hooking up and maintaining the equipment was Conrad's job. After a few months of trying to involve himself in both areas, the Buzzard wisely decided to do what he did best: keep his head down and make friends.

He chatted easily with the new team, entertaining them with stories from his own life until he found a point of connection with each one of them. He made a valiant effort to connect with the phlegmatic Leon. The young Russian wasn't unfriendly, but seemed to find the conversation too lightweight to be worth the energy. Dave had better luck with Ina, after discovering that the shy woman had been a professional musician back in the USSR. He put her at ease with respectful Southern charm and long rambles about his Daddy's gigs to which she need only smile and nod. He enjoyed it as much as she did, emboldening her to stumble out an occasional reminiscence of her own. Dave never noticed, but Leon liked him for this. Leon was fiercely protective of the pretty woman who always seemed poised to fly away and hide.

Dave's defining moment came when a prospective client demanded to speak with a member of the Pinnacle technology team about their system security. Scott Bell always said selling was all about image. He chose Dave as spokesman because the tagline Kippy'd stuck on the brochure was "America's Home Office." Of the three who knew enough to handle the questions, Dave was the only one without what Scott called "a foreign accent." Then he saw Dave in action. Dave had the frank, boyish charm of a baseball player in a Disney movie. He was someone you wanted to have a beer with. When he talked technology, even Scott thought he understood what the hell was being said. From that moment on, whenever Sales needed to trot out someone from IT, Scott had them call Dave. It made for some crazy days, but Dave's spidey-sense told him it could be important to him for the long haul.

Dave was hoping for a very long haul with Pinnacle. With Angie's career taking off and Anabelle not yet in preschool, he wanted a place where he could hunker down. Spreading himself around was a good move, but it wasn't going to be enough if his team couldn't get their shit together. Lately he'd been starting to worry that they never would.

Development meetings were like a game of *Sorry!*, pitting Leon against Craig Parnes, Sid Reilly and now Ken Aoki. The project that kept pumping up the testosterone levels was Bridge Mark II. It was a question of perspective. Leon saw it as a plan to build a better band-aid. The newer guys were chomping at the bit to tear down Bridge entirely and build something cutting edge from scratch.

Every meeting was a battle over how to design the bits Scott Bell's Sales team swore the market demanded and build them as slick and modern as possible, yet still plug into Bridge and operate.

For all that the middle ground was Dave's natural habitat, he wasn't designed to manage. He tried to mediate but would get so absorbed in giving equal emotional investment to both sides of an argument that he never managed to introduce them to one another. He did, inadvertently, help the developers to reach one splinter of agreement: they all shared an amused tolerance for his muddled efforts.

This morning, as often happened, Leon had a grim expression on his face. In and of itself, that expression might mean anything from anger or misery to a twinge of petulance or acid indigestion. Leon's face was rarely cracked by a smile. When something did amuse him, when he laughed and the light glinted on his gold tooth, the moment was as fleeting and transformative as a sunny day in Seattle. He wasn't laughing now. He wasn't doing anything but glaring, over folded arms, at the trio of scruffy hipsters who were jostling for position on the other side of the block of pushed-together tables. His jaded posture, combined with the ironic lifts at the corner of his mouth and one eyebrow, created the illusion of a man who was weary of and unamused by the vicissitudes of life.

Across the table, the new developers had the air of a secret club to which Leon Shnapik didn't belong. Ganz's cowboys would have been surprised to learn that most of them were older than this young middle-aged man, but they'd never learned anything much about him. As proof of their intellectual prowess, they had as few social skills as Leon. Casually surmising that his apparently conservative nature must correlate with out-of-date coding skills, they tended to speak over him rather than with him. Those of us whose view of human nature was somewhat less binary were not surprised that their dismissive attitude only made Leon more determined to stand his ground.

Avie Ganz, who should have taken the lead and moderated, was never around when you needed him. He was always running to some workshop or conference. As long as he was in the office on Thursday to deliver his weekly report, Kippy didn't seem to mind. Absences that would never be tolerated for anyone else were seen as an indication of his sparing no effort to remain balanced on the gossamer cutting edge of technology. There was no way this blessed state could last forever. Kippy would reasonably expect to see deliverables soon; he'd probably ask to be walked through a working demo any day now. Progress was being made at a granular level but, without a strong development lead, it was agonizingly slow. The clock was surely starting to tick, even if only Mike Ventura could hear it.

"We're supposed to start testing on the 15th!" Mike's palm came down on the table with such force that, had he been a lighter man, his ass would have consequently bounced up from his chair. These guys refused to see that, if someone didn't start playing hardball, they might lose the field. Ganz had insisted his Agile team didn't need a project manager on their backs. Mike was officially only their liaison to Fulfillment, but he couldn't stand by and watch them flounder. "What do you mean there's nothing to show?"

"I've got some code," Craig said defensively. "But it's not hooked up to anything. There's no UI."

"Well, where's the UI?"

Dave swiveled his laptop to face Mike. "I did some mock-ups in PowerPoint."

"How do you design an interface in PowerPoint? Don't answer. We have to get some tools for this team." Peering at the screen, Mike forwarded through a couple of slides with a noncommittal sigh. "Okay, at least this is something that Kippy can see. You do all get how important that is? If he can't see it, he doesn't get it, and if he doesn't get it he won't want to keep paying for it. So—diagrams? If I can walk him through a work flow…" Blank faces all around the table. "What are you guys doing here?"

"We're working Agile," Craig protested. "You don't write things down."

"I don't care how 'agile' you think you are." Sensing Leon's smirk behind him, Mike carefully avoided turning that way. "You're supposed to have plans and diagrams, or how can you show the big picture? Okay, look; here's what's going to happen. First of all, I'm going to manage some expectations. I will go into Kippy and eat some kind of shit to buy you time until Friday, when I'm going to promise—*promise* to have something to show him. And I'm going ask him to let me lose half the pile I've got on my plate so I can be on this project at 50 percent, no matter what Avie said, and put together a plan for moving forward. You know this is not going to make any of us look good, but we'll look a whole lot crappier if I tell him you've been working five months with nothing to show."

"Four months," Craig corrected, sulking. "Avie only brought Adam and Sid and me in four months ago. And it took a month for us to choose a scripting technology."

"Where's your fearless leader today anyway? How is he on vacation when he's supposed to have a product coming into test?"

"It's his Leadership course at NYU," Dave explained. "Two week intensive for the certificate. This is the only time of year they give it. Kippy was cool with it."

"Maybe he didn't know Avie's leadership focus was needed elsewhere right now. Okay, however you thought you were working, you're going to give me something I can walk in there with. When Adam gets in tomorrow, he stops everything to get a data diagram together. Maybe only high level, because I'll need it by Friday—insanity, having a DBA for only half a week— but after that he's going to keep drilling down for as long as it takes. Sid, you're on workflow diagrams: all three major processes, mapped so clearly a third-grader could follow them. And I'm not talking about a geeky third grader. Think your little cousin who wants to be a Disney Princess. If you can't make them pretty, don't worry; I will. Dave, I need real requirements on paper, not just some footnotes on a slideshow. I'll send you a template. Use it. Meeting over. Get to work."

Dave Broussard was not happy. "Mike, I have two RFPs to work on. Even if I were on this 100 percent, there's no way for me to churn out a requirements document in three days."

Mike nodded. "Just get something started. If I can show Kippy five or six pages, he'll get the idea. And it'll look impressive. That matters, you know. No point working your ass off if no one can see that you're doing it."

Δ

Arriving plus-punctually at 8:45 a.m., the new hires were asked to wait outside the glass doors. They shifted awkwardly on plastic bucket chairs, trying to appraise one another without obviously staring. They wished, every one of them, that they'd dared to stop for coffee on the way in. At 9:35, Chris finally emerged to welcome them and lead them to the conference room.

Our offices filled a single floor of a building that spanned the breadth of a New York City block. At our center was a bifurcated glass box. Kippy's office, the smaller portion of the box, was separated from the larger conference room by flimsy plasterboard. Despite the connecting door, meetings retained the illusion of autonomy. New employees would quickly learn that this hub was the only fixed point in the ever-shifting maze of the floor-plan. "Like a warp core," Freddie Vega thought, every time he passed it. "Like the inspection house in Bentham's Panopticon prison," Tully Mulhern explained to his enthralled roommates that evening; Tully had minored in Sociology.

Cubicle dwellers along the route glanced up to assess the passing newbies. Pinnacle was growing fast. With new people coming onboard almost every week, we were curious to see who might be joining our teams. One look was usually enough for a solid guess of who belonged where, but only one of today's batch was obvious: the wiry guy slouching along in cater-waiter white shirt, black pants and protean leather sneakers. His wildly patterned tie was clamped down with an actual clip in the shape of a guitar. Above his glasses, his ginger hair was carefully piecey with wax. Overall, there was a whiff of starving artist that stamped him as one of Edie's children. The other two, however, were puzzle enough to cause a buzz.

The young man with the old haircut was surprisingly tricky to place. He was a big guy, the kind always assumed to have played football in High School. That he was wearing a suit at all might have marked him as Sales, except no salesman worth his ambition would be caught dead in badly-fitting all-season toffee gabardine. The large podgy hand that wore a wedding ring was clamped over the handle of what could have been Ward Cleaver's original briefcase; taken together with the unfortunate suit, both accessories created equal confusion in the eye of the beholder.

The woman fit absolutely no place at all than anyone could imagine. Despite her mahogany bob, she was probably older than Edie, but she was clearly much younger than Ruth, Kippy's admin. She wore cheap black pants, like the cater-waiter; the enormous shoulder bag had seen hard service; but her jacket, like her haircut, was way too expensive for the room. She was the only one of the three who looked back into our eyes as she passed; we wondered what she was thinking, almost as much as we wondered why she was there.

So what did they see, our newcomers? What do any of us see?

Our offices were famously designed by Kippy's wife Marcy. Kippy always said that he knew he was a winner the minute Marcy accepted his proposal, because she had perfect taste. He meant this sincerely. He'd let her start picking out his shirts and ties even before he gave her the ring. He never stopped talking about the designer outfits she used to put together from Loehmann's, back when they ostensibly didn't have a pot to piss in. She had a knack for decorating, too. Not that any of us had ever seen it, but Kippy assured us that their place in Fort Lee looked like it was done by a professional. Long-time employees like Noble remembered that, when the senior Mr. and Mrs. Melcher began scooting down to Boca for extended winters, Marcy had been allowed to spruce up the old offices with fresh paint and a few tastefully-framed museum posters.

With perfect timing, Kippy gained control just as Wall Street led the country into the era of Lean and Mean. Offices services were ripe for outsourcing. Kippy expanded the scope of the original answering service and accounting agency and the company flourished, requiring him to take on a second office across the street and, ultimately, move everything to a larger building across town. The new offices, in a raw space formerly occupied by a ribbon manufacturer, were Marcy's first chance to spread her wings outside the home. They were her—and Kippy's—pride and joy. When family or friends visited from out of state, Marcy would take the train in from Jersey to share the grand tour and soak up their admiration first-hand.

Someone had told Marcy Melcher that neutral shades, being restful to the eye without encouraging relaxation, were conductive to work. As a result, our walls were the stewed color of boiled butter beans. So were the cubicle partitions and the fabric used to upholster the chairs in the conference rooms and executive offices. The floors were slightly darker, covered in a durable industrial matting approximately the shade of an old latte. One wall of the glass-fronted conference room was painted in what we'd heard Marcy describe as "an invigorating shade of green," symbolizing growth and, she'd assured Kippy earnestly, lots of money. The same green accentuated the reception desk and one wall in the break room.

Marcy had worked out the modern, open-plan design with the assistance of Walt Sacco's contractor cousin. To describe this as a maze for lab rats, while evocative, would be an over-simplification. The truth was more complicated. For one thing, there was no single "cheese." More discrepantly, there was no definite route. Any number of paths could be drawn through the cubes and demi-cubes, and Pinnacle was growing so quickly that desks were constantly being rearranged and reassigned, changing them. Vivian's walk to deliver the team's time sheets to Gene on Friday might be different from the one he made following Tuesday to deliver the checks.

We didn't have those cubes you see posted on Tumblr or Pinterest, the ones people decorate like tiki cabanas or college dorms. Even the full-sized cubes were smallish and, with the exception of those used by Chris and Finance, low-walled. In some areas, desks were arranged four-square, or else in strips of three, with only a ten-inch sneeze-guard of smoked glass separating the contiguous laminated surfaces. Marcy, who'd sold costume jewelry in Bloomingdale's before the birth of the legendary Alex, thought this was so much friendlier than having a lot of walls. What it was, was public. Without Chris ever having to tell us, we kept our work spaces clear of nearly all personal items. We only kept things out that we didn't mind anyone seeing—absolutely anyone, including passing clients. Novelty calendars were popular, not because we needed paper calendars, but because it was a business-related way of expressing personality. Other than that, we pinned only the occasional sports team logo and, for the few who had them, photos of smiling children. You never knew who would walk by and peer over your shoulder. Kippy and our President, Scott Bell, were particularly fond of doing this. Vivian Karlow, often accused of Russian paranoia, suctioned a purse mirror to the side of her monitor so that no one could sneak up on her; it became a trend.

The noise level was often impossible. Sales used headsets. Over on the Fulfillment side, so did Switchboard and Training, but the rest of Edie's people brought in their own headphones to shut out the constant chatter. Without a headset, you had to yell so loudly on the phone that half the room would overhear. As a result, we were constantly stumbling over one another in the toilets, in the stairwell, or in front of the building, trying to make a doctor's appointment or get an urgent call through to a loved one.

The trio of newcomers filed into the conference room and settled primly at one end of the long, blonde wood table to fill in their I-9's and various other on-boarding documents. Those of us who sat near enough the glass to have the abiding sensation of being cast members in an oddly demure season of *Big Brother* flicked them the occasional covert glance. When the paperwork was done, the pledges made uncomfortable small talk amongst themselves, marking time until their managers were through with morning meetings or whatever emergencies had cropped up.

When the door to the temporary IT tank was flung open, Mike Ventura shot out and headed straight to the glass box. Waving his blue mug and beaming as if he'd found the pot of gold at the end of the rainbow, he greeted the confused woman and escorted her out.

The two men had to wait a little longer. It was another half hour before Edie, freed from the latest crisis, smiled warmly and shook their hands. No one was surprised; it was so like Edie to put people at ease. The only surprising thing was that she claimed them both—the cater-waiter and the guy sharp-tongued Alex Silva had tentatively nick-named Baby Hughey.

Δ

"Mike Ventura." He stuck out the hand that wasn't holding the mug. "Nick's out of the office. He asked me to welcome you."

"Do you work together?" Judy Schreiber's new boss had implied he was on his own.

"Not directly. I like to think of us as allies."

She regarded him with open curiosity. Andreas had impressed her as what they'd once called, with straight faces, a "preppy." This solid young man, with his careful black beard, garnet shirt, and black and gold rep tie, seemed cut from a different cloth. She wondered how they fit together.

He seemed to read her mind. "We're both kind of the new wave around here. I'm a project manager." Mike had been the very first certified Project Management Professional that Kippy had ever met, no less hired. When he'd been brought on earlier this year, it had been part of the monthly address, Kippy waving that PMP as a seal of approval that proved the company was moving up to the Major Leagues. Since then, Mike had been preaching the gospel to all and sundry, campaigning hard to hire a team and keeping a weather eye out for talent. When Andreas had to be in Philadelphia this week, he'd volunteered to step into the breach and get the new assistant started. "Right now I'm stationed in IT, but I'm spreading the good word and hoping it catches fire." There was a twinkle in his eye, but Judy didn't think he was kidding. "The company is growing like crazy. It's a tremendous opportunity."

"A period of explosive growth," she nodded. She liked this Mike's enthusiasm. After having been caught in the death throes of her previous company, it felt good to be somewhere with positive energy. "I heard. Sounds exciting."

"Coffee first? Then I'll give you the grand tour. They're fixing up a desk for you outside Nick's office, but it's not ready yet," he noted apologetically. "They keep forgetting to tell Conrad about new hires. He can't keep up with the demand. Nick said you should feel free to use his while he's out."

Judy nodded again, her mind going in several directions at once. No desk was bad. Being able to use her boss's sounded like a vote of confidence, though not quite enough to balance out having her boss out of the office on her first day. It was nice of this Mike to show her around, but what was she supposed to do with the afternoon?

He steered her down the wide aisle that separated the Pit from the rest of the office. "So I know you're Nick's new assistant, but what is it you do?"

"Communications, and Corporate Events. That's what I did at Trowbridge."

"TWB, huh?"

"Mmm." He sounded sympathetic, but she was trying to put all that behind her. "Nick wasn't exactly sure what he was going to do with me," she added hastily. "I got the feeling I may be shared around."

Mike's grin grew broader. "Works for me. So I'm guessing you can put words together…"

Predictably, someone had just put up a new pot of coffee. While they waited for it to brew, Mike pointed out where things were kept in the break room and explained the unwritten codes of behavior.

"Don't forget to put your name on your food. And the date, or Bertha will toss it out when she does her Friday cleaning. And don't use the 'Pinnacle' mugs. Those are for clients and prospects only. If you hate styrofoam, you have to bring in one of your own. That's what we all do."

His mug, she noticed, was covered with what looked like blueprints of important buildings; she could swear she saw Fallingwater. So it was okay here to show a personality.

"The television has cable. Watch whatever you want at lunch, as long as everyone else in the room agrees. We've got some fierce sports rivalries on staff, but by and large people keep it friendly. News is fine, but we try not to discuss politics. Especially if Senior Management is in the room." There was that twinkle again.

She smiled back. It was difficult not to.

"And the bulletin board can be useful. It's supposed to be for HR, but Chris doesn't have the bandwidth to put much out there. So people have taken to using it for, oh, you know. Looking for a roommate, cat up for adoption, laptop for sale kind of thing."

Mike was gesturing to the cork board, but Judy couldn't pull her eyes from the wall. Painted in white against a fibrillating green was a quote she didn't recognize: "All life is a purposeful struggle, and your only choice is the choice of a goal." It wasn't one of the more inspiring inspirational messages she'd ever seen, but it connected with the question running through her head. "Did Nick…" She'd already picked up on this being a first-name-only kind of office. "Did Nick, uh, leave me anything…?"

Mike shrugged and grinned. "He's not much for planning ahead. Lesson one. But not to worry. I have a few ideas."

Mike's "few ideas" kept Judy running for most of the day.

His crack-the-whip tour of the floor paused only at the supply closet, where he handed her a cardboard file box and suggested she fill it with whatever she thought she might eventually need. "I know you don't have a desk yet," he observed, "but we tend to run out of stuff. For an office services company, we don't have a great handle on our own maintenance. You know, shoemaker's children kind of thing. Aha!" He snagged a pack of erasable markers. "Anything you don't see, put it on the clipboard with your name. Worse thing they can do is say no. But you better keep checking. I ordered these last month. Had no idea they'd come in."

In Nick's office, Mike slid her a list of telephone extensions. "Not for public consumption," he twinkled, proceeding to run down a quick who's-who-at-Pinnacle. Judy covered nearly four pages of a legal pad, her hand cramping to keep up with his commentary. Though everything he said was good-natured, he had a way of noting a few details that implied people's weaknesses, even as he described their strengths. She decided to be flattered by his spontaneous trust and hoped that, next time he ran through this roster with someone, her own character would hold up well.

There was a brisk tap on the door. Mike said to put away the list for now. Edie Brewer was starting a new assistant today, and she'd offered to include Judy in the first hour of his orientation. Mike had spoken of Edie with respect and affection, Judy recalled, stuffing the sheets of yellow paper discreetly into her bag. With another of his infectious smiles, he performed the introduction before hurrying off to the next appointment on his schedule. He'd see her again after lunch.

Δ

It was a simple relief to steal off for an hour's escape. Judy found a tiny cafe near the office that reminded her of the places where she used to hang out in her first life. The walls were splashed with bright turquoise paint and paved with mosaics made of broken dishes. A flea market's worth of printed oilcloth was stapled over the wire spool tables. Judy paid the androgynous waif in the knitted cap for a sandwich and settled into a corner of this oasis to pretend to eat. She was still too jittery to be hungry. She didn't try to imagine what ideas Mike Ventura might have for this afternoon. It was enough to sit quietly and sift through all the information that had already been thrown at her. Information and people.

It's a distinct and funny phenomenon, the way we react to people who remind us of people we've known before. We recognize this, even as it happens to us, but we can't resist it. Edie Brewer's pencil skirt and button-down cotton shirt had immediately brought to mind Judy's fifth-grade teacher; so did her straight spine, the faint sprinkle of grey in her sandy crop, and her quick twitch of a smile. Judy responded with the first natural smile of the day. She later learned that her response was far from unusual. Edie reminded almost everyone of a favorite teacher. It was how she'd been able to build her department. Her organizational skills, while formidable, would have meant nothing at Pinnacle without her gift for wrangling the packs of inexperienced young people who were Fulfillment.

Fulfillment. The core of Pinnacle remains in the original bookkeeping, answering service and data entry areas, though all of these have gradually expanded to reflect the changing needs of the market. The fact is that specific products continue to be added to the Pinnacle menu by the simple expedient of potential clients demanding they exist. Kippy had learned all he needed to know about the market from the single example of his own first successful sales pitch. He—and later Scott, and Scott's merry men—would schmooze with the clients, hear what they were griping about, and offer to do it for them for a price. When a client bit, then we'd worry about how to deliver.

Trailing behind Edie Brewer and the awkward young man, it came as something of a relief for Judy to be dealing with concepts that she could understand. Her first few weeks at Trowbridge had been like parachuting into Shanghai. At Pinnacle, things just about made sense. The services were easy to get a handle on. What she couldn't quite grasp was how the company was growing so quickly by doing them. There must be more to the office services industry than she'd realized. Working for the Vice President of New Product Development, she was going to have to correct this lack of vision as soon as possible. So much to learn.

Edie's overview brought an avid gleam to George Waters' eye. Waters was an ambitious young man, eager to work hard and make his way up. What he was looking for was a climbable ladder. Every job he'd had, he'd found the same thing: all they cared about were expensive suits and more expensive advanced degrees. The suit thing was ridiculous. A suit was a suit. It was there to prove you were thinking like a professional. As long as the jacket matched the pants, and you didn't wear a loud tie, that should be plenty. And he sure didn't get this fuss about an MBA. George Waters was damned proud of his BA from the College of Business at Stony Brook. Hell, he was proud of the Associates from Suffolk County Community that had started the ball rolling. George was the first person in his family to go beyond high school, and the family had done just fine all these years. He knew he had more smarts than any ten of those MBA's. Hell, he was smart enough not to waste thirty thou on a piece of paper! In the kind of place that shared his values, smarts and hard work should be enough to drive him straight up to the top. He was fed up with places that didn't respect what he had to offer, and fed up with the kinds of people who dumped all their work on George Waters and then paraded around taking all the credit.

Things would be different here; no more getting steamrollered or pushed aside. He'd known it the minute he'd got off the phone with Art Russo and checked out the company website. It was just a little clunky. George liked that. More significantly, Kippy Melcher's biography showed no advanced degrees. He was practically a self-made man, the kind who would appreciate a smart worker like George Waters. Going into his meeting with Russo,

Waters felt confident. The look of the office backed up his impression from the website: up and coming, with a lot on the ball, but not already there. Russo, from Staten Island, was an easy guy to talk with; he seemed to get where George was coming from, and talked a lot about the opportunities here. It was just going to be a question of matching him with the right one.

On his way out, Waters nearly ran into a pair of those damned expensive suits. He was feeling strong, so certain that Russo would call him back for a second interview that, instead of his instinctive scowl, he gave a pleasant smile. Damned fairy godmother must have been watching over him that day. Because he'd done his homework, he saw that one of the suits was Kippy Melcher. Didn't take an MBA to know to stick out his hand and say "George Waters, Mr. Melcher. An honor to meet you. I'm so inspired by what you're doing here at Pinnacle. It would be a real thrill to have the opportunity to be part of it."

Melcher had these blue marble eyes. Waters felt them taking him in. "Thank you, George. Ha! I'll be watching out for you."

Waters wasn't surprised when Russo called him the next morning. A new position had been added to the budget and required exactly his kind of experience. It was to assist Edie Brewer, who ran what sounded to him like the most important department in the whole place, the one that did the actual work that the rest of them were selling. It only got better when he met her in person. Edie reminded him of that Sunday School teacher who'd made him class monitor, no-nonsense but warm and encouraging. It was almost funny, how concerned she looked when she explained that he'd have to start down in the trenches, learning all the ropes. It was as if she'd been afraid this would discourage him. He liked it, feeling that she already understood that George Waters was someone of consequence. This morning had been the icing on the cake, Edie entering that conference room with a big smile on her face, her hand already stretched to shake his. After they parked that Tully kid in the Data Entry pool, she led him on a tour of the department. Their department. The warren of desks was the Promised Land spreading out at his feet. He felt expansive, smiling benevolently at anyone who glanced up as they passed. As right-hand-in-training to the manager, he could afford to. Edie's department was packed with scruffy kids who didn't even know enough to wear a suit to the office; no competition at all. He couldn't wait to go home tonight and tell Cathy.

Δ

Jeff Curry's cell phone vibrated. With a sidelong glance, he scooped it into his pocket. He hit "Save", pushed back his chair and jerked his head at Tully Mulhern. "Come for a smoke?"

Tully nodded. He'd stopped smoking after his dad's heart gave out, same time as he started cutting back on the beer. He felt less winded, that's for sure; but the big gain was to his pocket. When he quit, he banked the amount of every pack he would have bought. In only a year, he'd saved enough for the maple top Fender Jazzmaster that he loved more than his first girlfriend. The next year paid for his share of studio time. It was beside the point that Angels Share never finished the album, and later broke up; he had too much else to do with his money to go back. So he didn't smoke, not any more, but it didn't bother him to be around people who did. Right now, his head was pounding and he needed a break. He jumped up with alacrity, and followed Jeff to the elevators.

Tully hated the first day at any new job. There was too much to learn and never enough time for it sink in. Since his typing was good, Edie Brewer had him shadowing the team lead in the Data Entry area. Like a lot of the people at Pinnacle, Jeff seemed to be around Tully's age. His fingers flew with blurring speed. So did his tongue, and what he had to say was sharp. Tully kept his own face zipped; you don't go mouthing off on your first day in a new place. It was interesting to listen, though. Jeff had something to say about almost everybody. It was kind of a surprise that there were people willing to hang out with him.

As Jeff explained, the little group wasn't allowed to hang around the front of the building; it "gave a bad impression." We never knew if the prohibition came from building management or Kippy and Scott. There was a rumor out of Sales that Scott had once been seen, in the flush of converting a prospect into a client, pulling on a cigar. Even if that were true, cigars, just as in the days of the original railway and oil barons, spoke of power and money. The mystique of cigarettes had, like the health of the middle classes, fallen in a downward spiral.

The smokers had to congregate in the trashcan alley on the side of the building. In a city where a studio apartment the size of a college dorm room easily went for $1200 a month, real estate traded on the platinum standard. New buildings walled up the vestigial windows of the adjacent structures. The few alleys that remained were between pairs of large older buildings. The smokers were lucky to have one of these, and luckier still that Anthony let them use it. Of course, Anthony was a smoker himself.

There were eight or nine in the smokers' ghetto, though there was rarely enough coverage on any team for everyone to come down together.

Her eye on Tully's tie clip, the blonde girl, Dawn Kollist, passed Jeff her cigarette. "Musician?"

With one hand cupped against the wind, he touched it to his own and took a deep draw. "Yaaahhh," he drawled, answering for Tully. "Guitar. No band, though. It broke up."

Alex Silva pulled back the fiver he was in the act of passing to Mia Freeman. She shrugged. "Half right. Owe me a latte."

Tully felt awkward. Needing to do something, he pulled off his glasses and wiped them on his tie.

Orla Belton's pale green kohl-rimmed eyes crinkled kindly. "No offense. We're all in the same boat. Pinnacle is either your first real job or your day job, one or the other."

"Which is it for you?" he asked.

She shrugged. "I just wanted to live in New York."

Dawn offered her pack. "It's okay to bum. Payday isn't for two weeks. You can pay it forward when the next person starts."

Tully waved her off. "I only wanted some air. My head works better if I can clear it sometimes."

Mia cocked a finger in his direction, showing her approval. "Renee actually encourages us to take breaks. Twice a day; it's in the scheduling."

Jeff blinked in disbelief. "You're shitting me! Why didn't I know that?"

With a look of mock horror, Alex grabbed Mia from behind and pulled her to his chest. He clapped a hand over mouth. "You little fool, now they know our secrets! We'll have to kill them all!" She gave him a good-natured jab with her elbow. Pretending pain, he let her go.

"Asshole." She tugged the single curl that drooped over his forehead.

Alex slapped her hand. "But seriously." He maneuvered his phone so that he could check his hair in the reflection and make a minor adjustment. "We're not supposed to say. There's an impression that the Cs don't exactly see eye-to-eye with her on the breaks thing."

"Or almost anything," Mia added.

"Renee is nice." Diego Guzman said this about most people, but in this case he wasn't alone. Renee, the Director of Client Care, was a positive presence on the floor. Between her cheerful demeanor and the bright scarves tied perkily at her neck, a rumor persisted that she'd once been a flight attendant. "Why wouldn't they like her?"

"Alan likes her fine," Alex corrected. "It's Kippy and Scott she keeps butting heads with."

The only non-C who didn't like her was Vivian. We all knew this because Vivian had once made the mistake of confiding in Mia. The first secret of Pinnacle was that there were no secrets at Pinnacle. Hired for the assistant's role, Vivian had been breezily certain that she'd prove herself a shining star and the Cs would call off the hunt for a more experienced Director. Six months later, Renee was hired and Vivian never forgave her. It was foolish of Viv. Renee was supremely qualified for the position, with tons of impressive experience. Under her direction, Client Care grew and incidents of panic lessened. Renee told her people that client service should be "responsive, not reactive." It was a subtle distinction that Kippy and Scott, who tended to go ballistic over squeaky wheels, failed to grasp. This philosophical difference, coupled with an inability to have knee-jerk reactions to orders from on high, caused her friction with the CEO and the President.

"Not surprising she's getting grief about breaks," Jeff blew out a disparaging stream of smoke. "If you're not chained to your desk, they think you're not working."

"Come on, Jeff," Diego protested. He would. The general consensus was that Diego was too nice for his own good.

"Show me how I'm wrong. Here. Noble had this thing with his leg once. He had to get up and walk for a few minutes every hour. That was before we left 40th Street. The only place clear enough was this aisle that cut through Sales to Scott's office. Mia, remember how Scott went apeshit? Ran screaming to Kippy about how Noble was wasting company time."

"It's true," she agreed. "If Kippy didn't love him so much, Noble would have been toast."

"Yeah, so what is it with Kippy and Noble?" Dawn hadn't been around long, but she'd noticed that Kippy gave a little salute whenever he passed by Noble's desk.

"He was one of the first people Kippy hired," Mia explained. "When he first took over from his father."

Dawn was shocked. "How old is he?"

Jeff clarified. "He was still in high school or something. Old enough to drive. Kippy drives in every morning. Noble used to meet him at the office at the crack of dawn, take the car over to the garage and pick up him up breakfast at the deli. He came back after school and put in a couple of hours doing whatever until Kippy was ready to go home and he had to bring the car around again."

"What the fuck," Tully marveled.

"Right? So then he joined the Marines. Did five years. When he got out, he came back and told Kippy he was looking for work. Fuck knows why." Jeff was being flip. Everyone knew why, even Kippy. Noble was going for an MBA and studying for his CPA. "Anyway, after Noble came back, the business starting taking off. Out of nowhere. So now Kippy thinks he's a good luck charm or something. But he still makes him get his breakfast. Egg whites on an English muffin, yoghurt and a fresh OJ, from the place on the corner. Every day."

"I thought Bertha got his breakfast," Diego said.

"Lunch. Bertha gets his lunch." Jeff grinned. "Tuna salad on whole wheat toast, with a piece of tomato. It's good to be the king."

Dawn cocked her head at Tully and made a face, as one new recruit to another. He was relieved. He'd been wondering if he was the only one who thought it all sounded a little weird.

"So who's the new guy with the loud voice?" Orla suddenly remembered to ask.

"Oh, yeah! Baby Hughey! What's that about?" Alex's eyes glinted eagerly.

All eyes turned to Tully. He polished his glasses on his tie again, while he tried to figure out what they wanted.

"The one who came in with you," Diego smiled helpfully. "Joe something, Edie said?"

"George," Dawn supplied, flicking an ash. She had him in Procurement this afternoon. "George Waters. Edie said he's floating for now. He's going to spend a few weeks with each team. I think maybe he's going to be her assistant."

"What's his background?" Jeff snapped. Jeff had expected his experience as shift manager at the U Conn Co-op would get him on a management training track somewhere in the city; but somewhere turned out to be Pinnacle and all they wanted him to do was data entry. He'd been informed, as if he should be thrilled by the achievement, that he'd gotten the highest typing score ever recorded on the skills test. It hadn't been like he'd deliberately practiced; it must have been from all those papers he'd typed for spending money while he was still in school. Never in a million years had he dreamt this would turn out to be the only marketable skill that would come with a BA in Journalism.

"He's a suit," Orla noted, as if that said everything.

"You call that a suit?" Alex rolled his eyes. "I wouldn't let my cat wear that thing."

"So why isn't he in Sales?" Jeff wasn't going to let it go. "And if Edie needs an assistant, why isn't it one of us?"

"Stop taking this personally, Curry. It's a good sign." Alex took a final drag before grinding the half-smoked cigarette carefully out on the sole of his shoe. "They're putting in a layer of middle management. That means they're serious about all that corporate maturity stuff. It makes sense that they start with people who have more experience, but the company's growing. They'll need more and we're getting in on the ground floor."

"At my interview, Mr. Russo said that they were growing 20 percent every quarter." Dawn's parents had raised her to be anachronistically mannerly to those older or in positions of responsibility.

"Gross," Jeff said trenchantly.

"Huh?" Tully wrinkled his nose.

"As opposed to net. I bet he didn't factor in attrition."

"People come and go so quickly here," Alex agreed. "You'll see, children. Wait and see."

2 BUILDING BRIDGES

Dave Broussard did most of his mockups in the middle of the night, when he had to wake up anyway to feed Anabelle. Why waste a cycle? If Ventura got how he did it, he'd be blown away; not throwing him into remedial writing with this Judy, who didn't know javascript from a cup of coffee. The only upside was that it was her job to squeeze everything into that ridiculous template. Okay, maybe not ridiculous, but over much: this was proprietary software for a small company, not a NASA launch.

"So if they dirty the screen and then try to move forward, we want to have something that catches this and displays a message." Dave drew an X over the rectangle he'd already sketched on the whiteboard. For a guy known for his line of patter, it was pretty funny how he always felt more confident laying out his thoughts in pictures than putting them in words.

"What do you mean by 'dirty'?" Judy Schreiber's voice strained to stay even. This tended to happen around hour two, when the whiteboard sketches devolved into meaningless doodles. Dave used his X's and arrows and circles as punctuation, the way Mike Ventura used his hands.

"Dirty." Someone who knew the least thing about UI development wouldn't have to ask any of the things she asked. "You know. You change what's on the screen; you type a letter, check a box..."

"What if you click your cursor in one of the boxes, but you don't actually type anything? Is that 'dirty'? Or only if you leave a character behind?" Dave was frustratingly vague about almost everything, and Mike had cautioned Judy to be specific, especially about what she'd learned to call "behavior."

Dave had an impressive range of information in his head and creative solutions to problems, but he danced around details as if frightened to commit. To finalize anything, Judy had to go through a level of interrogation that exhausted them both. Mike swore that the results were worth it, that Kippy had loved the first eight pages. They had 22 pages now, about halfway through, based on what Judy could understand of Sid Reilly's flow-charts. That was a surprising lot. Judy had been nervous when Mike asked to "borrow" her for this job, but capturing requirements was just like blocking a play. What a joke. Every industry pretended to be so arcane, when you only ever needed a few dozen pieces of jargon to be an insider.

Mike arrived for his second ever 8 a.m. one-on-one with Kippy, armed with a satisfyingly thick folder of papers. The requirements looked impressive. So did the diagrams and workflows, for which he'd used the sacred Sales color printer. His walkthrough would culminate in a slideshow of Dave's mockups for the new UI. The Buzzard's knack for drafting attractive screen designs was unexpected from a perpetually disheveled man whose desk looked like a jumble sale.

"Nine months is long enough to make a baby out of a coupla cells, it ought to be enough to build a piece of software, right?" That was Kippy's opening gambit.

"Well..." As much as he was tempted to say "Yes" and throw Ganz under the bus, Mike's future depended on Kippy understanding that it took time to turn around a large, quality deliverable. "It depends on the application."

"Ha! My point!" Kippy grunted with satisfaction at being understood. "Took Leon a year and a half almost to build Bridge. But he was working on his own and he started out with nothing."

"And he did a stellar job," Mike hastened to observe. Kippy's respect for Leon was legendary.

"They're building on the back of that. Should take a fraction of the time."

"It's because we're leveraging Bridge that we need to move carefully. Consider all angles to find the best approach, so we don't risk damaging what Leon built. We're making Bridge scalable, so we can keep growing to support whatever work load Scott's team brings in, while allowing us to add the new features everybody's been asking for. Let me show you..."

Guiding Kippy through the stack, Mike carefully dialed down the technology references, focusing instead on the business value behind the decisions. He also tried to highlight at least one achievement for each member of the team. They were smart guys; all they needed was some decent wrangling.

It was a long hour. Kippy seemed pleased in the end, shaking Mike's hand and asking if he could keep the papers. Later in the morning, he stuck his head in the tank with a loud "Great work, you guys! Keep it up!" and a big thumbs up.

Everyone, even Leon, whose bacon had not needed saving, perked up. Sid gave Dave a hearty thump on the back. They decided to grab a quick one together at Whine Bar after work. Mike, they agreed, would not be allowed to buy his own.

Δ

Pinnacle was celebrating Hallowe'en. Kippy and Scott weren't too sure about all this kind of thing, but COO Alan Reisch sided with Russo. We'd onboarded a lot of new people. A silly party would foster a sense of fellowship and make people feel connected to the company that sponsored it. Russo's slightly hokey email, complete with animated apple-bobbing gif, invited everyone to come to work in costume. It included a warning:

```
"Our goal is for everyone to have fun, but remember that this
is a work environment. Bodies should be suitably covered — no
Baby New Years, no belly dancers. And no suggestive costumes.
If you are uncertain as to whether your costume meets these
criteria, please come and talk with me."
```

Naturally, people who would otherwise have never considered it began to think of ways to subtly subvert the dictate. In the ladies' room, someone overheard one girl say that she was planning to wear a grey wig, carry her crocheting and wear a ribbon saying "World's Oldest Hooker."

Judy Schreiber was delighted to not have to rush home to change before heading down to the Parade. She was expected there to cheer on some old theatre friends, who were going as the characters in *The Lion King* as interpreted by Picasso during his Primitivist period. Her own costume was an old favorite: Medusa. She loved getting extra use from the hours it had taken her to make the hair, tacking dozens of rubber snakes onto a cheap fiber-optic-studded wig. Fortunately, it didn't matter what she wore from the neck down. Her old goddess dress wouldn't be office-appropriate even if it did still fit. Anyway, an old jersey tunic and a pair of black leggings was fine. Plaster on some sparkly eye makeup and a slick of purple lipstick and she was perfect. Better than perfect.

With the median age of 27, Pinnacle was the first place that ever made Judy feel old. Wearing something crazier than most of the younger crowd turned her into a peer, however honorarily. She assumed the shadow over the edge of her desk was one of her new fans, and offered the bowl of gummy worms with a wicked hiss.

"Judy?" It was Ruth, Kippy's gatekeeper.

Surprised, Judy quickly adjusted her leer to a friendly smile. They often nodded politely to one another in passing, but the poor woman was usually too frazzled to converse.

Ruth seemed calm enough now. She smiled back, "Listen, Kippy is doing Executive Lunch today and one of the people who was scheduled is out sick. Would you mind jumping in?"

Judy had heard about Executive Lunch. Kippy and Scott took turns hosting a few members of staff every month. She was impressed that the CEO and the President wanted to get know the people they hired. It seemed a curious choice on Ruth's behalf, asking her to participate with a headful of snakes. "Dressed like this?"

Ruth's eyes held an unexpected twinkle. "I think it would be fun, if you don't mind. It is Hallowe'en after all."

"It's fine with me. I'm not the one who has to look at it. That's the secret of walking around in costume, you know."

"Really?"

"Harvey Fierstein once told me that."

"Oh! How exciting! You should put that on the questionnaire. He likes to know a little bit about you. I'll send it as soon as I get back to my desk. Noon sharp, yes? In the conference room. Is tuna okay or are you a vegetarian?"

"Turn anyone to stone yet?" The new guy with the Buddy Holly horn-rims flashed an admiring thumbs up.

Dawn Kollist stared in awe at the bobbing snakes. "I was going to dress up. Until I got invited to Executive Lunch, then I figured I'd better not. It's a little unfair. Though I feel like I'm kind of in costume anyway." She adjusted her shirt collar so that it fell outside the lapels of her blazer. "I wish I'd worn my Blue Fairy gown."

The older woman laughed. "If it makes you feel any better, I had no idea I was coming to lunch. I'm a last minute substitute."

"Did you have to fill in that questionnaire?" Dawn had found the questions pretty strange.

"Very roughly. I only had a few minutes before Ruth needed it back."

"I mean, 'where did you work before Pinnacle and for how long?' Wasn't that on the job application?"

"It was on mine," horn-rims nodded. "I started in Compliance last month."

"Are we all new to the company?" the woman asked.

"I've been here since July," Dawn offered. "I'm in Procurement. Try explaining that to your parents," she added wryly.

The quiet Asian-looking guy from Curry's team never got to say anything. Just as he was about to open his mouth, Kippy entered and shook hands all around. When he got to Medusa, the other three waited with bated breath for a reaction. None came. Kippy appeared oblivious to silver glitter eyelids and a headful of serpents.

"This is so great!" he enthused. Kippy face-to-face was as much a cheerleader as Kippy on a windowsill. "I really love getting to know everyone like this. Lunch will be here in a minute. So tell me," he focused on the quiet kid, "what department..."

The door flew open, shouldered by a short round woman with a large tray. The quiet boy jumped up to help her.

"Oh, she's okay, aren't you Bertha?"

The tiny dynamo shook her fierce eyebrows, set down the tray on the credenza and scooted out, returning momentarily to throw a handful of napkins and paper-wrapped straws down the middle of the table.

The interruption lost Kippy his train of thought. He pulled a paper bundle from the tray and started unwrapping. "Doesn't this look great? Place down the street makes the best tuna. Everyone take one."

Horn-rims looked a little uncomfortable. "Um, I was supposed to get a vegetarian sandwich?"

"Ha! Must be the one with the V on the wrapper. Here you are...uh...?"

"Will. Will Compton."

"Will. So what did you do before joining Pinnacle, Will?"

"I was at Brown. My degree is in Comparative Religion. I studied everything across the board...you kind of have to for the 'comparative' part, but my main area of interest was Islam." From behind his glasses, Will blinked blandly.

Kippy seemed to have a piece of lettuce stuck to his soft palate. "You're not a Muslim?" he gargled; "not that there's anything wrong with that."

"Presbyterian. Islamic studies seem especially relevant in today's world. But mostly I just find it fascinating. There's such a rich history around that culture, and we know so little about it in the West. I've been accepted into a post-graduate program at Columbia, but, well, it's expensive. They allowed me to delay entry for up to two years while I save up some money."

Kippy nodded his approval. "Don't go into debt if you can avoid it. One of my top five rules for success. And you're working for us in...?"

"Compliance. Also extremely interesting." Will took a bite of his sandwich to forestall further questions.

"Glad to hear it. And...Dawn, am I right?" Presumably the two women's questionnaires diverged enough that it was easy for Kippy to guess which was hers.

"Yes, sir. Dawn Kollist. I graduated Barnard in January. Then I took a few months off to visit my brother in Reykjavik. He's an energy consultant, working on thermal energy."

"Greenland must be a fascinating place. Pretty cold."

"Um, well..." Dawn's parents hadn't taught her what to do when your CEO confuses Iceland and Greenland. Before her stalling became a problem, she was saved by Kippy laughing at himself.

"Ha! That was a stupid mistake! It was summer. Of course it wasn't cold! So what department are you in, Dawn?"

"Procurement, sir."

"Excellent. Good place to get started. You like it?"

"I'm learning a lot," she replied promptly. "And I'm hoping in time to be able to move into Payroll Services, or maybe Training."

"That's what I like to hear! Ambition!" Kippy set down his sandwich and spread his arms wide, as if embracing the entire conference table. "You see, this is what Pinnacle is all about! Giving people a good start. We take young people like yourselves." He conveniently ignored that his left-hand neighbor was his near contemporary. "We train you, we give you the tools and experience, and as we grow, you grow."

Dawn made sure to nod with alacrity, to show that this was exactly what she'd been hoping for in a job.

Still beaming, Kippy returned his focus to the shy kid who'd tried to help Bertha. "So if that's Will, then you must be Kaymee Poole. Am I pronouncing that right? KAY-mee?"

"Close sir." He had a sweet smile. "It's more like Kah-EE-mee."

"You've all gotta stop calling me 'Sir'!" Kippy laughed. "You're making me feel like my father. Sir! Ha! Everyone at Pinnacle calls me Kippy, okay?"

"Yes, s... Kippy."

"So tell me about yourself, Kay-mee."

"I'm a musician, but I like to work multi-media. I studied at the Rhode Island School of Design."

"Like Talking Heads," Medusa observed. Kaimi reacted with pleased surprise. "I met them once," she continued. "At La Mama."

Kaimi's awe was evident but, again, he was cut off before he could get any words out. Poor guy.

"Well, Kaymee, you'll have to talk with Scott about all that," Kippy said. "He's the music buff. Me, I'm more of an action guy. I'd rather go to a ball game than a concert. Or a show—don't ask! My wife dragged me to something on Broadway last weekend. She said it won all kinds of awards in London. I couldn't understand a word they were saying. I fell asleep halfway through. Ha! So Judy, what did you do before you came to Pinnacle?"

"I was with TRB."

"Terrific! I met Milt Wardell at a conference once. Heck of a guy. Such a pity about what happened."

An interesting expression flitted across Judy's face. Dawn guessed she wasn't big on that description. "It should be a cautionary tale to the banking industry," was all she said.

"Ha!" Kippy said. A light flared in his eyes, causing them to glow like a pair of well-sucked blue raspberry Jolly Ranchers. "Let me tell you..." And he embarked on his passionate analysis of where Trowbridge Wardell and Benedetto had gone wrong. It filled up the remainder of the lunch, and touched on everything except the boundless cupidity of their directors, several of whom had played through his favored eighteen holes.

The costume parade started at the reception desk. Laughing and mugging, those of us gutsy enough to have gone all out marched down the center aisle to line up by the windows where Kippy gave his monthly address. There were lots of cheers from those who'd only dared a funny hat or wig.

We turned out several vampires and witches, and two versions of the guy from *Scream*; a gypsy, a flapper and a spot-on home-crafted Rainbow Brite. Wildlife ranged from a lion and a "magic" dragon to a (female) butterfly and a (male) bee. Because she was in HR, Chris' clever Q-tip costume was out of the running for a prize, as was Art's inevitable knightly armor.

The entire event had the whiff of class divide. No one in Sales wore so much as a pair of flocked red horns. Kippy and Scott were nowhere to be seen. Serving alongside of Ruth and Walt, Alan Reisch was the only of the C-level executives to even judge. Other than Art, who might have been said to have sponsored the event, the only vaguely managerial person to embrace the holiday was Mike Ventura.

After lunch, Mike had changed into a purple coat and trousers and a broad-brimmed purple hat. Now he swaggered down the aisle with his "diamond"-knobbed walking stick.

On one hand, he wore a knuckle-duster that spelled out PIMP. He'd blocked out one letter with square of black duct tape so that it now read "PMP." "Get it?" he said, flashing his bling at the onlookers. It was his certification: Project Management Professional.

When the judges emerged from their huddle, the cleverest costume was declared to be Alex Silva, who wore gym clothes with the word "No" painted all over the shorts and singlet. He said he was a "running nose". Mike was "funniest" and IT's tall Senior Developer Craig Parnes, in a rented Teletubbie costume, was "scariest." The award for "Best All Around," a twenty-five dollar Starbucks card, went to Megan from Reception who wore her old flag-squad uniform and painted her face white with black socket eyes.

Dawn and Will caught up with Judy.

"You was robbed," he said gravely.

"True that," Dawn agreed. "Seriously, you call that a zombie cheerleader? Where's the rotting flesh?"

Judy laughed. "Thanks for the vote of confidence. I'm glad I got to meet you today."

"Some weird lunch though, wasn't it?" Will waggled his eyebrows behind his glasses.

"Food for thought." Judy turned serious. "Will, why aren't you in the State Department or something like that? With your education?"

"Oh, I'm trying. No luck so far. I think it's my Mom's FBI file. She hung out with a kind of radical group in the 60's. You'd never believe it if you saw her now."

"No, I probably would."

He gave sober consideration to her snakes. "Yeah, maybe," he concluded. "Anyway, it puts a kind of question mark in my background. I keep trying. I hope they'll take me eventually, maybe even in time to put me through Columbia. *Insha'allah.* Meanwhile, I'm working on my Arabic."

They drifted off to join their friends.

Judy, wandering over to the cider and donuts, ran into Edie Brewer.

"Fantastic costume," Edie said. "You should have won something, but they just didn't get it."

"A headful of snakes? Not all that cryptic."

"Let's just say it's not a company of great readers."

"Funny your saying that. I got to talk to some of the younger people today, and I was struck by how bright and interesting they are."

Edie nodded significantly. "Oh the kids are great."

"Well, well, well, fine ladies!" Mike was still in character.

"Congratulations," Judy told him. "It's a great costume."

"So was yours. You got stiffed. Craig's was rented and the only reason it was scary was because he was in it."

"At least the judges understood that running nose. Who is that? He's very clever."

"Alex Silva," Edie said. "One of Renee's. So Mr. PMP, did you wear that to your morning meeting?"

Mike laughed. "Can you imagine Kippy's face? No, I changed after."

"I had Executive Lunch today," Judy said coolly, patting her wig. The other two looked at her, speechless. "It was Ruth's idea."

Edie turned to Mike. "You're right. She must be getting ready to retire."

Δ

```
From:        Kippy Melcher
To:          All Pinnacle Employees
Subject:     Exciting News!
-----------------------------------
```

Please join me in welcoming Gary Feldman as Pinnacle's first
Chief Financial Officer. Gary has an MBA from Boston
University and joins us directly from five years as
Controller of Kate Andrews Apparel.

Kippy Melcher, CEO
Pinnacle Management Services

Δ

Art Russo had suggested the LC hire an experienced professional to do what was called "train the trainer," to get the client-facing teams up to speed on new products and services. The same person could take over whatever was required for incoming staff: things like the mandated sexual harassment training which, despite the sound, was the exact opposite of teaching people how to molest one another.

At her interview, Kay Kuperman raised more questions about the company than most interviewees have the presence of mind to come up with and almost as many as they later wished they'd thought to ask. When Art called her back to meet Alan Reisch, she brought a whole slideshow outlining a program that not only covered NLRA and OSHA compliance but would introduce new employees to Pinnacle's history and what the various departments did. At this velocity of growth, it was the most effective way to quickly enfold groups of people into the corporate culture. That soundbyte alone was enough for Kippy. He loved that he had a company big enough to have a "corporate culture." He attached himself to the phrase like an American tourist in China who'd finally learned how to pronounce *xie-xie* so that it meant "thank you;" it became part of the business vocabulary that he trotted out on every conceivable occasion.

The deal was hardly sealed before Kippy volunteered to participate in Kay's new program. He was gung-ho to give a short but inspirational speech to all the new associates (she'd also explained that no one said "employees" any more). He was so enthusiastic that he told Marcy to re-configure the extra conference room for training purposes.

Kippy decreed that such a critical component of his corporate culture required an official name. Kay had assumed she'd put it down on the calendar as "All Aboard," like she had at her last three consulting gigs. Kippy thought "Spring Training" sent a stronger message of teamwork, but was ultimately convinced that it might not be effective throughout the year. By chance, Kay and Kippy ran into one another on the street one morning. He was passing his car keys to Noble. She was stiff and a little wired from her early morning effort to lose 20 pounds in time for her sister-in-law's wedding. The same word popped into both their heads, and Pinnacle "Boot Camp" it became.

It would take a while to put together the kind of program Kay, and now Kippy, imagined. Team presentations, and the Bridge training exercises for which Edie Brewer had lobbied, would come later. For the first iteration of Boot Camp, Kay prepared a half-day of activities, including a brief history of the company by Chris and Ruth, Kippy's meet-and-greet, and the Sexual Harassment Training that Art had bought from a company that specialized in these kinds of things.

Anything related to OSHA compliance had to be remediated company wide. Seeing the signup sheet in the break room, many of us decided to get it over with quickly. Returning from their ten-minute bathroom break, the initial group of seven newcomers found the room packed with Pinnacle associates of longer tenure.

Kay already had the dvd loaded, with the title frame frozen on the screen: *Sexual Harassment: What You Need to Know*.

Craig Parnes, who liked being authorized to take a break, sat up extra straight in his chair and folded his hands before him on the conference table. "I think it's very nice you're going to teach us Sexual Harassment, Mrs. Cleaver," he said, head bobbing, eyes round with virtue.

"Asshole!" Freddie Vega, from the IT HelpDesk, cuffed him across the ear. "She's going to teach us *not* to harass."

"Oh, shit!" Craig said. "Now you've gone and ruined everything."

Chris Keane, observing the training on Art's behalf, tried to shush them. "I know you think you're joking, but this is exactly why we have to have this training, isn't it Kay?"

Kay gave enough of a smile to show she wasn't angry, but not so much that she seemed to approve. "That's okay. This is a topic that makes people uncomfortable, so they try to break the tension." Now that she had everyone's attention, she slid into the script. "This is a topic that's very misunderstood and difficult to discuss. But it's such an important issue, something all of us need to be sensitive to. You each found a questionnaire on your chair. This is for you, not for me. So you have a record of what your perceptions were going into this training, because in about half an hour they're going to change. I'd like you to fill it out now. We're going to watch a short film together, and then we're going to discuss it. After that, there'll be a little quiz, so you can see what you've learned. Don't worry, you're not going to be graded!"

There was quiet, except for the almost inaudible scrape of pen against paper and a few snickers. When we seemed to be done, Chris turned down the lights and Kay pressed "Start."

Establishing shot: an office. Possibly the office of the company in Utah that made these videos. Unlike any office ever seen in New York, it is spacious with lots of empty floor space, squeaky clean and without a speck of clutter. There seem to be only six people working there: one Black, one Hispanic, one Asian, one middle-aged and the designated "hot babe" who, though it's difficult to find a respectful way to say this, is nothing to write home about. Action.

"Wow, would you get a load of that!" White Guy in tan pants turns to his identifiably Hispanic work buddy. His smile is broad and vigorous. "She must be new here."

Change camera angle to focus on the Young Woman. She toys with her hair as she chats with the Asian Man. Both pretend to laugh. He places his hand on her shoulder.

Camera lingers there.

Hispanic Buddy, off camera: "She's hot!" By his tone, he seems to be commenting on a serving of soup.

Return to previous angle: two men. It is now obvious that they are standing in front of a suspiciously silent photocopier that is being "used" by a grey-haired Older Woman. She glares at the stooges.

White Guy: "If I were Bob, I'd be reaching for those juicy melons!" He could not sound less sincere.

(Someone in the Pinnacle conference room has a minor choking fit.)

Older Woman: "This is an office, not a singles' bar!" Her huff marginally more convincing than her photocopying, she stomps out of view.

And so it went. A shot of the girl sitting at her desk, with one of the men reaching over her shoulder at an impractical angle to put down a file folder. The girl standing unsteadily on a stool by a file cabinet, one of the men reaching to "steady" her. And the grey-haired woman—who else?—complaining to the manager, an older Black man in a three piece suit.

Finally, the lights came back up.

"Well!" Kay said brightly. "Let's talk about what we just saw."

After that, we all wanted a shower. Since we couldn't have one, we settled for coffee and veered, as one body, toward the break room.

"Well if there's only one girl in the whole office, of course they're going to have problems," Dawn observed.

Will, moon-faced behind his horn-rimmed glasses, shuddered. "It was just such baaad acting. It made me want to go all *Mystery Science Theatre 2000* on it."

"It made me uncomfortable when the manager put his arm around Bob after lecturing him," Craig said righteously. "Didn't that make you uncomfortable, Freddie dear?"

"And that perfect demographic spread!" Dawn continued. "One of every flavor, like that ever happens."

"Since this training is all about sensitivity, I have to point out that the person doing all the complaining was the one middle-aged woman." Judy had been the only person over forty in the room. "I mean, how age-ist is that? Making her the bad guy?"

As sexual harassment training it might have been a washout, but as a team-building exercise, it was a resounding success.

Δ

```
From:          Arthur Russo
To:            Pinnacle Leaders; IT
Subject:       Employee Departure
------------------------------------
```

Effective immediately, Avie Ganz is no longer with the company.

Arthur Russo, Dir. Human Resources
Pinnacle Management Services

Δ

```
From:          Kippy Melcher
To:            All Pinnacle Associates
Subject:       Exciting News!
------------------------------------
```

Please join me in welcoming Wesley Peterson, Pinnacle's new Chief Technology Officer. Wesley has a long track record of establishing dedicated software development teams for companies such as DanTech, Kore Metals and Cobaltic Industries. His arrival comes at the start of a new phase in our company's maturation.

Kippy Melcher, CEO
Pinnacle Management Services

Δ

Everyone on the news was saying it was impossible, but it looked like the MTA might really go on strike. The old lady Martha Moon always met at the laundromat was a native New Yorker and she said it had happened before, twenty-five years ago. In those days, Mrs. Ceppos had been teaching downtown and her husband was a florist with his own van. They drove in every day, packing the van with strangers they'd pick up along Queens Boulevard. It had seemed like the right thing to do. People would congregate by the bus stops looking for rides, Mrs. C said. People who lived within a mile or so of any of the bridges walked right across them. "Like ants at a picnic, the 59th Street," she said. "I only saw the Brooklyn on TV, but that was something! Like those movies about Europe during the War, with all those evacuees. Oh, they'll strike this time, take my word. Where do you work, honey? You got a way to get in?"

Dad always said Martha was one of Nature's Girl Scouts. She was organized, was all; she saw no reason for panic or fuss. It was easy enough to keep fresh batteries in the big flashlight and the old radio. Even living in New York City, she always kept packs of jerky and a box of candles in the kitchen drawer, and a couple of gallons of water on the floor of the closet, in case of storms.

Incapable of doing nothing, Martha asked Chris about the company's plans. For example, her job was all phone and computer. Was there a way she could maybe work from home? She knew Sales had some software they used to remote in from the field.

Chris looked as blank as only Chris's golfball eyes could manage. Art hadn't said anything. "Anyway, there isn't going to be a strike."

"Maybe no," Martha allowed for the possibility; "but it's better to have things lined up and not need them, then need them and not have them."

Chris shrugged.

"Can you tell me who else lives in Queens?" Martha had learned that you had to be persistent when trying to get anything out of Chris. "Maybe I can find a ride."

"We're not allowed to share confidential personal information." Chris used her chirpy HR voice and, dipping her head, indicated the conversation was over.

Martha was on her own. She thought she remembered hearing that Freddie Vega lived in Queens. She wondered where.

"Elmhurst," he said promptly. "My cousin has a car he uses for weekends. Kinda beat up, but it runs. I'll ask if I can use it. You'd be right on the way." Martha lived in Jackson Heights. "Orla lives in Astoria somewhere," he added. "We can get her, too."

Martha gave him a high five. She might not end up needing it, but she always felt better having all her ducks in row.

Seemingly overnight, the media made a 180 degree turn from "impossible" to "inevitable." They dragged out old footage from both previous strikes. The Brooklyn Bridge really was something to see, just like Mrs. Ceppos said: thousands of people surging across, all kinds of people; and Mayor Koch at the head of the pack, shaking every hand and cheering everyone on. Bloomberg was going to have a lot to live up to, especially being such a committed straphanger himself. The news reports said some of the larger companies were chartering busses for employees. A spokesman from one of the banks spoke proudly about his company's remote office network that would allow them to work at full capacity from home.

We started getting nervous at Pinnacle. Hardly anyone lived in Manhattan, not on our salaries. Those who were in Jersey or out on the Island were okay; the commuter trains would be running. It was everyone in the boroughs, about 80 percent of us, who'd be stuck. One of the Training Services girls sent out a blast email: "anybody live in Williamsburg with a car?" Before long, there was a barrage of similar emails. After a couple of hours, HR sent out a blast calling for them to stop; the emails were distracting everyone from their work and the traffic was slowing down the network. Instead, our brand new office manager, unlucky enough to be starting work this particular week, would put a spreadsheet on the share drive; anyone who was looking for a ride, or had one to offer, should post there.

The spreadsheet didn't go up until the end of the day. Martha didn't need it any more, but she peeked out of curiosity. All it had were columns for people to enter name and zip code, and to tick off whether they were driving or riding. You couldn't even filter for your own zip until Gene Siriano took pity and made a few tweaks.

The day before the strike deadline, the Mayor had a news conference urging people in "non-essential jobs" to stay home from work. There was a small lift in spirits until Kippy called an emergency all-Pinnacle meeting in the Pit.

"I know there's been a lot of talk on the news," he said; "and a lot of gossip in the office. I want to make things crystal clear. If the Transit Authority workers go on strike, and I sincerely doubt they will, Pinnacle will be open for business as usual. You are each one of you responsible for finding a way to get to the office. We're not losers here. You are all smart, creative professionals who take your work seriously and our clients are depending on us. Are there any questions?"

There was a moment of stunned silence, while we all silently tried to see where letterhead orders and PowerPoint training fit into the "essential" hierarchy with heart surgery and running water.

Glenn stuck up his hand. He'd been the highest earning salesman often enough that his question was casually confident. "Some of us only need a phone connection and maybe a login to Salesforce. It would be great if we could work from home if there's a strike."

Ken Aoki, rumored to be the sharpest of the IT developers, put in his own two cents. "I agree. We've got the technology to support it. All my work for the next few days is coding. I could just as easily be doing it from home." That new CTO, Wesley Peterson, pursed his narrow lips. We didn't expect Ken would be sticking around for long.

"That's fine." Kippy's voice was cold. "If you don't mind working from home permanently. Pinnacle does not have a work from home policy and I have no plans to start one. It's sloppy. People working from home take no pride in their work, in their team. Teams need to be on site, with their managers. If you work for Pinnacle, you work AT Pinnacle. This is how we create the kind of professional discipline that makes us the greatest managed office services company in the world. Strike or no strike, I expect to see you here in a timely fashion, at your desks and ready to work."

The soon-to-be John Jay graduate who'd recently joined Will in Compliance raised his hand. "I live way out in Brooklyn, sir," he said matter-of-factly. "I need a bus to get to the train. Neither one's going to be running if there's a strike, and I haven't been able to find anyone out my way who's driving in."

"You can arrange with your manger to take a personal day." Kippy's face was turning that dangerous red color. Someday he was going to have a stroke in the middle of one of his speeches.

"But I'm willing to work all day from home," he said, doggedly. "I could even work longer hours if we needed."

"To repeat what Kippy said," Art Russo jumped in quickly, before Kippy could draw breath, "Pinnacle does not support a remote work policy."

"I don't see what all this fuss is about," Kippy said, running his hand through his hair. "Frankly, I'm disappointed at your attitude. All you have to do is get up a little early."

Freddie raised his hand. "Um, a question for those of us who are driving. There's basically no parking in the neighborhood on a good day, and this isn't going to be a good day. Will we be reimbursed if we have to use a garage?"

"The LC will take this under advisement," Art said hastily. "If anyone has any other questions, please come see me. Thank you everyone." He looked pointedly at Kippy.

Kippy nodded sharply. "Yes, thank you all. See you all tomorrow. Here."

After the meeting, Edie Brewer made a beeline toward Martha. Martha didn't work for Edie, but she'd seen her in action and liked what she saw. Like Renee, Edie was a hands-on manager. She was managing now. "I hear you have a carpool going through Queens," she said.

Martha nodded. "Me, Freddie and Orla."

"Great," Edie said briskly. "You've got room for another body. I have a kid who started last week who needs a lift. Gabe del Monte. I'll tell him to call you."

"Have him call Freddie," Martha said. "He's the one driving, so he'll have to figure out the timing."

Negotiations went on all through that night, buying the city another day of service, though everyone had to wake up at the crack of dawn to check the news to find out. Once she knew for sure she'd have a train, Martha managed to fall back asleep for another hour or so, but she was still pretty cranky for most of the day. Interrupted sleep did that to her. All the Moons were eight-straight-hours kinds of folks. It didn't help any that Kippy strutted around all day acting as smug as if he'd personally negotiated for World Peace. It made her almost glad to see the workers go out the next day. She hoped when she got to work she'd be able to rope in a mad desire to thumb her nose and stick out her tongue.

By the time she finally got to the office, "I told you so" was the last thing on her mind.

Since Freddie was driving, they'd left the timing up to him. Martha would be the first stop; he'd call her when he left his house. She set the alarm for 5:30. If Freddie called her earlier, she'd be able to jump out of bed, brush her teeth, throw on her clothes and be out the door before he got there. Just to be sure, she laid out her clothes on the towel rail in the bathroom. He called her a little after six, so she'd even had time to put on some eye makeup. That was always a good thing. With her coloring, if she didn't, she looked like an unfinished pastel.

At 6:15 a.m. in December, it's pitch black out; the stars are still in the sky. The corner was freezing cold. Martha was glad she'd pulled on her Uggs. This was so not a normal day. Anyway, the whole HR anti-Ugg thing didn't make sense. Why should anyone care what brand of winter boots she was wearing? Her feet spent all day under a desk, except when she walked towards the toilets and then all anyone could see were three inches of round suede toe.

There was a girl in front with Freddie, so Martha climbed into the back.

"This is Silvia," he said. "She's my boy Chiky's lady."

"Hi." The girl twisted her neck to breaking point to smile at Martha. "I was so relieved I can't tell you, when I heard Freddie had a car. Like he's saving my life!"

"Where do you work?"

"38th Street. So not too far."

"Silvia's actually got a really essential job," Freddie said. "Just like us, right?"

"I'm an assistant pharmacist," Silvia said. "Why, what do you guys do?"

"He's joking," Martha explained. "Our company only means life and death to six people, the members of our Leadership Council."

"Seriously. Why are you guys having to come in today?"

"Because the people we work for are bat-shit crazy. We coulda worked from home, almost everyone, but if they can't see us with their own eyes, they don't believe we're working. Silvia, throw Martha my phone so she can call Orla. We're picking her and Gabe up by the Seven Eleven. Maybe we can get a coffee or something."

When they were only a few blocks from the intersection, Martha had to call Orla a second time. The carpool restriction required there to be four in any car crossing into Manhattan. Everything by the bridge was stalled to a screeching halt as cars that fell short wove towards the curbs to pick up people who were waiting there, hoping for lifts. Naturally, once they were full up, drivers immediately tried to push back into the bridge-bound lane, cutting off the cars behind them that were trying to do the same thing. Up until that point, other than the early hour, the drive hadn't been too horrible. Here, traffic was moving in chevrons. It took Freddie fifteen minutes to inch those last five blocks to the meeting spot.

It took another forty to get across the river. By then, everyone was getting twitchy. It was warm in the car, especially in the back where three people in puffy coats were crammed in tight. Afraid he'd get sleepy, Freddie opened his window a crack; then it was warm with an icy draft across the neck. It was good that Orla brought bagels as well as coffee. Things would have been far worse if they'd been hungry.

It also helped that the new guy, Gabe del Monte, was really funny. Martha would never be able to recall what he said—she could never remember jokes or stories—but he managed to keep them laughing, even when some idiot stopped short and Freddie had to slam on the brakes and they all whiplashed forward.

After dropping off Silvia at the Duane Reade, they hit some good road karma. Orla spotted a vacant parking space a couple of blocks from the office: a legitimate space, with absolutely no signage preventing them from sliding into it. They let out a cheer.

It was 8:45 when they hung their coats in the closet and made their way to their various desks. It was a miracle. Martha thought there should be a 21-gun salute on the other side; but there was only Vivian Karlow, watching anxiously from her corner cube.

Viv rushed to greet her, visibly relieved. "Thank you so much for being here."

"How did you get in?" Martha knew Viv lived somewhere near Brighton Beach.

Vivian blushed. "I called in a favor. A guy who used to copy off me in college. He's at NYU Law now. I told him I needed a place to stay in the city or I'd lose my job. He lives downtown. I had to walk three miles this morning."

Martha didn't know if she was more surprised that Vivian had let someone copy her work or that she'd stayed with a man. Either way, her surprise must have shown.

"I slept on the floor," Vivian said defensively. "My back is killing me."

Of course she had. There was something strangely virginal about Vivian.

"Mia couldn't make it, but it looks like we're going to have the rest of our group. Alex is skating down from the Bronx if you can believe." Vivian almost laughed. "He called to say it's taking longer than he expected. Crescenzo's volunteered to take the late shift every day while the strike is on. I think our numbers are going to be fine."

"The phones shouldn't be all that heavy today. No one local is going to call. Half of them are closed anyway. And the whole country knows about the strike. They'll probably treat it like a natural disaster and give us a break." Martha knew the customers well enough to feel this was a reasonable assumption.

Vivian had a frown that was surely going to lead her to Botox someday. "It's not coverage I'm worried about. It's bodies at desks. Kippy and Scott are asking every manager for head counts." With Renee away on vacation, Vivian was the one who would answer for the Client Care turnout. For once, her priggishness was excusable.

Vivian hadn't exaggerated. Kippy and Scott took turns walking the aisles, counting noses.

It was almost shocking how many of us were sitting at our desks. By 11 a.m., almost anyone who had tried had made it in. We looked like we were about to collapse, but we were there. Not a whole lot of work got done that day; we were way too tired to focus on much of anything except how we were going to get home at the end of it. The biggest excitement was when one of Edie's guys arrived at nearly noon. It had taken him seven hours to get in from Flushing on the LIRR. The line for the station had stretched for blocks, with trains so packed that only a few people could cram into any car. It would have taken less time to travel down from Boston. Edie made him leave at 3 and told him to stay home until the strike was over. George Waters thought that a questionable decision; he held his tongue for now, but made a mental note to remember.

Freddie was leaving at 4:00, so anyone in his carpool was leaving too. Martha was grateful the decision had been taken out of her hands.

Vivian was clearly not happy. "Working hours are from 9 'til 6."

"I was here before 9," Martha reminded her. "Most people didn't get in until later. And I ate lunch at my desk." It had been two granola bars and a bag of chips from the machine. We'd all assumed the company would have the grace to spring for pizza today. It was the standard for state occasions at Pinnacle, offered with tremendous fanfare. We were shocked when noon came and went without anything from Senior Management. Not so much as the words "thank you." Nothing but smug smiles of head-counting satisfaction. "I think I did very well by Pinnacle today." We all had. Better than Pinnacle had done by us.

Martha got home at 7:30. Three and a half hours for a twenty minute ride. She didn't know how Freddie managed it without putting a fist through the dashboard. Every bone in her body ached. She was starving but the thought of food nauseated her. She got the shower as hot as she could take and stood under it, trying to think of a really good gift for them to buy him, she and Orla and Gabe. It was horrible to think they'd have to do this all over again tomorrow.

The next morning was worse. Much worse. Freddie picked her up half an hour earlier, and they didn't get in until after 10. Vivian shot her an ugly look. When Kippy did his next circuit of the floor, he made a big deal about stopping by her desk.

"Good morning, Martha." He always took a particular fatherly tone when addressing her. She'd put herself through college working for Pinnacle and Kippy seemed to have frozen her in a perpetual Junior year. "I was afraid we weren't going to see you here today."

"There was a little traffic," she said.

"Never blame circumstances that you can control. You should have taken that into account and planned to leave a little earlier."

If only she had a paycheck big enough where she could put some money away each month after covering her rent and student loan, she'd be able to tell him to take that paycheck and shove it.

They were spending more hours in Freddie's cousin's old car than in the office. It felt as if they were living there, on those sticky vinyl seats. Heading up Third Avenue, they were stalled so long that Gabe got out, went into a Subway, picked up sandwiches and brought them back without the car gaining a block. At 7:30, they still couldn't see the on ramp to the 59th Street bridge.

Orla popped the door. "I can't sit any more, I'm getting out. I'm only a mile from the bridge."

Gabe looked at Martha apologetically. They'd been talking about the last Terry Pratchett book, kind of hitting it off. "She's right. We're both really right over the river."

"I don't blame you," Martha sighed. "If I could, I would. I bet Freddie would too."

"I tell you what all of us are doing," Freddie said grimly; "and that's calling in sick tomorrow. And it's no lie either. This fucking drive is making me sick and I'm not doing it again."

Orla called from the other side of the bridge. "Good news," she said. "Once you get across, the traffic seems to be moving."

That was nice to know, since the car had nearly progressed as far as 56th Street and they'd picked up two uncomfortable strangers to make the body count. It was a quarter to nine before Freddie dropped Martha off at her front door. "Freddie," she said, giving him a giant hug, "I owe you so big."

He waved her off. "Call in now, so you can sleep in."

Half the people who'd been dragging in took Thursday as a personal day. Kippy and Scott must have been livid walking the aisles, though according to Crescenzo's IMs the phones were practically dead. Gabe, the crazy dope, ended up walking in all the way from LIC. Being with the company only a few weeks, he didn't dare call in sick. He was probably right about that. No matter how understanding Edie was, HR listened to a higher authority.

The strike ended that afternoon, but the trains wouldn't start running again until morning. Gabe was so exhausted that he couldn't face walking all the way back home. He hid out in the interview room until everyone else was gone, then stretched out across a row of chairs in the break room. Martha found him in the morning, when she came to make herself an instant oatmeal. Instead, she ran downstairs to get him a fried egg sandwich while he washed his face and combed his hair with a plastic fork. It didn't help much. Neither did his dropping some of the egg on his already sad-looking shirt.

Gabe tried his best to stay inconspicuous that day. It was his bad luck to have Scott walk by while he was standing at the filing cabinets. He snatched up a stack of folders to cover the front of his shirt, but it was too late. When it came to wardrobe, Scott had a gimlet eye.

"That's not proper business attire for Pinnacle," he said sternly.

"I'm so sorry, sir," Gabe thought it politic to grovel. "I had a little accident..."

"Before or after you slept in that shirt?"

The painter who lived in Gabe's skull couldn't help but observe that when Scott got angry, his lips narrowed to a wiggly line, but his forehead remained curiously unfurrowed. Had Scott had Botox? Who could he ask?

"I asked you a question!"

"I'm tremendously sorry. I couldn't get home last night..."

"The strike is over," Scott said, grimly satisfied.

"They didn't restore service until this morning. I walked here all the way from Queens yesterday. I was here all day covering for my team," Gabe hoped that this would buy him some appreciation if not sympathy. "I had to sleep in...uh, on a friend's floor. I didn't have anything to change into this morning."

"You should always keep a fresh shirt in your desk," Scott said, apparently unmoved. "All of my team does." Scott paused to consider what he'd just said. "Go see Glenn Levine. Tell him I told you to loan you his."

"Yes sir!"

There were only a couple of hours left to the day, but Gabe was afraid not to obey. Glenn took a Brooks Brothers box out of his file drawer. "Bring it back when you can," he said. "I keep two. I sweat like a pig in summer, you know?"

"Thanks," Gabe said. "I mean it"

"Hey, no problem." Glenn looked thoughtful. "You're pretty lucky. If it was one of us, we would have got fired for that."

"Seriously?"

Glenn nodded solemnly and pointed to a print-out on his cube wall. Ten Commandments of Sales. 'Appearance' was number three, just above 'Integrity'. Gabe's jaw dropped. "Think what you like," Glenn told him; "that man knows how to sell."

Δ

From: Kippy Melcher
To: All Pinnacle Associates
Subject: Goodbye and Good Luck!

As you all probably know by now, Ruth Berger is retiring
effective December 31. Ruth has been my administrative
assistant for nearly 20 years. She's always been at my side
helping Pinnacle to grow from a small answering service and
bookkeeping company to one of the top 12 managed office
service companies in the country, It's hard to imagine
Pinnacle without Ruth. She will be greatly missed.

Ruth will be attending our holiday party as usual, but we
wanted to give her a special sendoff all her own. I invite
everyone to please join us in the Main Conference room
Thursday afternoon at 5:30 for wine and cheese, to help wish
Ruth happiness and good health as she begins this new chapter
in her life.

Kippy Melcher, CEO
Pinnacle Management Services

Δ

Everyone loved the idea of the Holiday party, and this year the actual party
was as good as the idea.

Because he liked showing us he was smart and well-connected, we knew
some friend of Kippy's in the restaurant business had gotten him a special
price on the smallest room at Tavern on the Green. It was a quantum leap
from the back room at Whine Bar: a pretty room, darkish, banked with an
abundance of evergreen and poinsettia and festooned everywhere with
twinkle lights. Dave Broussard couldn't help but imagine himself in the shoes
of the team that had hung them, climbing a 12 foot ladder and twisting 20
yards of lights around a two-story window and then, wanna bet when you
plugged it in you found one light smack in the middle that didn't go on?
He'd had too many jobs like that not to be grateful that he didn't have to do
them anymore.

He gave himself a final check in the glass door before going deeper in.
The invitation, jointly signed by Kippy and Scott, urged "festive dress." Dave
thought his own attire struck just the right note: festive with a retro kind of
classy that put people at ease. Angela said he was putting on the pounds, but
the gold brocade dinner jacket still closed. It had already been second-hand
when his dad got it to play weddings and country club dances with Harry
Silver and the Goldtones, a bunch of broke jazz musicians selling out to put
food on the table. The Goldtones hadn't lasted long and the jacket ended up
in a box in the garage. Dave filched it when he went off to college. There
hadn't been a lot else for him to take. Luckily, he had that trick of making do
and turning strange gear into a statement of style. He'd gotten so used to
working the jacket that when he had to put on a real tux, for one of Angela's

56

work events, he didn't recognize himself in the mirror. He looked almost elegant in a tux, like someone he'd want to be. In the jacket, he was, like always, the Buzzard: a little goofy, a little edgy, and an all-around good guy.

With a final tweak to his hand-tied bow tie, Dave pushed forward, scoping out the scene. Guys who weren't in Sales had on jackets and ties. Okay, some of the ties were a little odd, but they were ties. Dave was pleased to see some on the necks of his own team. Exercising some leadership, he'd urged the guys to get hold of some dress shirts and flatly begged them not to wear chinos unless they had no other non-jeans option. He wanted IT to make a good showing. No heads had rolled except Avie's, but this new CTO could easily decide to clean house. He was making a lot of interesting noises, this Peterson. He had an IT resume, but he carried himself like Kippy or Scott. If they could hang on, this could be good for all of them. Not everyone was Ken Aoki, so smart he was like to cut himself, one foot perpetually out the door. Aoki must have felt him thinking. He threw Dave a salute as ironic as his hugely expensive leather jacket and collarless black shirt, festive but a bit of a red flag. Dave saluted back. He felt a wistful kind of respect for the guy. Dave had never been quite that cocky; he'd always been too aware of what he had to lose.

Heading towards the bar, Dave lifted a skewered shrimp from a circulating waiter. He wished he'd lifted a napkin, too. The sauce wasn't bad, but it was sticky. He needed to wipe his fingers asap. Kippy was holding court near the bar and he'd have to shake hands. He noticed Judy, standing with an awkward cluster of newbies who didn't seem to know one another. All those hours together had made them partners of a sort. He knew she was the kind who always had whatever you needed somewhere on her. Right now she had an extra napkin and some advice. "Order something straight. They're using those really sweet bottled mixers."

A well-crafted cocktail was a thing of beauty, but industrial strength corn syrup and citric acid was disgusting. Dave was starting to genuinely like Judy. He wondered what kind of scotch was on offer.

Part of the fun of the Holiday party was seeing how different people looked when they weren't being Business Casual. Dress shirt collars set off fresh haircuts. Jeff Curry, as though trying to prove he had management potential, preened in a well-fitting dark suit. Craig Parnes had shaved his stubble, revealing a surprising dimple in his chin. To match his gaudy eyewear, Fabian Mello decked himself out with scene-of-crime-tape suspenders and pair of taxi-cab yellow Docs. The women of Pinnacle had outdone themselves. At 5:03, the Training Room, which Kay Kuperman had volunteered as a dressing room, had been like backstage at Fashion Week, garments flying through the air amidst a frenzy of half-dressed women wielding makeup and hair products. The results decorated the room as effectively as evergreens and twinkle lights: girls in short, shiny dresses, walking like queens on stilts of black patent and silver lamé, hair piled high to show chandelier earrings. A few had decorated their false nails with rhinestones, setting off a light show every time they lifted a hand. Only Sales looked the same as they always did.

There was a trend that year for tiny little cameras in jellybean colors. A lot of the women had them dangling from their wrists. We stood around in giddy clusters, drinks in hand, admiring one another and snapping pictures, interrupted only briefly by the obligatory pleasantry with Scott Bell. While Kippy held the bar, Scott circulated among the enlisted troops, meeting and greeting. As the official host of the Holiday party, he made it a point to attest, especially to those whose faces he didn't know, that Pinnacle was like a family and that he cared about each and every one of us. As he circulated, Scott insisted on having his picture taken with every little group, usually bracketed by two women with an arm around each. "Don't forget to email me that one!" he told each photographer, flashing his widest grin, his skinny hazel eyes brimming with delight before he released his squeezes and moved on.

"Your new boss is headed towards us. How do you feel about being folded into IT?" Edie cocked her head questioningly at Mike. It didn't have to be official yet for her to know. There were no secrets at Pinnacle.

Mike shrugged. As much as he'd enjoyed the independence, he'd known it wouldn't last forever. He could never have reported to Ganz, but this Peterson felt substantial. "It might be good, to have a C-level exec for IT. Peterson has an interesting track record. Nick says he's helped two companies to IPOs. That's not luck, that's talent."

When something surprised her, Edie had an infectious laugh. "Come on, Ventura. Kippy is never going to go public. He loves it too much, all of this."

Mike knew what she meant. Kippy liked to have his hand in everything, and he lived for making decisions. Having to answer to stockholders would make him miserable. But the kind of cash that came with an IPO was a powerful incentive. "Never say never."

"Glad to hear you say that, Mike. I never do." Wesley Peterson smiled blandly.

Unless he had the hearing of a bat, he'd been too far away to have heard anything but the last bit through the crowd buzz. Mike grinned comfortably. "So what do you think of the party?"

"Impressive. Tavern on the Green? I'd say I'd made the right choice to come aboard the Pinnacle Express. Hello, Edie. I'd shake your hand, but mine are occupied." They were, with a pair of Old Fashioned glasses. "No jokes about two-fisted drinking please! I'm headed for the Russians. These are meant as an ice-breaker, for our prickly friend Leon. I understand how difficult it must be, after all he's accomplished, to have to answer to someone else. I need to make a connection. The man's a stone wall in the office. I thought perhaps the party atmosphere, some Stoly..."

"He'll appreciate the respect even more." Mike was beginning to feel a connection of his own with his new boss. "Ganz pretty much steamrollered him."

Peterson shook his head decisively. "Foolish. If we're going to work with the technology he built, we need to make that man the bedrock of this team." Behind his rimless glasses, his pale eyes were surprisingly sharp. "We have a lot of talent here, Ventura. We can do great things. And you're going to be key. I've watched how you relate to them. You're a good man."

Mike hadn't expected that. "Thanks. They're a good team That is, now they've got someone to lead them, I think they can be."

Peterson winked a smile. "They will. And don't they clean up well?! Broussard's jacket was a bit of a surprise, but Melcher and Bell seem to like it. I better hurry before these get too warm to be acceptable. *Dosvedanya*."

He strode swiftly away. Mike turned to Edie. She raised her eyebrows and lifted her glass. "To change?" she said.

At one end of the room, the floor had been left clear of tables in case anyone wanted to dance. When the salsa music came on, Renee Ochs, outgoing Director of Client Care, took the floor with one of her erstwhile staffers. She was letting loose a little tonight. She deserved a good party. Tomorrow would be her last day of work at Pinnacle. She'd only been there a year but, after butting heads with Kippy and Scott every step of the way, it felt like ten. Renee didn't understand those two. They'd hired her to impose structure and establish procedures, but every time she put something in place, they'd short-circuit it for some imaginary client emergency. They'd even shot down her call center skills training program, a program she'd polished at three other companies and for which she had reams of metrics proving success. What did they say was wrong with it? That it took too long! There was such a disconnect between what these men said they wanted and what they were willing to support. Renee felt that all her efforts had been for nothing. She was exhausted. Official word about her departure was going to be that the "decision was mutual," but Renee knew no one would believe it. The rumor mill would say she'd been cut loose, which was pretty much the truth of the matter. Her contract ran through the end of February but, cheap as they were, Kippy and Scott decided they preferred paying it out to having to argue with her for another two months. She didn't care; she was well out of it, and she already had some promising leads.

With unexpected skill, Diego Guzman led her into a spin. Renee twirled into it and flew out again, laughing out loud. She was happy as a clam to be set free.

Marla Cox had been with Pinnacle longer than almost anyone except Walt Sacco and Noble Landrum, and had done nearly every job in the place. She was also excellent with people. All of this made her an ideal Trainer. She loved her job. She'd recently had a quiet talk with Kay Kuperman, to find out if there were certifications she should maybe go for, to make a career of this. Right now, any plans had to be put on hold. Starting Monday, until they found a replacement for Ruth, she was the only one Kippy would trust to cover his desk. It was kind of a compliment, though she'd rather be training. Right now, as for every party since he'd joined the company, it was Marla's job to be Scott Bell's Lovely Assistant. It was another compliment she could have done without.

Scott climbed up on a chair so that we all would be able to see him; she handed him Mr. Microphone.

"Hello, Pinnacle!" he crowed.

No one turned a hair.

"Um," Marla said, tugging on his pants leg to get his attention. "It's not on."

"That's why I need you up here with me," he said, pointing to the nearest chair.

She sighed and pushed the chair over. It wasn't close enough for Scott; he reached for the chair back and pulled it as close to his as it would go. A waiter held the gift basket and helped her up. Her stilettos wobbled dangerously on the cushions. Marla was the kind of woman who looked good in anything. At nine months pregnant, she'd looked like some actress faking it with a basketball shoved under her shirt. Tonight she was looking particularly stunning, in a fitted cocktail dress that contrasted with the warm tones of her skin. The shoes matched. She started to ease them off. Unfortunately, in order to stay steady while she did, she had to lean on Scott's arm.

He seemed far too happy about that. "Much better," he said, slipping an arm around her aqua satin waist.

When she was comfortably bare of foot, she twisted gently away from him. "Oh, the awards!" she exclaimed loudly and bent to retrieve her basket from the waiter.

That was enough to get the nearest people to swing around and stare.

"We're good to go then," Scott nodded. He flicked the switch on the microphone. "Hellooo, Pinnacle!"

Anyone who hadn't noticed them before then turned around now.

"I am so excited to welcome all of you to our annual holiday party! Isn't this terrific?!"

Looking ahead to a short workday followed by a long weekend, loosened by a drink or two, and off balance from the sight of familiar faces in an unfamiliar setting, we cheered and applauded raucously.

Scott beamed. "This is our biggest party yet and without a doubt our best ever. On behalf of Kippy and myself, I'd like to thank you all for coming and for the great job you do each and every day. Now we've got a couple of awards to give out, including our coveted MVP award...."

A crew from Sales started chanting "Ro-ger! Ro-ger!"

Scott laughed. "I can see some of you have some side bets going on! You're gonna have to wait just a little, okay? Where was I? Oh, yeah. Awards, and some door prizes. What have we got in there, Vanna?"

He handed the microphone to Marla who cleared her throat, took a deep breath and rattled it off in an embarrassed stream: "two $50 gift cards from Best Buy, five $25 iTunes cards, and three PTO days."

"That's for three lucky people," Scott shouted into the cheers. "They get tomorrow off! But first—hold your horses—before we give away this great stuff, I'd like to say a few words about the company and the amazing year we've had."

Dave Broussard's attention was diverted by little Martha Moon pulling at his elbow.

"Dave," she whispered, "there's a situation."

It was never clear how, because none of them were able to remember much, but a couple of the younger guys had somehow gotten far drunker than their allotted drinks would account for. There was reason to suspect they'd gone somewhere before the party and gotten a head start; or maybe they snuck in a flask. It didn't really matter. The result was that Freddie, Crescenzo and some new kid in Payroll were puking their guts out. Martha, a little relaxed herself, had been wandering around looking for Gabe del Monte. She'd kept thinking about him, how he was tall, dark and cute in a giant puppy-dog kind of way. They could pick up last week's conversation; get to know each other a little better. The boys stumbled past her. She felt compelled to follow. They barely made it to the shrubberies. The situation was more than Martha could handle. She needed a fixer and Dave seemed like the logical choice. He was a good guy, not the kind to rat anyone out. Plus, he was a little older. He must have had some experience in his day. He had that frat house air about him.

Dave sized things up in a heartbeat. Crescenzo and the new kid were a mess, but at least they were upright; they could be sponged off and sent home in a cab. There was no way Freddie was going to get out on his own steam.

"Find me two people you can trust," Dave told Martha. "Conrad if you can find him. No one in Sales. And keep far away from anyone in HR."

"You don't have to tell me."

Gabe del Monte was grinning from ear to ear.

"Look!" he waved a piece of paper under Martha's nose. "I'm a winner! I won a day off from work. Tomorrow. Okay, it's a half day, and I have to take it tomorrow. But a four day weekend! How great is that?! I don't qualify for vacation for another two months."

"It's great, it really is." What lousy timing, running into him now. She needed to find Conrad.

"Of course it would have been really great if I'd had it last week, right?"

"Mmmm, yeah. Yes, of course." She couldn't keep her eyes fixed on his face.

"Am I keeping you from something?"

He looked so sad. Martha looked into those brown eyes and made a decision. She knew she could trust him. "Help me find Conrad Beale," she said, taking his hand. "Tall guy with red hair? I think we're about to pay Freddie back for all that driving."

Δ

Martha's place made the most sense. They didn't have Freddie's exact address and Gabe had a roommate. She paid the driver with the money Dave had slipped her and ran ahead to unlock the doors, leaving it to Gabe to pry the body from the back seat. It was a good thing he was about a head taller than Freddie, and looked like he was used to lifting heavy things.

While he stuck Freddie under the shower, she put a layer of garbage bags on the sofa and covered them with the oldest sheet she had, in case he started barfing again. She also rolled away her rag rug; her mom had made it.

Once Freddie was safely tucked up, the bucket by his head, Gabe could have gone home.

"I'll be fine now that the heavy lifting is done."

"That's not right," he objected. "You shouldn't be alone. I have a feeling you're not going to sleep."

"Too right. No point in even trying. I'll be jumping up every time I hear him turn over.

"I'd rather stay and keep you company." He said it the way a girlfriend would, or a cousin. There was something different about this guy.

"You want something to eat?" She started rummaging around in the kitchen. She knew there was a bottle of wine somewhere. "We kind of missed out on the party. I never even got to hear who got the MVP award."

"Mike Ventura," Gabe said promptly. "Conrad said, while we were getting them in the cabs."

"Mike's a good guy. Funny too. You would have laughed yourself sick to see what he wore for Hallowe'en."

She found the wine, and there was the cheese and cookies her sister had packed up and made her bring back from Maine. Gabe sat at her tiny table, looking around the studio.

"You've got a real home here," he said appreciatively.

"It's the L-shape," she said. "It's almost like having a bedroom."

"I mean the way you have things. A table. Curtains. That rug…"

"I'm guessing you and your roommate are doing the usual guy thing? Mattress on the floor, paper plates and a really expensive widescreen television?"

He laughed. "Not far off," he admitted. "Except for the television. Only a small one. We need the space. We're both painters, me and Josh. We were roommates in art school. He came up here and I stayed in Miami until…" he looked at his watch. "Wow. Eight months and five days."

She sensed there was more to say and waited patiently, sipping at her wine.

He looked at her and took a deep breath. "I was with someone for more than a year," he blurted. "I thought it was….I thought she was The One. I was…damn, I almost gave her my grandmother's ring. I was about to when she told me she was leaving me. She left me for her girlfriend." He shook his head as if trying to wipe out the memory. "It hurt like hell, and I felt so fucking stupid, pardon my French."

"What? Oh, you mean 'stupid'? Not my favorite word, but that's okay." Without him asking, she refilled his glass.

He smiled weakly. "Yeah, right. I had to change things up after that. Josh was always trying to get me to come up here, so I finally thought what the hell, why not. It made it easier, it did. Distance. But it still doesn't go away." He looked her straight in the eye. "I'm not ready to jump back on the horse."

She nodded, accepting what he was saying. He was a guy she could trust alright. "Who would blame you?" she said, as if there was nothing else going through her mind. She couldn't think what else to say. What might have become a very uncomfortable silence was broken by the deepest yawn she'd ever felt coming out of her. It practically sounded like the word "yawn."

The sympathetic yawn hit him immediately. They both laughed.

"We might as well try and doze or something," she said. "Sleeping Beauty over there doesn't seem to need us."

They kicked off their shoes and stretched out on her bed. Gabe seemed tense until she made a point of turning on her side, facing away from him. Before long, she heard the slow rhythms of sleep at her back.

She was wide awake. She turned over with exquisite slowness, so as not to jolt him awake. Her heart did a pancake flip in her chest. Martha was burned out on a pattern of falling madly in love, jumping a guy's bones and cleaning his house, and having her devotion thrown in her face when either he'd been "unofficially engaged since college" to a girl back home, or he met someone else on a business trip to Tokyo, or what he really needed in a girlfriend was someone who could pay half the rent on a $3000-a-month studio in Nolita. She never wanted to get her heart broken again. Ever. Now here was this guy, this kind of adorable guy with those tousled curls and that crooked sideways smile, someone she could trust. And he only wanted to be friends. No, she corrected herself; what he'd said was he was only ready to be friends. Well, she could be friends, too. Until he was ready.

A loud snore percolated up from the sofa. Martha stifled a giggle. "Thanks again Freddie," she thought.

Δ

```
From:        Arthur Russo
To:          Pinnacle Leaders; IT
Subject:     Employee Departure
-----------------------------------------
Renee Ochs has left Pinnacle to pursue other opportunities.
We wish her the best of luck in all her future endeavors.

Arthur Russo, Dir. Human Resources
Pinnacle Management Services
```

TUESDAY

3 MINOR RESTRUCTURING

All day Monday you ran on fumes. You got home, ate some kind of dinner, watched a little comfort video—maybe a stream of something you saw a million times already, like "The One With the Thanksgiving Flashbacks" or "I Borg"—and crashed. Waking up Tuesday, after a seriously good night's sleep, it's all "Hello, World!" You bounce out into the city like you're in a sitcom, with your own theme song. That's probably the best thing about Tuesdays. Other than that, it's nothing special. All routine. The muscle memories kick in, finally pushing the weekend out of your head.

There's so much to do that the hours flash by. If you don't watch out, there'll hardly be time for it to hit you that you've blown another week of daylight at that desk. Remember how you swore you'd do your own work at night? Okay, you've been too wiped out to pick up a brush, but you gotta try. It's not like you need natural light, not for what you do. And what about those galleries and museums you said you'd hit, now that there's enough money coming in to cover the rent and pay for paint? Last week you let everything get away from you again. This week, you're going to manage your time better. It's only Tuesday. You have all the time in the world!

Either you'll get that grant or you won't. You did the best you could with the new application, and yesterday you had it notarized and stuck it in the mail. There's no point in dwelling on it. Time to face the week.

You can sit down to new business now, after all yesterday catching up and squaring away. And there's something new all the time, now that the CTO is settled in and feeling his oats. The man speaks better Salesman than even the Buzzard. And Kippy eats it up, those big smiles and firm handshakes charming the dollars out of his pockets. Peterson's pushing out staffing requisitions as fast as Judy can type them up. If Andreas was right, he helped take his last two places public and is looking to three-peat and retire before he hits 55. Talk about a dream! In any case, what he's doing is definitely good for IT, and what's good for IT is great for the resume.

And with that big gap on your resume, you're lucky someone would hire you at all. Can't complain about good luck. Though you sure wish the old secretary had been willing to hang around a few more weeks and train you, so you wouldn't have to guess at everything. It'll be fine, once you get used to it. It just feels strange to be back in a regular office after so many years doing Rory's paperwork at the kitchen table. But with Swarthmore cutting his hours, how else are you going to get health insurance and try for a baby?

You can't keep a family on beautiful words. You don't want to throw it in his face, but sometimes he won't let up. Good thing he's one of those late-to-bed-late-to-rise writers. If you had to face that reproachful look first thing in the morning, you'd never make it out the door. Especially on Tuesday. It's crazy busy on Tuesday! As if it takes all of Monday for people to remember what they needed from you.

Well, they can yell your name as loud as they want. You are absolutely taking lunch today because you are absolutely hitting the gym. None of this emergency shit; none of those Monday excuses. Gym today for sure. If you drag the other guys, if you go together, there'll be no excuse. And Noble said he'd do a real Marine boot camp. Which would be radical, especially for Shawn. Can you believe that guy lost 72 pounds? All he needs is to get a little cut, so he can build up some confidence. Ventura looks like a heart attack waiting to happen. Wonder if he'd come with?

Because hey, you need all the energy and stamina you can find. This place gets crazier every day, especially since they fired your boss. The only one in the company who seemed to know what she was doing, and they got rid of her. Tuesdays. Business as usual.

#sameold

Δ

"Things are going to be a little different. Since being appointed Interim Manager, I've been looking at our points of failure and listening to feedback from the LC."

This was the third time in one meeting that she'd squeezed in her unofficial title. Vivian Karlow was that girl whose hand shot up the instant the teacher asked a question. That eight-grader who never had a spot, and whose hair had the preternatural gloss of a shampoo commercial. That classmate who volunteered to take attendance for the substitute, who ate the over-cooked green beans in the lunch room with apparent enjoyment. Mere self-satisfaction might have been forgivable. Her smug righteousness was not. Viv made it clear that Scott and Kippy, having finally seen the error of their ways, had anointed her to lead Client Care out of the darkness. "Our biggest pain point is we're not picking up calls fast enough. Certainly not for our marquee clients, Scott says."

"Marrrrrqueeeeee," Alex Silva purred. "Are those the ones that do the most business or the ones that scream loudest?"

Viv pretended she hadn't heard him. "We need to reduce Time-to-Talk. So we're doing a little restructuring. Martha and Crescenzo, you've been with us the longest; you have Depth of Knowledge." If there was one practical thing Viv had learned from years of academic pursuit, it was the importance of appropriate jargon. Renee Ochs might have forgotten that the CEO is always right, but her vocabulary had been exemplary and Viv had taken care to absorb it. "I'm making you our team for what Kippy calls White Gloves Service. You will be dedicated to handing these clients. They'll have a special extension—Scott's drafting the email now—that routes directly to you."

Chronically respectful, Martha raised her hand before she started talking. "But Viv, we can get through the queue faster if we're also available to help the new people. That's why Renee put the mentoring system in place, so we could keep the volume going while people learned."

Vivian's little lemon slice smile turned into a twist of dried out peel. "Scott isn't happy with that system. Keldorian was on hold for two minutes the other week. They were furious."

Mia objected. "That was the day we had three people out with stomach flu."

"That shouldn't matter."

"What if Martha and I both get stomach flu? Or strep throat or something?" Crescenzo was so obviously in earnest that no one laughed.

"Both of you have exemplary attendance records. And all that hand-holding is a waste of bandwidth."

"Bandwidth?" Alex sounded incredulous.

She ignored him. "From now on, I'll be training the new people myself. If people are properly trained to begin with, they won't be asking questions all the time."

"You have to ask questions when you first start," Martha pleaded. "It takes months to learn enough about the business to be effective on a call."

"Scott says it shouldn't." Vivian sounded almost reverent. "He's shared his training materials with me and I'm putting together something similar for our team. You'll see. So, Martha and Crescenzo, here is your White Gloves list. Companies, plus primary contacts for each service we fulfill for them, with emails and direct lines." She handed them each some stapled sheets of pink copier paper.

"We have all this in Salesforce."

"This way you have it right."

Δ

It was what the on-air weather people had taken to calling a "wintry mix," as though it were some delightful blend of cocoa and cinnamon and peppermint stick. It was the kind of cold air that felt hard when you breathe it in, with a dash of precipitation that couldn't decide whether it wanted to be snow or freezing rain. In the alley, the smokers huddled by the back door of the posh boutique in the next building. The overhang, a miserable strip of corrugated metal erected to protect incoming racks of inscrutable Japanese tailoring, served well enough on days like this, though the drumming rain drove everyone a little crazy.

Alex stamped his feet, keeping the circulation going. He was glad for the pop-top mittens Martha had given him for Secret Santa. So what if he sock puppet eyeballs looked a little wonky? At least his hands wouldn't freeze while he smoked.

"If I'd have gotten my fellowship, I'd be on my way to sunny Italy right now," Mia grumbled.

"Pathetic," Orla observed.

"Well fuck you very much."

"I mean Silva's boots. I told him to get thick bottoms. Insulation." Orla extended her foot for inspection.

"Grunge cliché? I don't think so. I like Martha's but they're disgusting in men's sizes. Either traffic cone orange or baby shit tan. I wouldn't be caught dead."

"My folks sent me these for Dia de los Reyes Magos," Diego admired his own black storm boots. "I'm liking them."

"Are they expensive? I'm still saving for a new mattress. Did I tell you I tried out one of those foam ones at Macy's? The ones where you can jump on one side and the glass of wine doesn't move?"

"You can't afford something like that!"

"I know. But the salesman didn't. He was pretty cute, especially when he had to bend over to read the price tag. Twice."

Mia's little shove sent Alex barreling into Tully, popping out the side door.

"What the hell are you doing out here?" Alex said crossly. "It's cold as a witch's tit and you don't even smoke!"

"I had to get out of there for a couple of minutes." Tully's voice was so muffled by his triple-wrapped Arsenal scarf that it was difficult to hear him. He pushed the wool away from his mouth. "Where's Dawn? I thought she'd be down here. Fucking Spurious George is on the rag and he lit into her for not being fast enough with Keldonian."

Waters was the kind of guy who was vulnerable to nicknames. "Baby Hughey" had been an involuntary response to his appearance. As the weeks wore on and his less fleshly qualities became evident, there had been a minor competition to fit a more suitable handle, a contest that Jeff's combination of writerly skill and bitterness had handily won. In fact, the only slightly exaggerated exploits of Spurious George were growing the audience for Jeff's blog in a way that his rants about stupid people on the subway and dueling Halal food carts had not.

As his rival continued to thrive at Pinnacle, what had begun as Jeff's knee-jerk resentment had ripened into a pleasingly solid vendetta. They were equally without charm, but while Jeff's loyalty and bull-headed insistence on honesty endeared him to the rest of us, Waters lacked any qualities that might redeem his endless toe-stomping. Management registered Waters' conviction of his own superiority as confidence and dubbed him a rising star. There was escalating discord between this perception and the effect Waters had on his coworkers. Discussing Waters' latest blunder gave us all—not only Jeff—the same kind of satisfaction as tracing "wash me" through the dust coat of a neglected Porsche.

"Since they gave him the official title, Spurious thinks he's king of the world. And Dawn's so conscientious. Look how fast Edie moved her into Payroll."

"Fucking conscientious doesn't get us anywhere. You know, before Spurious, Edie wanted to give me the Assistant spot, but they told her there was no room in the budget."

"Sucks," Tully agreed. "But at least Spurious leaves you alone."

Jeff gave a harsh laugh. "Yeah, well, he knows what he'd get if he tried the same crap he pulls with the rest of you."

"He doesn't pick on Orla," Diego noted.

"Sure he does. I just don't let it get to me like you all do."

"No," Diego disagreed. "It's not the same. I think you scare him."

Orla was almost as nice as Diego, but it was easy to see how the black hair and nails, the kohl-rimmed eyes and the visible multiple piercings might communicate otherwise to a man of Waters' Eisenhower-era sensibilities. "Maybe we should get Dawn some ink."

"Back in the day, if someone spoke to one of my sisters like Spurious speaks to Dawn, I'd have had him bloody behind the dumpsters. He was harsh, let me tell you. I think she was crying."

Orla stubbed out her cigarette. "Poor kid. I'll go check the toilets. Don't worry." She cuffed Tully affectionately on the shoulder on her way past. Everybody except Tully and Dawn knew it was only a matter of time before they'd get together.

"This sucks. Did anyone tell Edie?" Alex asked.

"As soon as she gets back."

Jeff twisted his mouth into his characteristic almost-sneer. "I still don't get how Brewer doesn't see right through that asshole. It's making me lose all respect."

"Curry, Curry, Curry." Alex lowered his eyes mournfully and shook his head. "You know exactly how." At the holiday party, Waters had been overheard dropping his origin story to Roger Didilian in a fit of beer-induced braggadocio. "If you were willing to hide your evil twin, maybe Kippy would have anointed you, too. Edie didn't choose him any more than we chose crazy Vivian."

"Vivian! How bad could she be?"

"Today she took the breaks off the schedule. They don't, ahem, dovetail with our productivity initiative."

"Then how are you down here?"

"Oh, we're still taking them. They're just not on the schedule. Unless you count the secret schedule Martha started so we can cover for each other."

Tully checked the time on his phone. "Maybe you should go back. What if Vivian notices?"

"The women of Client Care are going to be having a lot of embarrassing cramps." Like Alex, Mia had the knack of raising her eyebrows like finger quotes.

Tully turned to Alex, fascinated.

Alex shrugged. "I predict an epidemic of irritable bowel syndrome. It's not like we can do anything about her. Not with Scotty pulling the strings."

"You think Spurious is anointed? Scott stops by a couple of times a day and does that shoulder squeeze thing of his." Mia shuddered, her beads rattling in the cold. That Scott's attentions never went beyond hovering and drooling made them no less distasteful. "That man is such a creep! But Vivian acts like the Annunciation. The Fra Angelico one where the dove is hovering in a Glinda bubble overhead. She glows."

"Among other things, the bitch is totally OCD." Alex considered his half-smoked cigarette. What the hell. Just this one time wouldn't break the bank. He took another draw. "She gives new meaning to the words micro-manage."

"Give her time. Maybe she'll learn. If Renee hadn't left..." Diego started to say.

"Renee didn't leave," Alex and Mia chorused. She gestured for him to take the baton.

"She was pushed out," he continued. "After they tied her hands behind her back. Very Tony Soprano. So they can save a few bucks by putting in someone like Vivian, who doesn't cost anything."

"Renee was awesome," Mia sighed. "Not just the way she organized the work. The way she trained us, shadowing and role-playing...she made Client Care feel like a profession. Viv's taking apart everything Renee put in. Like that mean kid who breaks apart your Lego castle to build a house for a frog."

"That happened?"

Mia laughed. "Let's just say my cousin Derek was a real dick. He's at Lehman now."

Jeff tried not to be impressed. "Maybe you should set him up with Viv."

"He only dates Asian women. He says that way he doesn't have to take sides. His mom is whiter than Dawn."

"Then maybe you should set him up with Viv's new assistant."

Mia was already feeling a sneaking sympathy for Ann Ling. With Viv bossing her around from day one, the poor girl didn't have a chance. She changed the subject. "Speaking of new assistants, I shared an elevator this morning with the new Ruth."

"Another mother for Kippy?" Jeff fished a napkin out of his jacket pocket to wipe his nose; this weather really was a bear.

"Not so much. Younger, more like us. Black tights and orange shoes. She has that baby seal look: big sad eyes and dazed, like someone clubbed her on the head. Liz says Chris says she used to be a model or something. But she smiled and said hi. She seemed nice."

"So yeah, another week and Scotty's wet dream finally comes true." There was a round of muttered expletives. Covering for Ruth had kept Marla away from Fulfillment just long enough that Scott could claim that he needed her assistance more than Edie did. Once the new gatekeeper was trained, she'd be moving permanently over to Sales and under the President's thumb. "And with poor Marla moving over, Scott doesn't need Megan. They're bumping her over to us. So, Vivian asked for an hour a day of her time to start training her." Alex shook his head.

Tully was confused. "Isn't that good?"

"She's not doing it the way Renee did," Mia explained. "What Viv does is more like SAT prep. She gives Megan pages of client notes to memorize at night..."

"On her own time," Alex added dryly.

"Ma certo! And then she gives her these ridiculous quizzes. To what end? Everything's in Salesforce! All we need to do is look things up. Megan would learn more by shadowing one of us for a couple of days to see how we answer calls."

"Except," Alex interrupted, "that would mean she might have a few days at the start where she—gasp!—isn't handling a full call shift."

"Well, you said Viv has Scott breathing down her neck." Tully was inclined to be sympathetic to any manager who was doing the crying herself and Vivian was famous for her quivering lower lip.

"We all have someone breathing down our necks," Alex retorted. "That's no excuse for incompetence."

"Yeah, well I wasn't incompetent until Waters starting hanging over me and telling me I was." Everyone stared. No one had ever heard Diego say anything negative before. "He was standing so close behind me yesterday my neck began to sweat. He starts telling me he doesn't like the way we keep the logs. He's supposed to keep his nose out of what we do. You know how Kippy feels about anything changing on Switchboard. But does that stop him from putting in his two cents? And then what are we supposed to do?"

"Okay, okay." Mia held up her hands in surrender. "We are all equally fucked. Except we're more fucked than you are because at least Edie will be back in another week."

"Wait, so who's moving into Marla's Training slot?" Alex had to ask. "Not Pee Wee Herman?"

Tully laughed. "You mean Channing? Nah, we're stuck with him in Data Entry."

"Creepy." Mia wrinkled her nose.

"I don't know about creepy, but he's definitely obnoxious. He started bragging he went to NYU. Then Curry told him Will went to Brown and, like that, he switched to telling us how we could be more efficient if we had ergonomic keyboards."

"Just what we need," Jeff grunted; "another Waters."

Mia had a cheering thought. "It'll be like a fight between those two guys in Casablanca. You know, the Fat Man and what's his name, the whiny one."

"Peter Lorre" Alex supplied.

"The Fat Man always wins," Diego remarked, grinding his butt under the sole of his boot.

Δ

In short order, Alex ended the last call, unhooked his headset and logged off his computer. 8:30 p.m. Client Care's final shift lasted just long enough to make the few West Coast clients feel they had a full day. It was the one value-add of Renee's that Scotty insisted Vivian keep. It must play pretty well in the marketplace, but it was boring as hell to work. Now he needed a good long stretch. About the only benefit of doing the late shift was that you could do a downward dog for a solid five minutes and no one would complain or, just as important, watch. If Donny Rohmer didn't stop oogling his fine ass, things were going to get ugly. That is, uglier. How often do you have to tell a guy he's not your type before he leaves you alone? And there was no point in complaining to HR. Russo was nothing more than a recruiter dressed in HR doublespeak.

Alex followed his dog with a quick series of sun salutes. He was in no particular rush to head out. He was only popping down to the PT Cruiser for a drink and the scene, to unwind. He never made a date on late shift days; he knew he'd be too wiped.

Before he left, he'd pop by and say hello and goodnight to Fabian and the new girl on Switchboard. They still had hours to go, poor kiddies. Switchboard had been a big deal when Kippy's dad had started the company. Now it was a little ridiculous, but there were some old clients, mostly doctors, who wouldn't let it drop. Kippy must have been sentimental about it; there couldn't have been much profit. Then again, overhead was low. The night team was all people who were working their way through school and didn't want to stand on their feet all day doing food service. People like Fabian, in his giant yellow glasses that reminded Alex of Mom's Elton John album cover, the one signed "To My Tiny Dancer" that had made little Alex think maybe Elton was his real dad. Damn, he'd been a thick kid, hadn't he? Whistling gaily, Alex moseyed over to the cubes where Switchboard lived.

"Hey."

The voice from the floor was Gabe del Monte, tucking a stack of folders into the bank of cabinets near the men's room. "Me and Tully and the guys from IT are ordering pizza. You want in?"

"Huh?" Alex craned his neck, like a dog sniffing the air out the back seat window. How had 8:30 suddenly turned into prime time at Pinnacle? He could spot eight, maybe ten people at their desks and that was without being able to see IT. These days IT was behind that new little wall of office pods that reminded Alex, who'd done his share of days as a film extra, of the Winnebagos they used as dressing rooms on location. Marcy Melcher's designer had one weird eye. Like the way he clustered Kippy's office and the conference room in a hub with all those doors. What was that about? In case there was ever a wedding in the office, so the guests could "flow?" Alex was no designer, but he flattered himself that he knew as much about placement as anyone. It was part of what made him a damn fine director. Which he'd do again. This dry spell was temporary. It was a question of waiting things out.

"Pizza," Gabe repeated.

"Sorry. No thanks. I'm on my way out. What's going on?"

"Not enough hours in the day," Gabe sighed. "I spend all day transcribing pages, and there's never time to get the originals filed away."

"I hear that upgrade to Bridge is going to get us paperless." Alex was good at hearing things. "If they ever finish it."

"I'll still have to file everything."

"At least you won't have to sit on the floor."

"There is that. At least when Fulfillment does overtime, we get paid. The bright side of being hourly. Not like the IT guys."

Alex's laugh was a little rude. "IT? I wouldn't waste any tears. They get paid more than anyone."

"Maybe. But you couldn't pay me enough to work like they do. Fourteen-hour days? When do you have time for a life?"

"I'm guessing this *is* their life. It's probably really different to be making a living doing what you want to be doing."

"I can't even imagine what that's like. Believe me, I wouldn't be here if I didn't have to. I only asked for approval to put in the extra time because Josh moved out and I need the money. Too bad they didn't let me take Marla's old slot in Training. It wouldn't have been much of a hike, but it would help."

"You looking for another roommate? Isn't Tully looking?"

"He found a place in the Bronx. Even cheaper than Queens, and with a bunch of musicians in the building so he can practice all he wants with no one complaining. Me, I need my quiet. No, I'm hoping maybe I can make a go of it on my own. It would be awesome to have the extra space to paint. Of course, working so many more hours, I hardly have time. Catch 22."

"There are always the weekends."

"True that. You know what I love?" Gabe had a smile of pure radiance. When he smiled like that, Alex understood why Martha was getting a little silly about the boy. "That feeling when you get off the subway Friday nights, when you suddenly realize hey, this is MY time. It's like I can breathe again."

Δ

From: Arthur Russo
To: All Pinnacle Associates
Subject: Employee Departure

Conrad Beale is no longer with Pinnacle. Until we have filled this position, we ask that you please refer all requests for help to systemsupport@pinnaclems.com. They will be forwarded to the appropriate individual.

Arthur Russo, Dir. Human Resources
Pinnacle Management Services

Δ

From: Scott Bell
To: All Pinnacle Associates

Subject: Exciting Announcement

I'm so excited to announce the roll-out of a brand new
Pinnacle initiative: our own newsletter! A collaboration
between Sales and HR, "The Peak Experience" will be published
monthly, with articles on products and best practices,
profiles of key members of the Pinnacle family, and coverage
of our corporate events.

Our very first edition will be delivered to your desk later
today and will include:

- A Welcome editorial by Kippy
- A photo essay of Pinnacle's participation in last
  month's Office Services Alliance convention in Atlanta
- Senior Vice President Walt Sacco writes about
  Pinnacle's tradition of charitable giving

A newsletter is a great opportunity for us to shine a light
on our achievements, sharing good news across departments and
with our clients. It's also a great opportunity for you to
showcase your talents! If you'd like to contribute to "The
Peak Experience," contact editor Judy Schreiber.

Scott Bell, President
Pinnacle Management Services

Δ

From: Scott Bell
To: All Pinnacle Associates
Subject: Employee Departure

Nick Andreas will be departing Pinnacle to pursue other
opportunities. We wish him the best of luck in all his future
endeavors.

Please join us in the Main Conference room at 5:30 Friday for
wine and cheese, to say goodbye and wish him well.

Scott Bell, President
Pinnacle Management Services

4 RAMPING UP

From: Wesley Peterson
To: Pinnacle IT
Subject: Exciting Happenings for Our Team!!

Hello, IT!

As Pinnacle continues an impressive rate of growth, the LC is
recruiting management skills across all departments, ensuring
we operate at Peak Effectiveness. Here in IT, we're aligning
with this leadership initiative as we continue to recruit the
talent we need to accomplish GREAT THINGS!

I'm delighted to announce that Mike Ventura will no longer be
the only PM at Pinnacle, but will be heading up a new Project
Management Office! To jump start this critical team, we've
got offers in to a talented junior PM and to a BA with
significant process-mapping experience. I'm also pleased to
officially welcome Judy Schreiber who is now assigned to us
at 100% and is reporting to Mike. Working within IT, in
addition to managing the software development lifecycle, the
PMO will also be establishing Standards and Benchmarks for
Project Management THROUGHOUT Pinnacle. Congratulations Mike!

The big news is that we're bringing on a TOP FLIGHT pair of
Leaders for our Development and Engineering teams! Clifton
Speck, our new VP of Systems Engineering & Operations, comes
to us from Hoffman Consulting, where he's been leading
network and telephony projects. I saw Clif in action when he
was assigned to me for a data center migration project at
Cobaltic. When the LC approved someone at his level for our
team, I knew Clif was the perfect candidate and, lucky for
us, he's ready to make the move away from consulting and onto
staff.

Our new VP of Development, Eliot Tseng, has years of
Development Lead experience on large enterprise application
projects. We've already got a GREAT group of talented
developers on our team, and Eliot will supply the management
skills needed to optimize their performance.

In a few weeks, we'll also welcome our new high-powered
Security Specialist, Malcolm James! I don't have to tell you

how IMPORTANT this placement is, or what it says about the
maturity of our organization.

Attached are job descriptions for the positions we still have
available. We've still got PLENTY! If you know people with
the skills and experience to join us, knock on my door.
Remember, there's a hiring bounty, so you're not only helping
Pinnacle. If the person you introduce places and stays for
six months, there's a $1000 cash bonus in it for you!

You'll be meeting Eliot and Clif at Monday's all-IT meeting,
so save your questions for then! Have a great weekend, IT!
Monday is the first work day of an exciting future for all of
us!

Wesley Peterson, CTO
Pinnacle Management Services

Δ

"They just redid this bank, and we're already outgrowing it. I was going to
give you Aoki's old desk, but it turns out the Security guy is starting sooner
than we thought." Ginny Chicosky's new manager looked more sheepish
than you'd expect from a guy that big. "By the time you get out of Boot
Camp, Conrad should...I mean Clif. Sorry. I'm still getting used to some of
the new players. Clif's our new VP of Engineering. He and Eliot Tseng only
started a couple weeks ago."

Ginny tilted her head, regarding him with bird-bright eyes. The avian
impression was increased by the egg-shaped frames of her glasses and her
fluffy cap of blonde curls. "I worked with Eliot a couple of years ago. When I
was still with A-Ware, I consulted on a Kore Metals project with Eliot and
Peterson. Small world, huh?"

"Too bad he didn't think of you himself. Our CFO hates paying agency
fees."

"I guess that's why Peterson asked me not to mention it to Art Russo." For
a tiny woman, Ginny had a surprisingly hearty belly laugh.

Mike joined in. "Okay, let's get you some coffee and introduce you
around! We'll stow your stuff in my desk for now. You won't be sitting here
much this week anyway. After Boot Camp, I'm going to have you shadowing
for a couple of days. I need you to get a feel for what the Fulfillment teams
do. They're our primary consumers."

"What about clients?"

He nodded, pleased. "Them too. But Client Care can be the baseline for
that. Anyway, you'll start with Edie. She's got two new hires of her own, so

it'll almost be like a class. And Friday, Viv said you can sit with Martha Moon. She's one of our top Client reps. Plus, she's been here longer than most, so she can probably answer any other questions you may have. A lot of us have been here less than a year. The company is..."

"Growing fast; everyone says. That's why I'm here!"

Mike had sold this hard at the interview. A place that was growing would allow you to spread your wings and grow with it. It was a message that Ginny was ripe to absorb. She'd gotten restless at A-Ware, where they hired you to fit a particular skill gap and you stayed put until the day you left.

Δ

Scott held himself so straight he rose another three-quarters of an inch from his built-up black calf bluchers. He'd promised himself that, if this deal came off, he'd treat himself to another week in Mexico, even though he'd only just come back. Visions of tropical prints and spray-on bronzer danced in his head as he strutted through the door of Kippy's office, grinning like a cocktail waitress who'd snagged an investment banker. The news was so exciting, Kippy sent out a blast email calling for an instant all-Pinnacle meeting.

We snaked towards the Pit in a hesitant conga line, compelled to hurry, afraid to hear what might be announced. Why was Kippy call a Town Hall? Beyond the usual revolving door in Fulfillment and Client Care, the last couple of months had seen a few high profile slashings that had us all on edge. Avie Gans, Conrad, Renee...because no matter what the email said, we all knew Renee had been slashed...And that baldish guy in Sales, the older one. Everyone had assumed he must be Kippy's cousin or something. These sudden departures created a ripple of uncertainty that Management either didn't notice or didn't care to alleviate; not even Art Russo who, as the head of HR, might have been expected to address it.

But Kippy was smiling from ear to ear. And he wasn't on the windowsill; he and Scott were standing on either side of The Gong. The Gong lived in the Pit. It made a loud, brassy "nnnnnnngggggggggg" that set everyone's teeth on edge. Any deal over 50K per annum, the salesman got to take a whack at it, so that the whole company would know he'd landed a big fish. Old timers like Noble and Marla could remember when it only took 20K for a swing.

"Sorry to interrupt your day. I know you're all hard at work, helping to make this the greatest managed office services company in the world. Which is why I wanted you all here to congratulate yourselves when Scott rings the gong for the biggest sale ever in Pinnacle history!"

A few of the Sales guys nudged each other in an inside-joke kind of way. One of them gave out a loud "woot! woot!" Assuming this to be a cue, we started to applaud. Scott stepped forward, his grin slicing his face in half, and waved for us to stop.

"Hold your applause until after the gong, okay? Before I ring this one in, I want to give a shout out to the team who worked so hard to make this happen. We wouldn't be ringing this in without the help of Vivian Karlow of Client Care, Mike Ventura and Dave Broussard of IT, and as always, our rock, Edie Brewer. And now, without further ado, Pinnacle is proud to welcome Mama-San Yakitori!"

The resounding gong turned the announcement into a parody of the cheesy MSY commercial. We half expected to see the trademark Japanese woman, a gingham apron tied over her traditional kimono, shuffle out from behind Scott, fold her hands and bow. Once we fought back that image, we had to be impressed. Mama-San Yakitori might not be as big as Mickey D or even Taco Bell, but it was a national chain and it was on the rise. To think they'd chosen Pinnacle instead of a giant like ADP or Ceridian! It wasn't only Scott and Kippy who were excited. This was the kind of client that would put us on the map. We clapped and cheered like mad. Raises, bonuses, management tracks. Maybe even cubicles with walls high enough that you could make a personal phone call at your own desk. With a company like Mama-San Yakitori on our client list, the sky was the limit!

Δ

Mike Ventura played a kind of chess, hunching skill sets he'd need to have on tap. Like latching onto Judy even before Andreas left, and starting her writing training materials and SOPs. And putting in the request that got him Simran Bhalla. Watching with pride as his brand new hire steered the MSY implementation meeting, he remembered the blank looks that "BPMA" had gotten from both his CTO and the two IT VPs who had to clear all new hires. Maybe he shouldn't have been surprised. Business Process Mapping was just starting to trickle down to smaller businesses.

"Smaller"; he'd better not say that in front of Kippy! Kippy would die to hear Pinnacle described in any way as small. Instead of longing to be the likely successor to Warren Buffet, Kippy should appreciate the actual scope of his accomplishments. Sure he'd been lucky, inheriting a solid business, but he'd also been smart enough to see the writing on the wall and seek out new ways to keep it going. And then he'd been lucky again during the post 9/11 dip in the economy, when a lot of companies moved to outsource whatever positions they could. Trimming down the fat, they called it, "fat" being anyone who didn't directly generate income: admins; payroll clerks; messengers. If work had to be kept in house, well, they doubled the load. Take Mike's girlfriend, Kitty, an admin for an insurance giant. She used to work for one adjuster; but when her boss retired they assigned her to cover three, claimed they couldn't justify her salary for any less. They told her that all the younger computer-friendly adjusters did most of their own work anyway. That simply wasn't true; to keep up with the load, Kitty was working the same kind of crazy hours as Mike. Really, what Pinnacle charged for office services was probably about the same or even more than companies like hers they would have paid in salaries to keep things in-house; but this way companies saved a bundle on benefits and office space and, if they were publicly owned, kept the illusion of a happily slim payroll budget.

Kippy kept his own payroll as low as possible. The kids he hired came cheap. Mike had never worked with such a collection of artists and musicians and actors and writers. Misfits and broken toys. It reminded him of the community theatre where he'd met Kitty. *Anything Goes*. She was Reno Sweeney. His cousin dragged him in to help build the ship. She broke a strap on her tap shoe, and when she bent down to tape it, she fell over him and bam! He was one lucky guy, to have a girl like Kitty. She'd been a Tinkerbell once, until a compound fracture of the tibia pushed her out of Orlando. There were pins holding her leg together; she set off airline security whenever she went through. Another broken toy.

Like Mike should talk. He'd started out in wood with Uncle Ed, a kid learning how to hand cut and set inlays, and lay parquet. He came out of North Carolina School of the Arts with big plans for his uncle's business, but once the rich people and the museums had all the floors and door panels they needed, the money stopped trickling down. All the hot ticket designers who used to hire them moved on to sticking their names on paint cans or designing lines of accessories for Target. Uncle Ed retired to Tampa and Mike started working for Cousin Gio, the contractor. Things were none too busy for Gio either, and he suggested, not too gently, that Mike start looking elsewhere. Another contractor who hung out at the social club put Mike onto Project Management. Mike took to it like a duck to water. Now, he had a PMP certification, some good experience under his belt, and was in a place that was virgin territory for what he had to offer.

Mike made great strides last year, raising Kippy and Alan's level of enthusiasm for process and quality management and making a big fan out of Edie Brewer. His impact had been significant enough for Kippy to have made him MVP in December. Under the gung-ho Peterson, he expected to make much more progress with IT than he'd managed under Ganz. It was a good team, and the work ahead was challenging in the best possible way.

This meeting was a case in point: Client Care and Fulfillment discussing the list of requirements they'd gotten from Mama-San Yakitori. "MSY" as they were calling it. It was interesting to watch from the sidelines instead of running things himself. You could learn from delegating, something Vivian Karlow didn't understand. Mike had suggested that Viv send two representatives: one with deep Client Care knowledge; and someone newer, who'd probably be more comfortable about any MSY procedures that might deviate from Pinnacle SOP. That she'd brought only Ann Ling meant that Viv had appointed herself as the experienced member of the team, a move that seemed to support the buzz that, with all her noise, Viv couldn't make herself think like a manager. Edie, on the other hand, was surrounded by subject matter experts from each of her teams except Switchboard, the one service MSY didn't need.

Mike quietly watched the action unfold. The way Bhalla was handling all of them, Mike could see already he was a major bullseye. Over a series of meetings the dignified Sikh was going to figure out how to translate all those MSY demands into smooth, fulfillable actions. There was beauty in this, like cutting bits of wood and arranging them into a perfect parquet floor.

Δ

```
From:          Wesley Peterson
To:            Pinnacle IT
Subject:       What's Happenin' Now!
------------------------------------
Hello, IT!
```

We keep growing like grass on a Chia Pet. And what a lawn we've got! This month we've welcomed FOUR more teammates:

We are lucky to have wrangled Noble Landrum away from Fulfillment, where he's accrued nearly a decade of domain knowledge. That's even MORE than Leon and Ina! Add the Systems Analysis training and hands-on technology experience gained in Active Service, and we've got ourselves our own secret weapon. Semper Fi!

Clif's team is thrilled to welcome Senior Engineer Mac Fraser, who brings us MISSION CRITICAL Disaster Recover and Business Continuity experience. Mac joins us from the USAF. Uh-oh! Remember gentlemen, you're on the same team now!

Pinnacle enters a NEW ERA, as we institute Enterprise Quality Assurance. The team will be helmed by Misha Smirnov, whose formidable prior experience includes building QA from the ground up at Ryder-Kentish Industries and Auriole (you read that right, gamesters!).

In addition to his PMP certification, Harvey Mellen has an MBA, an MAEng and an impressive roster of experience. Harvey joins us directly from two years managing onshore-offshore partnerships for FischNet.

And to top it all off, I know everyone will join me in a heartfelt sigh of relief that we have FINALLY got our DBA, Adam LeFevre, onboard as a FULL TIME Pinnacle employee!

Everyone please remember to look through those Learning Tree booklets and discuss with your managers. I have a small budget for training, if we can satisfy the LC that we have identified specific skills necessary to support to our project pipeline.

Wesley Peterson, CTO
Pinnacle Management Services

Δ

"Okay, so you know how I love to read. And people are always asking me what I'm reading..."

"Hey, Kippy!" Donny Rohmer called from his desk. "Waddaya reading?"

There was a sycophantic ripple of laughter.

"Ha!" Kippy barked. "Glad you asked that, Don. It happens I've been re-reading an old favorite. *The Magic of Thinking Big* by David Schwartz. Terrific book. Gives you all kinds of tools that help you really focus on your goals and push through whatever obstacles are up ahead. I recommend it to every one of you. Because you're all leaders, you know. That's what we do here at Pinnacle, we build leaders. I want all of you to excel. I want you to have motivation and the skills you need. Which is why I'm so excited to tell you about my new initiative, the Pinnacle library! I'm kicking this off with a whole stack of books I brought in from home. I sent Shawn out to Bed Bath yesterday and he's already got the shelves up. That's right! I was so excited to do this, I couldn't even wait for Marcy to design something! Ha!"

Kippy was pleased by the unmistakably genuine laughs, even if he didn't get that we were laughing at Marcy and not with him.

"So we have a great new library, set up right outside the break room. Gretchen'll be managing it for us. She's got a spreadsheet that she's putting on the share drive...right?" He looked down and to his left, towards the column where his assistant habitually stood during the Town Halls.

She nodded. "I'll be sending an email with the link, later today." Her thin voice didn't make it very far into the Pit.

"Can't hear you back here!" George Waters called out.

Kippy leaned down and handed her Mr. Microphone. With an embarrassed flush, Gretchen took it and repeated: "I'll be sending an email later." She cleared her throat. It rumbled obscenely through the cheap amplifier. Now the color of brick, she continued without pausing for another breath. "Withalinktothespreadsheetandhowtocheckoutabook." She thrust the microphone back into Kippy's outstretched hand and melted into the pillar as much as her green mini dress and long black-stockinged legs would allow.

Kippy beamed. "Great! And if you know about a book you think we oughta have, I want you to shoot Gretchen an email so we can look into it. That goes for everyone, okay? Not just these guys in Sales! Ha! Seriously, we have so much talent in this room, and a team needs all kinds of talent for success. You know, when you get to be my age, you learn how important, how critical teamwork is. You think I'm going to start talking about the Yankees again, right? Well you're wrong! Because if they keep up the way they've been playing, this is not a team we want to emulate. Am I right? Anyway, you know how geese take off in that V formation? That perfect V shape they have? Amazing, right? They're birds; how do they do that?! Well no one really knows, any more than they really know—no matter what they say they do—about how any bird, any animals...salmon...How do they know exactly when it's time to fly south or north or whatever? Or how do they find the exact right spot to go back to year after year? But there's one thing scientists have learned and that's that this V formation is the most effective way of keeping everyone in line. That shape is what keeps the flock together, making sure they all get to their goal. Everyone is responsible for seeing they make it. No one can get lost because they all follow the leader, and the leader knows exactly where they're headed. If someone starts to slow down or veer off course, someone else pushes him back, gives him a little nudge. So even the slowpokes have to come up to speed. They look out for each other; help each other out, you see? The stronger have to keep encouraging the weak, and because of that V they can see who needs help. Think about that, how amazing this is. These are birds and they know this, instinctively! Ha! And they get where they're going, year in year out, right on target. Well, I want us to be the geese! This is going to be our watchword from now on. If you see your neighbor falling down, slipping out of line, you're responsible for getting him back on course. Because only if we work together can we reach our goal. If we work together, there's no limit to how high we can fly. Nobody can do it alone, not the strongest, not the smartest, and you know I don't claim to be the smartest! So get out there and be the geese! And together we'll get where we're going. Give yourselves a round of applause!

Δ

Dawn lit her cigarette off of Jeff's. "So I'm confused. We're not termites any more?"

"Guess not," he grunted.

"I don't know if I want to be the geese. Unless I can fly south to Disneyland."

"I'd rather be a happy little bluebird," Alex said.

"I want to know more about those salmon who fly south," Mia said.

"What?!"

"Diego, do you never pay attention?"

"I was. I just didn't hear…"

Jeff was exasperated. "You're letting yourselves be distracted by trivialities. What I want to know is, what's this goal that we're all flying toward? Other than making money for him and Scott." Giving Jeff the official title "Team Lead" had done nothing to settle his prickles. It was an empty title, a sop to his vanity. He was doing the same work he always had. Jeff was openly envious of Noble's transfer to IT. What he didn't say was that he'd put in for an IT Business Analyst slot, but that asswipe Peterson said his minor in Computer Science and all these websites he'd built for friends wasn't enough of a technical background. Maybe he didn't come with a string of initials after his name, like the guy with the turban, but his experience was as relevant as Noble's, maybe more since Pinnacle didn't need much in the way of combat readiness. Jeff definitely had more mad skills than whatshernameJudy, and they'd found a spot for her. Hell, if he could stomach the thought of working with Viv, he'd put in for a transfer to CS. Fulfillment was a dead end at Pinnacle and wasn't going to mean a fucking thing to anyone in the real world. Mulhern might be all juiced about moving over to Compliance, but it wasn't going to get him anywhere real. It was becoming clear to Jeff that the only way up was out. He wasn't going to law school, even if his Aunt Ronnie said she'd pay. He wondered what kind of Master's degree he could pick up at night that might get him a decent job with a real future.

"Well I know what my goal is. *Voglio andare a Venezia.*"

"How about a more immediate goal, people? Who's coming with me to Harry Potter tomorrow?" Dawn had been talking about the movie for weeks. "I got ten tickets and the only ones who said yes for sure are Orla and my friend Marina. I need a final headcount."

"I said yes," Alex reminded her. "And so did Peggy Guggenheim here."

"No," Dawn corrected. "You said the idea quote unquote had potential."

"That's his way of saying yes," Mia sighed and cuffed him on the shoulder. "So we make it five. And Mulhern is six…"

"Um…no. I went Saturday."

"Opening weekend?" Alex was horrified. "Are you insane?! With 12 million screaming tweens?"

"And their moms," Tully recalled ruefully. "Hey, it wasn't my idea. Martha and Gabe had an extra ticket and they asked if I wanted it."

"Wasn't that weird?" Dawn wondered. "Not that they're going to do anything at Harry Potter, but still..."

Tully's eyebrows made a quizzical knit. "It's not like they're a couple. They hang out together. In a group. Sometimes I go with them."

Alex shook his head sadly at Tully's naïveté. "That doesn't prove anything."

Tully laughed. "It's people like you who start all those internet rumors, the ones that Snopes has to debunk. No! There are these three blondes who moved in down the hall from Gabe, models with legs up to here. From Stockholm," he added wistfully, as if that clinched something. "Anyway Martha's got this long-distance thing with some guy back in Maine. He was supposed to be coming down for the weekend but couldn't at the last minute. That's why they had an extra ticket."

Alex was intrigued. As long as he'd known Martha, there had never been the slightest whiff of someone back home. She only went up there for the big family holidays, and for a cheap vacation week in summer. The one photo in her cube was her and her sister in a boat with their dad. And he'd been catching unmistakable signs of her longing for the Boy for months. His curiosity was definitely piqued.

Gretchen Kenneally flew into the alley on antelope legs, coat unfastened, cigarette already between her lips. Her breaks were always like this. You would think Kippy kept her on a leash. Alex held his lighter out to meet her.

"Three minutes," she said on the inhale. "On the way to Newark. Holland Tunnel. Reception always sucks down there."

"So what's with the geese thing?"

She tossed her head so that her long, honey colored mane flipped off her shoulders. It was gestures like this that supported the rumors of a former modeling career. "I have no idea where that even came from. He must have seen them flying over the golf course and someone said something. He found a poem, too. I have to have Graham turn it into some kind of poster for us to hang on the walls of all the conference rooms."

Δ

```
From:        Scott Bell
To:          All Pinnacle Associates
Subject:     Welcome to a New Leader
-----------------------------------

Please join me in welcoming Abby Witherspoon, our new
Director of Client Care. Since the departure of Renee Ochs,
we have been searching for the perfect candidate to fill this
challenging role. With experience at Khiels, Seagrams and
Fresh Direct, Abby has the perfect background to establish
```

the procedures that will bring Client Care to the next level. Vivian Karlow will be reporting directly to Abby.

Scott Bell, President
Pinnacle Management Services

Δ

Vivian Karlow would never understand what she'd done wrong. She'd been running the department since Renee had left. Longer, if truth be told. Once Renee's contract had been, ahem, renegotiated, she'd pretty much phoned it in. That Transit Strike nightmare, for example, had rested squarely on Vivian's shoulders. Since January, of course, absolutely everything had fallen to her. And she'd taken up the responsibility gladly. Renee's methods might have worked well enough for a retail catalogue, but Pinnacle's clients...not customers; clients. English might be Vivian's second language, but she understood the distinction better than Renee Ochs...Pinnacle's clients expected, and moreover deserved, a different caliber of service. Things like the White Gloves team were critical to providing this. Vivian agreed completely with Scott on this. She agreed with Scott on most things. Who knew better than Sales what the clients needed? Renee had been a fool to challenge their superior knowledge. And Renee had pampered the staff, as if they were more important than the clients, when it was so very much the other way around. It took months, sometimes years, to land a new client. The streets of New York were flooded with potential Client Care associates. Every single one of them was replaceable. Even, it turned out, Vivian. Even though she'd done everything Scott asked.

"I know you've been on your own since the beginning of the year." Scott had called the whole team to the big conference room. He addressed us with the earnest furrow that, combined with his habitual boyish grin, made him look like the Daddy from that commercial where the kids are making Mommy breakfast in bed. "I think you did a terrific job of trying to stay on top of things. You're all to be commended. And now I'm pleased to say there's relief in sight. You don't have to struggle alone anymore. Let me introduce you to your new Director of Client Care, Abby Witherspoon."

No one could look at Viv. Now she was what, one of us again? Dislike aside, it was hard not to feel some empathy. Sure, she drove everyone nuts with her endless drama, the eyes that leaked the same tears whether someone had fucked up a client call or the weather forecast left her without an umbrella; but no matter how ineptly, she'd been running the department for nearly six months. To Ann and Yan, she was the only manager they knew. Her limitations hadn't stopped Kippy and Scott from putting her in, and she'd held the fort. If Scott or Kippy said "jump", Vivian asked "how high?" The last bit was of course why she'd been left in charge for as long as she had. The poser was why she was being replaced now. And why in such a mortifying way.

Abby Witherspoon knew none of this. She smiled at everyone in a friendly, open manner. Younger than Renee, maybe about ten years older than most of us, she sported a look—well-shaped hair with a persimmon boost, smart black suit and gold silk shirt—unusually fashionable for Pinnacle. Her voice was low and a little cool. Was she going to turn out to be the maternal type? The military type? The I'm-one-of-you-except-that-I'm-not type? No telling yet. But she was definitely eager to make a good start. After Scott left, with a last friendly squeeze of her shoulder, she made sure to hear all our names and repeat them back. She said she'd be scheduling one-on-ones all this week.

She asked us to think about the top ten pain points for clients and the top five for ourselves. "Write them down, print them out and drop them in this box." She held up a fabric-covered file box from The Container Store. "Be brutally frank. It'll be out here by the photocopier, so I won't see you drop it in. Completely anonymous. Friday, I'll take the box home and read through them over the weekend, and next week the real work begins."

Δ

Wesley Peterson was a man of many parts. He had the bland face of a Nixon aide and the beautifully-shaped tight rear end of, well, a tight end. Because he hid them behind innocuous glasses, his eyes were wrongly assumed to be a watery blue; but when he scanned the ranks at one of his department meetings, it was momentarily clear that there was nothing watery about them. This was the measure of the man, that each time you caught him, depending on the angle, you saw a different stereotype.

Right now, he was beaming so hard at his assembled forces that it seemed his glasses would pop off his face. This was the first team meeting in the new eighth floor office space that had been built out especially for his burgeoning kingdom. Standing before his people, our faces glued to his every gesture, every heart beating to his breath, Wesley was Henry V in a Paul Stuart suit and $30 shave.

"Pinnacle is going places, gentlemen and ladies. And Information Technology is going to be right at the forefront. Our development and system support are essential to the health and prosperity of this company. But this is not all that we are. Not by a long shot! We've got Mike and the PMO creating order out of chaos, rolling out the message of process management and repeatable workflow. And Malcolm is rolling out a Center of Excellence, to make sure standards and policies for security and standard operating procedures are baked into all our systems. We can do so much to level-set corporate maturity to a new high, but we need the rest of Pinnacle to understand this. We need to cross-pollinate. The more that we can socialize this with our coworkers on other teams, the better for us."

Clif raised his hand. "Isn't that going to be harder, now that we've moved up to a different floor?"

Wesley cocked his finger in approval. "Absolutely! As much as I value our autonomy, I know the isolation puts us at a disadvantage. Believe me, I wish we could have carved out more space on four. But you know how crowded it's gotten down there. Someone had to move, and in practical terms, we're the only team that could be broken off. At least we're in the building. The distance just means a little more effort. From all of us. Yes, the Help Desk crew, the PMO and Malcolm have the most contact with the other teams, but it's lazy for the rest of you to think you're not involved. You would not believe how much of my time is spent proselytizing for IT, spreading the good word. I keep hearing how expensive we are, how much we're costing the company. We need to prove our value proposition. How do we do that? In a single word, 'excellence.' To start, I need you, every one of you, to display nothing less than consummate professionalism in the office. Always. In every way. You may have worked in environments where it was okay for the IT team to wear the same *Wired* sweatshirt two weeks in a row—this is not that place." Wesley flashed a quick, knowing smile. "We need to look sharp and act sharp. There's no other way to say this: we can't afford to be geeks. And we need to deliver on time and under budget. So let's take a look at our pipeline. Mike?"

Mike Ventura stood up and tapped the smartboard that Wesley had insisted be installed in our big collaborative space. His touch should have moved the slideshow forward, but it didn't work. "I think I need tech support," he joked. "Is there an engineer in the house?"

"Just use the mouse. Clif's team will check it over later."

"Right. So what we have here is a high-level view of what we've got on our plate. The timeline is this calendar year, through the end of December, plus projections for Q1 and Q2 of next year, so we can look ahead a full 12 months from where we are now. The horizontal bars represent individual projects, positioned according to delivery schedule. This is big picture. We get more granular on later slides, so you'll read it there. All you need to see here is scope. Okay now, the green bars are anything we've already got in the process...."

"Green? Since when is anything green?" Of course Craig Parnes would make a crack.

"Bear with me, okay? There are only so many colors. I wanted something distinct and strong so everyone could see clearly. It's not a status chart. Green just means there's some activity going on. That's all. And no, red doesn't mean it's behind schedule, Parnes. At least not by definition. Red is for projects we're already committed to, but haven't started working on. The gold, no surprise, is the Mama-San Yakitori enhancement."

"OnRamp," Wesley corrected.

"OnRamp. And anything blue...well...think of it as 'blue sky,' because those are things that the LC has come up with over the last two weeks and is pushing hard for us to add to the deck. And, tah-dah...You. Are. Here!" His smacked his hand against the whiteboard for emphasis. The board chose that moment to function and jumped forward three slides, creating an excuse for some much-needed nervous laughter.

After some wrestling with the board and the mouse, Mike returned the display to the original slide. Our stomachs, full of Wesley's infamous meeting donuts, sank. You didn't need Craig's sarcasm to see that the colors had nothing to do with status. The green bars ventured just over the edge into April, like dipping a toe in the Long Island Sound in the same month. There was a lot of red up there, with one bar, presumably the bar for the still-unfinished Bridge Mark II, stretching ominously back to February.

It took time, and multiple delivery cycles, for a team to come together well enough to make solid estimates. Assuming the stakeholders didn't keep adding things into the mix, with a few months of weekend work, the negotiated deadlines could be met. Our development team, as it stood now, was still new. Even the core group had been together only about a year. So the red was sobering but not disastrous. Wesley and Mike were managing expectations. No, the real menace was the Leadership Council's wish list, the things we were first hearing about now, the blue bars, one of which was hovering over May. It was May now! How was the LC first raising an enhancement they wanted for May delivery?

As Mike talked us through the rest of the slides, one project at a time, it became clear that the blue bars were not remotely "wish"ful, nor were they part of any previously unrevealed corporate plan. They were enhancements that some single client—or even worse, some prospect—suddenly insisted they absolutely had to have or they'd walk. Sales had a simple philosophy: "sell it now, don't worry how." Graham, the cold caller who sometimes filled in when we needed a graphic artist, said that Scott actually made them chant this at their weekly team meetings. Every time a "must-have" came in a loud enough voice, Scott or Kippy or even Gary Feldman would stamp it Top Priority and toss it in the IT inbox. They never considered how the new demand might impact already-scheduled or even nearly-completed projects. When some pet enhancement or module didn't get out in time to meet whatever impossible deadline the LC had pulled out of their collective ass, it was always IT's fault.

How this was "Operational Excellence" was a mystery to Judy Schreiber. That list of things Mike had just walked through was impossible. Judy could see her own plummeting stomach mirrored on the faces of the rest of the team. If she were Wesley Peterson, she'd be in a total fit of panic, not grinning like a kid holding a gold Wonka ticket. The LC and Sales were a kindergarten full of spoiled brats. They needed was a Super Nanny to march in and tell them a flat "no."

A person could only stay quiet for so long. Judy lingered in the area until everyone else had drifted back to their cubes. "Wesley," she said quietly.

"Yes, Judy. What can I do for you?" He looked at her kindly. "You seem worried about something."

"It's that roadmap. We're already over-committed. How could the LC add more? And those deadlines...we can't possibly meet those deadlines. Why do they keep throwing out dates without first asking how long it's going to take for us to produce something?"

He chose to only answer her second question. "Because we haven't been very good at estimating our work."

"You mean Bridge Mark II? That was before you got here. There was no one in charge and the Business kept adding new features every day. Wasn't the idea of building this team, of doing all this planning, to make sure that didn't happen again?"

"And to give us the team we need to build this company's technology for the future. Think of the confidence it shows on the part of the LC, to ask us to deliver all of this."

"But we already know we can't possibly meet these deadlines. And when we don't, we're only going to look worse than before. Leon and Craig just said that integrating the calculator widget for Keldonian will take two months. They both say so. When do Leon and Craig agree on anything? And it's on the schedule for three weeks from Friday."

Wesley nodded solemnly. "At my first team meeting, I told everyone to think of Pinnacle as a start-up. You remember? I meant that. This company's been around for 40 years, but our piece of it, we're a start-up. Everyone has to pitch in and do their part. It's going to be shoulders to the grindstone for the next year. A lot of late nights and weekends at our desks."

"But when we know we're going to fall short, when they ask for something that's not humanly possible, wouldn't it be better to sometimes tell the LC 'no' up front?"

Wesley gave her an avuncular smile that made her feel about five years old. "Before we can do that, we need to prove ourselves. Once we have a track record of getting out dependable deliverables on schedule, then we can afford some pushback."

Δ

Abby Witherspoon had hoped that the promise of anonymity would bring her more insight into team dynamics, but the dearth of volunteers didn't really surprise her. Happy or unhappy, they were a team and she was the outsider. It would take time for them to learn to trust her. Not too much time, she hoped. She knew Vivian had been her predecessor's assistant, and Scott Bell said she'd been very helpful to him in the interim, but she sensed some hostility. She had to tread carefully there and was already feeling the strain.

She looked around at the assembled faces. They seemed bright and, with that one notable exception, enthusiastic. At least she could address the client issues; they'd been more forthcoming about those. "I hope you all had a good weekend. I, however, had a lot of reading to do." she patted the fabric-covered box and laughed, encouraging them to join her. There were a few minor titters, but more feet-shuffling and nervous glances as they wondered who might have said what about whom. Abby needed them at ease. "It's clear you guys work well together. Nothing but nice things to say about each other. Which is great, because your insights about our clients...and thank you so much for being so frank; this helps me a lot...what you say, and what I see in Salesforce, shows me we've got a lot of hard work ahead of us. The first thing I want to do is break you into teams, one for each business sector: Retail; Manufacturing; Professional—that would be doctors and lawyers, that kind of thing; Food Service... I think you see where I'm going. Each team with one very experienced support executive as lead, one of the newer associates—think of it as a kind of mentoring system—plus as many others as we need to staff-up proportionally to call volume."

There were a number of encouraging nods, significantly from those who had the longest tenure. Abby caught Alex Silva slipping a low five to Martha Moon. Alex liked to play the clown, but she'd already sensed he was one of her best associates. She gave him a smile.

Vivian gave a soft little cough. "Um, historically Scott has expressed concern about the level of support for our marquee clients. That's why we established our WGS team...that's White Glove Service..."

Ann and Yan, the newer members of the department, listened attentively as Vivian spoke. All other eyes stayed on Abby, who was learning plenty about team dynamics now.

"Yes, but do they pay more for that service? I can tell you: they don't. From the numbers I've seen, their business-to-call ratio isn't high enough to justify having two bodies dedicated full time to supporting them. And frankly if it did, two wouldn't provide sufficient redundancy."

Abby was not in the market for a rival. She needed an ally, a stout right hand she could rely on. It had been part of her contract negotiation that she be able to leave early when necessary and work from home when her son had a sick day. Caleb's dad was hapless at best, and now that he'd moved to Albuquerque, she had the full parenting as well as the main financial burden.

The financial part seemed well in hand. The way Kippy Melcher talked, Pinnacle was going to be the next ADP. After being part of the second wave at both Khiel's and Fresh Direct, she was looking forward to getting in on the ground floor.

Vivian sat impossibly straighter than her usual rigid posture and folded her arms across her chest.

Abby held up a hand to forestall the next objection; she wasn't going to let one hard nut ruin the brownie. "Scott expressed the same concern to me. I explained that with the kind of team coverage I propose, all our clients get better service. We get a better educated, more nimble support team. And there's rarely an issue with coverage, because unless we have the kind of massive disaster no one could plan for, there should always be someone available who at the very least has knowledge of the special needs of that sector."

Vivian would learn to support her, or she'd find someone more willing.

Δ

"Does anyone else smell smoke?" Ginny Chicosky's voice cut through two collaborative sessions and a good half-dozen pair of earbuds. Popping up from our seats, we craned our necks to sniff the air, straining our eyes for a sign of smoke, then twisting to sniff in another direction.

"*Meerkat Manor*," Craig Parnes cracked. The cube walls on eight were higher than the ones downstairs. For those of us significantly shorter than he was, all that could be seen were our heads.

We were laughing until Adam LeFevre called out sharply, "definitely smoke! Everyone out, now!"

There had been one fire drill, the day after IT took possession of the space. No one paid much attention. No one ever did for these things. We knew where the stairwells were and not to take the elevator. What else did you need to know? There wasn't going to be a fire, anyway. We were more concerned with getting back to our desks to unpack before Kippy came up to inspect the addition to his kingdom.

Despite this, and with all the managers downstairs in a budget meeting, we moved with the coordinated speed and efficiency of Alabama's '61 defense line. Everyone scooped up their phones, and headed for the nearest exit. Freddie Vega, whose desk was closest to the men's room, popped his head in to make sure it was clear. The women, all three of us, were already accounted for. While Adam rang Donna, the office manager, to let her know we were vacating, Sid Reilly pulled out the red phone to call the alarm in to the FDNY.

We flew down the eight steep flights, trying not to trip on the glow-in-the-dark nosings. At the bottom of the north stair, Ginny was confronted with a metal door labeled "No Exit. Alarmed." She looked over her shoulder at the chain of evacuees coming down behind her. "Fuck that!" she muttered, and pushed hard against the pressure bar. The door flew open, accompanied by the abrasive blare of a siren. We spilled out into a sparse lawn, the surprising inner courtyard of the condos that abutted our building to the east. It was a small space, filled with lawn furniture and toys. Leon tripped over some kid's scooter; his reaction was to furiously kick a nearby basketball, so hard that it flew over Sid's head and through the fire door just before it slammed shut.

"This way!" Ginny, who hiked on the weekends, had found the way out. She led us past the glass-box extension of someone's ground floor living room (judging by the mess, someone who didn't expect anyone to be looking in on a weekday).

"Worse than my ex-husband." Judy was heard to mutter. "If I could afford a place like this, I wouldn't be trashing it with pizza boxes and dirty underwear."

Politely trying not to trample the border of decorative grasses, we filed along the beige brick wall to a patch of tarmac that held the recycling bins. A wrought iron courtesy gate was all that stood between us and the sidewalk. Fortunately, it was unlocked. We passed through and, instinctively, continued walking around the block until we ended up in front of our own building. The half of our team who'd used the south stair were waiting for us there, along with the residents of the seventh floor who'd vacated, according to FDNY-coached procedure, when our alarm had gone off.

Adam said the firemen were already upstairs. It was probably nothing. Art Russo suggested we take an early lunch and meet back in front of the building in an hour.

We split off in threes and fours, everyone too wired to want to be on their own. It was the first really warm day. It would have been a good day to walk, but no one went very far, as if proximity were somehow dictated by the circumstances. We all came back early.

Freddie noticed Orla grabbing a smoke in the alley with a couple of others from four. He ambled over to say hi. "Pretty exciting stuff," he said. "Those idiot construction guys, I bet."

"Better than that," she grinned.

"Much better." Jeff Curry had a nasty laugh. "The people who used to rent your floor? They offered Feldman a deal on the air conditioning units, because they wouldn't need them in their new place. Naturally, he bargained them down. Wouldn't stop talking about how he made a killing, because they were practically brand new."

"How do you know this stuff?"

"Gretchen. She loves telling Feldman stories. He drives her crazy over Kippy's expenses. Like she says, it's Kippy's own money so WTF? Anyway, the bargain AC? Turns out they were reconditioned, not new, and the FD had already forced a couple of rounds of repairs. When they came to inspect before you guys moved in, the FD gave a conditional pass, contingent on repairs. Said they'd be back in a month."

"And what? There was still a week to go, so Feldman didn't call the maintenance guys?"

Jeff looked at Freddie in admiration. "Exactly."

Freddie's cheeks rose up and crunched to slits. This happened any time he grinned or frowned. It could be hard to tell the difference between two equally fierce expressions. Only the small crinkles at the corners of his mouth gave it away. "Yeah, that's what he does every time Clif has to order new hardware. He refuses to get that it takes a few months for HP to build us a blade to the specs we need. Feldman waits 'til the day before we need it to sign the PO. And then the LC complains to Clif about the delay. Every time. So it was the AC? The fire?"

Jeff nodded. His was definitely a smile. "Just a little smoke. You guys caught it fast. But it looks like Feldman's going to have to fork out for a fine now, not just a new unit."

Δ

After Simran's analysis was complete, there was no pretending that all MSY needed to come on board was wizard data-entry and a few special id fields. Without the faintest idea of what they were promising (beyond the client's desire to have it), Sales had sworn to MSY that we would "seamlessly integrate" our payroll and benefits support technology into their existing Human Resources Information System. They'd also guaranteed a Procurement dashboard that would mimic the interface of MSY's current internal system, so that overworked storefront managers wouldn't have to learn a new method of placing orders

Wesley Peterson, who liberally sprinkled his emails with exclamation points and often spoke in upper case, proclaimed the news to be an Exciting Challenge! MSY would justify the new framework his team was still tweaking for Bridge Mark II, and would be the proof of concept for Modular, Client-Customized coding that was the Future of Pinnacle! "OnRamp," the name that Wesley Peterson had wittily assigned to this new technology product, was state-of-the-art, automated and scalable—all of Wesley's favorite words, which were fast becoming Kippy's as well.

Though Mama-San Yakatori was a third as large as all our other clients put together, Kippy told Edie Brewer not to worry. OnRamp, together with the Bridge adaptations required to hook it up, was scheduled to be delivered by end of July, a luxurious 45 days before MSY was to go live. And Gary Feldman had agreed on an MSY Addendum to Edie's budget that allowed for a few new hires to be added as of the OnRamp release. Buffer time for training; what more could she need? Kippy, who got frustrated when he couldn't find the "Any" key on his keyboard, assured her that implementation would be a piece of cake. Peterson had explained it all to him: the integration would be "grabbing" data directly from MSY's existing HRIS system; there was no need for weeks of manual data entry before payroll could proceed. Edie's people would only check their regular Bridge work queues. Payroll, Compliance, Procurement; it would all be there, automagically.

Edie thought this sounded awfully like putting all her eggs in one basket. Preferring to be safe rather than sorry, she turned to the one person in IT who didn't make her feel like a Luddite idiot and asked: "What if the technology can't cover everything after all? What if there's a delay? No offense, but if IT were FedEx I'd still be waiting for my Christmas presents."

When Mike Ventura was embarrassed he couldn't help being a little defensive. "Why does Sales keep promising things before finding out if we can execute them?"

"That was rhetorical, wasn't it Ventura? Listen, I'm not blaming anyone. I'm only considering the worst case scenario. With or without OnRamp, MSY is going live the day after Labor Day. I'll be tickled pink if your guys are ready, but if not, I need to have a Plan B."

She was right, of course. Edie usually was. The anticipated spike in daily Fulfillment tasks was daunting enough. If OnRamp wasn't switched on Day One, Data Entry would also have to manually input thousands of records—all those names, rates, W2 information to be entered at the last minute—and Pinnacle would be dead in the water before MSY paid us a penny.

Mike and Edie spent the night on the phone, hammering out the options. There could be manual work-arounds for most of the automagical things the technology was meant to handle. It would be a strain on Fulfillment, but it was doable if—and this was the Big If—if the payroll data was already in Bridge. Was there some way, without OnRamp, to avoid all that input? Adam and the developers had a sample set of MSY data in their sandbox, to develop the real-time data exchange. Mike thought if we could leverage this to write a bulk data conversion program, then we could do a data scrape from MSY the night before go-live, run the conversion, and upload it to Bridge. We'd have to carve out a big chunk of time to write and test the conversion program, plus however-many days of Simran collaborating with Edie's people on the work-arounds, but our asses would be covered.

Mike's delicate task was to put this to Peterson in such a way that he'd understand CYA was for mutually-assured survival and not a departmental pissing match. Edie didn't envy him. She'd noticed Peterson's political side. "Do you want me to come in with you?"

She could hear the lopsided smile in his voice. "No need. If Peterson says we can't afford to lose the hours, he's as good as admitting there isn't enough time to deliver OnRamp. I just want to give him a way to save face."

As implied by her increased consumption of soothing dairy products, Edie's hunch about an OnRamp delay only amplified the more she thought about it. Instead of waiting for the allotted new hires, she decided to pull together a team that already knew Bridge like the backs of their hands. By telling them now that they'd be working exclusively on MSY starting July, there'd be enough time for knowledge transfers to their replacements.

There was no formal announcement about the dedicated OnRamp Fulfillment team, but of course we all knew about it in a matter of hours. At its head was Archandra Gosh. Archie, who'd been hired to fill Marla's old Training slot, had only been at Pinnacle for two months. Some questioned her appointment, Jeff Curry in particular, but there was a compelling reason for Edie to put her at the helm. Archie's dad owned three KFCs and a Baskin Robbins, and she'd worked them from the time she was eleven. If anyone at Pinnacle knew anything about fast food management, it was Archie Ghosh.

Abby Witherspoon had nothing but blithe assurances from Scott Bell that, thanks to technology, the massive jump in Fulfillment from MSY would cause nary a blip on the Client Care front. In fact, he implied that under her experienced guidance, CC would be working so much more efficiently by September that, if MSY were not on the horizon, they would have probably soon considered the team overstaffed. Despite that, he'd convinced Gary Feldman to approve salary for one more CC associate and, with a little extra wangling, managed things so that Abby could bring her new hire on board a month before MSY, to get up to speed. Wasn't that great?

Though the numbers didn't quite make sense to Abby, she was new enough at Pinnacle that she was trying not to tread on any toes; at least not any C-level toes.

It was only when Edie approached her about adding a couple of associates to a dedicated MSY team that Abby finally grasped the scope of what Sales had promised and IT had committed to deliver. The risk Pinnacle was taking, starting a client of this magnitude on untried technology, was breathtaking. If Edie's worst case scenario came true, frustrated MSY managers and HR contacts would be choking the phone lines. The strain on Client Care would be immense. Even the best-trained new hire wouldn't make a dent. Abby had to put an experienced CC head with Edie's team ASAP.

On paper, Vivian would have been an ideal candidate, combining Pinnacle domain knowledge with some managerial experience. In practice,

Abby didn't trust her as far as she could throw her. And right now, she was more than ever tempted to do just that. Vivian supported Scott's contention that, mostly due to her own historic efforts, there was no need for concern. Before the advent of Abby, she, Vivian, had done everything possible by giving IT the benefit of her insights. The very metrics Scott was using to determine manpower were based on her reorganization earlier in the year. Abby's more recent restructuring, Vivian's bitter smile implied, had yet to be weighed and found wanting.

Abby itched to get rid of the girl, but was waiting for Vivian to provide an excuse that Scott would accept. It would almost be worth putting her on MSY. If Edie's predictions turned out to be correct, she'd flounder so badly that Scott would boot her out himself. Tempting, but Abby would be shooting herself in the foot.

It was shocking how many sleepless nights she spent on this. By rights, if Peterson failed to deliver, it should be IT that took the hit; but she'd spent enough client-facing years to know that the first blow fell to whoever was on the phones. She needed to have the right people in place, to make certain the blame didn't fall to her. She was leery about disturbing solid client relationships by reassigning her most experienced people. As for the newer ones, maybe she was being paranoid, but she couldn't completely trust anyone Vivian might have trained. The more Abby contemplated the scenario, the grimmer it seemed.

Δ

```
From:        Arthur Russo
To:          All Pinnacle Associates
Subject:     Changes to HR
-----------------------------------
```

By now I'm sure you all know that this has been my final week at Pinnacle. Family reasons compel my relocation to Boston, a decision that was not made lightly. It has been a privilege to work with Kippy, Scott and Alan to build this team of bright and talented individuals. I will miss all of you!

I am pleased to announce that Kay Kuperman is assuming the position of Director of Human Resources. Kay has done a superb job establishing training here at Pinnacle and working by my side. Her appointment ensures a seamless transition for the company and for all of you who know her so well.

I wish everyone at Pinnacle the best of luck in the future.

Art

5 TEAM BUILDING EXERCISES

"I sure as hell won't miss him looking over my shoulder."

"For what, Curry? It's not like there's anything interesting on your desk."

"I don't know about that," Jeff smirked. "There's all the patient records we're transcribing for that plastic surgeon. *People* magazine might find some of those names verrrrry interesting."

"So this is where you all go." Everyone jumped. No one ever arrived from the other end of the alley. "What are we talking about?" inquired Judy Schreiber.

"Celebrity facelifts," Alex informed her.

"Channing," corrected Dawn, stepping back a little to make room in the circle. "The mysterious move to Finance."

"I know!" Judy's eyes widened in appreciation of the topic. "Where did that come from?"

Tully sucked in his lips and shook his head. "No one seems to know."

"And we're sure as hell not giving him the satisfaction of asking," Jeff added.

"What are you doing out?" Dawn peered into the recycled paper tote bag, Judy tipping it to accommodate her. "Ooo! B&N run!"

Judy sighed happily. "Not a single meeting all day, and hardly any emails. Do you know how much work I got done today? Enough to have an actual lunch hour."

"Well you, yeah. Peterson and Ventura are both at the offsite. *My* boss spent the whole morning sulking because he wasn't important enough to be invited." Dawn drew two fingers down each cheek, miming tears. "I'm only here now because he's on a webinar with Lutz & Lutz."

"Vivian's not there either. She's been holed up in Abby's office all day with the door closed." Alex grinned wickedly. "We started a pool for whether or not she'd call in sick." Everyone looked at him expectantly. "Oh, come on, people! Viv doesn't know how to call in sick!"

"But isn't it great when the Cs are all away, how peaceful it is?" The always cheerful Diego positively beamed.

"I never even heard the phrase 'C-level executive' until I came here. You said it, Curry, and I swear," Orla smirked; "the way you did I thought you meant all the execs were C-level students."

"Probably true." Jeff shrugged. "Maybe I can get a blog out of that."

"Speaking of which," Judy reminded, "you promised me you'd sanitize that post on cubicle etiquette, so I can put it in the next *Peak Experience*."

"I liked that one." Mia gave him an approving pat on the head. "You actually can write when you're not crazy ranting. You may end up making some money yet, Curry."

"Well, if they're never gonna promote me, I need something," he noted with unusual equanimity. "Fucking bastards wouldn't even give me a lateral move to Client when Reggie left, because Scotty doesn't like me. Not that any of them do, except Edie. But they have no problem promoting assholes. No offense Archie."

The official OnRamp Team Lead stuck out a good-natured middle finger.

Diego was curious: "I don't get how people make money off a blog. It's not like you pay to read it."

"Ad placement," Jeff said succinctly. "If I'm reading Google Analytics right, a couple hundred more followers should do it for me. So everyone keep sharing those links."

Dawn squinted happily at the cloudless sky. "Such a gorgeous day! Don't you miss having class outside?"

Tully draped a casual arm around her shoulders. "Isn't that what an offsite is?"

"Dunno. What do they do at a management offsite anyway?" Orla practiced her smoke rings. She was working on a chain.

"Three-legged sack races?" Alex suggested. Mia smacked him on the arm. "Hey! No bruising! I need to look good on the pier this weekend."

"We did some at Trowbridge," Judy recalled. "You hire these facilitators. They lead what they call 'team-building exercises.' Pretend projects, games, anything collaborative. Who knows? Maybe they do have sack races."

"You're shitting me." Jeff was so appalled he lit a second cigarette.

"I wish."

"People get paid for this?" Alex marveled.

Judy nodded. "Disgustingly well. They also give inspirational speeches. Unless your budget runs to a name keynote speaker, which I somehow doubt Pinnacle's does."

"New pool!" Archie fished a dollar from her pocket and waved it in the air. "I say Kippy probably gave the speech himself." No one could disagree. She shoved the dollar back.

"How do you get a gig like that? The facilitator thing?"

"The ones I met were either failed actors, or they stopped short on their clinical psych degree, right before the dissertation."

Alex seemed unusually thoughtful. "You may have just given me a new career path, if Show Business keeps letting me down."

"I forget you're an actor." The playwright stuck out her hand to shake his.

He turned it into a high-five. "So did the casting agents. Baddum-bum! Anyway, what I really want to do is direct. No, seriously."

"Hey, Judy!" It occurred to Orla that there was a rumor she could have confirmed. "Is it true? The story about Craig and Sid?"

"You mean about the SOAP guy?"

His cigarette dangling between his fingers, Alex slapped both hands against his face in mock horror. "Please don't tell me people have started outsourcing their laundry to us!"

"Simple Object Access Protocol," Jeff drawled. "It's a web service framework." Everyone stared at him. "What? I keep saying I've got some tech chops. Not my fault no one believes me."

"I didn't have a clue what it meant," Judy confessed. "Still don't. I only know Craig and Sid insist it'll be the crowning glory of OnRamp."

"I thought OnRamp, was almost done." Archie was particularly sensitive to any whispers about the application she was expected to own in another two weeks.

"I think this will be for OnRamp version two," Judy reassured her. "Once MSY is up and running, they plan to expand it. Peterson says the speed and convenience will be a great talking point for Sales." Wesley was always emphasizing things that would be great talking points for Sales.

Tully scratched his head, a new habit since he'd decided to shave it. We couldn't tell if he was being thoughtful, or if the stubble was itching him. "So if this SOAP thing is so great, why not use it in the first place?"

"Feldman wouldn't okay the budget."

Orla blew out a final smoke ring with her last good draw. Watching it dissolve, everyone contemplated a favorite Gary Feldman story.

It was time to go upstairs, but Jeff had to know: "Okay, Jude. So what's the SOAP story."

"Right. The story. Well, first we lost the best candidates because of how long it took to get a green light from Feldman. When this guy said yes, Craig and Sid were over the moon. Which in Craig's case, you know, means slightly manic."

"What 'slightly'?" Orla snorted. In daylight, the rings of kohl gave her pale green eyes a spooky transparency. "We went to a concert together once...Okay, it was a date. Gogol Bordello. I swear, he's more intense than they are."

Judy knew nothing about Gogol Bordello, but she assumed that someone who looked like Orla would have a pretty high threshold for intensity. She nodded. "Exactly. Anyway, this guy is going to be the answer to all their prayers. They had him start Monday, so he could go right into Boot Camp."

"What actually goes on in Boot Camp?" Alex had been curious about this, but he kept forgetting to ask. "Archie, you did it. Tell us old timers."

"Damn!" Tully looked at Alex in shock. "I'm an old timer! Where the fuck did the year go?"

"I'm a year," Dawn touched him on the nose. "You have two months yet. This is Pinnacle. Anything could happen."

"Sssh! Don't scare Archandra! I want to hear about Boot Camp."

Under seven attentive pair of eyes, Archie cleared her throat. "Um, well, Kay starts off with a history of Pinnacle. And then Kippy stops by to say hello and shakes everyone's hand."

Alex stuck out his free hand and grabbed hers. "Amanda!" he exclaimed, pumping enthusiastically. "Welcome aboard! Client Care. Great! Our clients can never get enough care! Ha!"

Archie looked at him in wonder. "How did you know he called me Amanda?"

Everyone howled.

"I'm a genius." Alex shrugged modestly. "So what happens next?"

"They show this very weird sexual harassment video…"

"I still think that sounds like the exact opposite of what it is," Dawn muttered.

"And after lunch, you spend the rest of the day watching presentations. On day two…"

"Wait!" Judy interrupted her. "You have to stop there for my story. So Sid and Craig promised their guy that they'd feed him a nice lunch Tuesday, to make up for having to sit through all that. They took him to the Thai place."

"Which one?" Diego asked. "The place on the corner, or the fusion place across the street?"

"The one two blocks away. The good one." Everyone murmured appreciatively. Of the five Thai restaurants within lunching distance, that wasn't merely the best, it was the most expensive, the only one where the lunch special was more than nine dollars.

"Did they order dumplings?" Diego sighed.

Judy nodded. "That's what Sid says. And summer rolls and Thai tea. Everything." And they probably had a pissing match to see who picked the hottest curry; it was the way of IT team lunches. "Anyway, they get back, and the guy tells them to go ahead up; he needs to make a quick phone call before the afternoon session."

"That's the last one," Archie recalled. "After that, you go to your department for the rest of the day, and that's it."

"So when it's 4:00 and this guy doesn't show up at his desk, Sid goes looking for him. Josefina...have you met Kay's new assistant? I like her. Anyway, Jo said he never showed up for the afternoon presentation. Then right around 5, Kay gives Wesley a call. The guy emailed her that he decided not to accept Pinnacle's offer. Ginny looked him up on LinkedIn today. We think he never quit his other job, that he must have taken a couple of personal days to test the waters."

Δ

```
From:        Wesley Peterson
To:          IT
Subject:     Here Comes the Cavalry!
-----------------------------------

As necessary as it is for Craig and Sid to siphon off some
bandwidth for SOAP training, I know we've all been feeling
the pinch. Well, Help is On The Way!

I'm excited to confirm that we've got a Green Light to
temporarily take on extra resources! Through Aprotek, the
same shop we're using for Misha's QA team, we're getting
access to not 1 but 3—count 'em, 3—developers! This should
enable us to get OnRamp out the door, with all those Bells
and Whistles!

As with QA, they'll be working U.S. hours from Pune. The
knowledge transfer can begin as soon as Clif has the secure
VPN hooked up.

Keeping pushing forward!

WJP
```

Δ

"I've been reading a terrific book. *Masters of Enterprise*. By...Grant? Wait, who is it Gretchen?"

"Brand," she corrected, her fingers continuing to fly across her Crackberry as she, momentarily, glanced up in his direction.

"Right. Emma bought it for me for Father's Day. Did I tell you she's going to Chapman in the fall? Smart kid, right? Gonna be hard having her all the

103

way out there. Anyway, this book. Terrific! It's like a history of American business, going all the way back. All the greats: Carnegie, JP Morgan, Vanderbilt...I'm talking about the original Vanderbilt, Cornelius, not Gloria! Ha!"

Judy was shocked by the sound of her own laughter. It was only a little chuckle, but it sounded explosive, probably because she was alone. Most of her coworkers were too young to know who Gloria Vanderbilt was. If anyone asked her, she wouldn't bother mentioning the jeans commercials and the winged hair; she'd just say it was Anderson Cooper's mother.

Kippy beamed at her happily. "After them, Brand moves on to people like Disney and Sam Walton. All the way up to now. You know to who? To Bill Gates and Oprah. Oprah! Ha! But don't laugh. Oprah is a phenomenal business woman! She had what? An afternoon talk show? And she leveraged it into an empire. We could learn a lot from Oprah. We can learn from all of these people. The point is, to people like this, people who really make a difference in the world, it's not about making money. Though I'm not going to pretend money isn't important. Ha! But the important thing is to have a passion for what you're doing. Like we do at Pinnacle. I wake up every morning and let me tell you, I jump out of bed. I can't wait to get to the office! That's why I'm here so early, even after fitting in my run. Ha! And why I hate to tear myself away all day. Every waking hour, I'm thinking what I can do to grow this company and make it the best it can possibly be. Sure it's my company, but it's more than that. I swear, I'd feel the same way if I were doing this for free. Because..." His voice dropped dramatically, "I believe that much in this company."

The vocal sincerity was accompanied by a sweeping gesture at the crowd, occasioning a scattered outbreak of coughs and throat-clearing.

"Because Pinnacle is my passion! And it should be your passion, too. If you're not passionate about what you're doing, you shouldn't be doing it. We spend too much of our lives working to have it any other way. Am I right?"

Kippy was clearly gratified by the unusual strength of the murmured agreement. He leaned forward, his broad grin foreshadowing that he was going to put the icing on the cake.

"No matter what your job is, your main objective is to grow our business. We get bigger, we get stronger. That means more opportunities for everyone. Sure, raises and bonuses, but, much more important, career opportunities. Opportunities to grow, to lead! And in case that isn't incentive enough, I'm sweetening the pot. Any one of you who brings in a prospect or even a lead that turns into a client? You get a referral bonus. A thousand dollars when the client signs, and a percentage of the first year's business. No matter what your job is. Except Sales of course. You guys are already taking a big enough bite out of the gross. Ha! Only joking. You guys are the greatest. You know I know that. But all the rest of you, the offer holds. Gretchen'll send out an email later today with the details. Now give yourselves a round of applause…"

Δ

There was the same expression on every face, a combination of surprise and wariness at finding ourselves in Central Park, in our weekend clothes, surrounded by the people we saw in the office every day. Not all the people, of course; far fewer than Kippy and Scott had anticipated when they gave Kay Kuperman the green light for her first Pinnacle event.

The LC thought a company picnic, spouses and children included, was a grand idea. However, by the time Gary Feldman signed off on a budget, the only Sunday for which they could get a park permit was the weekend before Labor Day, not a weekend to deliver maximum turnout. No matter how strongly Senior Management "suggested" we attend, a lot of us didn't. Some of us were leveraging the weekend to stretch five PTO days into a ten-day vacation. Some had expensive shares in summer houses and weren't about to give up the next to last chance to use them. If you did plan to be in the city, while your significant other might be kind of curious to meet the people you were always talking about, you weren't about to drag in: your parents, who'd finally worked up the nerve to visit the Big Apple and picked out this weekend three months ago; or your cousin Evan, who was stopping off for a few days of downtown music and ethnic food before heading across country to Willamette; or that hunky Croatian you met backpacking in Norway, who took an impulse tour of the USA and miraculously showed up at your door Wednesday.

A little fewer than half of us made our way to the Stranger's Gate, found the first of the yellow balloons, and followed them along the path to the Great Hill. The path was for foot traffic only. The early birds, meaning anyone who'd hoped to pop in, say Hi, and go on to do something productive and/or genuinely amusing with their precious weekend time, found themselves commandeered to help Shawn and Jo carry the food from Noble's double-parked van on Central Park West to the picnic grounds. Thanks to some confusion about what the permit did or did not allow, about the only definitive thing Pinnacle had on site were a pair of long folding tables, presided over by Donna, our office manager. Clif Speck had a boom box set up with an entire cordon of speakers, until the Park Police came by and told him they were in violation and had to come down. The volleyball net was okay as such, but no stakes could be driven into the ground to hold it and there wasn't a viable pair of trees in sight. Chris Keane hopped the train down to Modell's, hoping to find poles with inflatable or foam feet, and returned with a compensatory stack of Frisbees and some balls.

Between general reluctance to attend and Sunday morning hangovers, we trickled in slowly, inevitably sorting ourselves into shapes that echoed our work groups.

Sales clustered around the slatted wood Park picnic tables, benches and table tops serving equally well as seating. Whether by memo or mind meld, all wore striped Polo (not merely "polo") shirts, and baggy khaki cargo shorts with a Blackberry in one capacious pocket and a personal phone in the other. The few wives were uniformly petite and toned in white capris and sleeveless shirts, with the exception of Glenn Levine's wife who flaunted her excuse in a pink bundle slung across her chest.

A patchwork ground cover bloomed from the yards of blankets and beach towels wisely lugged from home. Fulfillment Acres was abutted by slightly tidier beds laid down by Client Care, the boundary between the two being colonized by those who routinely socialized across tribes. Tully brought his one acoustic guitar. So did Lily Sheehan, a fairly new addition to CC who was delighted to connect with the artistic crowd. At the outside edge, facing the water fountain, Noble and his wife sat with Marla and Marisol from Finance, whose kindergarteners took to each other so immediately and completely that there would be crying when it was time to go home. Soft strumming mingled with the children's giggles and the comfortable buzz of people who were used to gossiping with one another.

IT, their demographic yielding the highest per-capita number of spouses and children, formed an awkward cluster under a large tree close to the path. Wesley Peterson had been pretty insistent: the deliverable was to show up and make sure Kippy noticed. Peterson himself was still unaccounted for, but the team had turned out in full force. Ginny Chicosky's husband Tim offered congratulations on the Phase One OnRamp deploy with only the faintest touch of irony, before taking off with the six-year-old twins and their Razors.

Kay circulated, pushing hard for us to mix things up. Like all the organizers, she wore a bright yellow polo shirt stamped with what appeared to be a melted iceberg. To any foolish enough to comment, she dropped coy hints about a stash of similar shirts. The Buzzard made a crack about Kippy and Scott shooting them into our waiting arms from a t-shirt cannon. Kay's customary ebullience momentarily deflated. Had he guessed right, or was she was regretting not having thought of this herself? He couldn't wait around to ask, because his impossibly adorable daughter chose that moment to go running toward a patch of grass where Frisbees were soaring at lethal height for a toddler.

Dave's wife Angela, her linen smock revealing that next year's model was under production, sank exhausted into one of Mac Fraser's lawn chairs. The other was occupied by Mac's enormously pregnant young wife. In contrast to the Broussard family revelation, we'd all been hearing about the Mac-in-progress from the time the poor woman had peed on a stick. Mac, having married late, was enchanted by everything about marriage and children. He hovered protectively behind Cindy's chair, bestowing delighted smiles on any rugrat who came within view.

One apparently winged preschooler nearly escaped onto the path, stopped by the intercession of Mike Ventura's big hand grabbing the straps of his little Oshkosh overalls. The child's breathless and grateful mother was, surprise! Abby Witherspoon. We knew Abby worked from home once a week, and a few of the CS crowd had spotted some refrigerator art on her bulletin board, but she'd never actually spoken about her son to anyone at Pinnacle.

Abby preferred not to mix work and family. Distasteful as it was, the fact was that female managers couldn't afford to be seen as maternal. Even if it worked for her department, as it did for Edie Brewer, it did her no favors with those higher up. When Scott and Kippy made this picnic non-negotiable, Abby's instinct was to get a sitter; but it seemed cruel to Caleb, as well as sad for herself, to sacrifice an afternoon of shared park time. She decided to bring the baby and keep a low profile until she could reasonably disappear down to the zoo. Squatting to administer an admonishing smack to his denim tush, she realized she'd found the perfect foxhole with IT. She went to retrieve the stroller from where she'd parked it by the water fountain, temporarily leaving Caleb in the custody of Ventura and his girlfriend.

Kitty was as baby-besotted as Mac Fraser. She looked from the two pregnant women to Caleb to Mike, then repeated the cycle, her grey eyes moist with dreams. Mike never stopped talking about this girl: how beautiful she was, how talented, how funny, how sweet. The big teddy bear was the kind of guy who fell hard when he fell. We'd been waiting to meet her and judge whether she deserved him. We hoped so, because it felt like Mike was getting awfully close to the altar.

Kay used Mr. Microphone to declare the buffet officially open. We hoped that was the only action Mr. Microphone was going to see today. Alex Silva grinned at Archie Ghosh, who pulled a dollar from her jeans to start a pool. They needed a piece of paper. Too bad Gabe del Monte hadn't come; he would have brought some pencils and a sketch pad. We had to make do with Orla's kohl stick, and the paper bag that had concealed a couple of six-packs until Shawn spread the word about the official (from Pinnacle), secret (from Park Services) coolers of beer. Gabe was in Long Island City today, showing at some parking lot art fair. He'd paid the non-refundable registration fee back in April, long before Pinnacle decided to have a picnic. A small posse, led by Martha Moon, was heading out to Queens later to cheer him on.

By unanimous acclaim, Martha was the possessor of the absolute best picnic blanket in the Park. Padded, waterproof on the bottom, and soft and plaid on top, it folded into a block the size of a three ring binder. We'd never seen such an elegant accessory outside a catalogue. Because it was Martha's, from the legendary outlet shop in Freeport, we could admire it generously and delight in the naked desire that briefly washed over Mrs. Kippy's face during the Royal Progress.

No one had spotted their arrival on the scene, but our C-Level executives were now in evidence. Wesley Peterson liked a good party. Having scored beers for himself and the pleasantly attractive Mrs. Wesley, he joined his team in their prime shady real estate. Seen from a distance, in jeans that had seen some serious wear, both the Petersons blended right in. Scott Bell, despite the occasional yearning glance at the beach of blankets, also kept to his own kind. Gary Feldman—jacketless, tieless, but ever vigilant—stuck close to Kay, Donna and the supplies.

Kippy and Marcy wore matching jeans, of a wash so even that they must have been dry-cleaned, with white cotton shirts and Nikes. She wore a Yankees cap and designer sunglasses. Kippy sported those new Ray Bans that people who don't know better mistake for the classic style. Making his way from one small bunch of merry makers to the next, our CEO was beaming like a lighthouse. "Isn't this terrific?!" he trumpeted as he pinned each new group with the fierce wattage of his smile.

"What a day! Perfect weather! Couldn't have ordered it better." With so little shade available, ten degrees cooler would have been nice. Kippy wasn't standing still, so perhaps he didn't feel it. "Martha! Enjoying this?"

"Very much, Kippy," Martha obediently replied. "It's great. It's so nice to see you, Marcy."

Apart from Sales, who were always trying to score points, few of us would have had the guts to address Mrs. Kippy. Martha had been with Pinnacle for so long that it was probably a reflex.

"You too, Martha." Despite her obvious envy of the picnic blanket, her smile was friendly. "I'm always in sucha rush when I pop in. I never gedda chance to say hello to anya you." It didn't take a Henry Higgins to determine that Marcy Melcher had been raised in one of the Five Towns. "So, hello! Hi." She stuck her hand out to the nearest person, who happened to be Alex.

"Alex Silva." He took the hand and shook it. "Pleasure to meet you." We were impressed that, two IPAs on an empty stomach notwithstanding, he stopped there. One of Alex's favorite rants was about Marcy Melcher's taste in décor.

"Alex. Mia. Fabian." Kippy was working his way down the receiving line, with Marcy doing the handshakes. "And this is Megan. Megan started at the front desk and now she's in Client Care. See, Marce, this is what I'm talking about, giving young people the opportunity to learn and build a career!"

"Wondaful!" Marcy gushed. "You must be so proud!"

Megan, who'd earned her undergraduate degree in Archeology and read both Latin and Greek, flashed a tight smile. "Thank you, Mrs. Melcher."

"And this is Orla, right?"

"Orla Belton." She gave Marcy's hand a hearty shake. Although budgetary constraints were causing the masterpiece to be done in stages, Orla's defined biceps were already encircled with a snake that would have done Cleopatra proud. We enjoyed watching it ripple. Marcy moved quickly to the next person, who happened to be Orla's boyfriend. "And this is Carl. My partner."

Carl's black muscle shirt, donned in a show of respect for an office gathering, did nothing to conceal the considerable extent of his own ink. "My goodness!" The words popped out of Marcy's mouth before good manners took over. "You have...I like your...is that a skunk?"

He peered at his own forearm to locate the creature in question, then grunted with some satisfaction. "Honey badger. One of my own."

"Carl's an artist," Orla said proudly. "Actually this is also one of..."

"Impressive," Kippy said hastily. There was still one person left and he greeted her gratefully. "Amanda! Marcy, this is Amanda. Just started a few months ago, and already a rising star."

"Very nice to meet you, Mrs. Melcher." Archandra Ghosh smiled serenely, ignoring the coughing fit at the other end of the line.

"You too. Well, we should let you all get on with your lunch."

"Enjoy yours as well." Archie closed the conversation on the highest note she could muster. "Thank you so much for hosting such a lovely picnic."

"What a great group of kids," Kippy whispered, or so he thought, to Marcy as they moved on.

Alex could hardly wait for them to be safely away. "Why the fuck didn't you correct him?"

Archie flipped her heavy braid over her shoulder. "I didn't have the heart. He seemed so happy. And after Orla and Carl, I needed to make sure he stayed that way."

"I don't know about the rest of you, but I'm getting my proud ass over to the tables before the locusts from Sales wipe us out."

Somewhere around a quarter past one, our slice of the park was as full as it was going to be. As neat in blue cotton trousers as in her usual pencil skirts, Edie Brewer drifted to the end of the buffet queue and pretended she'd been politely holding back until youthful hunger had been appeased. She'd only just arrived. Having carefully weighed her options for a reverse commute on a beach day, she'd opted for the car, then lost an hour thanks to an overheated van breaking down on the Hutch. The only garage she could find with parking was down on 94th Street. Arriving while she could still blend into a food line was the first break she'd caught all day.

She couldn't stay long. The agency rates for Sunday were extortionate. Phil refused to let her pay them so he was home alone, except for the dog. Checking her watch, Edie swore under the breath she was still trying to catch. She'd better get her face seen, pronto, so she could head home.

Edie nearly collided with the other latecomers. These were easily the most attractive couple at the picnic, if not in the Park. Donny Rohmer, returning from the beach just for this picnic, was tan and buff. His cargo shorts were pressed and tailored to fit properly. The entire package, the white—not striped—Polo, the polished Docksiders, could have been an ad for Ralph Lauren. To the amusement of every openly gay man at Pinnacle whose ass he had ever ogled, Donny was accompanied by a would-be Victoria's Secret model in a floral sundress, strappy heels and the same sunglasses as Mrs. Kippy.

One of Ginny's sons, using the buffet line as a human slalom course, pulled his scooter to a short stop. "Mom! Are they twins like us?" Harry didn't need Mr. Microphone. His piping treble could probably be heard at Stranger's Gate.

Everyone turned toward the sound. It took a couple of beats for most of us to catch up, probably because young Harry's line of sight was at such a different angle from ours. Scott was also wearing a white shirt with fitted khaki shorts. Both men wore their wavy brown hair in a kind of pompadour, and both had their sunglasses secured by red sports retainers. They were of similar build. Today, they were even of similar height. That gave us pause, as Scott was usually taller.

Scott approached Harry and ruffled his hair. "Adorable!" He pretended to laugh. Tim ran up and whisked his son away with promise of frozen yoghurt. The moment over, we all went back to whatever else we'd been doing.

Hank Iversson from Procurement crossed over into Sales. Hank, whose family manufactures doorknobs or something like that in Minneapolis, was the only person we knew of who'd put in for the referral thing. He'd also said he was thinking of asking for the next Sales Assistant opening. We'd thought he was joking, but there he was in khaki shorts, albeit in a Twins t-shirt, sharing a beer and a laugh with Glenn and Roger.

Tully and Lily finished their sandwiches and resumed their strumming, wandering into a Dylan song they both liked. They sounded good together.

"Maybe you guys should start a band," Dawn murmured from her patch of sun on the blanket next to Tully.

"I'm already in a band," Tully reminded her.

"I play solo," Lily said.

"But are either of you getting any work?"

The two musicians looked at each other and shrugged. They weren't.

Tully leaned over to kiss Dawn's hair. "She's got a point."

"Of course I do." She yawned happily and allowed herself to doze to the sounds of their jam.

Freddie Vega found a soccer ball in the box and pulled together a pickup game, with players from every department. It was a triumph of team-building that registered with no one at C-level, and it was a hell of a lot of fun.

Abby Witherspoon bundled Caleb into his stroller and made a discreet exit. So did Edie Brewer. Shawn and Chris folded up the volleyball net that had never been used, and started on the tables.

Tim had caved into the boys' badgering and taken them down to the boathouse, a treat Ginny was glad to have an excuse to miss. It was pleasant by the large shade tree, chatting softly with the remnant of the IT contingent. She kept a weather eye on Angie Broussard and her daughter, curled up napping on a faded crib quilt. Ina Hochmann, who missed having babies at home, was enjoying the opportunity to fuss over Leon's and speak Russian with his wife, a woman shyer than she was. Leon's three-year-old clone, having refused to settle down for a post-lunch rest, sat on his Baba's shoulders and grabbed at the leaves that were just out of reach. The Buzzard returned from schmoozing with Sales over by the coolers. Between his fingers, dripping bottles dangled by their necks.

Ginny accepted a beer. "Do you think Scott looks different today?" She couldn't stop thinking about it.

"*Da*! He looks like Donny Rohmer!" Leon snickered. "He's a smart one, your son." His own son snagged a leaf at last and stuffed it in his mouth. Some fatherly radar, or maybe it was the child's joyful tug at his hair, communicated this to Leon who reached up with one arm and dug it out.

"I ought to have died of embarrassment, but I only wanted to laugh."

"I would stick with laugh." Mike touched his bottle to hers in salute. "Best moment of the day. Anyway, no one knows he's yours."

"Tim thinks fast. It's an air controller thing." Ginny took a thirsty swallow. "Damn. Scott may not know who he is, but Peterson does. He remembers when I was pregnant."

"Wow! You've been with the company a long time." Mike's girlfriend Kitty seemed impressed.

"Only a few months. I was working with Peterson on a contract job back then."

"Peterson was laughing," Mike assured her. "Don't let it get to you."

"Seriously though, why does Bell look different?"

"He's short." Leon chuckled again. "Look at his feet." The incident had put Leon in an exceptionally good mood. He wasn't particularly fond of Scott, who chose to act as if he couldn't understand a word that Leon said.

Ginny flicked herself on the forehead. "Idiot! The man wears lifts!"

Mike looked at her blankly. "What did you think?"

"I wasn't thinking. I mean, I never thought."

Kitty had a clear line of sight to the Sales huddle. "If he usually wears lifts, he isn't today. He's got on flat sandals."

"No way!" Twisting to see, Mike nearly gave himself whiplash. "Damn! I don't believe it!"

"Expensive ones. If he usually wears lifts, you'd think he'd have boat shoes, like that other guy."

"Don't!" Ginny started giggling helplessly.

"That's not the point!" Mike was seriously pissed off. "Didn't I ever tell you about the sandals?" Apparently not; the faces around him were uniformly blank. Mike took a fortifying gulp. "Last summer, on one of those really hot days? It was broiling out, so I wore a pair of sandals to the office. Not flipflops, not those Teva things. Good looking. Polished leather. I love those sandals. I got them in Italy. They have that look, you know?"

"They do," Kitty nodded her agreement. "Sophisticated. Think Marcello Mastroianni."

"No joke, they really are that nice. So I'm on my way out of a meeting, when Scott grabs my arm and says 'don't you ever wear that to work again.' I have no idea what he's talking about. I'm wearing, you know, what I usually wear to work. I must have looked confused..." By way of illustration, Mike stroked his beard. "He points down at my feet. There's this look on his face, like he's never been so disgusted in his life. And he says 'you should never see a man's toes in public.' And then he...what was that word in all the *Peanuts* cartoons? Harumph. That was what he looked like when he walked away; like he was thinking 'harumph!'" Mike had drunk just enough beer to allow him to toss his head and give a magnificent shrug, mimicking Scott having a hissy fit. "You should never see a man's toes?? And now he's wearing sandals??"

"To be fair," Ginny said, once she'd blown the beer out of her nose, "that was the office and this is a picnic."

"He didn't say 'office'," Mike grumbled. "He said 'in public.' And mine are really nice sandals. Nicer than what half the women wear to work."

"Maybe you should talk to Kay about a Sexual Harassment suit," Dave suggested, deadpan.

"It's not a suit, it's sandals," Leon cracked.

No one had ever heard Leon make an outright joke before. Once it had sunk it, the laughs were so loud that they woke Dave's daughter, who in turn woke Angie, who looked at her watch and decided it was time to go.

Which by then most everybody except the soccer players had also decided. The First Annual Pinnacle Picnic had come to an end. Though we didn't yet know it, so had the Last.

6 FAILOVER

From *The Peak Experience*

Pinnacle Rolls Out Cutting Edge OnRamp Technology!

For more than forty years, Pinnacle Management Services has alleviated the burden of office administration with our comprehensive suite of service products. Our reputation for client satisfaction is unparalleled; yet we continue to explore new avenues to make your experience even better. Now Pinnacle takes the pain out of getting started!

With Pinnacle's game-changing OnRamp technology, onboarding is a breeze! Using a secure, encrypted data pipeline, OnRamp seamlessly integrates our proprietary Bridge Mark II fulfillment system with your internal HRIS or other record-keeping system. The user-friendly OnRamp dashboard provides high-availability, intuitive access to the features you need most. Customizable...

Δ

Edie wasn't happy to be proven right, but she was relieved not to have been caught napping. She continually lit mental candles to whatever saint had inspired Mike to think of that data scrape. If they hadn't done it, Mama San Yakitori would still be waiting for the typing to finish. Instead, MSY was up and running. No, the conversion hadn't gone as smoothly as they'd hoped. They'd had to push the client roll-out four days. The first weeks had been woefully rocky, despite all Simran's work-arounds. Still, they could hang a big "Mission Accomplished" banner over the radiators in time for Kippy's next monthly address.

If she and Abby and Mike hadn't put the contingency plan in play, MYS would have been dead in the water. Thanks to all the Sales bells and whistles the LC dumped into the project over the months, the initial deliverable of OnRamp had more holes than a block of Jarlsberg. Instead of kissing their feet that the launch wasn't the disaster it might have been, Kippy, Scott and Feldman dismissed everything except the grumbles they were hearing from MSY.

Grumbles were unavoidable. A stopgap was still a stopgap. The best manual process couldn't keep up with this volume of work, not at current staffing levels, and Feldman wouldn't unglue his ledgers.

"I already approved two hires for you." It was difficult to call it a glare when his brows were so furrowed that his eyes were slits.

"That was assuming we'd have OnRamp," Abby protested. It was her two hires he was talking about. "Orders are crawling. My phones are ringing off the hook with complaints. I need four bodies on MSY, not two. Where am I supposed to get them? My crew is perpetually understaffed; I have no surplus to steal for this."

Feldman turned his prune visage on Edie. Yearning for the pleasure of punching it raw, she returned his look as blandly as she could manage.

"Gary; you know as well as we do that our budgets were done before MSY was a gleam in Scott's eye. And the exceptions you approved were based on the existence of a functioning OnRamp." Collaboration was one thing, but she wasn't about to fall on any swords for Peterson. "Which is why you only let me add one body to each of my teams." Edie had been told that, with OnRamp taking on so much of the burden, that should be more than sufficient to cover MSY.

"You don't need more staff. Your staff is 12 percent over what it should be. And you," he stabbed the air in Abby's direction; "yours is 10 percent over. According to your own metrics."

Vivian's metrics, as "supervised" by Scott, had been submitted well before Abby arrived at Pinnacle. As for Edie's, Feldman, who had no personal experience of the effort involved for any of the Fulfillment services, regularly insisted her headcount was far too high for the volume of work.

"Our people are moving heaven and earth to make this work. They can't do any more than they do, and we've run out of bandwidth to steal." She'd already thrown more bodies at MSY, making up the shortfall by redistributing their work. As a result, nearly everyone in Fulfillment was working outrageous overtime and scarcely drawing breath. It was an unsustainable solution to the mess.

"I have no latitude here. We're already well over budget."

"Because of two Client Care associates?" Abby couldn't contain herself. The man was making sounds that meant nothing. "You realize, don't you, that you're paying 15 percent below market rate for that role."

"We hire the inexperienced, and train them," he replied stiffly. "That training is worth much more to them in the long run than a few extra dollars."

It was stunning logic.

"I don't care what their previous level of experience was. These people do a tremendous job. To our clients, they're the face and voice of this company. How can we not value the work they do?"

"We've had several unanticipated OpEx line items that have strained our cushion. I will approve no additional hires." Before Abby could further object, he stood and leaned over his desk, his hands pressing hard enough to turn his knuckles pale. "And I don't have to explain myself to either of you. You're supposed to be problem solvers, ladies. So solve the problem."

Δ

```
From:        Kay Kuperman
To:          All Pinnacle Associates
Subject:     Congratulations!
------------------------------------
```

While we continue to grow in all segments, our Payroll Services business has experienced particularly explosive growth over the last three quarters. To better maintain Operational Excellence in this area, George Waters will lead this team in his new position as Manager of Payroll Services and Data Entry. Please join me in congratulating George Waters on his promotion.

Kay Kuperman, Dir. Human Resources
Pinnacle Management Services

Δ

The main conference room was crammed to bursting. The LC was there, of course, and all Senior Management the next level down. Then the IT team leads, who even Feldman had to agree needed to be there. The rest of the room filled up, one diffident body at a time, with certain skilled worker bees that the managers, closer to the ground than the LC, anticipated would be roped into this project: Jeff Curry, for example, who knew more about Bridge than anyone except Leon and whose promotion Waters had been systematically sabotaging; old-timers Noble Landrum and Martha Moon; Mike Ventura's entire team.

"This is a landmark day for Pinnacle!" Kippy stood, not on a windowsill but only at the head of the long table. With everyone else either seated or pressed flat against a wall, the top of his head was still the highest spot in the room. "Almost exactly ten years ago, people I knew in business were shocked when I decided to build, from the ground up, a software application that would revolutionize the way we do business in our sector. It cost a lot of money. And it was going to take more than a year before I'd find out if it would even work at all, never mind pay for the investment. People thought I was nuts. Walt thought I was nuts, didn't you Walt?"

Walt Sacco smiled and bobbled his head. If Pinnacle was a family, Walt was the uncle who sleeps on the sofa in the TV room. "Absolutely thought you were nuts, Kippy."

"Ha! Everybody did. People at the country club, my alumni association, everyone said to me, 'Melcher, why do you want to throw your money away on a bunch of computers?' And I told them, 'I am looking at the future and the future is about technology.' Now I don't know the first thing about technology, am I right Leon?"

Every eye in the room turned to where Leon sat, arms folded, face more than habitually sour. He bent under all the stares. He didn't say a word but nodded, opening his mouth enough for a fleeting glint off his gold tooth.

"Hey, I don't have to, right? I only have to be smart enough to hire a genius like this guy. And I am exactly that smart. I told Leon what I wanted and did he ever do an amazing job. Him and Ina. They built us Bridge, and we've been driving our business across that Bridge ever since. Ha! Amazing work. Let's have a round of applause for Leon and Ina." Kippy started the applause himself, his hands held above his head like a prize fighter's. A dull flush crept into Leon's sallow cheeks. Beside him, Ina ducked her head so that her hair swung forward to cover her face.

"So, ten terrific years. Growing...no! Exploding! We have almost twice as many people here as we had last year at this time. I know, I can hardly believe it myself. And this is just the beginning. Scott and his team are going after more and bigger fish out there every day. So I'm looking into the future again and I say we need to build a bigger better Bridge! Now Wesley Peterson says it's traditional for development projects to have a code name, so today ladies and gentleman, I'm announcing the launch of Project Verrazano."

Jeff couldn't stifle his snicker. Fortunately, Kippy thought it was an appreciative laugh and joined in.

"Ha! Yeah, it's pretty good, isn't it? Project Verrazano is going to take Bridge and grow it, to match our growth! All those enhancements you've all been asking for, we're gathering them all up. But that's not all. We're going to build this next generation of Bridge with resources I never even knew existed ten years ago. We're gonna have a whole new best-in-breed platform, with OnRamp baked in right from the get-go. And a whole new Expense and Travel Management product. Great, right? But now you're asking how we're gonna do this. So let me tell you. By partnering with Centient, an exceptional team of professionals specializing in researching and organizing projects like this. These guys, well, when I saw their presentation, it blew my socks off. They have a whole blueprint for doing this kind of thing. You know the way those journalists were embedded with the troops? We're going to have a team from Centient embed themselves here at Pinnacle. These Centient guys are going to be eating Pinnacle, sleeping Pinnacle, learning our business inside out. They're going get to know what we need so well that we won't even have to ask for it! Wait 'til you see what these guys can do! Ha! I'm not going to make you wait another minute. I'm going to turn this meeting over to Jim Dagny of Cenient."

Even standing, the man who inclined his sandy crewcut in acknowledgement would have been invisible if he hadn't been introduced. He smiled pleasantly. "Hello. As you've just heard, I'm Jim Dagny and I'll be heading up your Pinnacle Centient team. I'd like to introduce you to our Business Analysts, Kamlesh Patel and Pradnya Sawant." A timid pair in navy blue suits rose halfway from their seats to bob their heads before retreating behind their open laptops. "Over the next weeks, they'll be spending a lot of time with you. We'll be organizing some group meetings to familiarize ourselves with your functional areas. Be sure to put your information on the sign-in sheet that's circulating now. Name, team, role. This will help us identify our subject matter experts, and that will be key to our success. If someone would please get the lights? Thank you. I'll begin by showing you a short video presentation about Centient, after which I will walk you through the timetable of our knowledge-gathering process."

Ventura and the Buzzard weren't big buddies, but today they went out together for lunch. Without discussing it, they ended up somewhere further uptown than anyone at Pinnacle usually ventured. Even so, they looked carefully around them before choosing a table toward the back of the restaurant but facing the entrance.

"They're big," Mike volunteered. He knew it was the first thing Dave wanted to know. Before Pinnacle Mike had worked with, or in the vicinity of, most of the respected local players. "They're newish on the scene, but they've racked up some impressive jobs. During the meeting, I sent a message to a recruiter I used to work with. He said they're doing work for Greenpoint Savings Bank, Fortunoff...I'll forward you the list. They've got a small presence in Providence, but most of their team is in India. I bet Len Strauss brought them in."

That made sense to Dave. No one was clear how bullet-headed Leonard Strauss was connected to Kippy or to Pinnacle. He blew in every other month or so and, while he was in town, he had the use of a conference room as an office. The only thing that anyone could gather was that he was a player, possibly a marriage broker, in the US-India business market. Even Will Compton, an indefatigable googler widely considered the biggest brain at Pinnacle, had been unable to learn more. Noble thought Strauss might be with the CIA. Whatever he was, Kippy always seemed a little cowed by his presence.

"I wonder how much this is costing."

"Let's see. They sent us a team of three to start..."

"To start?"

"Did you look through any of that material they handed out? It's like a build-your-own-IT kit. System architects, DBA, a usability specialist..." Mike ticked them off on his fingers. "Kippy must have felt like a kid in a candy store. I wonder if he realizes how much this is going to run him."

Dave snorted. "Come on. It's got to be a fixed bid. Even if Kippy got carried away, Feldman would reel him back."

Mike looked troubled. "Yeah, I bet they're all feeling smug, thinking they're getting away with something."

"You agree, they're looking to break us down."

"I think that's in their heads, yes. They've had this team over a year now..."

"What do you mean? We just finished staffing up!"

"You know that, I know that. But the LC looks around and sees a lot of the same faces who didn't deliver BM-II..."

"Maybe if they'd stop changing their minds about what's supposed to be in BMII..."

"...And only gave them part of OnRamp." Mike held up a flat palm. "I'm playing Devil's Advocate. Doesn't matter that they started asking us for a carport and then added on a mansion. To them, it's us that didn't deliver. Now Centient comes galloping in on a white charger to save the day. Only with a company like Centient, you want their best people or nothing. You lowball them and they send you the B team."

"So we're getting the C team." It was a statement, not a question. Dave waved his hand at the waitress. "I'm betting no one would notice if we had a beer."

Δ

```
From:        Kippy Melcher
To:          All Pinnacle Associates
Subject:     Name the Project!
---------------------------------
Hello, Pinnacle!
```

At today's Monthly Meeting, I shared some news about a software development project that is going to change the way we do business.

This is the application you'll be using every day. We think that ALL of you should have a chance to give it a name! So put on your thinking caps, Come up with a name that expresses who we are, and the excellence to which we aspire. Each suggestion should be backed up with a few sentences that explain why your idea is the one to choose.

Email your suggestion to Gretchen (g.keneally@pinnaclems.com) by EOD Friday, November 30. And don't forget to sign it, because there are prizes! That's right! There's a $500 cash prize for person who comes up with the winning name. The four runners up will each be awarded a $50 gift certificate at Best Buy.

The contest will be judged by the LC. In case of a tie, the date/time stamp of your emails will be used to decide the winner, who will be announced at the Pinnacle Holiday Party.

Kippy Melcher, CEO
Pinnacle Management Services

Δ

The day of the school's Thanksgiving pageant, Ginny arranged to come in a couple of hours late. The floor seemed unusually quiet when she arrived. Peterson's door was closed. So was the door to the conference room. Mike wasn't sitting at his desk. She could swear she'd double-checked her Blackberry during breakfast; she hoped she hadn't missed a meeting. Ginny logged in and eyeballed her calendar. No, nothing. And the only thing in her inbox was the overnight QA status report from Misha's Aprotek team. Before she started updating the project plan, she'd grab some coffee. And she'd stop by Mac Fraser's desk to show him the video. With all the war paint, even she could hardly pick out Harry from all the tribe, but TJ was adorable as a singing ear of corn. Mac would get a real kick out of it. Maybe she'd show it to the Buzzard later, too. She wondered if Leon knew about Thanksgiving pageants yet; his two were too tiny and he'd grown up in Belarus.

Mac wasn't at his desk; disappointing. His monitor was off and she didn't see his usual "redneck coffee," as he called his morning can of cola. She'd have to stop by later. She hoped he was okay. Mac wouldn't be taking a sick day unless he were dying. Except for the day he'd earn between now and New Year's, he was out of PTO. Fiscal Conservative though she was, Ginny admired countries with things like paternity leave and child care. Tim, who knew more than she did about that kind of thing, said taxes in those places were obscenely high; it still sounded nice. Maybe poor Mac had just been up all night. She remembered what it was like with a newborn. Maybe Clif Speck was letting him work from home. He occasionally did that for his guys, keeping it quiet so no one on the LC caught on. Clif managed information better than the CIA. Every time he excused a missed task by saying "my bad," she wanted to brain him, but she really kind of liked him. Ginny was predisposed to like most people, unless they did something cruel; cruel was unforgivable. Clif was a pretty decent guy. She hadn't seen him yet today, either.

Something didn't feel right. Mac's Air Force badge and the framed photo of Cindy and the baby were missing from the cube wall. The lights were off on his CPU. Ginny didn't like what she was thinking.

She made her way back to her own aisle, jumping when the door to the ladies' room banged open. Someone grabbed her arm and pulled her inside.

Xu Lin-Fai was the most reserved woman Ginny had ever met in her life. She made Ina Hochmann look like an extrovert. Cal Jiang, who was making it his mission to Americanize her, said it was a Mainland thing. Right now, she was too upset to be shy. She pulled Ginny over to the sinks and whispered fiercely, "they fired Mac!"

"For what?!" Despite her almost-hunch, Ginny was momentarily stunned. Mac was an Eagle Scout, clean in thought, deed and, in front of women, word. He never ever defaulted on an assignment. More critically, he was a single thread on the SysOps team. "Nobody else here knows how to do what Mac does. This makes no sense."

Lin-Fai shook her head. "Not Mac only. So horrible! Also Ho..."

Judy burst through the door, relief washing over her white face. "Oh good, you're here. I was afraid..." Her hug was as disconcerting as Lin-Fai's volunteering information. Ginny and Judy worked well together, but they weren't what you'd call BFFs.

"I just got in. School play. What the fuck is going on around here?"

Lin-Fai was so upset that she forgot to cringe at the language. She shrugged helplessly. "Chris came. She left with Mac and Hossein. The managers are in a meeting with Wesley Peterson. All of them."

Judy leaned on the tampon dispenser and took a deep breath. "I was upstairs, picking up some toner from Shawn. Chris was closing the door to the training room. There were a lot of people in there. Shawn said layoffs. Company wide."

"But the company is making a lot of money," Lin-Fai whispered. "Kippy always says."

"Well, what they say isn't always real." Judy was equally shaken. This was how it had started at Trowbridge, the beginning of the end. It wasn't supposed to happen to her again.

Ginny snorted impatiently. She'd never heard of a mass layoff coming without some warning. And Kippy wouldn't be shelling out so much on Centient if he didn't have sufficient capital. "I don't get it. You should hear what they say in some of those Verrazano meetings with Edie and Client Care. We're short-handed everywhere. How can we be laying people off?"

No one had an answer. There wasn't one.

Ginny's next thought made her furious. "It's Thanksgiving week! How do you lay people off during the holidays? What kind of people do that?!"

That question was clearly rhetorical.

"I guess we should get out there," Judy finally said. "Wesley will probably call some kind of all-hands soon."

Ginny made a sound something like a laugh. "I can't wait to hear how he's going to spin this one."

Wesley didn't. Clif, Eliot and Mike each met with their own people to give the official word.

Δ

On Sunday, Kippy had called an emergency teleconference of all Senior Managers to announce the LC's decision: it was imperative to cull the herd; ten percent across the board. Only Sales was exempt, it being counterproductive to pare down your sales team when your most urgent need is to ratchet up income. It was up to the managers on the ground to select their sacrifices. Effective tomorrow.

"It's Thanksgiving!" The words were out before Edie Brewer knew she'd thought them.

Anyone else's head would have rolled, but Kippy liked Edie. He respected her even when they didn't agree, an increasingly frequent occurrence since he'd beefed up his layer of Senior Management. "Don't think I'm happy about this," he assured her. "But we gotta tighten our belts. And we had to get it in before December 1."

"Um, Kippy...?" Clif Speck eased into his own objection. "Most of my guys are single threads. Anybody we give up, we lose a critical skillset."

The other managers, without exception, found the courage to toss their own protests into the pot: they also couldn't afford to lose a single body.

"The decision's been made!" Whatever forbearance he'd kept for Edie, Kippy lost it now. Over the phone line, Edie could hear the red face and popping eyes in his voice.

"If you're single threaded," Gary Feldman interjected; "that's poor management on your part. As is the almost constant whining about being understaffed. We are extremely generously staffed for our volume of business, which is why we're in the position of needing to trim down."

"Exactly!" Kippy swung back to his habitual cheerleader mode. "Lean and mean! That's how we win this race! You've all got some hard thinking to do, so I say we reconvene in an hour."

An hour later, Gary Feldman polled the managers. The atmosphere on the phone lines was heavy and soiled, reminding Edie of a documentary she'd seen about the McCarthy hearings. Naming names.

She cleared her throat to give up her own. Larry Oester and Emma Koutsos were a case of last in first out. Rose Urban was the most dispensable of the Switchboard operators. The hardest cut, the one to which she'd devoted most of the last hour, was to Training. All her kids were smart and hard-working, but the Trainers were the cream of the crop and each had a wealth of institutional knowledge. It would be serious hardship to lose a single one of them. She decided not to. "And Andre Lewis from Procurement," she stated. "I'll be transferring Molly Pacquin from Training into that slot."

There was silence. It was a bold move. Training was the most expensive Fulfillment team. By replacing Andre with the more expensive Molly, Edie might be adhering to the letter of the directive, but not the spirit. Trying not to shudder, she waited to be challenged.

"Ha!" The ever-impatient Kippy exclaimed, before Feldman managed to object. "Creative problem-solving. Great! Who's next?"

George Waters was. He offered his two names without the slightest reluctance: Ethan Farkash from Payroll; and Jeff Curry. Edie was appalled. She suggested he reconsider. She suggested it so strongly, she very nearly begged.

Curry was enormously effective in his role. He had close bonds with his team. He'd trained nearly all of them. They respected him. Prickly as he was, many, including Edie herself, were even fond of him. An organization is a body of sorts. Its beating heart is a core group of people who build a sense of community, the ones others rally around. Only rarely are they in positions of management, but a wise manager identifies them and makes good use of them. Pinnacle had a few such key souls: Noble Landrum; Alex Silva; Martha Moon; Dave Broussard, if only for his ubiquity. And yes, Jeff Curry.

Edie had learned to understand George well enough that if she tried to explain this, she knew he'd decide she was criticizing him for lacking this same inscrutable quality and take offense.

George was an able enough young man. He had potential. He was also conceited and a bully. Now that the LC had rewarded his limits with this promotion, he would never change. It was a pity. As long as he'd remained her assistant, there had been some chance Edie could gently steer him into good management behavior. She'd chipped through hard cases before. Look at what a fine Team Lead Jeff Curry had turned out to be, despite all his bitching and moaning. Jeff Curry, who George had selected as the Data Entry team's sacrificial lamb.

All Edie could do was underline Jeff's more quantifiable achievements. George was offended anyway. She was questioning his judgment. He was, he emphasized, Manager of that team and "other managers" (was that a sneer she heard?) should respect his decision.

At which point Gary Feldman weighed in: "I'm sure Waters is considering cost-containment. You know, Curry's the most expensive body on that team."

Feldman's condescension always made Edie want to tear her hair. They were on a WebEx, so for once she could. She also made horrible faces at herself in the side of the toaster. "Yes, I know that Gary. I also know what a bargain we have, considering his expertise and the management load he's assumed."

"Moot point," Feldman continued smoothly. "We allowed you to insert a supervisory layer, Edie, because you had too much on your plate. Since we've put Waters here on top of these teams, the position is redundant. "

George had a valuable rabbi. It was Wesley Peterson who'd made the bigger splash at first, spreading heaps of charm and expansively validating Kippy's projections of future grandeur. Pinnacle enjoyed a flutter of happy excitement. But while almost everyone's eye had been on Peterson, Edie's included, Feldman played at some kind of three-card Monte and the prize flickered out of sight. Despite Kippy's insistence that business was booming, things gradually disappeared from Pinnacle: little things, like red pens and the break room supply of aspirin and band-aids; big things, like budgets for professional development. The worst of the pseudo-economies, even worse than the infamous eighth floor Air Conditioning units, was the way Feldman played Chicken with technology, refusing to release Clifton Speck's purchase orders until months after they'd been cut, squeezing Payables for pennies of interest that surely came nowhere near what was lost each time the network crashed.

Feldman had become the power behind the throne. He opposed Edie at every turn, with an antipathy that was almost chemical, pulling away from her like a salted leech. Edie, who could usually get along with anybody, wasn't used to having an enemy. She responded in the only way she knew, by ignoring him and focusing on her job, working even harder. The games she wouldn't play, George Waters would. Edie made the critical mistake of allowing her perception of George as an awkward, green kid to blind her as to how he might be turned against her. Feldman adopted him, pumped him up, egged him on. Where George Waters had been difficult before, he was impossible now.

Edie knew when to throw in the towel. Jeff Curry was gone.

Δ

On the day of what would be immortalized as the Thanksgiving Massacre, in every space could be used for a meeting, managers cleared their throats to recite that, while Pinnacle was still strong, we were not invulnerable to the dip in the economy: expenses continued to rise, income was not meeting the forecasts and Receivables were becoming difficult to, uh, receive. To create greater financial cushioning against what was anticipated to be a weak first quarter, the Leadership Council had made the tough decision to preemptively reduce staff by ten percent. This was a hard call, but the right one to make in the current climate. Like us, the LC regretted the loss of our coworkers. Perhaps, if the economy picked up quickly, we'd be able to hire them back in a few months.

The party line was delivered with reasonable conviction, apart from the tacit agreement that there was something particularly cold about doing this right before a major holiday.

Only George Waters, Manager of the Payroll and Data Entry teams, appeared to revel in the announcement. Followed by a shuffling conga line of direct reports, he swaggered into the large conference room. From the other side of the floor, amassing her own troops in the aisle where Compliance sat, Edie Brewer saw this and suppressed the desire to run after them. These teams needed real leadership now.

Waters preened before his sullen audience. Edie turned resolutely away. There was nothing she could do. She had a couple of dozen other lives to concentrate on, people she could help.

Δ

By 2 p.m. we all knew it was true: Data Entry had staged a walkout. Nothing like this had ever happened before. Definitely not at Pinnacle, and even people as old as Walt Sacco and Judy Schreiber had never heard of it happening outside the movies.

It was crazy, but something had to be done. The loss of anyone from Data Entry was crippling; lose Jeff and it was all going to collapse. Jeff, faster and more accurate than anyone else, did the work of two people. More like three, Fritz Kennedy suggested, when you consider that all the leadership stuff was almost a full-time job and Jeff still pounded the keys like he always had.

The team elected Tully Mulhern to take their grievance to HR. He walked out dejected; Kay Kuperman didn't have the power to do anything except refer the group back to their manager, the person who'd caused it.

Quiet Kaimi Poole returned from Edie's cube looking as if he wanted to cry.

No one remembered whose idea it was, but it felt right. There didn't seem to be anything else they could do. So it was decided: everyone went out for lunch and not a single one came back.

When Waters figured it out, he was incensed and Dawn Kollist got the worst of it. Whatever it was Waters had about Dawn, it didn't help that she was dating Tully.

Dawn washed her face and treated herself to a comforting bag of greasy, spicy pseudo-Doritos from the machine. On the way back to her cube, she saw the LC assembling in the big conference room and sent up a quick prayer to the patron saint of office drones that it was payback time. It wasn't hard for her to find reasons to walk by and bear witness. She refilled her coffee in the break room, decided she needed to consult Gene Siriano about an Excel formula, discovered a sudden need for supplies to clean the surface of her desk. Each time, she flashed an eye through the glass and basked in the spectacle of executive fury focused on an impotently flailing, scarlet-faced Spurious George.

This was no time for stamping feet and pointing fingers. George Water's tantrum served only to underline that he was in over his head. Following Alan Reisch's admirably calm suggestion, the LC sent George home early while the rest of them focused on damage control. It was critical they act immediately. Edie Brewer hoped her former assistant would maybe learn something from this experience. It was a reflexive hope; in her heart, she knew it was unlikely. He would blame everyone but himself.

Feldman naturally skipped past any leadership failure on George's part and placed the culpability square on the team. "I refuse to be held hostage by a bunch of divas. Fire 'em all. Effective immediately. Or wait, don't. They walked out. When they try and file for Unemployment, we refuse it. On grounds." The last two words must have tasted delicious to him.

Kay Kuperman's usually sunny face, mottled and puffy from a sleepless night, blanched a stark white.

"Is that really warranted?" Alan Reisch spoke hastily, presumably to prevent Kay from toppling over. "I can't condone what they've done—they've certain overreacted—but I understand their frustration. Edie and I both warned against cutting that team."

She agreed as neutrally as possible. "They're such bare bones, any loss puts them at risk."

Kay's shoulders heaved and she spoke on a sigh. "One of the team came to me this morning. I couldn't help him."

Poor Kay! She wasn't equipped for something like this. Edie was seriously worried the woman wouldn't make it through the day. Turning to face her, she tried hard to look supportive.

Kay cleared the waver out of her throat and continued. "He said, the one who came in, that even with all the overtime they've been putting in, they're barely keeping up, and that without Jeff Curry it would be impossible. I know you said there had to be a cut from that group, Gary, but I think maybe Jeff was the wrong person to choose." She slumped back against her chair, visibly exhausted from having her say.

"He was the most expensive," Feldman replied testily. "Waters may be rough around the edges, but his thinking is sound. Data Entry should have been phased out years ago. We can't charge enough for that service to cover their salaries."

Edie was tired of this particular dead horse. "We keep the compensation as low as we can," she reminded him. "Which is why it's so difficult to hire for that role."

"Ridiculous," he snapped. "It's typing. Any monkey can do it. Pick people at random off the street. We can have a new team here in less than an hour."

Scott Bell, of all people, shot him an impatient scowl. "Get real, Feldman. It's not about the data entry we bill for. This team does all of our own input. It takes...wait, Edie...how long to train them to set up a new client in Bridge?"

"Three weeks. Until then, they need close supervision." It would be a nightmare, bringing on an entire new roster.

"Three weeks. All my new accounts! We can't afford to shut down the pipeline for three weeks! We need to get those bodies back in those chairs!"

Kippy suddenly stood. Edie knew he liked to think that Pinnacle was Santa's Workshop, filled with merry busy elves who looked on him as a benevolent father. It was his fondest illusion, reinforced by the extreme youth of much of his staff. He'd sat here in peculiar silence, his blue marble eyes bulging with astonishment at what she suspected he saw as a shocking betrayal, only galvanized to action by the enormity of Scott's projected three weeks loss. "Scott's right! We gotta find out what these people want and get 'em back to work!" He brought his fist down on the table, a gesture that seemed to surprise him as much as it did everyone else. He looked down perplexed, then frowned and beat the table again. The second bang put the fire back in his eyes. "Right! Action! So how do we bring them back? Edie, you know these kids. What'll it take?"

They'd handed the team over to George to manage, but she was still the one they turned to in a crunch. "I think we need to bring back Jeff Curry,"

127

she said proposed cautiously. She believed that would be enough. This wasn't a planned walk out. None of these kids could afford to be unemployed. They wouldn't cut off their noses to spite their face, except maybe Curry himself. "If he'll come," she added.

"Then that's what we do." Before Feldman could voice an objection, Kippy stared him down. "Now. That's what we do now. Anything else can wait. You tell that to your boy Waters when you bring him up to speed."

Feldman nodded curtly. Edie found that Kenny Rodgers song running through her head. Hold, fold, walk, run; Feldman knew the drill.

"Edie, you know Curry. You call and ask him if he'd be willing to meet with me tomorrow. I wanna talk with him face to face. That's how you negotiate! Kay, you call the other kids. Tell them we're doing it. Say we want them back tomo...no, day after tomorrow. Ha! Give everyone time to cool down. Okay then. All we gotta do is hang on 'til then. Can't be caught dead in the water. So how do we cover? Good thing we can always rely on Edie!"

Only Feldman didn't seem to agree. Everyone else faced her with flattering attentiveness. The solution was already in her head. "Give me anyone who's ever worked in Data Entry. For the rest of today and all day tomorrow. That means Marla, Scott; okay? Also Martha and Noble." The callous timing would work in their favor now: it was always a little quiet before a holiday. Scott and Abby nodded.

Peterson gave a smart thumbs-up. "Anyone else I have that you think can help, you just say the word. This gets top priority. Would Judy be any help? Broussard maybe?"

She thought briefly. "They'd slow me down; I'd have to show them too much. But if we really get stuck, I might ask to borrow Ina. And Kay, if you can handle things without her, I could use Chris Keane." That would give her three, maybe five sets of hands as well as her own and maybe Archie Ghosh. They'd be nowhere near as quick as the regular team and not even Marla knew any of the recent bells and whistles, but it would be enough. There'd still be a mountain of backlog, not to mention their own work piling up on the side; but the most critical jobs, the few that would lose them clients or stall an implementation, those would get done.

The next morning, Jeff Curry arrived at 9:30, late enough that a lot of us were at our desks to see him walk into Kippy's office. He wore a suit. Orla said he'd had a haircut. Alex said it was just that he'd combed it for a change. He was in with Kippy for almost an hour. Anyone who was looking up when he left saw them shake hands. Kippy had a broad smile on his face. Jeff's smile was more serious. He looked older, somehow.

Dawn managed to be on her way to the break room and cross his path. She paused and tilted her head, questioning.

"See you guys tomorrow," he said gruffly.

He strode quickly out the door without saying another word. Dawn turned her head and gave the nod to anyone whose eye she caught.

Data Entry had won. In our hearts, we knew it was a hollow victory. With Spurious George still Manager, everyone on the team had a price on their heads.

Δ

```
From:        Chris Keane
To:          All Pinnacle Associates
Subject:     Thanksgiving Jeans Days!
-------------------------------------
```

Many of you have asked if you can wear jeans tomorrow….Yes you can! So for those of you who will be working Friday, we have 2 (two) jeans days this week!.

On jeans days and on regular days, we ask that you adhere to the following guidelines.

Please continue to avoid the following when in the office:

- Clothing/jeans that are dirty, torn or frayed
- Sweatshirts — with or without hoods
- Uggs (Winter's flipflops)
- Hats, caps or berets. This applies to men and women, unless you require head-covering for religious reasons.
- Revealing clothing, including mesh/transparent panels.
- And remember…Clothing should be pressed and never wrinkled.

Please note: if you are meeting with clients or outside vendors, or when interviewing candidates, you are representing Pinnacle. Proper business attire is expected.

Enjoy the Thanksgiving Holiday!

Chris Keane, HR Generalist
Pinnacle Management Services

7 DISASTER RECOVERY

```
From:          Scott Bell
To:            All Pinnacle Associates
Subject:       Holiday Party
-----------------------------------
```

In view of some regrettable incidents that occurred last
year, I feel it necessary to remind you all that Thursday's
Holiday party is an office event. Bear in mind that you are
representing Pinnacle at a public venue, and comport
yourselves accordingly.

This year, a two-drink maximum will be strictly enforced. If
you are not working on Thursday, or have an early shift, do
not use this as an excuse to start the party early! Please
respect these limitations. If you notice any over-indulgence
among your peers, we ask that you have the good sense to
intervene.

Our Holiday party is meant to be an enjoyable experience for
everyone. Please do not spoil the fun of others with your bad
behavior!

```
Scott Bell, President
Pinnacle Management Services
```

Δ

We'd expected the Holiday party to be cancelled. Tully was probably right: there must have been a large, unrefundable deposit, and with the money already spent, the LC might as well have something to show for it. Anyway, Kippy had a thing about the Holiday party.

"It's my way of giving back to all the terrific people who make Pinnacle the greatest managed office services company in the world. I bet you're thinking I oughta say 'in the US.' Ha!" Kippy gave a hearty slap on the back to the one new face in the attentive circle.

"Or maybe North America?" Ian Sefton was in from Toronto for Scott's all-day sales conference and, therefore, for tonight's festivities. So were the remote salesmen who covered California and Texas.

"Get that man another Molson's!" Kippy chortled, raising his glass of seltzer in salute. "But seriously Vijay, you could look the whole world over and not find a company that does what we do, not at our level of excellence. What do you think?"

The wide-eyed young programmer had a hint of supplication in his smile. "I cannot pretend to have the experience to know what to say, Mr. Melcher. I can only say that I have been most impressed with those members of Pinnacle with whom it has been my pleasure to work."

"I love the way this guy talks," Kippy said. "Call me Kippy. Everyone does."

Vijay's prominent Adam's apple convulsed. "Kippy, yes."

"Have you met everyone?"

"I have only arrived. Dave Broussard introduced me to the development team. I am pleased to finally be meeting them after having worked together for so many months."

"Any surprises?" Roger Didilian winked a heavy eye. He was perpetually implying hidden meaning in the most ordinary statements.

Craig Parnes' new Mohawk was probably a surprise but Vijay was too polite to say; no one in the New York metro area had been this polite since 1962. "They are all very pleasant. I am greatly looking forward to meeting the others. Most of all, Edie Brewer, who was most helpful with OnRamp."

Vijay had been one of the three short-term Aprotek consultants. It was unclear when or how, but he was now working for Centient where his domain knowledge of Pinnacle made it a no-brainer to assign him to our project. Someone (not Jim Dagny) had suggested bringing him to New York to shadow our in-house team and increase that knowledge.

"Great gal, Edie. Works harder than anyone in the company except me and maybe Gene Siriano. Ha!" Kippy often espoused his respect for Edie and Gene. "Glad we gave her young Waters to help her out. Doing a terrific job, Waters. I spotted him, you know. Right off the bat. I could see he was an up-and-comer. Focused. Not like some of the young people here. Not that they're not all great kids, but they're missing that thing that comes from being settled down like Waters, or Didilian here. Like yourself, I hear. That right?"

Confused by this flurry of pronouncements, Vijay wasn't certain what the question was.

Gretchen's vivid red lips came close to Vijay's ear. She looked almost intimidatingly elegant tonight in her sparkly black sheath, but her touch on his arm was kind. "He's heard that you're married," she whispered.

"Oh yes." A relieved smile spread across his face. "I have an excellent wife."

"Good man! I have an eye for talent; never lets me down. Dave!"

The Buzzard's champagne brocade jacket made it easy to pick him out in the shadows at the far end of the bar. He pointed to himself and clownishly mouthed "Me?"

"Vijay here wants to meet Edie. You seen her anywhere?"

"Sure. Come on, Vijay." He hadn't seen her, but knew she was somewhere around; it was bad form to leave before the MVP had been announced. He could have searched directly for her, but he thought Vijay would enjoy some general socializing along the way.

Dave needn't have concerned himself. The combination of jet lag and party had Vijay floating in a happy haze. Only a few hours in New York and he was already in the famous Central Park, where trees sparkled with fairy lights. He could see them through the glass walls of this elegant room. Mr. Kippy Melcher, Founder and CEO of Pinnacle Management Services, had spoken with him as an equal. And Craig Parnes said that on Saturday, some of the team would pick him up from his motel in New Jersey and give him a grand tour of the city. His wife had not been pleased for him to leave Aprotek. Six more months and he would have been promoted from Junior Developer to Developer, that's for sure. But Mr. Leonard K. Strauss had assured him that he would do even better at Centient. Mr. Strauss said that his knowledge of Pinnacle would be valuable there, and enable him to move ahead more quickly. And indeed they had already brought him to New York City for three months to work with the in-house team. What more proof did Meeta need?

At least someone was having a good time. That it was a subdued party had nothing to do with Scott's admonishing memo; we were still unsettled from the Thanksgiving Massacre. We made the most of our two drinks by ordering straight scotch or rum or vodka; if we didn't like it straight or over rocks, we kept it strong by mixing it ourselves with something from the soft drinks table. Anyone who'd been to last year's party said the dinner was going to be meh, so we grazed from the circulating trays of not-bad hot hors d'oeuvres and foraged from the decorative tower of cheese cubes and grapes.

No one wanted to be there. We were only at the restaurant to show our faces. IT checked in with Peterson to prove they'd changed into what he called "business festive;" it could be hard to tell when he was being serious. Since Sales tended to flock together, Scott would be sure to see everyone at some point. Every single one of us made sure to circle past Kippy to say hello or at least nod and be spotted. We went through the motions until it was late enough to drift off to the after-party that a couple of the Sales guys had organized at Whine Bar.

The only thing we still really wanted to talk about, we couldn't; not in such close proximity to C-level ears. It wasn't just the smokers who found their way to the shadowy bit of frozen grass by the front door.

"I keep wanting to say 'let them eat cake'."

"Don't you think that's kind of exaggerating. It's only, what, a dozen people? And they had to bring back Jeff Curry."

"Don't look at the number. It's not like we're Bloomberg. Look at the percentage. Ten percent is a big cut. No wonder it's like a wake in here."

"It's the timing that makes it worse. So fucking heartless. I still can't believe they dumped Mac Fraser. The man just had a baby."

"Vivian gave her two weeks. Ann told Alex."

"I wonder if there'll be any kind of email about it. Will it say 'no longer with' or 'decided to explore other opportunities?' Should we start a pool? What do you think?"

"I wonder if they knew beforehand. Maybe otherwise they would have cut her with the others."

"Maybe they wanted to make us nervous, so we'd work harder."

"Unless they get me a pair of robot hands, I can't do any more. I was at 150 percent before the cuts. Our whole team was."

"You know the only reason Farkash was cut was because George Waters hates his face."

"If that were true, Dawn and I would both be out."

"You're here because he hated me more, Mulhern. If George Waters wins MVP, I'm quitting tomorrow."

"A, you know he is. And B, you can't afford to."

"I don't give a shit any more. I only came back because I couldn't let you guys down. Not after all you did. But I am this close to getting out. You should be too. You know Spurious is never going to forgive any of us. I figure it's just a question of whether we jump or get pushed. I already spoke to my folks. I can move back to Weston and live in the basement while I work on my blog. Did I tell you have I have over four thousand followers now? And *Daily Beast* invited me to submit."

"There still hasn't been any 'why' about this, has there?"

"I can't say where I heard it, but word is that we burned up a lot of money on OnRamp, and MSY isn't spending as much as Scott and Kippy thought they would."

"You think that'll teach them not to sell stuff we don't have?"

"Yeah, right. And Scotty's gonna keep his hands to himself."

"Oh, stop bitching and moaning. Everything is peachy. After all, we can wear jeans tomorrow. Ow, Belton, enough with the hitting! Did Freeman leave me to you in her will or something?"

George Waters was the MVP; to the surprise of practically no one except Edie, who blinked as if someone had suddenly turned on a very bright light. After all that had happened, she'd cherished some hope that her own nominee, Archandra Ghosh, would get the award. Phil was right; she really didn't understand the rules of the game.

George accepted his award to token applause. Seeing his audience beginning to break up and drift away, Scott held up his hand like a crossing guard and made another noisy exhale into Mr. Microphone. "And now, the moment you've all been waiting for."

We hadn't been waiting. We looked up at Scott, his freshly-whitened teeth piercing through the dim lighting, and wondered what he was talking about. "Drum roll please!" What sounded like a toddler jamming with kitchen utensils was Chris, armed with a pair of drumsticks and an electronic drum. "The winner of the Name-the-Platform contest!"

We froze in shock. The Massacre had made us forget all about the contest. As they were announced, each of the 4 runners-up stumbled over to shake Scott's hand and receive a Best Buy gift card from Marla, resplendent tonight in strapless coral dupioni.

"The winner," Scott continued, after the spattered applause died down, "submitted what he described as 'the pinnacle of North America.' Denali! So we'd like to present this award to…"

"I thought Mount McKinley was the pinnacle of North America," Tully muttered.

"Denali *is* Mount McKinley. And a much better name."

Will Compton gave a small salute as Jeff Curry bounded up, with the first real smile he'd flashed all year, accept his prize from Scott. On a wooden plaque, under the optimistic words "Pinnacle Denali, September 1, 2007," they'd mounted a photo of Mount McKinley and a bit of brass engraved with his name. Kippy stepped up to shake his hand, so any photos we took showed all three of them arranged behind the giant cardboard check for $500. Jeff wondered how much it had cost them to make up that big giant check. The real check, Kay whispered, would be in the envelope with his January 15 pay stub. His severance pay, he thought; he'd have to postpone his promise to quit, just for a little while.

Δ

"I'd really didn't want to be here New Year's," Martha sighed. She'd taken the bus up to Freeport Saturday, but she'd had to come back the day after Christmas instead of staying through the week as originally planned.

Client Care had harbored some hope that with Vivian leaving and Ann moving into the assistant slot, maybe they'd get Megan back. Losing her to the Massacre had been a blow. But Scott didn't liked the way she'd answered him about a problem at MSY and wouldn't hear of it. So they were two people short and barely managing, even before Mia's mythical grant finally came true. For their sakes, the thoughtful Mia gave the company a whole month's notice. She was told not to bother coming in the next day. Typical Pinnacle, cutting of its nose to spite its face. If only Mia had been less professional, if she'd worked until the last minute and then just walked without notice, Client Care would have had another body through mid-January. Instead they were down three and Martha was told—not asked—to postpone her time off. At least Abby was human enough to apologize.

Gabe gave her a friendly head-rub. "I understand," he said sympathetically.

He thought she was feeling bad about missing New Year's Eve with her boyfriend, the imaginary Clark. Martha had been looking at a shoebox at the moment she realized that Gabe would only ever feel comfortable hanging out with her if he thought her affections were otherwise engaged.

She'd done too good a job. She and Gabe did everything together. They liked the same music and the same movies. They liked celebrating holidays that weren't their own. She liked his art, and he liked her cooking. They'd been doing all this for a year now and Gabe thought they were the best of pals. He really didn't have a clue. The same way he didn't get how that exotic Latin charm was like catnip to the three blondes from Stockholm who lived down the hall. He really thought they were knocking on his door in their wispy nighties because they needed his expertise with hand tools. Gabe was a sweet, adorable fool; which was why, on the most romantic night of the year, she wanted to be anywhere but where he was.

She sighed, louder than was wise.

"Cheer up, kid," he said. "We'll do something fun together. You know what I've always wanted to do? Go to Times Square! Wouldn't that be great?!"

It would be Hell in every possible way, Martha thought. Standing in the freezing cold for hours, squashed by the crowds, getting progressively more deaf and tired, and all the while trying to pretend she was having fun. On New Year's Eve with the man she loved "Absolutely, bud," she said.

It was more fun than she expected. It wasn't really all that cold out, not if you'd grown up wearing layers of goose down and ThermaTek, and Gabe was so tall that he kept her from being trampled.

He bent his mouth to her ear. "It's great, isn't it?!"

She nodded happily. Maybe all she needed was to step outside herself for a few hours. Times Square had the energy of the Vegas Strip, all those lights, music pouring in from every angle. They could look right up at the big giant video screen and see everything doubled back at them. The excitement of the crowd buoyed her up. It was impossible to feel depressed, or even a little tired, with so much laughter around. And rather than making her feel her own lack of romance, the very public displays of affection had a frankness and innocence that were somehow cheering.

"Only a little longer. You warm enough?" he asked.

"I'm fine!" she shouted back up into the noise. "But I'm getting hungry!"

He tapped his temple with his forefinger. "Planned ahead! I picked up Chinese this afternoon."

"But I wanted peanut butter!" It was a joke of theirs, that Gabe never seemed to have anything but peanut butter in his refrigerator.

"Oh, look!" he said, tilting her a little backwards so that she would look up and see what he saw.

They'd been caught by the cameras and were up there on the big screen, standing in the middle of a crowd full of wildly, sloppily, passionately embracing couples. Two pleasantly good-looking people: he with a tumble of black curls and an engaging sidelong smile; she, neatly elfin with, when she smiled up at her gigantic image beaming over the city, a dimple that could drown a mosquito. It was like watching a couple in a movie. It was magical.

Still looking up at the screen, he pulled her back so that her head was pressed against his chest. On screen, the tassel on her silly knitted hat came up just up to his mouth. She watched the girl on screen gently reach up and brush the tassel away from his lips. He watched the boy on screen kiss the gloved finger. The girl tilted her head back to look into his eyes. He leaned down and kissed her. Somehow, she turned around to face him, their lips never unlocking. Her hat fell off and was never seen again. Only the pulse of the crowd, a million people shouting "Ten, nine, eight...." broke them apart.

"Clark..." he began

"There is no Clark, idiot," she said, smiling brighter than a ball made of 504 Waterford crystal triangles dropping from the top of a tall building into a screaming crowd.

The next time one of the Swedish blondes knocked on Gabe's door, Martha opened it wearing only his José Bernal t-shirt.

"Anything I can do for you?" she grinned.

Δ

From: Wesley Peterson
To: IT
Subject: New Year, New Names!

As a sign of our renewed pledge to keep moving forward in the
New Year, Pinnacle is eliminating the BORING conference room
monikers of yesteryear in favor of BOLD new values-driven
naming. In addition to Kippy's ENERGY, we've got ADVANCEMENT
(Main) and PERSISTENCE (Training Room).

Down here, we've got FOCUS and, best of all, our main
Collaboration Space is now DEDICATION, which is how we do
what we do! You gotta have Dedication to deal with the slings
and arrows of every Phased Development project! Don't let
anybody tell you we haven't earned this great Conference Room
name, and we can enjoy it for the unbridled testimony to IT
wonderfulness that it is. Of course, Dedication applies to
all the rest of Pinnacle too, so they can gladly borrow our
room anytime they want to be inspired!

WJP

Δ

Kippy wanted some kind of regular project updates from IT. There was no
need to drill down to the granular level. Kippy's technical references were
mired in 1985; he still said "software" and "programmer" instead of
"application" and "developer." No, all he needed was a high level view of
where they were headed and how well they were moving along. And he
didn't want this from the CTO; he wanted it from someone on the ground. At
least that was how Wesley Peterson packaged the assignment. Peterson said
he'd considered sending Leon, because Kippy trusted him, but Denali was a
complicated project and Leon's English wasn't up to the gentle massaging
required to make some of these updates palatable. What the team needed
was someone who could talk their CEO through the project in plain English,
but with a little finesse.

Mike Ventura was just that kind of regular guy and, as Project Manager of
Project Verrazano aka Denali, he was high enough in the scheme of things to
be the logical point of contact. Mike wasn't so sure. He was so close to being
under the bus that he could smell the exhaust fumes. It was clear to all of us
that Denali was a hot mess. The day that Kippy reached the same
conclusion, he was going to remember who'd been bringing him that news.
It was no wonder that Peterson would go to great lengths to avoid being that
person.

The trick wasn't to manage expectations; it was to defuse them. Despite
the fanfare and Kippy's Opening Game enthusiasm, anyone could see that
the only thing Denali was doing better than BM-II was burning money. In
fact, Kippy had already spent as much on Centient in three months as he'd
spent on our entire in-house development team for ten, and without a

reciprocal boost in production. The scribbling on the white boards had degraded from workflows to a second-grader's introduction to triangles and parallelograms. At what turned out to be her final SME meeting, Megan Newell had cracked that she was submitting 'Perseus' to the naming contest, because results would have to find their way through a hell of a maze to get out. The only person who could maybe do something about this was Peterson, but Peterson seemed resolved to give Centient enough rope to hang themselves. Whatever Jim Dagny said in the weekly Thursday morning status call, Peterson gave a bobble-head nod and said, "Jim, we're in your capable hands."

The Buzzard had been right on the money when he'd said we were getting the C team. Dagny's crack team of analysts now extended to half a dozen: business analysts, process analysts, even a User Experience analyst; wizards, one and all, at taking existing tables and diagrams and reformatting them to fit on Centient-branded pages, but not so much at actually analyzing anything. Any attempt at feedback—say, for example, correcting their misconception that the Switchboard team was the same as the Client Care call center—set them off into a frenzy of progressive signoffs that could take a business week to put to bed. Other than Vijay, who everyone knew from before, the developers they'd met were fresh out of school. Craig and Sid would break out into frantic one-armed pushups during conference calls, to keep from exploding with frustration. The one thing the Centient resources excelled at, across the board, were metrics. Their devotion to metrics was such that any project activity played second fiddle to the monitoring thereof. Every task was recorded and measured to levels beyond even Harvey Mellen's most OCD fantasies. Before Mike lost Harvey to the Massacre, he'd nearly lost the poor guy to apoplexy.

Mike dragged himself to his weekly one-on-one with his stomach in his boots, which in his case was no small load. He sometimes wished he were the kind of person who could turn something like this to his advantage. If he came out too strong against Centient, he'd have to explain why his own boss wasn't pushing back. Mike unfortunately lacked whatever gene it was that carried the necessary back-stabbing, conniving trait to lead a palace coup. He'd just keep walking Kippy through whatever minor progress might have been made, beat the drum about how well OnRamp was working these days and the great job our own guys were doing on the Travel Management product module, and hope Kippy didn't ask the wrong questions that Mike would be too honest not to answer. Exactly what Wesley Peterson was counting on him to do. For now.

8 REBRANDING

"How many C-level executives does it take to handle an MSY complaint? None. You need an advanced degree."

The joke had been making the rounds for weeks. Sitting in on the LC weekly status meeting, listening to them natter on about an issue that was never going to change, Kay Kuperman couldn't get it out of her head. She'd first heard it from Jeff Curry before he quit, along with his theory that Pinnacle deliberately stocked its phones and keyboards with the extremely gifted and the over-educated. "Cost-containment," he said flatly. "Keep down the overhead by hiring people who are looking for a job, not a career." It was a caustic observation from such a young man.

The Kappas would be shocked if they only knew that Kay, the once and future Sunshine Girl, thought he was probably right. She hadn't been able to get back to her usual cheerful self since Thanksgiving. For a company that paid a lot of lip service to transparency, there was an awful lot that happened under cover of fog. Kay was the head of HR—make that Talent Management (the LC had renamed it, when they'd renamed the conference rooms)—and she hadn't heard so much as a whisper about the layoffs until they were all but executed. When she'd first heard what the teleconference was about, she jumped to the conclusion that own name was on the list. She'd collected her senses quickly enough to ask about the severance package she'd be expected to administer. The line got so quiet she'd thought she'd lost the connection.

Gary Feldman eventually coughed and brushed her aside. "No need to worry. New York is a no-cause state. Just process their final pay periods and have them sign off on the COBRA option."

The coldness of it knocked her sideways. If Mats hadn't been between jobs then, if he weren't still, she'd have volunteered to go. In any case, it was only a matter of time before they pushed her out. Her assistant, Jo, had enough experience in a prior junior slot to be more qualified for the Director position than Kay and, with ten fewer years in the work force, she'd be cheaper. Just as Kay had been cheaper than Art Russo. Now that her eyes had opened, Kay couldn't help wondering if the Russo family had really relocated to Boston. Maybe it had been a cover story to save face for Art. That was the sort of thoughtful gesture she could see Alan Reisch making.

It was Alan who'd invited Kay and the other two women to the LC status meeting, because this was the topic: "We're losing people." Alan had a way of shaking his head that made him look like a sad old basset hound.

"Good." Feldman seemed pleased. "I keep telling you we need to keep the numbers down."

Scott seemed honestly confused. "You never have a problem with my numbers."

Feldman nodded approvingly. "Because you cull the herd every quarter."

The quota system that determined the fate of Sales associates seemed brutal to Kay, but she supposed it was standard practice. Certainly no one from Sales ever showed up at her door to complain. Alan must have agreed. "Sales is used to competing. They work on commission. But we don't incentivize Fulfillment or Client Care. It's not as if there's any bonus for them..."

"Their bonus is that they get to have a job!"

"Gary, Alan was only making the point that Sales is a different kettle of fish." Edie Brewer's tones were always reasonable. "If we want to stop the attrition from my team and Abby's, we either need to create career opportunities, or we have to do something to raise morale."

Did Edie seriously think that was going to happen? Kay was surprised at her own cynicism. No she wasn't.

"I have no problem with attrition." Feldman was positively grinning. "Makes it easier for me if they self-select."

"It's the best ones who are self-selecting. Abby and I have lost key people since the November cuts."

"Even I've lost two." Wesley Peterson had been unusually quiet until now.

"And we're paying top dollar for yours. So don't tell me it's about money."

"We're not paying more than they can get elsewhere," Peterson countered mildly.

"They feel there's no future for them here." Kay spoke up bravely, hating how helpless she felt. "It's a dead end. That's what they say at the exit interviews."

Kippy objected. "We give them a break. We train them. If that's not enough, if they think they've outgrown us and want to move on, then I've done my job. I'm fine with that."

"We're hemorrhaging institutional knowledge." Alan had the drained look of a teacher whose students couldn't make the connection between the alphabet and reading. Even his mustache drooped. "This costs us. No matter how easy it is to refill the position, we lose months every time we have to break in someone new."

"It's a good three months for CS," Abby agreed.

"Edie's point is well-taken, Kippy." Peterson took the bull by the horns. "We should address the morale issue."

"I speak to these people every month, from my heart. I know them by name, every single one of them." Kippy's eyes popped, and he started rising out of his seat. "I gave them a great holiday party! That was no cheap thing, but I did it to cheer them up. That's what we do for them. This company is a family. Remember that great picnic we had last summer? And we've got that Talent Show coming up. We'll do more stuff like that, right Kay?"

She flashed a meaningless smile. "Working on it." Pinnacle was supposed to be her chance to build an employee engagement program from the ground up, to help create the kind of corporate climate that got a company on the "Happiest Places to Work" list, but everything she'd proposed since the picnic had been shot down by the LC as being either too expensive (Feldman) or having "potential Compliance issues" (Kippy's Jiminy Cricket, Walt Sacco). In a cross between desperation and a joke, Kay, herself a former chorus girl, threw out the idea of a talent show. Kippy loved it. So did Scott, who probably had some fantasy of Pinnacle cheerleaders or Rockettes. Feldman was away that week, on an off-season Canadian cruise with his wife. The email went out, garnering so much enthusiasm that when Feldman got back he had no choice but to roll with it. Since then, he'd plunked Kay firmly in the "enemy" category.

Kay was burned out from trying. Eventually Kippy's enthusiasm for company events was bound to die a natural death and she'd be off the hook. At least she still had Boot Camp. Chris and Jo both kept offering to take it over entirely, but Kay refused. It was the only thing she had to hold on to. Her eye strayed to the clock on the wall. "I'm so sorry. I've got a Boot Camp starting in the Training...in Persistence in five." She stood and gathered her things, hoping her relief didn't show. "I hate to leave this discussion; but really, it all only serves to remind us how important it is to give our new associates a solid launch."

Kippy nodded vigorously. "Absolutely. You go ahead. I'll be there for my bit. You can always depend on me. Ha!"

"I know. And I appreciate it." She got out of the room while she could still keep that smile plastered across her face.

Δ

After the initial flush of enthusiasm, the LC members delegated their Boot Camp presentations to appropriate, if less impressive, underlings. Mike Ventura ordinarily covered IT but right now he was in Florence proposing to his girlfriend. Peterson asked Judy Schreiber to take it. She was the logical choice, considering she'd written the presentation in the first place.

We were staffing up again, inching back to pre-Thanksgiving numbers. Maybe a dozen people were grouped around the training room tables. Maybe less; it was hard to count and talk. The configuration in this room always reminded Judy of third grade. So did the shiny first-day-of-school faces and extraordinarily neat grooming. Except for the two new salesmen, this was probably the last time these people would wear what she thought of as banking clothes to the office.

She wondered about the woman in the raspberry tweed faux-Chanel; it was a good faux, but Judy's mom had trained her to shop at a near-competitive level. The suit wasn't the only thing that seemed a bit off to her eye. Chanel Woman had such a plastic smile that you expected it to throw off those cartoon sparkles they sometimes paint into toothpaste ads. The IT presentation was scattered with mild puns and couple of geek cartoons, meant to put the audience at ease; this one flashed her teeth like a stand-up comedian's girlfriend fluffing the audience. When she wasn't smiling hard, she showed she was listening hard, leaning forward in her chair, her chin perching on her manicured hand on the edge of the table, her nose pointed attentively up at the screen. It was quite a performance.

"Any questions?" The animation on the final slide had run its course. The only arm that shot up was Chanel-esque. What a surprise. Judy nodded, casting her own brightest smile. "Yes…," she peered at the folded paper tent on the table, "Milla."

"First I want to thank you so much, on behalf of all of us, for your informative presentation. Entertaining and informative." Flash.

"Thank you," Judy murmured. "It's a pleasure to introduce our department to you all."

"So much fascinating information to absorb! I wanted to ask you…" Milla tilted her head to one side in the manner of a winsome child performer. Her slightly oversized head reinforced the similarity. "What I'm seeing here is that Pinnacle produces its own proprietary software at the enterprise level, which doubles as service fulfillment device and information radiator. But it's not evident how either output set can be leveraged to generate performance metrics. Which is clearly detrimental for internal operations in the attempt to forecast scalability."

Judy tried to shovel her way through the jargon to get to the actual question. What was the point of this empty statement? To impress the rest of the room?

Wesley caught her on her way back to her desk.

"How did it go?"

"Fine." She made it noncommittal.

"Sit. I want to hear all about it."

She sat. "Nothing much to say. I think I kept their attention."

"That's because it's a really terrific presentation. I think you hit the nail right on the head with that one."

"Thanks."

"They're a good group. I met them yesterday. Kippy's out of town, so I had to cover for him and do the cheerleading." Wesley all but winked. "So." He leaned forward and fixed her with his surprisingly penetrating stare. Now she was going to find out what he really wanted to know. "What did you think of Milla?"

"Who is she?" Judy blurted.

Wesley pushed back in his chair and gave an open-throated laugh. "That is our new VP of Fulfillment."

"You're kidding me. Why was she even taking Boot Camp?"

"Kippy insists everyone do it. This program is dear to his heart. So what did you think of her?"

"Um...very enthusiastic. She has a lot of energy." Something didn't make sense. "So if she's the VP...?"

"Edie will be her direct report. Yes. Milla Kristol has a tremendous resume. Kippy and Scott tried to bring her on in August, but she was on an acquisition team at her last company. She had to stay through the end of the year or forfeit the completion bonus. Don't let her enthusiasm blind-side you. She's a very heavy hitter. We're lucky to have her onboard."

Judy regarded him thoughtfully. He was spouting the party line. The only unusual thing is that he was doing it without even a brush of sarcasm. Mike wasn't being paranoid. Peterson's handling of Centient wasn't playing out the way he'd planned; he was getting nervous.

Wesley's head was still facing Judy's, but his eyes were focused on an invisible spot beyond her shoulder. "I'm sure she's going to have a lot of interesting ideas. She's used to getting results and we're going to deliver and support her. This will be a good opportunity for IT to shine."

Δ

From: Scott Bell
To: All Pinnacle Associates
Subject: New Days for Operations

We are excited to welcome Milla Kristol as Pinnacle's new
Vice President of Fulfillment Services. Milla brings an

impressive range of experience in establishing Operational
Excellence at other service providing companies. She will be
a tremendous asset to our organization as we continue to
increase in both size and maturity.

Edie Brewer will be reporting directly to Milla.

Scott Bell, President
Pinnacle Management Services

Δ

"We think we know about hard work. Ha! Well let me tell you something. My grandmother was 36. A widow, with four kids. In the Depression. Lived way up in the Bronx. You know about the Depression, right?"

Kippy craned his neck so that he was staring directly into the camera. Ever since Clif started taping the Monthlies, there had been these kinds of asides. We wondered whether he thought he was addressing future legions of Pinnacle employees, or maybe only preserving these pearls for his own kids.

"My grandmother, she got a job cleaning bathrooms at the Plaza Hotel. And let me tell you, she knew she was lucky to have it! The Depression wasn't like these hiccups we get now. Oh, no. Whole country was at a standstill. Back then it took a nickel—a nickel! Ha! Can you believe that?— to ride the subways. I told you she lived in the Bronx? Well, she made friends with the garbage men on her route. Every morning, she left at 4:30 a.m. to catch a ride with them down to 102nd street. Then she'd walk from there, walk three miles to the hotel, just to save that nickel. And all the kids found jobs too. Whatever they could get. My aunt Betty sold candy at a movie theatre, used to sneak all the other kids in the side door. Probably worth more than whatever they paid her! Ha! Eight years old, my dad started helping this blind newsstand guy sort out his paper deliveries. This was when you used to have morning and afternoon editions of the papers. Imagine this little kid going to work every day, before and after school! This is the work ethic that built this company! That made me who I am. Now when I first started working for my Dad, he sent me out to sell. What an experience! Just a great way to learn about business. I have incredible respect for people who sell. Let me tell you, it's hard work! I went out there...I was going to be the best salesman that ever was! You're laughing at me, aren't you Roger!"

"Laughing with you Kippy!"

Because Roger Didilian had a long, slack-jawed face and liked to joke around, a lot of people got the initial impression that he wasn't too sharp. If they were lucky, they learned their mistake the easy way.

"Ha! Because you know I'm right! Because that's how you gotta approach everything. If you're teaching, be the best teacher; if you're collecting garbage, be the best garbage man. One of my first big sales, I'll never forget, was a chain of stores. They sold all kinds of things for the house. Kind of like a Pier One kind of place. Dishes, candles...I remember lots of pillows. And those bead curtains people used to hang in the doorways. Hey, it was the 70's. Ha! Well, it was really already the eighties, but all that stuff was still around. Anyway, they had six places, one in Brooklyn Heights, one somewhere in Queens, and the rest here in the city. A family-owned business. They liked doing business with other family-owned businesses and the wife, who handled everything on the office side, she was a shrewd old lady. Ha! Listen to me. She was probably wasn't any older than I am now! Take that as a warning all of you! Well, I was selling our services like they were gonna...I don't know; cure cancer or something. I'd talked my Dad into branching out, so a lot was on the line. I could see the old lady liked how hard I was trying. She put a hand on my shoulder, like this."

No one was standing next to him on the windowsill, so Kippy cupped his hand gravely over a block of air.

"Then she says to me, 'You seem like a responsible young man.' Well I did, because that was something my Dad pounded into me and my brother Brian from the time we were kids. 'If I sign your contract, I want you to do something for me.' So I said 'what?' Because I wanted to make that sale, right? And she said 'I volunteer for Muscular Dystrophy. I want you to donate $50 dollars to them. Not your company's money. Your own money. Out of whatever commission you're going to make on this sale.'" He paused to let the gravity of the request sink in.

Somewhere in the room, someone stifled a sneeze.

Kippy tapped thoughtfully against his temple and continued. "Understand that in those days, $50 was a lot of money. Not just to me, let me tell you. For 50 bucks I could take Marcy to a Broadway show plus still have money left over for soup and a sandwich at Carnegie Deli. But I really wanted that sale. The old lady could see me thinking about it. She pointed her finger at me and said 'I'm doing this for your own good. I don't want you ever to forget how important it is to give. Even now, when you're just starting out in life, there are so many out there who are so much less fortunate that you are. I want you to get in the habit of giving back, it doesn't matter whether it's one dollar or fifty.' Ha! So how come she wasn't asking me for a buck?!"

He grinned expectantly. We laughed on cue.

"Right?! But you know, she was right. Don't wait until you're rich and successful. You have to reach into your pocket when it hurts and give something. Even if it's only a dollar or two. You'll see. It makes you feel good about yourself, that you have the power to help somebody else. So I decided, we're going to do this together, as a company. Every month, we're going to pick a charity and whatever you all put in, the company will match you dollar for dollar. Just think! We've got what, a hundred and twenty…"

"One hundred seventeen," Chris piped up.

"One hundred and seventeen amazing people here. If everyone gave just $5, that's more than $500. And double that for matching! We do this together, we could give $1000 to a different charity every month! How amazing would that be?"

Δ

Gabe del Monte was a serious kind of guy. Once they'd decided they were dating after all, it didn't take long for him to want to make things permanent. He told his parents right away he was planning it. Where he got stuck was on the ring. After what had happened before, he felt superstitious about using his Grandmother's.

Josh came to town, ferrying some of his students around the museums. He stuck around for a couple of extra nights, sacking out on the floor of the apartment like old times. His was the moral support Gabe needed to get the nerve to check out the price of diamonds. They were ridiculous. Even chips discounted on 47th Street turned out to be too rich for Pinnacle salaries. Gabe felt that the toe of his sneaker was stuck in a crack on the sidewalk to romance.

"Maybe your Grandmother was trying to stop you from the last one," Josh said, sharing out the last of the bottle of Patrón. "Maybe she's looking down at Martha and saying, 'now this is a nice girl who'll make my Gabriel happy'."

"You think so? I mean you really like her, right?"

"I think she's great," Josh said. He pulled Gabe close and knuckled him on the forehead. "I ever find a Martha, maybe I'll consider settling down."

This was pretty unlikely. Josh liked to say that the best part of painting was the way it attracted women, both the leggy model types who were willing to cook him meals and do his laundry, and the bored older women who had more lucrative ways of supporting a struggling artist. The thought sometimes crossed Gabe's mind that his best friend took his art too lightly.

Δ

Gary Feldman had begrudgingly booked the cheapest place he could find for the Talent Show, a dank movie theater that was partially closed for renovation. Ventura and the Buzzard figured out the primitive lighting board, Clif Speck hooked up a projector and strung up a few mikes, and we were good to go.

146

To remind us it was a business event, Scott kicked things off with a pocket history of the company, ending with a slideshow of inspirational cartoons illustrating the year's corporate goals. Or, as Freddie Vega whispered under cover of the obligatory applause, "corporate gooooooaaaaals!"

After that, it was nothing but pleasure. Our chef, Diego Guzman, had led a baking marathon over the weekend, so we settled in with sacks of cookies to enjoy. We finally found out what Chris Keane's element was, because she was introducing each act and filling the time in between with genuinely funny patter. With all our dreamers and wannabees, it wasn't surprising that we packed a deep bench of talent.

Despite the proud assertions of the radiant Martha Moon, only Mia had known how good Gabe del Monte's work was. Now we watched in awe as a slideshow of his paintings ebbed and flowed to Kaimi Poole's hauntingly beautiful original score, played on electric cello. We finally heard Ina play, too. It had taken all the Buzzard's charm to coax her onto what was, we now clearly saw, her natural habitat. It was the work of a Russian composer most of us had never heard of, dark and jagged, and you could have heard a pin drop in the hall until Kippy led a standing ovation.

Every team had someone representing except, of course, Sales, who were too protective of their dignity. Under the polished direction of Alex Silva, Liz Dorn and Fabian Mello presented an affecting scene from one of Judy Schreiber's plays. Hank Iversson turned out to be a pretty good magician. Molly Pacquin showed pictures of her award-winning ceramic work. Craig Parnes and Fritz Kennedy gleefully whipped out "Dueling Banjos."

The biggest surprise of the evening was Donna DiPinto's belty, bluesy contralto. A tall woman who dressed like everyone's cliché of a librarian, the office manager was fabulous and downright hot tonight in a slinky white beaded gown. Inconspicuously accompanied by the versatile Buzzard, Donna let those pipes rip and no one wanted her to stop. She turned that rented multiplex screening room into a jazz club; you could almost smell the cigarette and candle smoke.

It was an act no one wanted to follow. Still, Tully Mulhern jumped up on the stage from the front row, a feat that garnered a splatter of surprised hoots and laughter. "Ladies, Gentlemen and Sales," he said, grabbing the mike. "Get ready for some music that's going to change the world! I'm Turlough Tully Mulhern..."

Lily Sheehan appeared behind him, carrying two guitars. She handed one to Tully, exchanging it for the mike. "And I'm E. Lily Sheehan Esquire. " She winked at us and nodded at Tully, who put his head next to hers.

"And together," they roared, to a growing rumble of knowing cheers; "we are Stail Fiáin!!!!" Tully struck a clashing chord and two figures moved out of the shadows; despite Walt Sacco's compliance reservations, Scott had signed off on allowing them to invite their keyboard and drummer to the event.

"That's Gaelic for Wyld Stallyns!" Dawn called from her seat. It was unnecessary. None of us spoke Irish Gaelic, but we all knew our Bill and Ted. We shouted happily and kept it up throughout the five-song set that ended the first and only Pinnacle Talent Show, the only other booster activity Kay was ever able to push through the LC.

Δ

```
From:         Wesley Peterson
To:           IT
Subject:      Departmental Change
------------------------------------
With the transfer of Mike Ventura to Operations, effective
immediately, Ginny Chicosky will cover managerial functions
of the PMO. Please address all communications to Ginny.

WJP
```

Δ

The PMO met up at the Thai place across the street. There was no need to go any further. It wasn't as if either Peterson or the new VP were going to turn up, and no one else mattered.

Mike had already ordered a few plates of dumplings, which arrived together with the rest of the team.

"What the fuck?!" Ginny said, sliding into the seat opposite.

Simran looked at her, astonished. "You didn't know either?"

Judy fell into her chair. "I know what you said, Mike, but tell me you didn't see this coming."

Mike's expression was difficult to describe: a bit of a grin, a bit of sorrow, a lot of what looked like resignation...The Germans probably have a word for it. "You see what Peterson's been doing. He thought he could get Centient to go kamikaze without us getting caught in the shitstorm, but it's not possible. As far as the LC goes, IT owns this thing. Doesn't matter if we're not in control. I did what I could to protect our guys, but Kippy started asking direct questions. It was Avie Gold all over again." He addressed this last thought to Judy, the only one who'd been there to see it.

She nodded her understanding. "Then why isn't Peterson going? Or is he?"

"Oh, he's staying just where he is." The waiter set a beer in front of Mike. He took a generous swallow. "He made it all about me. That I misinterpreted things. That I was maybe in over my head and was trying to deflect responsibility. Threw me right under the bus. Only Peterson forgot why he chose me for his messenger to begin with. I was MVP my first year, you know. A golden boy. Not for long, but there's this residual thing. Kippy still thinks he likes me. So I get another chance to prove myself, assisting this new woman with Fulfillment."

"That's not a bad thing." Ginny tended to be optimistic, or perhaps she was contemplating her own apparent rise up the ladder. "She sounds pretty strong. There could be some good opportunity there."

"Wasn't Edie also an MVP?" Simran remembered having heard this, perhaps in Boot Camp.

Mike laughed. "Is the BA looking for patterns?"

The face beneath the turban wore no corresponding smile. "I don't have to look very far." Recruited at the peak of Peterson's empire-building, Simran Bhalla had chosen Pinnacle over an offer from an attractive internet marketing startup. Because his wife worked for the DOT, their health insurance was covered and he had the luxury, unusual for a father of four, of choosing the startup. Then Peterson counter-offered with promises of professional development and quick advancement, not to mention bonuses in keeping with Pinnacle's staggering growth. It turned out that the enticing bonus formula never met the minimum net profits necessary to pay out. There was certainly no point in waiting for a payoff now. Soft market or not, it was time to start looking elsewhere.

"Simran's got a good point. They brought this woman in over Edie, and now they're transferring you. How can that not mean something?"

"And the playwright kicks in her two cents. It doesn't mean anything, except that I'm grateful not to have to plan a wedding from Unemployment. Let's order, people."

"Seriously, Mike. Kippy's got a short attention span. It sounds like he's just surfed from IT to Fulfillment."

Δ

From *The Peak Experience*

Getting to Know VP of Fulfillment Milla Kristol

Pinnacle's new Vice President of Fulfillment, Milla Kristol, has truly lived the American dream. Having emigrated as a child from the still powerful Soviet Union, Milla was raised to appreciate the freedoms that permit focus and hard work to bring high achievement. She graduated Summa Cum Laude from Oberlin College, where she earned a Bachelor's degree in Economics and was elected to the Phi Beta Kappa honors society. Milla also holds an MBA in Management.

Milla has accrued an impressive track-record of establishing Operational Excellence at service-providing companies. During her tenure at Randall Stephens, she was instrumental in a process improvement initiative that cut turn-around-time by 40 percent, while proportionally reducing cost...

Δ

```
From:       Kay Kuperman
To:         All Pinnacle Associates
Subject:    Leadership Development
-----------------------------------
```

Hello Pinnacle Associates!

President's Day is nearly upon us and in honor of this day that honors the leadership of our great nation, we're proud to announce a new Pinnacle Leadership Development Program called Phi Beta Kippy.

These 1-hour seminars, which will occur 1x a month for a total of 10 sessions, will be personally facilitated by Kippy Melcher. Each month, he will address a different topic on leadership and business and share the many powerful lessons he has learned in his years of experience. The seminars will function as a roadmap helping you to develop hands-on business acumen and leadership skills.

The first session will begin Thursday, March 1st at 2 p.m. The schedule for each month will be determined based on Kippy's travel schedule.

To ensure the greatest benefit to all participants, there will be only 12 spots in PBK this year. They are open to all Pinnacle associates, but a high volume of response is anticipated. If you are interested in being considered, write a brief (600 words or less) description of why you want one of those spots to be yours! You must email this to your manager, ccing me, by end of business Friday.

As you consider whether or not you would like to apply for this series, keep in mind the following:
- Attendance at each session will be mandatory, except where there is a valid medical excuse. If you miss one session, you will be asked to leave the series.

- Lateness will not be acceptable. All sessions will begin precisely at the time announced.

- At times there will be outside reading or learning assignments, all of which will be mandatory.

We will notify those selected by end of the day Monday, February 26th, so that you may plan your week accordingly.

This is just the first of what is planned as an annual Leadership series, so there will be an opportunity for a new group of employees to attend the program each year.

Thank you for your interest in Phi Beta Kippy and good luck!

Kay Kuperman, Dir. Talent Management
Pinnacle Management Services

Δ

"I want you tell me, where do you think you'll be—no, where do you WANT to be in five years' time?" Kippy ran his eyes around Persistence, drilling into each face in turn. "No rush. I'll give you a minute to think. Ha!" He flipped his wrist and punched a button on his chronograph. He sat with one thigh on the desk, foot dangling, the other leg reaching for the floor, watching the seconds tick by. Gretchen, manning the video camera, thought to pan the group but decided not to. All those worried faces. She didn't want to get anyone into trouble for their private thoughts.

"Okay." The timer's snap was an exclamation point. "Time. Who's first?" He stuck out a finger. "Ann."

Ann Ling fluttered a hand past her brow, as if the smooth oval of her face had ever been disturbed by a stray hair. "Um," she whispered, "I'd like to be teaching. Special Ed. That's what I'm getting my Master's in. At Columbia. When I have it, then…well, I hope I can get a job." Too late, she realized she'd just told her CEO she didn't plan on staying with his company forever. She swallowed hard. "Um, I'm sorry."

"No, no, don't be sorry!" Kippy enthused. "That's an admirable plan. We need dedicated individuals who want to help all our kids, but especially those special needs kids. Good for you! A round of applause for Ann!"

The enthusiastic applause made Ann blush and emboldened everyone else to speak the truth.

Noble Landrum smiled with his whole face. "I probably have one more Deploy coming up before five years, and I sincerely hope to have finished my CPA by then."

151

"And we all thank you for your service to our country," Kippy put in. "Which I...which Pinnacle has been proud to support."

"I appreciate that. My dream is to combine my military experience, which you know is where my heart is, with my accounting skills and work in Washington. Next time I get back, I should have my twenty years by then. And my new son or daughter," his grin nearly touched his ears, "should be ready to start kindergarten."

This burst of applause was entirely spontaneous; everyone loved Noble. Kippy dismounted from the desk to shake his hand.

"Congratulations!" he enthused. "Being a father, it's the greatest thing, the most amazing thing that will ever happen in your life. No matter how successful I am, the only success that means anything is to be a good son, a good husband and a good father. Because if you can do all that, you're a good man. And if you're a good man, you're a good boss. Gene, let's hear from you."

"Five years from now?" Gene Siriano smiled impishly. "Oh, I'll still be sitting right here, doing what I do. While continuing to learn from you how to make some very sound investments. So that in ten years time I can retire early to my house in Mexico."

"You have a house in Mexico?" Kippy was surprised.

"Bought it two years ago before the area really caught on. Costs me practically nothing, and I rent it out for most of the year so it pays for its own upkeep."

"That sounds great!" There was no mistaking the naked longing in Diego Guzman's voice.

"Is that where you want to be, uh...Diego, right?"

Diego nodded. "On a beach with a pina colada? Oh yeah!" Everyone tittered nervously. He threw his hands up in mock surrender. "Hey, my uncle owns a restaurant in the DR, right on the beach. I always wanted to work for him, since I was a kid. But my mami, she said 'nuh-uh, Diego, you going to college'. And then once I finished, it's 'you gonna waste all that education grilling up some fish?'" Someone laughed. He nodded. "I get it. But that's really what I want to be doing. I love to cook. And I love the beach."

"So you want to own a restaurant," Kippy nodded rapidly, pointing a finger up and down in time with the rhythm, showing he was working on understanding a knotty problem.

"Not really. One thing I learned at Cornell is what kind of headache that is. I mean, who wants that? And the kind of investors you need to have...not to mention what you gotta do to get them. What I want is just to cook. Thing is, unless you have your own place, you never know where you are. Which is why my uncle's little place would be, like, perfect. I go down there and work with him, and someday when he feels like quitting, the place is mine." Diego's face shone with satisfaction. "I got it all figured out. All I need is to finish paying off my college loan and I'm home free."

Here was something Kippy could latch on to. "Very important point, Diego. A lot of young people are tied down by those massive college loans. And for what? If you have that entrepreneurial spirit, you don't need college at all. Look at Bill Gates..."

"He went to Harvard," Ginny Chicosky reminded.

"He dropped out!" Kippy jumped with excitement. "And look what he accomplished! Ha! Built one of the greatest business empires in the world. He did so well without college that they're giving him a degree this year. It was in *The Financial Times* this morning. Let that be a lesson to all of you. Okay, not every one of you is going to be a Bill Gates and you probably do need to have a degree to get started in the business world, but does it really matter where you earn it? I think a lot of money is wasted on going to these fancy colleges, when a community college is just fine."

Ann started twisting her Columbia University lanyard into knots.

Ginny decided not to ask about Kippy's kids at Brandeis and Chapman. Rather than mentioning the gaming company she and her friend Mona were trying to jump start, she declared that she hoped to be heading a PMO, expediting development for a cutting edge company.

Eric Channing leaned back in his chair, so that he could keep his head straight while tilting his eyes upward towards the future and Kippy. His pin-striped suits and power ties were a little less ridiculous since his transfer to Finance, but they still looked a bit much next to Gene's famous sweaters. "Over the next five years," he mused aloud, "I plan to avail myself of the splendid opportunities at Pinnacle, like this leadership course you're so generously offering us, while earning my MBA at the Zicklin School of Business at Baruch College, an excellent program that I'm enjoying tremendously. Meanwhile, I will continue to work hard and do everything I can to help this company grow and move forward. I plan to gradually earn my way up the ranks to management level, and in five years' time," he concluded with a satisfied smirk, "my goal is to be a VP at Pinnacle." He shifted his weight and his chair jerked him upright.

"That's the stuff!" It came out almost as a shout. While Kippy shook Channing's hand, a circuit of exasperated eyebrows and smirks passed through the room.

"I don't know about five years." Hank Iversson couldn't help himself. "But in 15, I'll probably be President of Iversson Brothers. Once Uncle Ray retires and my Dad gets booted up to Chairman."

Kippy's focus swerved to fix on Hank, who smiled complacently. "Iversson Brothers? Isn't that a client?"

"Yes, sir. Our family business. I'll be fifth generation when I sign on."
Usually Hank said 'when they chain me down.' He was in no hurry to settle
down to manufacturing upscale period reproduction hardware fittings in
Minnesota. He'd fought long and hard to be allowed to come to New York
and sow some wild oats. Client Care wasn't particularly wild, but at least he
was in New York; and at least he'd managed to transfer out of Fulfillment. "I
brought the referral in to Sales this summer. Payroll, Procurement and
Compliance. We're billing close to 4K per month." Hank still hadn't received
the promised Referral bounty.

"Excellent!" Kippy didn't note the unsubtle hint. Glenn Levine did. It was
his name on the contract. Kippy spotted him thinking and turned the laser on
him. "Glenn! You're an ambitious guy. What are your plans?"

Glenn turned a little red in the face before managing to mumble "I want
to do what you've done. Build a business."

"And you know, if anyone can do it, it's this guy," Kippy said. "One of
our top salesmen, week in, week out. Doesn't take no for an answer."

Glenn looked down, uncharacteristically embarrassed. He'd raised the
subject of Iversson Brothers with Scott last quarter. He'd have to pin him
down again and get it resolved.

Earnest Chris Keane pitched in with something convoluted about how
important she felt the role of an HR generalist was to the morale of a growing
company. It sounded as if her five year goal were to do exactly what she was
doing, but with maybe an assistant.

Keith Ansell said something innocuous. Ansell was a team lead in Payroll.
George Waters had hired him to take Noble's old slot, and was grooming
him to be his right-hand man. Ansell had been Waters' nominee for PBK, but
Kippy asked George himself to be part of this class. It was a major
compliment that Kippy added an extra slot to accommodate them both.

While the rest of them babbled on, Waters sat confidently at the back of
the room, waiting for Kippy's attention to light on him. In his opinion, the
only ones who weren't making asses of themselves were Levine and
Channing, and Channing was too full of himself for George's taste. Donny
Rohmer and Archie Ghosh spoke up next. He supposed that, as MSY Team
Lead, Ghosh had to be included, though he didn't personally see the point of
her. All small talk and walking on eggshells. He hadn't yet seen her do a
single thing that a straightforward kind of guy couldn't have done a whole lot
more efficiently. Little Martha Moon said something sweet about feeling that
Pinnacle was her second family, and how she was happy to be part of it.
Weak, but probably true. George had no gripes with Martha, who seemed to
be competent enough. Kippy had a soft spot for her, like he did for Noble
and Marla. It didn't matter to George if Kippy favored the real old timers;

none of them were in his department. What was important was Kippy's opinion of George Waters, MVP and rising star of Fulfillment.

"George," Kippy said. "We haven't heard from you. I've been watching you grow since you joined the company. Impressive, impressive work. Where do you see yourself headed?"

"Like you say, Kippy. I've been growing here, and I want to continue growing, along with the company. Pinnacle has a bright future and I plan on being part of it."

"I have no doubt that you will. You keep up like you have been and sky's the limit. Except my job! Ha! So, you're all probably wondering why I asked you this, why I wanted to hear where you saw yourselves in five years...Gretchen! I didn't ask you! What about you?"

Gretchen startled. She had to quickly pull the camera back into focus, using her other hand to try and wave him on. "I'm only here to help out."

"So help me out by telling me. Five years from now. Where do you want to be?"

"I never thought about it," she admitted. "I guess I kind of play things by ear."

"Honest. Ha! I like that. But you know, if you want to move ahead in the world, you have to find your passion. That's why I started today with this question. For me, Pinnacle is my passion. Now back in my college days, I was an English major. I know, you're thinking that's a strange choice for a business guy; but back then I hadn't found my passion yet, my focus. And I was always a voracious reader. I never need to apologize for that. Best gift you can give yourself, a love of reading. And with libraries it doesn't even have to cost a dime. Ha! Today, I gotta say I mostly read for business, to keep learning. Because you never stop learning. You get to be my age, you'll understand that. All sorts of books. Anyone read *Moneyball?*"

Hands shot up into the air. Glenn's of course, Noble's, Hank's. Ginny's, to the surprise of some. Eric Channing nodded rapidly and tried to look knowing.

"Great book. Terrific. You really get inside his head," he tapped his head intently. "I'm gonna put together a reading list for you, so the rest of you will be reading it soon. Also *Lessons for Corporate America*. Warren Buffett is a genius. But I'm starting you with the single most inspirational book about business that I ever read. And I read it for an English class. Ha! Gretchen, where'd you put it?"

Gretchen handed him a Barnes and Noble bag. He dug in and started passing out books, like the Santa at a children's hospital.

"My absolute FA-vorite book of ALL TIME! It's all about what would happen if the leaders, the people who make everything in this country keep moving, just stopped. Packed it in, went on strike. How the country, how the entire world would just grind to a halt. Because that's it. It's just this small percentage of people in the world who get things done. The best and the brightest. The innovators. The ones who do the work."

Gretchen looked at the copy Kippy handed back to her. She'd read it in college, too. *Atlas Shrugged*. That wasn't exactly how she'd remembered it.

Δ

The door to what had once been Nick Andreas' office was closed. Since Nick's time, it had briefly been used by Wesley Peterson. After IT moved downstairs, it was a spare room, often grabbed by the office-less for a quick meeting. Now someone had stuck a tack into the hollow-core door and dangled a sign from a bit of string: "In Conference." Edie, arriving on time for her 4:30 introductory meeting with her new boss, was irresistibly reminded of Lucy's booth in Peanuts: "the Doctor is In."

She knocked politely. Perhaps someone had forgotten to flip the sign after the last meeting; perhaps it had been set prematurely for her own.

"Busy!" The voice on the other side of the door sounded exasperated, which was hardly a fair response to a first and timely knock.

Edie instructed herself not to be annoyed. It was important that she remain open-minded. Yes she'd been surprised...okay, make that shocked, at being told, just hours before the email went out, that the LC was inserting a layer of management between herself and the COO. Alan's expression had been as apologetic as his words. Even he didn't seem to know what this new VP of Fulfillment was meant to accomplish, other than receiving Edie's reports and parroting them back to him. "But she has a tremendous resume," he assured her. "I'm sure she'll be bringing a lot of value to the role."

His shoulders sagged so pathetically that she felt compelled to try and cheer him up. "I look forward to learning from her." Trying not to make it obvious, she ran to her desk and called an emergency Department meeting. She didn't want her kids to hear this from anyone but her, and she had to put as good a face on it as possible. George Waters, she noticed, was the only one who didn't seem surprised. Edie stood for a full five minutes by the closed door before deciding it was ridiculous. Whatever the current meeting was, it was running over. She could just as easily wait in her cube. At least then she could get some work done. Milla would buzz her when she was ready.

Almost five more minutes passed before the phone rang.

"I was under the impression that we had a meeting." There had been no 'Hello,' no preamble at all.

"I knocked. Your meeting was running long..."

"You should have waited."

"I did!" Edie was surprised into sounding flustered. "After a while, I thought it made more sense..."

"Now we're wasting time. Please join me now. And in future, I'd appreciate if you'd be patient enough to wait a minute or two before disappearing."

Edie wasn't used to being hung up on. She stared at the receiver before putting it down so violently that Archie Ghosh's desk, in the adjacent cube, shook.

Archie poked her head around the partition in time to see her manager heading away, in the direction of the private offices. There was an angry thrust to Edie's always swift stride. Sitting in her chair, Archie felt that momentary dip that happens when you stop yourself from falling. Something had happened. She wished she knew what it was. She picked up her cell phone and sent a group text. "needacig." it said; "whoever. NOW."

.

WEDNESDAY

9 PROFESSIONAL DEVELOPMENT

Wednesday. Humpday. Get past this day and you're halfway through the week. Mom got sad when you said that. "Why are you wishing your life away?" she asked. You kind of shrugged. You aren't really. Except for the work part, life is too good to want to wish away a minute of it. Sitting under a tree and smelling the flowers, reading a good book, planning a someday trip with your boyfriend to…oh, Paris, maybe…though on your budget it'll be more likely be a long weekend in Cleveland, at the Rock and Roll Hall of Fame…Good stuff. Even the job wouldn't be so bad, if only Spurious George didn't have to pump himself up by making other people feel like miserable ants. Someday Tully wasn't going to be able to control himself; he'd punch the guy out, and then you'd both be out of work. And you don't want that. You like earning a living, feeling like you finally started your adult life. Even a boring job feels good. Though you can't stop wondering what it would be like to have the kind of job they always told you about, all your teachers, the media. They promised you were going to use your brain, that what you did for eight hours a day would matter. "So go somewhere else," Mom says, as if half your friends from college weren't still looking for any kind of paycheck at all. You're lucky. You know that. Especially at EOD Wednesday, with only two more days to go. Anyway, work is work, right? No matter what they say?

Work is work. It's nothing. Wealth, now that's where you want to go. The trick is figuring out how to game it where you are right now. People here are too pathetic to catch on. Anyone with half a brain could see right off the bat that most of the jobs here are for crap. Waiting for a career to tap you on the shoulder? You could be sitting around forever. If you're savvy, you map your own trajectory, only do what moves you forward. Now Waters, he gets it. Focus on the one C-level exec no one's kissing up to and figure out how to get in his pocket. Note to self: watch Waters. Make the right noises, dress for success. Get what you can out of the experience, and move on. It's all bullshit. A means to an end. Wednesday, Sunday; it's all the same.

Why does it have to be Wednesday already? The guys have been working round the clock and it's nowhere near ready to go. This project sucks. You've massaged the timeline a million ways and you're still not seeing a happy end. Maybe if you had two more bodies to throw at it…no, even if Peterson pulled a budget out of his ass, it's too late now. It can't be done. It has to be done. The lease on the colocation site runs out Tuesday midnight and you have to be cleared out by noon, down to the last bolt and Velcro strip.

When you think how much you used to pack into the front end of a week! Running from meeting to meeting; herding cats and pulling heads out of clouds; moving the work along. You don't know whether to laugh or cry. Here it is Wednesday, and you haven't done a worthwhile thing all week. At least with a contract job, you walk in the door with a clue about why you're there. Now you're twiddling your thumbs while your new boss figures out how she wants to use you. If she wants to use you. You can feel your desk moving another cube closer to the door every day.

Just keep your head down and keep on being charming. That's always worked for you before. No point wasting charm on Peterson; he's high on his big dreams. Dreams are nice, but what if they don't pan out? You grew up around too many risk takers not to know: nobody gambles to lose, but the odds are sure against winning. Peterson wants to dig his own grave, that's his business. He's not going to drag you down with him, like poor Ventura. You've got more than one string to your bow. So you do your own work, and you don't push back. And meanwhile you pay the nanny to stay an extra hour while you catch a beer at Humpday Happy Hour with Roger and them.

You were too busy to notice. Now, for all you go around pretending that everything is great just great, it's too late. Phil disagrees, but you can feel it in the air. It turns out getting things done doesn't count; it's the show you put on. You wish you could change your spots, but it's too ingrained. You can't do anything except your best. Bringing order out of chaos. Working at 150 percent at minimum. Caring so much that you sometimes wake up in the night knowing you've been dreaming about the office. You used to be able to take some satisfaction from getting results. And respect; at least you used to have respect. It's like waking up on Wednesday morning and suddenly the shape of the week has changed. Except not all change is good.

#humpday

Δ

As usual, Edie arrived exactly on time to find Milla Kristol's door closed and the card on it flipped to "in conference." Milla's meetings consistently ran over. Waiting made Edie feel like a naughty child outside the Principal's office, a dynamic she'd come to believe was deliberate; the VP of Fulfillment was putting the Senior Manager in her place. The undeclared challenge was transparent, but push-back was counter-productive. If Edie weren't standing there when the door opened, everything she said during the meeting would be declared indisputably wrong. The fourth of six children, Edie's earliest lesson had been to pick her battles. This one wasn't prudent to fight.

She'd quickly formed the habit of picking up something to work on while she waited as long as necessary. It was just one of the ways that she tried to adapt to the new regime. She was relentlessly friendly and cooperative with the new VP, even in the face of cryptic directions with unfathomable goals. For a solid week, she devoted every night plus large chunks of both weekends to revamping her reports to mimic the less-functional "information radiators" Milla was used to receiving at her last job. Milla declared the new reports "too cluttered," covering each page with bold red slashes. Never one to make rash judgments, Edie was tempted to say that Milla Kristol was somewhat inflexible. Everything seemed designed to make it progressively more difficult for Edie to manage her department. She longed for the days when she'd answered only to Alan Reisch.

Waiting, Edie perched on the edge of Ventura's nearby desk. They didn't exchange more than a rueful smile. Since he'd moved back up to eight, they'd made it a point to appear only remotely collegial with one another. They had a sense that if they appeared too chatty, their mutual boss would take it amiss.

Though her eyes were on her printouts, Edie's body remained on alert for the door's opening. The wait wasn't long today. She'd only begun to resolve the Compliance team's routing issues when her ears picked up the click of the knob disengaging the latch. She sprang up, clutching her leather folio to her chest.

George Waters opened the door. Instead of exiting past her, he remained inside, his hand on the knob, gesturing for her to come in. He was practically licking the cream off his whiskers.

Edie deliberately cleared her throat, so that Mike would look up. She knew he could see past her to the figure in the doorway; it was another benefit of being narrow. Edie plastered a smile across her face and strode in.

George shut the door behind her and took a seat, joining her meeting. Avoiding Edie's eyes, he turned his full focus across the desk where Kristol flashed her expensively whitened teeth. As usual, her smile stopped without reaching her eyes.

"Excellent. Now that I have you both...As I've been explaining to George, Edie, I've monitored Fulfillment since I arrived and it's obvious that the work would be better covered if we redistributed the load. Yes? George has done a fantastic job with Payroll. Well, MVP and all that. Gary Feldman is a very big fan!" She crinkled her nose at this delightful news. Setting her peach silk dupioni elbows on her desk, she put her hands together prayerfully. She leaned forward, caught her chin on her fingertips and cocked her head in Edie's direction. "I can see George has the bandwidth to take on more responsibility, and he's certainly proven that he has the aptitude. It would be a waste of resources not to take advantage of his talent. I'm recommissioning Fulfillment as two separate departments. In addition to what he has now,

George will take Compliance. It's so tightly integrated with Payroll Services, I don't understand why it wasn't given to him in the first place. Which leaves Switchboard, Procurement and Training for Edie. Much more balanced. Much more efficient." Her hands made a jazzy little flourish to underscore the announcement, and she sat back in her chair. Above another empty grin, her eyes narrowed.

Edie nodded slowly; it was all she could do; it was a done deal. Less than two years since she'd started training him in the basics of maintaining her department, the department was no longer hers. Milla wasn't even making them equals. She was assigning the higher net portfolio, and therefore the balance of power, to George. Nothing had slowed his climb: not the controls that had gone by the wayside; not the meaningless quotas he'd imposed; not the way he continued to confuse bullying with management, a tactic Edie found as unproductive as it was offensive. Despite her intercessions, errors were on the rise, as was staff turnover. Somehow, George had convinced the LC that it all added up to increased productivity. Had they forgotten the Data Entry walkout disaster? Apparently. He was keeping that team in the re-org. All of Edie's experience, her skill, her gift for managing people, meant nothing. She turned her head enough to see the face of her former assistant. George had to know he wasn't qualified for this, that he hadn't earned it. He wasn't stupid. Wasn't he even the tiniest bit embarrassed?

Δ

What a mess. Ginny splashed her eyes with the coldest water she could bear, trying to get the grit out. Three hours of sleep was almost worse than none at all, but with another 12 to 14 hours to go she'd had to grab what zzzs she could. She'd have saved herself the Brooklyn commute by sleeping on the office floor, except for the mice. She didn't mind mice as such, but to wake up because of those little feet scampering across your face....brrr! Too bad Peterson hadn't managed to deliver on his plan for a team lounge, but even when things were good Pinnacle considered it a waste of money if it didn't directly deliver a sale. Of course, to order to keep all those delivered clients happyhappyhappy, technology deployments had to be done in the wee hours, something a couple of sofas might help. But you couldn't expect the LC to see that. Kippy once told Clif Speck, "you work when there's work to be done. That's why I pay you those ridiculous salaries." They were ridiculous, alright; just not the way Kippy thought. Ken Aoki'd run some figures before he walked: for the most part, Pinnacle was paying IT about 20 percent below market average. Ginny sometimes felt guilty that she'd gotten almost her asking price. It was sheer luck that, after losing three consecutive candidates to better offers, Mike was able to shame Peterson into raising the budget for her.

She pulled a sweatshirt over her damp face and went to kiss her family. Tim slept like an octopus, sprawled all over the place. She tried to nudge his leg back up on the bed without waking him. Poor guy needed all the sleep he could get. A solid weekend playing Daddy Daycare. He must be as much of a zombie as she was. Lucky it was one of his off weeks. She tiptoed into the twins' bedroom, leaving behind some goofy cookies on their pillows to prove Mom had been in tonight. Today that is; it was 3 a.m. 3 a.m. and she was heading straight back to where she'd been at 10 the night before.

She hoped the migration was going better now. Everything so far was completely FUBAR. Like the whole thing with the security guy being a temp and insisting Clif's security pass was invalid. Sure, it would be invalid—come Wednesday when the lease would run out; that's why they were migrating the data center to another site this weekend. Asshole! Meanwhile, bam! An hour killed getting it all ironed out. And that was just the tip of the iceberg.

Her Crackberry hadn't gone off again since Freddie's reminder to pick up breakfast. That was hopeful. If everything was back on track, there's be some reports from Pune to start checking when she got in. Not that good numbers guaranteed smooth sailing. The Aprotek QA people were skilled enough, but their use cases missed things that a tester with business knowledge would have caught. This was the downside of farming work out. In a weird kind of way, it was probably just as well the budget only covered the contractors for a few hours. The rest of the testing, the meat of it, would be her migration team plus some business-side SMEs Edie had identified; all of them working most of Sunday to finish up on time. Edie's kids were lucky; the Giant Security Fuck Up had bought them a few extra hours of sleep. They wouldn't have to drag in until 7 a.m. and at least they'd get some overtime out of it. The upside of being a poorly-compensated hourly worker. Her team wouldn't get anything for giving up their weekend. Until she started at Pinnacle, she'd never heard of a place that didn't give comp time. It was time to polish up the resume and start looking for a new place.

Ginny felt a touch of nostalgia for the days before motherhood. Back then, if a show was too toxic she'd jump ship and wait to catch the next one. She couldn't do that now. They needed two steady incomes. Until she found something new, she had to hang on here one day at a time.

The next 36 hours would be a good start, if she came out okay on the other end. She wasn't expecting perfection, only to have things up and running in time for start of business Monday. If there were tiny glitches, they'd do a patch after. There was a limit to what the company could reasonably expect from a half-sized crew working with racks that were older than her boys and not much better behaved. The infrastructure here was a wreck. All they were doing was rearranging the deck chairs on the Titanic.

Ginny felt like she had a hangover, but with none of the fun. Damn, this was so much harder since she'd hit 40. She was pathetically glad she'd begged Judy to come in later. There would be someone fresh to take over the monitoring tasks for Adam's round. Judy was a blank slate when it came to engineering, but she was super organized. And she had a weird gift for whipping guys into shape. They humored her, like she was their favorite aunt. With Judy covering the checklist, Ginny would be able to keep what was left of her brain focused on the test results.

Stumbling up the subway stairs, Ginny started walking east. "Bagels, bagels, bagels," she chanted, keeping it in the front of her head until she could find an open bodega. Butter, cream cheese, jam. Juice, absolutely; get that blood sugar balanced. And better pick up a can of coffee. The office stash tended to run out somewhere around this time of month. It was a mystery why no one ever upped the standing order. No it wasn't; ordering another pound of coffee would shake Feldman's budget all to hell. Channing had probably created some algorithm to determine how much they were expected to consume. Problem was, despite the pinstriped suit, Channing thought like a student. He had no idea of how to apply his accounting classes to the real world. How would he know to factor in the amounts needed to sustain all-night coding sessions or overnight production deploys, not to mention the late nights Fulfillment and Client spent trying to catch up on their mountains of paperwork once the phones were down for the day? Too few people serving a growing load of clients meant more work per person. How come Channing couldn't make that calculation? Why couldn't Feldman or the LC? Of course they could, but for some weird reason they chose not to care. It made no sense to Ginny. Keeping your operating staff perpetually lagging behind sales was not how to keep your clients happy. The only ones who would be happy were the people looking at the bottom line. Pinnacle's bottom line must look golden. She would almost buy into that perpetual rumor that Kippy was planning to go public, except that this was hardly the economy for an IPO. Plus, who in their right mind thought a managed office services company could grow enough to be worth the investment? You had to give Kippy credit. He'd taken his dad's old answering service and turned it into something that could be competitive in the 21st century. He was no sweetheart; on the other hand, you probably had to be a bit of a shark to make that kind of money.

Lin-Fei met her at the door to help with the bags. "Freddie is with Mal and Clif at new data center."

When they had Malcolm James on staff, they wouldn't reach into their pockets to keep him. Two months later, they needed his skill set and Peterson had to call him in as a consultant. It was hard not to laugh about that. She hoped Mal was charging them through the nose.

"Simran's not here yet?" Lin-Fei shook her head. "What about Craig? Out for some air?" In preparation for the migration, Parnes had slept most of

Friday—but probably not since. It would make sense for him to shake out the cobwebs.

Lin-Fei blinked uncertainly. "I think he maybe sleep in conference room." She made a long diagonal point towards Focus.

Ginny wanted to knock herself on the head for not having thought of it herself. The conference room tables were big enough that even lanky Craig could stretch out. Hard as they were, she could have had an extra hour or so of sleep if she'd thought of it. Genius! Next time she was going to bring her sleeping bag and stake a claim on Energy, upstairs.

"Oh well," she said. "Hope he caught enough zzzs because it's time for his wakeup call."

"No!" Lin-Fei grabbed at Ginny's wrist to stop her. She looked terrified.

"Look, I know we don't need him for another twenty minutes or so, but he'll need time to clear his head."

"There are sounds. In the room." Lin-Fei whispered so low Ginny had to make her repeat it.

"What kind of sounds?" she asked, once she'd finally heard.

Lin-Fei shrugged. She seemed to be growing smaller before Ginny's eyes. "I hear sounds like maybe he have bad dreams."

"Oh for Pete's sake!" Ginny said. "It's probably indigestion. I bet he scarfed down an entire pizza before putting his head down. Well, let's put him out of his misery." She strode determinedly across the floor. Lin-Fei stayed put, clinging to her desk. Ginny could feel the stare boring through the back of her head; she refused to react. Shy and modest was one thing, but the girl needed to get a grip.

Ginny's hand was almost on the handle of the door to Focus when she heard the sounds for herself. She snatched back her hand in the nick of time, and jammed it in her mouth. She didn't know whether to laugh or scream. Nightmare? Hell no, the little shit had a woman in there! Her first priority was to get well clear of the door, as quickly as possible. Then she'd have to figure out a way to tell Mr. Big that he and his babe weren't alone in the office. At least now she could understand what was going on with Lin-Fei.

"Not bad dreams," Ginny said succinctly.

"No?" Lin-Fei seemed relieved not to have to deal with the information all alone.

They stared at each other. Ginny started to laugh. "Who's in there with him?"

Lin-Fei shrugged.

Ginny really wanted to know. "Well, either it's one of Edie's team or he brought someone from in from outside. I don't know which is worse."

Her Crackberry went off. The guys were headed back from the colocation. No time like the present.

"OKAY!" Ginny practically yelled, grinning broadly at Lin-Fei. She stomped across the floor, making as much of a racket as she could. "Malcolm and Freddie should be here in about ten minutes. With good old CLIF, our favorite Veeee Peeee!!!" She banged and clanged everything she touched in the kitchen. "Guess I'd better get that coffee going! Hey, Lin-Fei!" she sang out, making a megaphone of her hands. She poked her head through the doorway and called out again. The girl finally caught on and called back. It wasn't loud, but it was audible. "Hey, give me a hand with these bagels, would you? Freddie needs his breakfast!"

Freddie had time to partake of a cream-cheese slathered toasted bagel and all the gossip before a rumpled Craig joined them in the kitchen, yawing ostentatiously.

"I was trying to get some sleep, assholes," he said, going for the coffee.

Behind his back, Malcolm wrapped his arms around his own shoulders and mugged a parody of ecstasy. Coming from a man the size of a small mountain, it was painfully ridiculous. Lucky thing Ginny'd taken those Heimlich and CPR classes after the twins were born. The piece of bagel flew out of Freddie with such force that it dented the Worker's Compensation poster on the kitchen wall. Once he'd caught his breath, it was hard to get him to stop laughing.

Assuming the hysteria was due to the near death experience, Craig pounded Freddie affectionately on the back. "You're fine, bro'. Chill."

"Yeah." Clif Speck replaced his habitual genial smile with the weight-of-the-world look he wore when presenting to the LC. "Maybe you should take a lie down, Freddie. Craig, got any ideas where a brother could stretch out for while?"

Freddie doubled over with mirth. A whoop came out of Ginny before she could cover her mouth. Even Lin-Fei showed signs of amusement.

Craig looked from face to face and turned scarlet. "Fuck you!" he yelled, stomping out of the room.

"Not interested!" Malcolm yelled back.

About 15 minutes later, Lexi from Procurement "arrived in the office," her coat open and a scarf in her hand. She looked a little smudged.

"Oh bagels! Awesome!" she said brightly. "I'm starving!"

Lin-Fei ran out of the room. No one had ever heard her laugh out loud before.

Δ

```
From:        Wesley Peterson
To:          IT
Subject:     Major Happenings!
------------------------------------
```

Hello, IT!

In recognition of her sterling efforts, Ginny Chicosky has officially been named Director of the PMO

WJP

Δ

"I've already talked about this with the gang in Phi Beta Kippy. Which is a terrific program, by the way. I hope all of you get to be part of it someday. Because you're all leaders! I really believe that, and I believe it's my job to see that you reach your maximum potential. Isn't that what I always tell you, Donny? Where's Donny Rohmer?" Treacherously close to the edge of the windowsill, Kippy leaned out to scan the crowd. Clifton Speck stepped away from the video camera with both hands held up as if to preempt a fall.

We shuffled uncomfortably in our ranks. At yesterday's quarterly culling, Donny Rohmer had landed at the bottom of the Sales herd for the third consecutive month. PBK Leadership notwithstanding, his head hit the chopping block. Most of us knew this, but apparently no one had mentioned it to Kippy.

"You model the way, Kippy!" Eric Channing piped up before Alex Silva and Archie Ghosh had time to start a pool.

"HA!" Kippy's eyes popped appreciatively and swerved to fix on Channing. "Good one, Eric! Eric's referring to one of the five practices in *The Leadership Challenge*. We've been reading it in Phi Beta Kippy. The idea is that leadership is something you can learn, not something you're born with. Well, maybe some of us come with a little something baked in. Ha! But even if you're a natural leader, there are tools here to help you ramp it up. Five major disciplines. What Eric just said? Modeling the way? That's just one. Which of my Phi Beta Kippy guys is going to tell us the other four? Not you Eric! Ha!" Kippy craned his neck again, seeking out the students hiding among us. It was hard for a tall man with military posture and a regulation-shaved skull to disappear among a crowd of geeks and artists. Kippy's face lit up. "Noble! You tell them!"

Noble lifted his chin and cleared his throat. "Share the Vision," he called out.

"Share an *inspired* vision." George Waters threw the correction over his shoulder from his favored monthly meeting post, almost under Kippy's nose.

Noble didn't move a muscle. He continued to look straight ahead, eyes fixed on the perpetually scrolling display of incoming deals. "Share an inspired vision," he repeated, loudly but without inflection. "Challenge the Process! Enable Others to Act! Encourage the Heart!" We half expected him to end with "Sir, yes Sir!"

"Exactly. Terrific, terrific book, *The Leadership Challenge*. I encourage all of you to read it. We've got a copy in the library, right Gretchen?"

Gretchen stuck up two fingers.

Roger Didilian shot up his own stubby-fingered hand. "I've got one of them right here." He waved it clumsily, the book's pages flopping dangerously off the stressed paper spine.

"Good for you, Roger! Glenn, you'd better start watching your back, or Roger here is going to be number one!"

"He's going to have to run pretty hard," Glenn observed. "I read it last year."

We gave Glenn a big laugh for thinking fast on his feet.

Ginny Chicosky raised her hand, as if signaling she wanted to be called on. "I noticed online that Kouzes and Posner are going to be doing a seminar at the Javitz this summer. I'm planning on signing up."

"Terrific idea, Ginny! There's a lot you can learn from these guys."

Ginny nodded, her pale face shining with enthusiasm. "I was hoping I could make this my professional development for this year..."

"Talk to me offline." Wesley Peterson spoke from his place by the pillars without raising his voice. There was an edge to his voice; not much, but enough that any of us who heard turned to see what it might mean. Peterson's face was unreadable.

"So you heard what Noble said. That last one, Encourage the Heart. Critical for success. You have to lead with the heart. Your heart has to be in everything you do. Like me. You can't keep me away from this place, I love it so much! Marcy said next time she redecorates my office, she's putting in a bed! Ha! And I want all of you to feel that same kind of excitement, every day. So what I want you to do is think about what you need to make you happy. Here, in this place, where you spend so much time. You're gonna think about it, and you're gonna send your suggestions to Kay. And the LC and I are gonna go through that wish list and see what we can do to give you whatever it takes for you to succeed. Now we're not some Silicon Valley startup, so don't go asking for, what? Skateboards in the hallways? Whatever it is those guys do. Ha! Crazy some of them. And no, Roger, I'm not buying a corporate jet! But I am going to give you what you need to achieve excellence. Because enabling others to act? That part goes hand in hand with the heart, am I right? We want each and every single one of you to be as happy to be here every day as I am. Because, like I always say, happy people mean happy customers. And happy customers mean a happy bottom line. Ha! Isn't that right Scott? Gary? Well, we know Gary has a different idea of a happy bottom line than maybe you and I do. Ha!"

Δ

From: Gary Feldman
To: All Pinnacle Associates
Subject: Employee Departure

Kay Kuperman will be departing Pinnacle, effective April 30, to pursue other opportunities. We wish her the best of luck in all her future endeavors.

Please join me in congratulating Josefina Vargas, who will be taking over leadership of our Talent Management team. Josefina, who has an extensive background in Human Capital management, is working with Kay to ensure a smooth transition.

Gary Feldman, CFO
Pinnacle Management Services

Δ

From: Josefina Vargas
To: All Pinnacle Associates
Subject: We heard you!

In response to the Employee Wish List collected last month, we are pleased to announce that Pinnacle's dress code now extends to JEANS EVERY DAY!

We ask that you respect the fact that Pinnacle is a work environment. Like all office-appropriate apparel, jeans should be clean and neat. Patches, holes and fraying, however fashionable they might be, are not acceptable.

Josefina Vargas, Dir. Talent Management
Pinnacle Management Services

Δ

"I need bodies." Ginny took a deep pull on her iced tea, as if something in it could kick her body into cloning itself for the help she needed. "My own projects already had me at over 100 percent. Now I'm supposed to keep doing all that and also be the magic Project Management fairy on Verrazano, make a two-year FUBAR disappear all by myself. How am I supposed to do the work of two full-time PMs?"

"The same way that I became Harvey when they cut him." Simran poked a fork in his salad. "I have never understood why HR doesn't handle contractor management. Or Finance, perhaps."

"Because those are both Feldman's teams and when Verrazano crashes and burns he wants Peterson to own it."

"Did you know we're going to have to replace the name Verrazano? Kippy and Gary say they can't patent the platform under that name." Judy was also doing the work of two or three. As well as putting out the newsletter and laying the groundwork for documenting the new platform, they were turning her into the default admin for the LC. A corporate communications team? What had Nick Andreas been smoking back then?

Beneath the French blue turban that matched today's tie, Simran's usually smooth forehead furrowed at this puzzle. "What is there to patent in an internal fulfillment system? There would be no more logic in another company using Pinnacle's system that there would be in our purchasing a platform from someone else."

Judy dipped another fry in the puddle of ketchup. She'd gained twelve more pounds since joining Pinnacle, possibly because you couldn't have a private conversation without leaving the office and leaving the office almost always involved eating. "I guess they think anything that cost them this much money must be something for the books. 'Ha!' So to speak."

"They have no idea what things cost in the real world." The catchphrase had become so automatic; Ginny no longer knew she was saying it. "So wait, why don't they use the name that won the contest?"

"Because Jeff quit and spoiled it for them?"

In a company with an endless stream of exits, this one was unforgettable. Like someone in a movie, Jeff Curry had climbed on his desk and called out at the top of his lungs: "Attention Pinnacle Drones! I am not a termite! I am not a goose! I'm a FREE MAN! And I am OUT OF HERE!!" Without waiting for a reaction, he'd grabbed his messenger bag and taken off, stopping only to Frisbee his nameplate through the opening of George Waters' cube. It was bridge-burning, but Jeff no longer cared. You can only keep a man down for so long, especially a young healthy man with no dependents. Jeff had been ready to go before Waters cut him. He'd only come back for the sake of his team, those goofy idiots! He'd known Kippy's hints were bullshit. There was never going to be a promotion or a raise. Instead, they'd declared him the winner of that ridiculous contest and made a big ceremony out of passing him a $500 check and a $20 plaque. Just as he'd sworn, he made his stand as soon as the check cleared. The word "Denali" was poison for now.

Ginny snagged one of Judy's fries. "Well they can call it the Weapon of Mass Destruction for all I care. I just can't keep working this way. I know they could care less about me, but they ought to really care that Verrazano or Denali or whatever..."

"I'm sure the LC can come up with a brilliant acronym," Judy sighed.

"Does it matter?" Simran posited. "The platform will never exist, not if we continue with Centient. Their development team in Pune is a joke. I've spoken with them offline. They're trainees. Except for Vijay, they've all come straight from school. I know more about coding than most of them."

"You can't get out what you don't put in," Ginny agreed. "They piss away money on all the wrong things. Without an architect, even the good code from Craig and Sid is almost worthless. And the equipment? We're working off stuff the guys have duct-taped together and it's not holding up. We can't support our business load any more. When MSY was getting ready to roll out? Clif practically spoon-fed this to the LC, and they did everything short of sticking their fingers in their ears and going 'la-la-la-la.' Until we had those crashes and lost Keldorian."

"Which was IT's fault, of course." Maybe just one more fry? Judy heroically pushed the plate away.

"Of course."

Simran smiled. "And now we are getting new blades. I have a contract for an HP Consultant to come in for a day to help configure them."

"I heard." Ginny gently nudged the fries in her own direction.

Judy was astonished. "Seriously? New blades? Isn't that the action item Clif's had owing for two months?"

"The PO has been waiting for Feldman's signature since January."

"Heel-dragging as usual. Damn that man hates to let go of a penny! Apparently Kristol calls Clif on the carpet this morning and starts ragging on him because 'his' network is holding back her turn-around times. Her turn-around times, do you believe this? The whole network could collapse like a house of cards and she's having kittens over a few seconds here or there. Kristol drags Clif into Feldman's office and bam! Don't you think the PO gets signed on the spot?" It was more of a snort than Ginny's usual hearty laugh.

We were starting to see more and more evidence of the iron will that lurked beneath Milla Kristol's hyper-feminine business suits and candy smile. When it put her up against Feldman, we could only cheer, but some of us were already worried how far her claws would reach.

"According to Clif, that's when the yelling started," Ginny continued. "You know how the LC thinks it's like buying a laptop at Costco? Like all we have to do is pick it up, drive it home and plug it in. Feldman was already pissed, because he had to spend money. When Clif reminded him it'll take two months for the computer fairy to grant his wishes, he exploded. Clif said he was surprised we didn't hear it down on four. Wait 'til the LC finds out that even once the blades get here, the guys first have to configure them. And that they'll need a weekend cleared to bring everything else offline so they can plug them into the mix."

"So we have to rework the whole deployment schedule once Clif has a delivery date? That'll be fun." All the impossible deadlines would automatically become a week more impossible. It would be hilarious, if it weren't going to cause hell for IT. Judy laughed anyway.

"There is irony here. The LC is always talking about growth. They should not be surprised that they have to invest in it."

"They think they are. None of them ever spent this much money in their lives, not on anything." Judy remembered some of the budgets she used to manage at Trowbridge, just for internal corporate events. The numbers would probably leave Gary Feldman flat on his back on a cold slab. "How much would you say this is costing, this thing with Centient?"

"From the contracts I manage, I would estimate the engagement is easily running to a million."

"And that's only since November. What about the money they lost by not letting us finish BM-II? I never understood why they pulled the plug."

"You know what it reminds me of? TJ has a mild ADHD. He gets really into something for a while. Then he loses interest, knocks it over and moves on to the next thing."

Sometimes Judy seemed to be hearing chorus after chorus of some campfire song. "When I came on, it was the first shot at updating Bridge. Mike was shoveling away, trying to salvage something from the whole Avie Gold thing. He was so happy when Peterson arrived. Poor Mike."

"When we came on, things were starting to move. It was exciting, right Simran? If they'd given us another six months instead of pulling the plug..."

"Another six months and stopped adding features." Judy didn't know how to code, but she knew about meeting deadlines.

Simran, who'd never quite put the OnRamp debacle to bed, could only sigh. "My mother-in-law says that she raised five only children. I think Pinnacle Senior Management was raised that same way."

"I'm not a quitter, but if Peterson doesn't get me some help, I'm may have to tell him I'm out of here. Tim's in solid at JFK; and my old consulting company keeps calling, so I should be able to pick something up to tide me over until I can find a better place."

"Why don't you?" If Judy thought she could get another job in this economy, she'd be out there in a heartbeat. She envied the tech types she'd met at Pinnacle. It must be nice to have one of those focused skill sets that you can sell as a consultant.

"I wanted to see this through. It would be good for the resume, to show I pulled together a team and led something this big. Of course, if I go into Peterson, I have to be prepared to walk. If I don't mean it, he won't take me seriously."

Wesley Peterson did take her seriously. Ginny was a little surprised how much.

"See?" Tim said that night, toasting her with a bottle of Blue Moon.

"I reminded him that we were still carrying Mike's old job in our budget. Then he said he'd rather hire two juniors."

"Is that going to help?"

"A lot more than nothing." She took a long cold swallow.

Tim ruffled her hair with his free hand. "That's how you negotiate."

"He asked me to give him a week to talk it over with the LC. I get the feeling they're watching him now. No more blank checks."

"But you think it'll go through."

She nodded. She did think so. But when she'd put Peterson on the spot, there was a look his eyes that bothered her. A slight narrowing. And his smile was a little tight in the corners. For a split second his face had seemed like a mask, something calculating behind it. Maybe she'd imagined it. She felt foolish saying anything to Tim. It was probably only her own reluctance to negotiate. She'd been self-conscious with Peterson. She was projecting her discomfort onto him, reading something into his face that wasn't there. The big thing was that she'd won her point.

Δ

```
From:        Josefina Vargas
To:          All Pinnacle Associates
Subject:     Prospect Visit
-------------------------------------
```

Please note that tomorrow H & R Block will be on site. Roger Didilian will be conducting this prospect on a tour of all departments. In view of this, be advised that the dress code for tomorrow is strictly Business Casual.

Josefina Vargas, Dir. Talent Management
Pinnacle Management Services

10 TOTAL QUALITY MANAGEMENT

```
From:          Milla Kristol
To:            All Pinnacle Associates
Subject:       Business Process Center of Excellence
------------------------------------
```

In support of this year's announced corporate goal of "Increasing Operational Effectiveness by Reducing Fulfillment Data Processing Turnaround Time by 10 percent While Decreasing Operator Error," I am excited to announce the establishment of a new Business Process Management team. I have engaged with Total Quality Management specialist Lloyd Baptiste to establish this new Fulfillment Center of Excellence, which will be led by Project Manager Mike Ventura.

Milla Kristol, EVP of Fulfillment Services
Pinnacle Management Services

Δ

They'd hopped a cab to the serenely pale Japanese restaurant that bore the name of a famous television chef. It was the kind of working lunch that Mike Ventura associated with Wall Street or the Entertainment industry, not with a place like Pinnacle, but Lloyd Baptiste had an expense account; it was part of his deal.

Baptiste ordered them a round of Asahis and, without looking at the menu, rattled off a few things to the waiter. Mike admired the confidence and bonhomie radiating off his new....what? Technically they both reported to Milla Kristol. Not boss then. Mentor maybe. Did it matter? The man across the table was a breath of extremely welcome fresh air, bringing the first hint of optimism Mike had felt since Peterson had anointed him the messenger of ill tidings.

Baptiste brought tidings of his own, about how Trim/Delta, a peerless methodology for supporting a cycle of continuous improvement, was changing the world. A certified Trim/Delta Sensei, Baptiste was qualified to sponsor his new best friend Mike for certification and coach him through the process. Together, they would build a team and be Pinnacle's Lewis and Clark through this new business frontier.

Comfortably mellow from his unaccustomed midday beer, Mike leaned back in his chair and allowed Baptiste's monologue to wash over him. It felt good to feel positive again. A tiny voice in the back of his head insisted that Trim/Delta had no more chance of being seriously accepted at Pinnacle than his PMI practices, but Mike was willing to learn it and give it a try. Trim/Delta was gaining enough traction out in the world that Milla had made it a priority to pull in Lloyd Baptiste. If nothing else, the certification would look good on his resume.

Mike's eyes danced around the restaurant, coming to rest on an elegant platter of fishy sculptures making its way to their table. Lloyd obviously did not come cheap. How the hell had Milla gotten Feldman to open his wallet? The moths must have been terrified! Mike laughed out loud. Baptiste shot him a wink, probably assuming he was laughing at the size of the sushi platter. If so, he wasn't far wrong. Exile from IT still felt wrong, but Mike was beginning to see an upside.

Δ

```
From:        Josefina Vargas
To:          All Pinnacle Associates
Subject:     The Peak Experience
-----------------------------
```

Hello Pinnacle!

From now on, *The Peak Experience* will be coming to you electronically, on our brand new intranet! Just click HERE to read this month's issue:

- Total Quality Management: Lloyd Baptiste, Director of TQM, explains how
- Pinnacle Previews Denali at OAA convention
- Pinnacle's White Gloves Compliance service: get the facts!
- How Do You Get to Carnegie Hall? (an interview with Pinnacle's own Ina Hochmann)
- Pinnacle Walks for a Cure (a photo essay by Chris Keane)

Josefina Vargas, Dir. Talent Management
Pinnacle Management Services

Δ

It began first thing in the morning and quickly rose above the usual eighth floor din, a rumble from the center of the cluster of desks that housed the dedicated MSY team. It gradually leaked into Fulfillment, into every team except Training. Traffic from OnRamp into Bridge had slowed to a trickle. CPU by CPU, each stroke of the "Enter" key invoked the spinning rainbow of the "wait" gif. Ripping ourselves free of the mesmerizing death spiral, we shot off messages to the IT Helpdesk: "STAT!" "SOS!" Some of us preemptively tried rebooting, which is what Freddie Vega was probably going to tell us to do anyway. It didn't help. We were limping; we were stuck.

Client reactions started pouring in faster than we could handle them, jamming up the phone lines. By then we knew what had happened. A major expansion initiative had brought on three dozen West Coast Mama-San Yakitori storefronts in a single day. Our load-balanced routing system, which Clifton Speck's team had begged to upgrade, but which the technology scholars on the LC had determined was already much more powerful than Pinnacle required for current volume, folded under the onslaught. The Dev team had planned out an automated failover architecture for OnRamp that would have mitigated the equipment's inadequacies. Except it was never developed. The LC had forcibly sidelined this unglamorous functionality, preferring bandwidth be applied to producing the custom color schemes, "best in breed" survey tool and interactive Procurement image gallery that Scott swore were absolute necessities for Sales.

It was a perfect one-two punch: MSY was effectively knocked out cold; and the rest of our business was backed up for miles. The finger-pointing began almost at once, in every direction but up.

"We should see this as an opportunity." Milla Kristol's eyes were steely above her patented broad-mouthed smile. "An ideal pilot for TQM. The results will be extremely valuable for planning out the Pune Fulfillment center. And I believe you'll find that this proves my point: that we ought to include one or two Client Care people in the mix, for back up."

This was the first Mike Ventura heard that Pinnacle had any plans in India beyond hiring IT consultants. He could see the attraction of expanding somewhere cheaper than New York, but why wasn't Pinnacle looking closer to home? Sure Data Entry clerks would come even cheaper in India, but the complications of such a remote staff were massive. A recent *TechRepublic* piece said Omaha was "the Call Center Capital of the United States." Why not try Nebraska? But if Mike had one takeaway from his tenure under Peterson, it was the wisdom of keeping his thoughts to himself. He'd keep his mouth shut and focus on shadowing Lloyd Baptiste through the task at hand.

Baptiste took over Advancement for the day, forcing Donna to hastily reschedule all other meetings. Working with MSY team lead Archie Ghosh, they'd begin with the "5 Whys," a diagnostic approach Trim/Delta shared with other methodologies of the Kaizen family tree; then apply the ACE bandage (for "Add, Change, Excise") to whatever fail point was identified.

Mike felt guilty about making lemonade out of this disaster, but he couldn't help his excitement. As interesting as Baptiste's monologues and the assigned readings were in the abstract, they failed to prove the value of Trim/Delta. Today would be a whole different thing. He'd see the methodology up on its feet, watch it unveil hidden stumbling blocks that would lead to fresh thinking and inspire out of the box solutions.

He listened carefully to various members of the MSY team as they rotated through to say their piece. The ideal would have been to bring everyone around the table together but, as certified by the first revelatory series of "Whys," the tiny team was stretched to provide sufficient coverage even when everyone was on the floor at once. Actually, all of the results of Mike's first practical Trim/Delta exercise only confirmed what everyone at Pinnacle below C-level had known all along, that our resources perpetually lagged behind our volume of work.

Mike didn't mind getting answers he already knew. On the contrary; it gave him confidence that Trim/Delta was worth adding to his toolkit. If it made the LC loosen the purse strings, it would be downright miraculous.

Δ

```
From:          Kippy Melcher
To:            All Pinnacle Associates
Subject:       Welcome Our New All-Star!
----------------------------------
Hello, Pinnacle!

I am so excited to announce that Leonard K. Strauss will be
joining Pinnacle's Leadership Council as our new Executive
Vice President of Business Development. I know you've all
seen Len during his regular visits to our offices. Len is a
longtime colleague and has been instrumental in identifying
opportunities for business growth and operational expansion.
Len's decision to join us full time is confirmation of
Pinnacle's success.

Kippy

Kippy Melcher, CEO
Pinnacle Management Services
```

Δ

There were more people than room for extra chairs. Though she'd given her desk chair to Lloyd Batiste, there was no doubt who owned this meeting. Milla perched atop the credenza, cocking her head winsomely at her growing circle of direct reports. She'd apparently learned her perching technique from old Audrey Hepburn movies. Her legs slanted to one side, knees neatly together, the lower heel finding purchase on the handle of a drawer. Pastel shoulders hunched ever so slightly, she pitched forward, keeping a protective hand curled on the edge of the cabinet. She gestured with her other hand, her left; the occasional spatter of mirror-ball sparks from her outsized eternity ring somewhat dented the waifish veneer.

"Before I forget." She flashed a typically mirthless smile, connoting that Milla Kristol never forgot anything. "Next week we'll need to bump this meeting up to Thursday. I'll be attending the Executive Offsite on Wednesday, and I have requested that Llllloyyd" she caressed the name of her prized possession, "accompany me."

Working an ever-present wad of nicotine gum didn't stop Lloyd Baptiste from delivering a winking grin. He leaned back comfortably, disregarding the ominous creak from Milla's chair. "Looking forward to it. Mike here's given me the low down on the last one."

Eyes and lips narrowing in concert, Milla turned her attention to Mike Ventura.

"It was a pilot, really, last year. There was a pretty large group." The big man shrugged it into the past, his lightness of tone seeming to mollify her.

She nodded sharply. "Yes. Well, I expect whatever the program was then, it will be much more rigorous this time. Keyed to the needs of Upper Management. Pinnacle is quite a different company now."

Milla's status meeting was dependably uncomfortable, but at least Edie didn't have to scrape herself out of bed at the crack of dawn to get there. That was one stress she didn't miss at all. She was surprised, though, to find herself missing her contact with Kippy. Kippy must have missed it, too. He gave her his most manic grin whenever they ran into one another. Like now, on her way to top off her coffee after the Weekly.

"Big plans for the Offsite!"

"I'm sure it'll be great. I look forward to hearing Milla's report."

He seemed puzzled. "You're on vacation next week?"

Now it was her turn to be puzzled. "It's a smaller group this time. Only Upper Management."

"*Key* managers," he said firmly. "You're key. You should be there."

She smiled as noncommittally as she knew how. They each told the other to have a good day. A few hours later, there was an email from Milla, inviting her to the Offsite. Inviting Edie and George. Had Kippy suggested George, too, Edie wondered; or was that Milla's addition, making the point that Edie was now no more "key" than her former assistant? Edie sighed.

Either way, the invitation was more political than made her comfortable. Between Milla and George, she'd be walking a tightrope all day long. Not only that, she'd have to wake up before 5 to get to Tenafly on time.

Δ

The invitation to the offsite said "casual." Dave had decided to interpret this as chinos. He couldn't imagine any of the LC showing up in jeans, so he wouldn't either. Angie told him to wear the striped shirt she'd bought him last summer for her company's Hamptons clambake. He felt like a twat in it, but she insisted it was more executive than the old white linen shirt he wanted to wear, the one he'd picked up on the French Riviera back in his yacht crewing days. Literally on the Riviera. Some stoned rich asshole must have stripped it off for a midnight swim and left it behind on the sand. It was a thing of beauty, that shirt; so obviously expensive that the label was superfluous. After all these years, it was now a little tight and he had to roll back the cuffs an extra flip to cover a nasty rip in one sleeve, but it still made him feel like a million bucks. Even so, he had to bow to Angie on this. All his brushes with big money had been at play. It was Angie who was rubbing business shoulders with people who made the LC look like peasants.

She was right, of course. If he'd needed any confirmation, he got it from the once-over Peterson gave him just now at the station. That kind of "hmmm" face, as if Peterson was surprised he looked so sharp. Or maybe Peterson was surprised to see him there at all. Technically, the offsite was for "Director level and above." The newly-dubbed "Product Owner of RFPs and Demos" didn't qualify. It was Scott Bell who'd insisted on including him.

This was Dave's fourth title in the three years since Avie Gold had hired him on with the meaningless title "Assistant to the Director of Technology." He'd been "Senior Business Analyst" and, after that, "Technology Process SME." The work he did hardly changed at all, certainly not the part about him being the guy that Sales turned to for...what was it Scott always said? "The only person down there who makes any sense." This was more critical than ever, the way the way the tide was rolling with Peterson's not-my-problem attitude to Centient. Angie even suggested he push a little harder, maybe switch departments. He didn't want to. He'd never been much of a hunter and he'd learned he wasn't much of a closer. He'd never make the cut. It was safer for him to work with them than to be them. And Scott plenty appreciated the Buzzard right where he was, giving his guys all that tender loving care. The invitation to the offsite was proof.

"I see it. Over there." Peterson ducked between a pair of Disney-on-Broadway posters, to the nearest stairs.

Dave followed him down to the parking lot, to a silver van that had a "Pinnacle" placard propped under the wipers.

George Waters had already claimed the shotgun seat. It was the best option to accommodate his bulk, but you'd still have thought the guy would want to make a few points by leaving it for one of the C's. Not the Buzzard's problem. He did the sporting thing and climbed all the way to the back, where Gretchen was folded into the corner, intent on her phone. Probably emailing Kippy to let him know the trains had all arrived and they were on their way.

On his way indeed. Whatever the day was about, it didn't matter. He'd made a good call. Unlike poor Mike Ventura, Dave was here today, and he meant to make the most of it.

Except for the kind of retirees who golf on a Wednesday morning, they were the only ones in the clubhouse. After a baffling T'ai Chi warm-up on the grass, the full breakfast menu was on offer. This was a pleasant surprise to Dave, who'd expected they'd all have to eat a la Kippy. A good New Orleans boy, he wouldn't risk the French toast, but he took a chance on the pumpkin pancakes with some of that applewood smoked bacon. People's breakfasts seemed weirdly in character. He could have bet money on skinny Milla Kristol starting her day with dry whole wheat toast and half a grapefruit, or that Walt liked home fries with his scrambled eggs and sausage. George Waters, who wasn't at all a yoghurt or egg white sandwich type, was clearly sucking up. Dave wondered if the facilitator, a horse-faced beach blonde named Kelly, was paying as much attention to the food choices as he was. She should have been. Not counting Gretchen, who'd be hanging on the sidelines in case Kippy had a sudden urge to make a call or read an email, she had sixteen people to wrangle and she had to learn them fast.

The facilitator swept a calculated glance at the plates. People were not quite finished eating. She jumped up from her seat and tapped her knife against her water glass.

"Everybody, forks down!" She smiled hard at the disgruntled faces. "Time to get started! Everybody follow me!" Taking for granted that they would, she bounced away from the dining room.

"Here we go!" Kippy crowed, hard on her heels.

Everyone else pushed reluctantly away from the table and trickled after. Across the foyer was a large game room, a card with the Pinnacle mountaintop masking-taped to the door. Inside were four long tables and a bunch of folding chairs. Kelly waited at the far end.

Once everyone had filed in, Gretchen closed the door and Kelly clapped her hands in apparent delight. "Al-right! Let's play global thermo-nuclear war!"

Dave quickly scanned the group from the corner of his eye. Not a twitch. He swallowed down his own instinctive laugh.

Kelly seemed disappointed at the lack of reaction. "No *War Games* fans in the house I see. Oh, well. We'll just have to do something else instead. Let's have four teams..." She stretched a bisecting arm over their heads. Dave made sure to scoot closer to Scott. Clif shifted towards Feldman, of all people. Fascinating. Peterson was definitely a sinking ship.

"Spread apart," Kelly urged. "One group to a table. One, two...four. Nope. Too many over here." She frowned and pointed at Waters, who was trying to edge closer to Kippy, Milla and Lloyd; he hadn't noticed Josefina, on Kippy's other side. "You. We need someone for the table at the end."

Everyone watched as Waters shuffled over to join Wesley, Walt and Alan, who was looking droopier than ever these day. The reject table, Dave thought, grateful to have secured his spot at Table #2. Close enough to feel Edie's shoulders heave, he thought maybe she was suppressing a laugh.

"Perfect! Now it's even. Okay, here's a little exercise in manufacturing supply chain management. And this...." She held up a piece of copier paper. "This is your product. So! Who here knows how to build an airplane?"

Δ

```
From:        Wesley Peterson
To:          IT
Subject:     New Teammates!
----------------------------------
Hello, IT!

Please help me welcome two new members to our PMO.

Joseph Biro comes to us from Metropolitan Life, where he's
been working as a Senior Business Analyst. Joseph will be
working under Ginny as Product Manager on Bridge, and will be
fully responsible for business analysis and patch deployment
management on that application.

Danny Zill is a recent graduate of SUNY Stony Brook where he
majored in Information Technology and Communication. Danny
will be our new Business Analyst for all non-Denali projects,
including Binder enhancements with our partners at Shelby.

WJP
```

Δ

"I hear del Monte's moving to Training." Diego's dimples quivered with excitement. "That's a nice bump up."

"Depressing thought." Archie didn't find the compensation packet particularly generous, and she was a team lead.

"I wouldn't mind it." Dawn was planning to go after the next opening herself. "It definitely looks better on the resume than anything else here."

Cheap progressive lenses didn't work so well in alleys. Gretchen squinted between the girls at the new arrival. "Hey! Since when do you smoke?"

"Always." Hank Iversson's tone seemed disproportionately defensive. "Long time."

"Not on my watch." Gretchen's hair seemed to toss itself. She didn't actually say "tsk tsk" but everyone seemed to hear it.

"Yeah, well I quit when I moved to New York." He tried to sound as fierce as his gel-spiked beer-colored hair. "I was doing pretty well until the MSY explosion."

Archie nodded empathetically. "I'm a pack a day since then myself."

"Welcome aboard." Orla raised a fist in his direction.

Hank sheepishly bumped knuckles. "I thought if I didn't make it a social thing, it would be easier to quit again, but I don't know. I feel like a criminal, blowing smoke out the window in the stairwell."

"Damn!" Gretchen hardly ever had time for more than a few puffs before her Blackberry went off, like an ankle monitor ensuring her house arrest. She handed her half-smoked cigarette to Hank. "Your mother would kill me."

He accepted it gratefully and took a deep drag.

"So Hank, you know everyone, right?" Orla apparently had decided to act as hostess. "Except these guys. These are Danny and Joe. New in IT."

"Hello, Danny and Joe. My name is Alex and I am not a workaholic." Alex assumed the ponderous air of someone addressing a crowd. Now that he was actually billing a few hours a week as an acting coach, he'd become more theatrical than ever. The gig had come via Gretchen's old modeling friend, who'd been very impressed with the scene he'd directed for the talent show. Which proves you can network absolutely anywhere, even at Pinnacle.

Orla ignored him. "This is Hank Iversson. He's Client Care, like us." Her skull-ringed index finger did a connect-the-dots between herself, Alex and Yan Cheung.

"For Abby Witherspoon. We saw the presentation in Boot Camp today." The one called Danny had wavy black hair and the bright-eyed look of the recently-graduated.

"Is Boot Camp still a thing? I mean without Kay?" Archie turned to ask Gretchen, but she was already gone.

"It was when I started," Yan said. "Jo was doing it. I guess she still is."

"Josefina Vargas." The one called Joe had a nod as decisive as his mustache. "Director of HR."

"Talent Management," Dawn corrected. "It used to be HR, but we got upgraded from Resources to Talent."

"Some of us have always been talent."

Orla gave Alex the traditional punch in the arm. "Skyped with Mia this morning. I had to tell her about Kaimi. She said to give you that."

"What about Kaimi?"

Orla flicked open her hands, spreading her fingers into starbursts. "Poof!"

"Kaimi Poole? Shit!"

Diego's face sagged. "I saw he was out. I figured he was stretching his PTO with the three-day weekend, so could go home to visit."

"Nope, he's gone alright," Dawn confirmed. "No explanation or anything, but he's gone."

"Fuck!" Alex brushed angrily at his flop of hair. "Am I the only one who sometimes feel like we're living in a banana republic? People getting disappeared all the time?"

"Uh-huh. You know why Tully didn't come down? He's up to his eyeballs helping make up the backlog in Data Entry."

"Well," Diego sighed sympathetically; "he can probably use the overtime."

The sound Dawn made was too ugly to be a laugh. "Nope. Waters moved him off Payroll into Kaimi's spot. It's Rex and Noni who are getting the overtime, covering Tully's work."

"What the fuck?" Orla marveled.

"I think it's because he stood up for me again," Dawn explained. "But Tully says Spurious is taking revenge for Thanksgiving."

"Now?! That was months ago."

Dawn agreed. "Spurious doesn't usually wait to react."

"Hmm..." Alex stroked his soul patch. "Tully was the one who went to Kay that day. And Kaimi went to Edie, remember? It's certainly starting to sound like revenge served cold."

This time it was Diego who smacked him. "You're scaring the newbies!" Diego smiled sweetly at Danny and Joe. "Don't let him. There are so many great people here. You'll see."

"Speaking of great people," Alex focused narrowed eyes on Hank. "How is it that our lovely Gretchen knows your mother?"

"Huh?"

"Your mother would kill me?"

"Oh that." It was hard to shrug it off with everyone staring at him. "We kind of grew up together. In Minneapolis. Her mom worked for my dad. She used to babysit me sometimes."

"Seriously? Damn! Where's a straight man when you need one?"

"I'll play straight man," Dawn said. "What do you want me to say?"

Alex made a dismissive slice with his hand. "No, doll, not straight man. Straight Man. Do you know how many male individuals in this place have a raging fire in their scrotums for our lovely Gretchen? Half of Sales would die to think Hank here had been naked with her."

"I was never...fuck!" Hank hated how his face went from white to red at the least provocation. "It's not like she changed my diapers or anything. I was already in school."

"Never admit that," Alex admonished. "You string those Sales guys along and maybe they'll sit on Feldman hard enough to get you your referral bonus."

Joe Biro grabbed onto the familiar phrase. "They told us about the referral program. And the health club subsidy."

"And the Disney apartment," Danny piped up. "Seriously, can anybody use it? Not only managers?"

"Oh, yes! Gretchen has a sign-up sheet." Archie had her name down for Labor Day. It wasn't the perfect time to be going to Florida, but her cousins would be visiting from Toronto. "Three bedroom, two bath. Roger says there's a nice pool in the building."

"There is," Alex agreed. "I went there instead of LA this year. Nice place and super convenient. Definitely a perk. The referrals, not so much. Hank here fed them his family business...how many months is it now?"

"Almost a year. Right after the company picnic." Before grinding out Gretchen's cigarette, Hank used it to light one of his own. "Uncle Ray signed the contract in October. Fucking ironic. I left Minneapolis because I didn't want to work for the family, and here I am, running interference for all their work anyway. And I'm still waiting to see a dime from the referral."

"It's Feldman." Orla made a dismissive gesture. "Hates to let go of a dime."

"Yeah," Yan chimed in. "Like the health club? It's the one across the street, which isn't cheap. And it's not a subsidy or a special rate or anything. It's a reimbursement thing. You have to log every time you use it, and someone there has to sign off. If you don't go at least three hours a week, you don't get reimbursed. I go a lot. But I'm sticking with the Crunch on 23rd. I mean, to have someone sitting on my head that way? I don't know. It's so..." Yan couldn't think of the word he wanted. He screwed up his nose instead.

"Infantilizing?" Orla supplied.

"Is that a word?" Diego asked.

"English major, remember?"

"There's a lot of that," Dawn told the newbies. "Get used to being treated like you're 14. Did everyone hear about the popcorn? You know that thing around 3:30ish?" Dawn's desk was nearest to the break room, but everyone knew what she meant. It was that late afternoon energy drop, the rush to the snack machines. Recently people had started microwaving popcorn, on the principal that was a marginally healthier option.

"What about it?" Yan was a big fan of popcorn.

"Kippy doesn't like the smell."

"The popcorn smell or the fake butter smell?"

She shrugged. "No idea. But I hear they're banning it. No more microwave corn. We'll probably get an email tomorrow."

"At least we have our jeans," Orla said sanctimoniously, patting her black denim leg.

"Unless a client's on the floor," Diego reminded.

Joe Biro was glad he'd waited to quit smoking. He'd just learned more in five minutes than he could have learned in a month, and all without using up his vacation time. Pinnacle sold itself well, but it was turning out to be one weird shop. Guess he wasn't going to be handing MetLife his notice after all.

Δ

```
From:        Josefina Vargas
To:          Pinnacle Leaders; IT
Subject:     Employee Departuro
-----------------------------------
Joseph Biro is no longer a Pinnacle employee.

Josefina Vargas, Dir. Talent Management
Pinnacle Management Services
```

Δ

```
From:        Kippy Melcher
To:          All Pinnacle Associates
```

```
Subject:          Employee Departure
-------------------------------------
```

Alan Reisch will be departing Pinnacle, effective June 30, to
pursue other opportunities. We wish him the best of luck in
all his future endeavors.

Pleas join us in Advancement at 5:30 Friday for wine and
cheese, to say goodbye and wish him well.

Kippy Melcher, CEO
Pinnacle Management Services

Δ

July 4th this year fell, idiotically, on a Wednesday. We wouldn't even have a long weekend.

Gabe and Martha were desperate to get away. Work was a treadmill, and they were being torn to pieces between her sister in Maine and his mother in Miami. They needed to hide out somewhere for a few days and just chill.

The ad with the last-minute holiday promotion for Vegas was too much for Martha. She didn't wait to ask Gabe. She grabbed it. It was too late to put in for PTO; they would both have to call in sick for the other two days. It was the naughtiest thing Martha had done since shoplifting a barrette from the dime store when she was eleven. It proved how exquisite the need was, that she didn't even care.

Slow already from the delayed holiday schedule, the subway got stalled on the way to the Air Train. Running through Jamaica station, Gabe lumbering like an elephant with a carryon case tucked under each arm, they missed a shuttle by a hair and had to wait forever for the next one to pull in. After leaving themselves two hours for a one hour trip, they barely made it to the airport in the nick of time.

They pushed through the throngs at security, tall Gabe opening a path, tiny Martha scattering worried smiles and apologies thick with the word "very", and managed to reach the gate before final call. It didn't matter: their flight was overbooked; their seats had been given away and the only two left were center seats in rows at opposite ends of the cabin. Martha, sensibly, burst into tears. The check-in attendant, watching how sweetly Gabe held her close and stroked her hair, said that if they'd wait a couple of hours for the next one, they could be bumped to First Class.

Somewhere over the Grand Canyon, buzzing with free champagne, Gabe had an idea.

Martha Evangeline Moon and Gabriel Famosa del Monte were married on July 5th, in a chapel on the Strip where Marilyn Monroe had once married someone. As a wedding gift, they gave themselves three days of peace. They didn't call their families until they were back home.

First thing Monday morning, Martha paid a quiet visit to Jo Vargas' office to ask about paperwork. Jo was extremely discreet. It was weeks before the rest of us found out.

11 UNDER THE BUS

"What did you say you want?"

Judy was so busy driving the poor guy at Brooklyn Bagels crazy, Ginny was surprised she'd even remembered to ask.

"Everything."

"...and four everything bagels."

Humming with satisfaction, Judy drew a line across the fold-softened paper. Her list. She said the friend she was visiting was homesick for nearly everything. You had to wonder why he'd ever moved. Judy'd said something about there being more opportunity. It made no sense. Ginny couldn't imagine Prague had more of anything than New York.

"Is that it?"

"Just about. All I need are the Ritz crackers. I can pick up a couple boxes on the way home and I'm good to go."

"You're kidding me!" Ginny's mom had used to make Ritz cracker pie, soaking all the crackers in lemon juice so they almost tasted like apples. It was the kind of thing Ginny and Tim had left Dickson City to get away from.

"People want the strangest things when they can't get them. Would you believe his Mom overnighted me a couple of Red Sox t-shirts? Because," Judy raised her fingers in air quotes; "when they make the Series he's going to need them."

Ginny's laugh always surprised people. It busted out of her, so big that sometimes, like now, she had to tip up her glasses to wipe her eyes. "Don't say that in front of Tseng. He's killing himself over the Angels."

"Maybe that wouldn't be such a bad idea," Judy said darkly. "This whole Centient thing...I wish I weren't going away right now..."

For last month's quarterly meeting of Kippy's mysterious Board, Peterson had tasked the IT managers with hammering out massive reports. Then Judy turned out *Reader's Digest* slideshow versions for them to present to a conference room full of stone faces. Ginny's report was a cost analysis of Centient. It was a joke; she had nothing to do with that relationship; the only one on the offshore team she was even allowed to talk with was Vijay, who liked to think of himself as one of us and would call with questions.

Peterson didn't say a word to anyone after, but there was an undercurrent on the floor. IT felt shaky. Everyone seemed to be opening accounts on LinkedIn and connecting with each other. Simran and Craig had both asked

Ginny to write them recommendations; she'd asked Mike Ventura for one and was updating her resume. Things didn't feel good, but there was no point in brooding over it.

"Don't let it ruin your vacation," she advised Judy. "Tim and I are taking the boys to Hershey this weekend. And having fun. Even if I get canned."

Judy looked stricken. "Don't say that!"

Ginny smiled philosophically. "Always better to be prepared. Something's happening. I can smell it. Peterson's had two fails. He needs someone to throw under the bus."

"Okay, but why you?" Judy objected. "Why not Eliot? He's a nice enough guy, but he's worthless. I never yet saw him do anything remotely constructive."

"He was Peterson's hire. It looks bad to fire one of your own hires for fucking up. He needs someone less directly connected."

"You knew him before."

"It's not like he brought me in. I once did some work for hire at a place where he and Eliot worked. It's a small world."

Judy wouldn't let it go. "But you're the only one who's ever managed to deliver anything on time and in working order. You're the best person on his entire team. It's not even arguable."

Ginny shook her head. When it came business, she sometimes felt decades older than Judy. "No point in sweating it. By the way, I put in your performance evaluation yesterday."

"Damn, that sounds so grim."

"Just practical. Hey, whatever happens, happens. It's not like we have any control here."

No control. But knowing helped; information was something. "So if anything does happen here, to anyone, you'll email me? I'd hate to come back to any nasty surprises. Though I guess I could get an email from Jo Vargas telling me not to bother coming back at all. Like they did with Jen Kramer on her honeymoon."

Ginny chuckled. "Exactly. Hey, cheer up! You're going to have a great time. Drink lots of beer for me and don't even think about this place."

Δ

Morning was hellish. More like Monday than Friday. By noon, Ginny was envying Judy's vacation big time. Peterson was holed up behind closed doors, but he emailed her a packet of reports he wanted updated by end of day. She'd have to stay an hour or two late to get it all done. Good thing Tim preferred driving at night to skip the traffic. The boys would sleep in the car; maybe she would too.

There wasn't time for lunch, but she was starving. Fastest was to run down to the deli, put together a salad, and eat at her desk. Gretchen must have had the same idea.

"Kippy already leave for the weekend?"

Gretchen whirled around with an embarrassed smile. "How did you know?"

"You're picking it up, not waiting upstairs for a delivery."

"He's in the tunnel. Plenty of time." She tapped her Blackberry. "I can even wait and walk back with you."

"Crazy. I don't know how you deal with it."

"I'm used to crazy. I live with a writer. Anyway, except that he hates being out of touch, he's pretty nice to me. And he's good about my going down to Asheville every July." Gretchen's novelist husband ran a writing workshop every summer. It was her job to manage the meals and laundry. The month away represented all her PTO time plus, we assumed, compensation for the tons of overtime she put in at the other end of that Blackberry tether. It was impressive she'd been able to negotiate for this. Then again, men were always pretty nice to Gretchen. Some guy in Sales swore he'd seen her in an old *Sports Illustrated Swimsuit Edition*. "And when I told him I was pregnant, all he said was congratulations."

Ginny almost dropped her change. Gretchen looked her usual willowy self; though now that the words had been said, Ginny could see that maybe the loose cotton sweater was covering something.

"Oops!" Gretchen blushed. "Don't say anything, okay?"

"I won't. But...Wow! Congratulations!"

"Thanks. I mean, people know I've quit smoking, but I've been keeping it quiet. Until it kind of speaks for itself, you know? Not that it should matter to anyone except Kippy. But who knows anything anymore? I'm glad if I had to slip up, it was with you."

"Dependable is my middle name."

"I know. We're really going to miss you."

Ginny had to force herself to take a few steps away, so that the drag queen with the granny cart could open the deli door. It didn't matter that she'd sensed this coming, it was still a sock in the ribs. It always is. She tried to control her reaction, but some signal reached the other woman.

"Oh, shit! You didn't know!" Gretchen looked horrified.

Ginny could only shake her head.

"Oh my god, I feel awful!" She clapped her hand over her mouth.

"No, don't." Ginny managed to push it out. "It's not like it's coming out of left field. I just...not..."

"I thought it was, you know, one of those mutual agreements. 'To pursue other opportunities.' I mean, everyone thinks so highly of you."

"Obviously not everyone. Hey, you were just the messenger." Ginny held up her hand before Gretchen could start apologizing again. No pregnant woman should have to look so sad. "No, this is good, really. Now I'm ready for it. I won't stand there like a deer caught in the headlights. That's a good thing. So when are they cutting me loose?"

"Today. That's another reason why...I mean, it's lunch already. They always terminate," Gretchen gulped at the word. "Um...they always do this in the morning."

"They probably don't usually have a pile of work they want someone to finish before clearing out their desk. It must have been a hell of a decision, throwing me under the bus when there's so much Peterson needs me to do." The laugh came out spontaneously, unnerving Gretchen. "It's okay, I'll be fine. And I owe you one, Gretchen. Thank you."

Δ

Between the elevator and her desk, four different people caught hold of Judy. "I know," she assured them; "she told me." Throughout the day, people kept pulling her aside, but not Wesley Peterson; not even Elliot Tseng, his second in command. Her manager had been fired while she was out of the office, and no one in Management thought it was important to tell her.

The week wore on. There was Peterson's usual weekly all-IT meeting, where nothing was said. Simran, who knew only as much as she did, led the project meetings, the same as if Ginny were on vacation. The Denali status meeting was cancelled from Outlook, Judy never knew by whom.

She tried to block out the eerie silence. She had a full plate, and the work was the work. Truth be told, she'd always more or less managed herself except for things like performance review. And what about that? Personal feelings aside, there was an HR issue here. Whose direct report was she now, officially? Nobody's, it seemed.

By the end of the week, still officially uninformed, Judy couldn't take it anymore. She poked her head through the door of Peterson's office.

"So, big changes," he said. He smiled—smiled!—and nodded, but he didn't gesture for her to come in, the way he usually did when there was far less cause for conversation.

Judy nodded back. Wesley returned to whatever it was that he was composing on his laptop. If it was another of his little presentations for her to polish up, the way she was feeling about him right now she'd probably scream. She kept walking, heading for the ladies' room. A toilet stall was the only place you could get any privacy at Pinnacle without actually leaving the building. If she left now, she was afraid she'd never come back, and she couldn't afford to do that.

Half an hour later the email arrived, not just in Judy's inbox but to everyone in IT.

Δ

```
From:        Wesley Peterson
To:          IT
Subject:     Major Happenings!
-----------------------------------
Good afternoon, IT.
```

As you all know, with recent deep scrutiny of our delivery progress, a series of realizations began to be made across the organization regarding the true scope/impact of the Denali platform project. We have discovered gaping holes in our processes, and shortcomings in our own performance, as well as that of our chosen partner, Centient. Rather than allow ourselves to be demoralized into stasis because of these realizations, we have chosen instead to mobilize around these challenges and troubleshoot our known issues across the board.

As we begin to properly identify and escalate project risks along the way, I want to give you some insight into actions we've begun to take to assure that Pinnacle's technology needs continue to be met on a CREDIBLE, PREDICTABLE and RELIABLE basis. We have begun this transformation with the dissolution of the Project Management Office. Virginia Chicosky's termination for cause last Friday, driven by recent realizations about the depth of our ineffectiveness in governing and managing the Denali/OnRamp projects, underscores the seriousness of personal job performance for all of IT. During her tenure as a Project Manager, Ms. Chicosky did provide various results. However, she failed in the highly responsible role as Director of the PMO, and lost the position because she wasn't able to lead the building of an effective organization, driving on-time, on-budget & in-scope programs with at least the core processes, quality measures & staffing necessary to make IT consistently successful with complex programs. Further, Joseph Biro chose to abandon his PM post just a couple of weeks into the job. We don't need this sort of weak commitment among our IT

Teammates, so it was best for Joseph to show himself in this way early on and opt-out of the Team as he did. Despite lots of rhetoric on the subject in the past, we have little in the way of effective processes actually rolled out. I myself have embarked on a complete REBUILD of this vital governance structure. We will soon be operating under an IT-wide style of production management that will help us set aside the 'silos' of our past, and lead us to a more mutually aware approach to yielding large new Technology Development Programs. This will be a challenging and yet REWARDING PERIOD FOR ALL OF IT because we will finally start to realize and benefit from TEAM-THINKING without reservations about whether or not our particular team's concerns have been addressed in "The Plan"...because THEY WILL BE, FINALLY!!

I remain FULLY CONFIDENT that by helping each other to break things down into workable pieces, and by holding ourselves accountable for our own actions as progressive professionals working together, we will successfully evolve a far more effective and enjoyable first-string shop to which we will all be proud to have actively contributed.

WJP

Δ

Except for Clif Speck, already in his usual place behind the video camera, the people in IT were almost the last to file into the Pit. We tried not to stare too openly. It was hard to be discreet when we were buzzing with curiosity. None of them looked well.

Re-orgs happened regularly. Except for a few nakedly ambitious types like Waters and Channing, no one below C-level enjoyed the constant shuffles, but we'd learned to ride them out with a good amount of philosophy. This one felt different. None of us knew what had happened on four, except that it was something big and Ginny Chicosky was gone. We hadn't seen it coming. Ginny got things done, and she managed it without raising anyone's hackles. She was in PBK, which was supposed to mean she was up and coming. She should have been solid. Rumor had it that when IT was told Ginny was out, Noble Landrum actually knocked on Kippy's door and asked to take a meeting. Weirdly, that was the only rumor we'd heard. Even the chattier members of IT, people like Judy and Freddie, were keeping mum. Or maybe they didn't know any more than we did. So we gave them all their space this morning and let them try to disappear into the shadows while we turned our eyes to Kippy on the windowsill.

"I know you have a lot on your minds, but before I open the floor to questions...Ha! That's right. No speech today. I'm here to hear from you. But first, I want to hear a round of applause for our terrific Sales crew!"

Obediently, we began to put our hands together. Kippy stopped us.

"Wait, let me finish. I'll tell you when. So these guys...and Lisa. Ha!"

Our one Sales woman shot fast thumbs up over her head. There were a few laughs. Kippy knew how to break the tension in a crowd. He grinned like a game show host. "These guys and Lisa, he repeated; "well, what they're doing is so extraordinary, I'm telling you I'm blown away. The numbers coming in? They're through the roof! I don't usually point people out, but I gotta make a special mention of Roger Didilian. Where's Roger?"

"Silver Spring," Scott called out from his usual post, by his own office door.

The hand that wasn't holding Mr. Microphone pumped the air. "Ha! Of course! With our new client, Boxer Trading! Most of you don't know that name. But I bet you all know Bamboo Barge, am I right? Well, Boxer Trading is the parent company, and Roger just got their Business Operations division to sign with us."

"And Dave Broussard!" Scott bounced over the built-up soles of his mirror-polished shoes.

Kippy pointed to where Dave was standing with a bunch of Sales. "That's right. Can't forget our IT maven. We had some tricky technology questions from Boxer. Dave jumped right in, helped clinch the deal. It's only a foot in the door for now, but when we deliver the kind of quality service that Pinnacle is famous for, this is gonna end up being even bigger than MSY. You catching this, Clifton? I wanna be sure Roger gets to see it later."

"We're rolling, Kippy!"

"Ha! Okay then, NOW you can applaud!"

We actually wanted to applaud. Bamboo Barge was a national chain. Even a small contract could lead to some major numbers. We wondered how Roger had conned them into it. Obviously not by giving MSY as a reference.

"Terrific, absolutely terrific!" Kippy beamed. "I would say I feel like Terry Francona, except I'm too good a Yankees fan."

Someone in Sales let out a big "Woot! Woot!" We got to laugh again.

"Okay now, settle down. Getting serious. We had a little setback with MSY. I'm not going to pretend we didn't. Not with this crowd. You're all bright, gifted...You know when we have a rough patch. Thing is, we always get through it, together. And that's why I wanna make one more announcement before I open the floor. Pinnacle can't succeed unless every person in this room is working at peak excellence and we all pull together. We can't afford to be average. We can't be the kind of people who think 'good enough' and then just sit back. We need to go above and beyond. Now, when people give more than 100 percent, I want you to know we notice. Me and Scott, Gary, Milla. You can be sure of that. All of us, we do. Wesley here. Len...And if what you're doing is really extraordinary, well, we think you deserve more than just a pat on the back."

We were starting to get excited. It was no surprise, after the Thanksgiving layoffs, to walk out of a performance review with a bump that didn't even cover inflation. A bonus would be extremely welcome. In the wake of the MSY deal last year, we'd each gotten a check for one percent of salary. A few hundred bucks wasn't a lot, but you could certainly do something with it. We all stood a little straighter and leaned in.

Kippy caught the ripple of intensity and spoke to it. "So moving forward, we're going to give out a limited number of options."

It was worth being near Feldman, just to watch his face turn an even paler shade of his usual pasty. Alex Silva said later that Channing reached out to catch him in case he passed out, but Alex was a drama queen. We did believe Marla, though, when she said Feldman closed his fist so tight that the pen he was holding cracked right in half, and that Feldman didn't even notice it until Gene passed him a handkerchief to mop up the blue.

"Only to reward really extraordinary achievements," Kippy clarified. "Which, since you're no longer going to stop at being average, means I may have to give away a big chunk of Pinnacle. Ha! Okay, then. Opening the floor to your questions. Eric?"

Channing's feverish eyes made him almost animated. "First let me say thank you, Kippy. This is a tremendously generous offer you're making." We still weren't sure what, if anything, this all meant, but we pitched in with some applause. Kippy looked modestly at his shoes. "My question is, what will the criteria be for earning options?"

"The details are still under discussion." Feldman choked the words out so quickly he almost swallowed them.

"Of course official guidelines need to be vetted by the Board before we can socialize them."

Jo Vargas was almost as horrified as Feldman. "There are compliance issues that have to be considered."

Kippy looked as if they'd taken away his pony. "Yes, well, we have to finalize the details. You know, options are like getting a piece of the company. If we were to maybe go public someday, they'd be very valuable. We'll only give them at a certain level, and I hope every one of you will work to get promoted to that level."

We weren't satisfied, but even Channing knew we weren't going to get any more. He nodded and shrunk back into his usual pose.

"Other questions? Anybody?"

The silence went on a bit too long. "So what are you reading?" Clif was nothing if not dependable. All of us, including Kippy, laughed.

"Michael Raynor's new book. *The Strategy Paradox*. Terrific stuff. About unpredictability, how leaders have to make strategic decisions when the future is uncertain. Very timely. Brilliant guy, Raynor. He says the worst thing you can do when things are unpredictable is to stand still. Right? Just what I always say. And I don't have a PhD from Harvard. Ha! You gotta take risks, no matter what. That's part of being a leader. Making decisions. You can hear me say this: I never make a bad decision. And I mean that. Because it's always better to do something. For example, it was not a bad decision to hire Centient. We may have lost a year and—Ha! Gary's gonna kill me for saying this—and a lot of money, but we learned a valuable lesson. We need to rely on ourselves, not on some so-called experts. Which is something we wouldn't have learned if we didn't give it a try. So I stand by what I said. I never made a bad decision. Only sometimes I don't get the results I want."

Δ

```
From:          Josefina Vargas
To:            Pinnacle Leaders
Subject:       Employee Departure
------------------------------------
```

Noble Landrum is leaving Pinnacle, effective September 30, to pursue other opportunities. We wish him well in all his future endeavors.

```
Josefina Vargas, Dir. Talent Management
Pinnacle Management Services
```

Δ

```
From:          Milla Kristol
To:            All Pinnacle Associates
Subject:       Congratulations to George Waters
------------------------------------
```

Please join me in congratulating George Waters, our new Vice President of Fulfillment!

```
Milla Kristol, EVP Fulfillment Services
Pinnacle Management Services
```

Δ

The wheels kept snagging on invisible threads, or maybe it was the weight of stuff piled on the seat that was causing the resistance. Judy gave it one final shove. Her cargo wobbled down the inner aisle, almost reaching the right cube.

"Tah-dah!" She straightened carefully. She resisted putting her hand on the small of her back; it would make her look like an old lady, not a good idea if you wanted to keep working.

Mike Venture looked up from the battered cardboard file box he was unpacking. Her offering was an ordinary black office chair. He blinked. "Huh?"

"It's yours. The one you said you had all broken in. Noble took it over when they shipped you upstairs. You may as well have it back."

"I thought the goodbye party was Friday."

"He's officially gone Friday. But his wife is getting a sonogram this morning. Anyway, he said you can have it now."

"What's this stuff?" He peered into the black plastic container weighing down the seat. "Aren't these my books?"

"The ones you left for Ginny." There was a relish of satisfaction in her voice. When the world swings out of orbit, you do what you can to restore the balance. "Also some PMI booklets that were Harvey's. No one else needs them. If you don't, just dump them. Speaking of which, please note that I'm giving you a trash can."

Used paper was supposed to be disposed of in the shredder bins. With so many people eating at their desks, any desk-side trash containers that pre-dated the security policy were a precious commodity. Mike was suitably grateful, quickly dumping out the container and hiding it in the shadows. The contents scattered across his desk, an explosion in a Staples warehouse. "So what's this for?"

"I'm the scavenger queen. After HR boxes up the personal stuff, I go through the desks. I set up our own supply shelves in Harvey's old cube. Keeps us from having to run upstairs every time we need a pack of Post-its. Plus, there's the stuff Feldman won't okay any more. Like the good headphones—they only give them to client-facing now, you know. And dry erase markers. Why are there never enough of those? Makes sense not to let anything go. Think of this as a housewarming present. Welcome back to the hood."

"Don't you need these?" he pointed to a shrink-wrapped packet of spiral notebooks.

"We've got plenty. If you don't need them, maybe someone else on your team will." They'd shifted half the floor last week, clearing out the end aisle of desks for Lloyd Baptiste's TQM group. There was enough room on four for either TQM or Finance to move and free up some space on eight. Feldman gave a pack of reasons for why it couldn't be his team, so Milla had to migrate her Center of Excellence. They were always walking around anyway; it didn't much matter where they technically sat. Judy eyeballed the other cubes curiously. "Where *is* your team?"

Mike shrugged. "Lloyd's not in today. The new kids, Hugo and Khosi, are shadowing Fulfillment this week. It's not like they have anything to move. Freddie never had a place to set up their boxes downstairs."

"Khosi? Is that male or female?"

"Oh very female." Mike waggled his eyebrows. "And she's African. I mean *African* African. You should have seen Scott's face when they were introduced. I think Marla's finally going to get some peace."

"Someone ought to warn her. Khosi."

"I tried. You should have seen the look she gave me. Like she pitied me for being so stupid. She's a little scary. You can see the wheels going round."

"Has Peterson seen you yet?"

"He passed me on his way to the men's room. Smiled. You know. That smile. What did he say when they told him we were moving up?"

"No clue. By the time he called an all-hands to tell us, he was passing out new floor plans and telling us how great it was for IT. That having TQM here would put us in closer touch with Fulfillment and Client Care, keeping us an integral part of Pinnacle…No, wait, I want to get this right. Not integral…"

"And here's my roommate!" There was genuine warmth in Mike's voice.

Edie staggered towards them from the elevator, followed by Freddie and her monitor. Mike hurried to grab her heavy box and set it on the desk across from his.

With a wan smile, Edie let her laptop case drop onto the outside arm of the L.

Judy darted a glance over her shoulder. No one else was in view. She gave Edie a quick hug. "Are you okay? I couldn't believe when I heard. George Waters? What is it the kids say? WTF? "

"Could have been worse," Edie sounded matter of fact. "They could have cut me loose."

"Kippy respects you too much," Mike said.

"And Feldman knows I'm cheap. Cheap enough to make it worth milking me for whatever they can get. I'm supposed to be 50/50 between TQM and whatever Milla thinks she needs out of me for Fulfillment. Not exactly calculated to make me feel secure."

"Sounds to me she's basically admitting Waters can't do the job." Judy's nose did what it does when you smell vinegar.

Edie shrugged. "Does it matter? What is it you said when Peterson pushed you out? My desk is still moving closer to the exit."

Mike sat back in his old chair, pushing it until it creaked. "Yeah. Probably. I don't think I have too long, not with Baptiste bringing on all these kids. But I'm learning a lot. I'm not putting on a happy face. You'll see. This Trim/Delta thing could be good. I mean out there."

"I hope you're right. I'd better learn fast. I can't afford to be out of a job."

Δ

It was, hands down, the biggest party in the history of Pinnacle goodbyes. Noble Landrum had been with the company so long that he knew pretty much everybody, and anyone who ever met him liked him. Even newbies who'd only heard about him wanted to wish him well. Everyone below C-level who was at all worthwhile—and a few dubious characters like Eric Channing—showed up.

Mike Ventura's people were waiting at the odd table that was usually the last spot in Whine Bar to be claimed. It was wedged in the back, between the vestigial wooden phone box and a server station that no one had ever seen used. Hands filled with beer bottles, Mike elbowed his way through the sea of bodies.

Ginny grinned and patted the stool next to her. "You sure you want to be seen with us?"

"Could be dangerous," Mac Fraser agreed. "Screw your career if they catch you with us undesirables."

"Screwed already," Mike said pleasantly, tapping the neck of his bottle against each of theirs in turn. "Salut."

Mac missed these good people. Ten months was a long time. Ten scary months. Hardly anyone seemed to be hiring. The ones who were told him he was over-experienced for what they were offering. He'd finally realized that was a euphemism for old. The only solid offer he had was for military contractor work in Afghanistan. There wasn't much to decide. He hated the idea of leaving Cindy alone with Junior, but they were practically throwing the money at him. One tour would pay enough that the bills would be covered for three years. Plus, a part of him was calling out to be in country again with his guys. He'd shown up early tonight to talk things through with Noble, the only one who would understand. He felt easier in his mind now; he could enjoy the rest of the evening. "Slàinte mhòr."

They all took a deep swig.

"I was hoping to see Edie," Ginny said, savoring that first swallow of hoppy goodness.

Mike shook his head. "Hey, I tried. She never comes to these things. Not even for Noble. She took him to lunch yesterday instead."

"And Judy? She SM-ed me she was leaving at 6 on the dot."

"Probably got caught by Len Strauss. She's helping with something about the website. With no more PMO, I guess they decided she has the bandwidth."

"To do what? And where does she have bandwidth? She had a pile of work that I know of."

Mike shrugged. "She was only working at 110 percent. You know how it is. Got to be at least 150 or they think you're slacking off. She'll be here soon. Strauss has this charming habit. The minute she's headed out the door, he finds something that needs doing asap; something small. Just to prove he can make her stay."

Mac had no idea what they were talking about. "Who's this Strauss?"

"Kippy's pal," Mike said. "The one you used to say reminded you of the Penguin."

"Right! Dick Cheney! Came in every few months and took over a conference room. Used to drive what's her name, Kippy's lunch lady, crazy, always barking orders."

"Bertha. Still does, only now he's got a permanent office. And a title: EVP of New Development."

"Not that anyone knows what that means," Ginny added. "I still say he must have a piece of the company."

"Or at least options." Mike joked at a pair of blank faces. This was after their time. "Aha! The man of the hour!"

Noble pushed towards them with a couple of beers. He set one in front of Ginny with a flourish, then scooped her off her chair in an enormous hug.

People noticed. Noble was a big guy, and he was, as Mike Ventura said, the man of the hour. Whoever didn't see for themselves heard about it later. The rumor was already out there, that he'd quit because of what Peterson did to Ginny. A matter of honor. Not that Noble, with his residual loyalty to Kippy, would admit it. He said he was shortening his commute; they would be moving deeper into Jersey, closer to his wife's parents, after his son was born. It still seemed interesting timing, that a job in Cranbury materialized so soon after Ginny's dismissal had gotten him as angry as clamped-down Marine discipline every allowed him to show. And now there was that hug; and him buying her a beer, when tradition had it that his money was no good here tonight.

We still weren't clear on the details, but we knew Ginny had been equally as blameless as Edie. Edie. If throwing Ginny under the bus was a thunderbolt, then the Bizarroland restructuring of Fulfillment was a seismic event. Even those of us who weren't in Fulfillment were feeling the aftershocks. No one at Pinnacle was more respected than Edie. More than respected, Edie was beloved. It had been unsettling enough when the Execs hired Milla Kristol for the VP slot instead of promoting Edie. That Kristol was determined to marginalize her, and that the LC was letting her pull it off, was so incomprehensible that we tried to believe it was some kind of joke.

"Maybe..." Diego Guzman fortified himself with a large gulp of beer. He was tiptoeing into heresy, but somebody had to say it. "Maybe Waters has some good ideas that we don't know yet."

His friends shook their heads in sorrow at the extent of Diego's need to look on the bright side. Whatever brilliant innovations the new VP of Fulfillment might have up his sleeve, he was currently fully occupied with finding fault and taking umbrage, moving his pieces all over the map with no apparent goal beyond displaying his power. Timid incoherent Bentley Wang had been dragged into Training while Dawn Kollist, who would have been great in the role and had asked for it, was left kicking her heels in Payroll.

"Good ideas?" Tully wheeled on Diego. "You mean like my new job, Onboarding SME for Boxer? Effective Monday, I'm working downstairs with the TQM people."

"Hey, congratulations!" Diego didn't get why Tully and Dawn looked so upset. The job even had a title, almost.

Tully downed the last of his club soda and took a silent poll to see who wanted another round. "I don't fool myself," is all he said before diving through the crowd towards the bar.

Dawn watched after him, her eyes glossy with concern. "It's bogus, you'll see. Waters'll backfill Tully in Payroll. When the implementation is done, there'll be no slot for him."

"He'll be on the Bamboo team!"

"There isn't going to be a Bamboo team." No matter what she said, Archie Gosh's voice remained cool and tranquil. It was why they called her the Client Whisperer. "Milla says the MSY team has, ah, failed as a POC for client-specific cross-functional service. They won't repeat it. I expect they'll soon be taking us apart. Maybe cut us loose."

"The work has to get done, with or without the team. They'll reabsorb you. Tully'll be out on his ear. All because of me."

"Waters definitely has a thing about you." Before his transfer to Client, Hank Iversson had seen it with his own eyes.

"Getting me to cry totally shoots his wad. After that, he's almost nice for a couple of days, like he gets it out of his system."

"It's fucked," Lily Sheehan agreed absently, keeping one eye trained on the guitar cases in the corner. Stail Fiáin had a gig in Brooklyn later tonight.

"It's abuse," Orla chomped down decisively on an orange slice. "I don't know why you don't get HR to do something about it."

"I don't know why I don't go to the moon for the weekend." Dawn rolled her eyes. "What planet are you living on? I reported it to Art Russo, way back. Then I went in to Kay. All they did was listen and look sad. Pathetic. Art came right out and said Kippy was 'very enthusiastic about Waters' potential'. I swear, that's what he said. And he said things would get better once Waters 'did some growing up.' Okay, I'm paraphrasing that bit. But you get the idea. No power to actually do anything. Neither one of them. Neither does Jo. At least Jo had the good grace to get really angry; I felt like less of a moron. She said she'd try to get me transferred to something else. Of course, with Waters running the whole shebang now, there's nowhere for me to go except Client Care. Which I just don't see happening. I worked at FAO Schwartz one Christmas season. I'm so not good at that 'customer's always right' thingy."

"Why the fuck do you hang around?" Hank Iversson, who had a family business he could run to at any time, was one to talk.

"Why do any of us?"

It was a question we didn't like. Maybe it was because we didn't identify ourselves by what we did here. Most of us only wanted to make a decent living so we could have a life. Combine that with the general resistance to change. On our worst days, when we felt the urge to do some random searching, we were easily discouraged. It seemed impossible to match our Pinnacle roles to other job descriptions. The jobs we fit were few and far between, and there was so much competition for the ones that did. A lot of us had friends at other companies who'd been laid off, or knew people who'd gotten new degrees in the spring and still couldn't find a job. Now that things at Pinnacle were getting scary enough to get us off our butts, we were starting to realize we might have left off leaving too long.

"Maybe somewhere else would be even worse. At least here we have each other." Diego put an arm around Dawn's waist.

She brightened. Diego had that effect on people. "I can deal with the Waters shit most of the time. It's only when Tully hears him and goes all Celtic sticking up for me. I keep telling him not to, but you know how protective he is. Waters figures by moving him out he can bully me in peace. Well let him enjoy it while he can. I've been working on my resume. First of the year, I'm going to start looking."

"First of the year? Waiting for your bonus?" Orla smirked. "I wouldn't hold your breath. Iversson is still waiting for his referral."

For all his own griping, Hank always turned defensive when someone else brought it up. "End of the year," he mumbled, turning redder than two beers warranted. "Scott promised me."

Dawn patted his arm. It was a night for benevolence. "Well, Kippy keeps telling us how well we're doing. It'd be a shame to cut out and hear I'd missed out by a week or something."

Even those of us who found change the hardest to contemplate were giving it some serious thought. If business was so great, why was Sales suddenly sweating to hit a monthly quota instead of competing against their own personal best? Thanks to Roger Didilian who, eccentrically refusing to regard everyone outside Sales as losers, actually spoke to the rest of us, we all knew that everyone who didn't meet it was getting that black mark that could lead to being cut, a new tactic that explained the hunted expressions on a couple of older salesmen who relied on a steady trickle of small accounts. With work volume rising for Fulfillment, the happy-path result of Sales feverishly driving cash cows to the slaughter, why were team leads told there was no question of new hires, and instructed to hold off on backfilling spots left open by attrition? The MSY team was burning through overtime at such a rate that Feldman had given them a hard limit, and they still couldn't hack themselves out of the weeds. Client Care, left holding the ball, was drowning. As for IT, it wasn't clear that there was a Pinnacle IT department any more. With the plug being pulled on the Centient disaster, the developers and engineers were estimating that a prolonged present at Pinnacle was no more guaranteed than a future and had begun swapping the names of contract recruiters, buffing up their resumes and restyling their hair. Craig Parnes had already been seen on the floor in a shirt that had buttons and a collar.

Despite a firm January 1 start date for Bamboo Barge, and with Baptiste and his TQMers pawing at the gate to make it a proof of concept for a shiny new onboarding procedure, we felt the skies darkening overhead. It was the end of an era; the era when, even if we were only termites and geese, we'd had a sense of being part of something growing and vital. Tonight, we clung together. Noble was taking a piece of our heart with him, or maybe he was just confirming that it was already gone. We would see him off in style.

Whine Bar was packed to the cheesy reproduction rafters. Everyone jostling, drinking, laughing. Jokes that would never be so hilarious when retold. Flashes of brilliant insight and invention that could never be recalled. The Buzzard, whose brain was packed with useless information, started a raucous trivia contest at the bar. Shouts rang out from where Roger and Cal Jiang were having their weekly drunken darts game. Occasionally, Donna DiPinto's gutsy contralto cut through it all with a phrase or two of blues; someone had bought the office manager one too many rounds.

If she hadn't been safely stowed on a stool by the counter that ran parallel to the bar, little Martha Moon would have risked being crushed. Or was she Martha del Monte now? People might not say things outright, but we were pros at picking up clues. The client-facing people who were all on that Facebook thing together said Martha's page only said 'in a relationship.' We searched for confirmation in the way that Gabe fetched her mojito, or in the way she smiled back. We wanted them to have made it legal. We all need something good to think about.

Δ

From *The Peak Experience*

Grooming the Talent Within: Milla Kristol interviews new Vice President of Fulfillment George Waters

At Pinnacle Management Services, our mission is to exceed expectations and establish new benchmarks for excellence. We inspire our talented associates to go above and beyond, provide the tools that enable them to do so, and reward their success. George Waters is a shining example of our corporate culture. Mr. Waters joined Pinnacle as a Fulfillment Associate, initially learning his department from the ground up. As he grew, his talent and dedication were acknowledged by a series of promotions that matched his ever-increasing skills. Recently, I was delighted to appoint him to a newly-created position as Vice President of Fulfillment.

Milla Kristol:

George, let me begin by congratulating you on your new role. And let me add that your promotion is richly deserved.

George Waters:

Thank you Milla. I'm grateful for the confidence that the Leadership Council has shown in me, and especially for your own support. I've learned so much working with you. Your innovations have brought Fulfillment Services into the 21st Century. For example, the improved qualitative metrics and our Trim/Delta Center of Excellence. I really believe the sky's the limit for Pinnacle.

MK:

I agree George. By committing ourselves to continual improvement through Total Quality Management, Pinnacle ensures that we are always striving to provide our clients with the best possible...

Δ

There was finally an upside to Spurious George's temper. When he ripped the pages from Fabiano's hands, if he hadn't yelled "it's this kind of incompetence that's cost us MSY!" it might have taken weeks for us to learn that we'd lost the biggest client Pinnacle Management Services had ever landed. He did yell it; so it took minutes instead of weeks. His red face turned purple when he realized what he'd yelled, and he stomped into his new office. The hollow core door slammed shut behind him with an anticlimactic bang. Fingers snatched up mobile phones and raced across keyboards. Dawn and Raney rushed from their first row seats to the ladies' room, plucking query-faced associates from desks along the way. Freddie, plugging and unplugging through yet another desk shuffle, understood why he was moving Archie Gosh's CPU to George Water's old desk on the border of Training; he made a big show of searching for a "missing" splitter before zipping down the fire stairs to four. The bush telegraph kicked in. Chris Keane drifted over to Gene Siriano's cube and received a button-lipped nod. Gabe del Monte brought his wife a coffee and nodded eloquently at Abby Witherspoon's closed door.

Work poured in. We tried to settle down to it as if it were any other day. Orders were processed, clients soothed, payrolls checked. All the while we felt a twitching in our shoulders, waiting for a carrier pigeon to land with the latest word. A mid-day ripple: closed doors around the office perimeter opened to emit grim-shouldered executives; they converged in Advancement, followed by Bertha with a tray of sandwiches and Kippy's preferred unsweetened iced tea. Bertha was the only visitor to those precincts, conveying coffee and cookies, emerging with empty trays.

They were closeted in Advancement all that day. Not a word was formally released, not the next day, not ever. The MSY group, quietly broken up, was reabsorbed into their original teams. Kippy never called a company meeting. There was no global email announcement. Only gossip and rumor trickled down. It was said that Waters, called to testify, stated flatly that he couldn't be expected to answer for the failure of a project for which he'd only recently taken over responsibility. Kippy supported him; therefore everyone else, including Peterson, who saw no hypocrisy in doing so, agreed. Feldman demanded to know why Milla's expensive Center of Excellence had not resolved the outstanding issues. We heard that Milla shrugged this away, initially implying that Client Care should have been able to manage expectations while TQM analysis was ongoing; then switched gears and fixed the blame solidly on IT for failing to complete OnRamp on schedule the previous year. Feldman, always pleased for the opportunity to blame IT, tabled his anti-TQM project for a later date and jumped on the bandwagon. Word was that Peterson, sniffing danger, countered by expounding on the subsequent flow of successful OnRamp enhancements, produced despite the diversion by Centient of valuable resources that he would have allocated to produce still more; and that he slyly underscored

Milla's original contention that Client Care was not performing to Pinnacle standards of Operational Excellence. We knew that no one dared to blame Feldman for limiting their resources; budget time was upon us and Feldman could easily bite back. We knew that no one would ever blame Sales for over-committing in the first place.

How did we know all this? We just did. The same way that we knew that Milla Kristol had married her first boss, after stealing him away from his original wife, and that Len Strauss had been with the ATF. The same way that we knew about Scott's little trips to Mexico. First secret of Pinnacle? There are no secrets at Pinnacle. People watch and listen. People talk.

Δ

```
From:          Josefina Vargas
To:            Pinnacle Leaders; Client Care
Subject:       Employee Departure
-----------------------------------
Abby Witherspoon is no longer employed by Pinnacle. Ann Ling
will assume responsibility for Client Care until that
position is filled.


Josefina Vargas, Dir. Talent Management
Pinnacle Management Services
```

Δ

What Kippy said at the December monthly meeting was that the economy was a little soft, but he assured us that this was no reason for concern. On the contrary: a soft economy was actually good for Pinnacle. As companies trimmed down, they had more need to outsource their office services to us. Kippy went on to give major kudos to Sales for what was looking to be the best fourth quarter in Pinnacle history, and to announce that Len Strauss had been put in charge of an exciting new initiative to beef up our public website. Bearing in mind this continued pace of expansion, we must be more committed than ever to Operational Excellence. The TQM team was setting up a "Waste Basket" on the share drive, to collect ideas for places where those of us "in the trenches" might have spotted an opportunity for process improvement. There would be appropriate bonuses, of course, for any suggestions that might be acted on. Our ripple of suppressed snark, as we mentally adding this to the list of uncollectible bonuses and bounties, only registered as attentiveness to Kippy.

He beamed. "And to continue supporting our overall professionalism, to rise to new heights," he continued, with a nod in Gary Feldman's smug direction, "Pinnacle has a new non-fraternization policy!"

We turned as one body to stare at Jo Vargas, so quickly she couldn't conceal her shock. Once again, the Leadership Council hadn't thought it necessary to discuss human resource issues with the Director of Talent Management. How was she supposed to handle this? There were several existing couples at Pinnacle. One less, now that Tully Mulhern had indeed been canned, but at least three others. Was Jo expected to terminate one of each pair? If so, there was no way she was going to can her own assistant, so Liz Dorn would be out. And Gabe del Monte, because Kippy would never let her get rid of Martha.

Before Martha and Gabe could reach her, Jo was already in Kippy's office, listening to Feldman pontificate about best practices and elevating Pinnacle's standing in the marketplace.

"Every top company has this on the books. It's an anti-harassment policy. You should be all for it."

"Yes. But how have you decided to handle our existing couples?" Jo demanded.

It hadn't crossed Kippy's mind that there might be existing couples. Perhaps he thought, subconsciously, that relationships were a luxury his young employees couldn't afford. He turned to Feldman for an answer.

Feldman gave a non-committal shrug. "That would appear to be a Talent Management decision."

"Ah, so do I terminate Gabe del Monte or Martha Moon?" Jo knew how sentimental Kippy was about Martha.

"Martha?! That great little gal? Don't blame this del Monte kid for asking her out."

"Married," she informed him. "They got married over the summer."

Feldman didn't blink. Because he insisted on signing off on all Pinnacle payroll adjustments, he'd known immediately when the del Montes had changed their W4s and made one another the beneficiary for their life insurance policies.

"Isn't that terrific! He's the tall kid with dark hair, right? Well spoken. One of Edie's. Ha! Good for him! He'd better make Martha happy!" Kippy seemed oblivious that his new policy might have the opposite effect, just as he was always forgetting that Milla had sidelined Edie.

"One of our top Trainers, I understand. George Waters gave him an excellent review last quarter. It'll be a shame to see him go."

"A shame," Kippy echoed, his brow furrowed. "But we can't lose Martha. Knows everything there is to know about the business. Hard worker, too. And loyal."

"Mmm." Jo sighed portentously. "Well, she's always been extremely professional. I'm sure she'll understand it's for the good of the company. Maybe not right now, but in time. Assuming she decides to stay."

When the policy email went out, it included the rider that existing relationships would be grandfathered in as long as (a) they were reported to Talent Management by the end of the week and (b) one member of the couple did not directly report to the other. Four other couples came forward to register.

Δ

Email exchange between Judy Schreiber, Technical Writer and Leonard K. Strauss, EVP New Development

```
Monday, 14:26 PM
From:          Leonard K. Strauss
To:            Judy Schreiber
Subject:       White Papers for public site
-----------------------
As I expected, it took ten minutes to find writers eager to
take this project on as piece work and at a very reasonable
price. Expect two papers on payroll management by end of next
week. That is what I mean by results. We will publish
whichever is better.


===========================


Wednesday, 20:19 PM
From:          Leonard K. Strauss
To:            Judy Schreiber
Subject:       Grace Scott white paper
-----------------------
Attached is our first white paper. The other candidate did
not meet expectations. I doubt John Cooper is his real name.

This one is good enough. Clean up the English and check we
have sufficient iterations of the SEO keywords provided by
OptiSearch.


===========================


Thursday, 8:57 AM
```

From: Judy Schreiber
To: Leonard K. Strauss
Subject: Grace Scott White Paper - question

Len,

I've edited Grace's white paper and verified the keywords, as requested. Edited version is attached.

I've also taken the liberty of reformatting the document to give it a more polished appearance consistent with Pinnacle-branded collateral. If this format meets with your approval, I'll create a style guide we can provide to experts who are contracted to write future white papers.

I notice that the paper includes no identification of Grace Scott other than her name. Do we have a title? Professional association? Other websites usually post a brief bio of some sort at the top or end of the white paper, with a link to the guest expert's own website or related professional page. That would be our opportunity to get a backlink on that person's page. Ravi from OptiSearch has emphasized that these backlinks are as critical as the SEO keywords for raising our presence for the search engines. What information do we have for Grace Scott?

===========================

Thursday, 15:52 PM
From: Leonard K. Strauss
To: Judy Schreiber
Subject: RE: Grace Scott White Paper

On reflection, I don't think bio's etc of the writer make sense when they don't add credibility to the article. In this case, I don't think it will. Do you still feel it's worthwhile to pursue?

===========================

Thursday, 17:55 PM
From: Judy Schreiber
To: Leonard K. Strauss
Subject: RE: Grace Scott White Paper

I agree with your point about credibility. In Grace's case, I
don't know anything about her background to be able to decide
if it adds value — does she have anything we can spin?

```
===========================
```

Thursday, 18:07 PM
From: Leonard K. Strauss
To: Judy Schreiber
Subject: RE: Grace Scott White Paper

```
-------------------------
```

A bottle

Δ

It was the same pretty room as last time: evergreens, twinkle lights, white
glass balls frosted to sparkle like moonlit snow. Gossiping in clusters,
laughing self-consciously in their unaccustomed finery, were many of the
same faces. Martha Moon del Monte watched her tall, adorable husband
weave his way back through the crowds with their refilled glasses.

"Why is it always a surprise that so much can change in a year?" she
thought aloud. "Do you realize? At last year's party, we weren't even
dating."

"Yes you were, you just didn't know it," Alex Silva teased. "Aw, made
you dimple! You guys are too cute. I'm thinking we should start calling you
Gartha."

"Gartha?"

"Like Brangelina. Or we could go with Marbriel. Your choice. Personally
I think it sounds too much like a Disney villainess, but it..."

"Why can't you use our regular names?"

"I am trying to drag this place into the 21st century. No one else has
anything that remotely works. I mean we've got half of Dully over here. Or
do we use their stripper name, Tawn?"

The margarita sputter wasn't pretty, but it was the first laugh anyone had
pulled out of Dawn all evening. If Waters hadn't given his people a mandate,
she wouldn't have come at all. Everything about this party seemed calculated
to emphasize that Tully was no longer part of it. She'd rather be home with
him tonight, and she felt no need to pretend otherwise.

"What about Orla and Carl?" Archie Gosh proposed. Orla had come in
after Thanksgiving with a ring tattooed around her marriage finger.

"Seriously? Orrrrlll? I sound like a fucking a pirate."

"They'd probably like that," Will Compton observed.

210

"You're probably right."

"Who would like what? Miss me gorgeous?" Gabe dropped a light kiss on Martha's upward-tilted face. "Okay, so who would like what?"

"Most people would like a lot of things," Alex said. "I, for example, would like Neil Patrick Harris and a villa on Lake Como."

"Mmmm," Archie agreed. "Except I'd rather have David Beckham."

Will put on his quizzical face. "I don't know. World peace sounds kind of nice."

"Then you'd never get a job with the State Department," Dawn observed.

"Touché."

"I'm happy with what I already have." Martha dimpled again.

They all turned expectantly to Gabe. He paused, thoughtfully. "If we have to say...well, I might like a jacket like the Buzzard's."

Alex couldn't stop himself. "A Cuban in a gold brocade dinner jacket? Who are you, Ricky Ricardo?"

Dawn waited for the hoots to die down and lifted her glass in the direction of the bar. "Me, I'm a simple girl. I'd just like it if Pinnacle stopped picking assholes for MVP."

We followed her eyes to the far end of the bar, to where Eric Channing, brazen with approbation, his award clutched in his shield arm, had worked his way between George Waters and the CFO.

Feldman stood at his usual party station, one foot on the brass rail, one elbow on the bar. One eye was trained, always, on the bartenders; the other flickered over the faces of those who found it expedient to court him at this social occasion. As well as the two most recent MVPs, there was Clifton Speck, carefully buttering the side of his bread that faced away from Wesley Peterson's pavement. The always prudent Gene Siriano, and other members of the Finance department, took it in turn to pay their own respects. Cradling two fingers of something that was presumably not one of the lesser brands whose consumption he was monitoring, Feldman occasionally nodded at one or another of his petitioners, causing the others to visibly recalculate their positions.

Above the general din, we could hear cheers and woots from the long table claimed by Scott's merry men. There was probably an arm-wrestling tournament going on. We didn't bother to verify. There usually was, at this point in the evening, once the awards had been given out and Marla allowed to mingle with the rest of the party. Arm wrestling fit with Scott's attitude towards good clean manly fun, and the guys built up a good thirst for Roger and Craig's secret after party. We weren't surprised to see Khosi at Scott's elbow; with Lloyd's apparent acquiescence, she'd honed in on Sales almost from day one and Scott, predictably, was thrilled to have her around. That the Buzzard had joined the wrestlers was confirmation of how hard he was working to be seen as Scott's man. He would have had more fun if he'd disappeared into the dark far corner, where Peterson had gathered the remaining developers and engineers and was plying them with drinks beyond the quota. The laughter from that direction sounded a lot more genuine than what came from the other Executive orbits.

There was one of those odd pockets of silence that eventually occurs in any noisy gathering. A loud "Ha!" rang out, drawing our eyes back to the bar where Kippy, pop-eyed with delight, held court at the other end from Feldman. As spouses were not invited to the annual holiday party, Gretchen acted as his consort for the night. This didn't please Milla Kristol, who'd chosen to join the preeminent retinue rather than setting up a lesser one of her own. We could see the industrious vivacity with which she appreciated whatever sally of Lloyd Baptiste's had caused Kippy's reaction. She visibly shook with laughter. There was a laser flash from her hefty diamond as she chose to steady herself with a clutch at Kippy's forearm. Marcy Melcher would have been highly satisfied by her husband's instinctive recoil and the momentary strain of politeness around his smile. Baptiste, lolling against the bar with his usual nonchalance, must have felt the eyes watching. He looked out into the party and winked, perhaps to someone in particular or maybe just to anyone who might notice. He grinned and resumed his spiel, adding gestures. Milla wisely chose to show sudden hilarity by lifting both her hands to her mouth. Kippy laughed again. Even the usually stone-faced Leonard Strauss cracked a smirk.

"Must have been one hell of a funny story." Judy Schreiber stabbed her toothpick at a passing tray and speared a steamed dumpling.

Mike Ventura's hand wiggled a mezzo-mezzo flip. "Sometimes it's just the way Baptiste says things. You should hear our weekly meetings."

"We do," she noted drily. "Focus isn't actually sound-tight. As Craig Parnes might be able to confirm." Though the identity of his partner had been politely concealed, most people in IT knew about the conference room assignation back in April. Even without that, we knew his clever bad-boy persona had cut a fair swathe through the women of Fulfillment and Client Care. When the new non-fraternization policy was announced, there was a scramble to start a pool for how long it would take him to get caught.

"Oops. I'll tell him we should take it down a notch."

Something about the CEO's chuckling posse caught Judy's eye. She craned her neck for a better squint. "I didn't realize Gretchen was that far along."

"Is she pregnant?"

"Oh, come on!" It was men, Judy thought, the oblivious sex, who'd come up with those stork and cabbage patch stories. "I know it's a babydoll, but you can see how she's filling it out."

Mike eyed the float of silvery tissue. "So that's a babydoll! When Kitty was describing bridesmaid dresses to me, there was something about a babydoll, just in case one of her cousins got pregnant. I had no idea what she was talking about. Very educational things, weddings. I can't believe how much I've learned about porcelain."

"And crystal?"

"No. That I taught her. It was my first love when I was a kid. Glass. Seriously. I found this place in Brooklyn where I could sweep the floors and learn. Loved every minute. Then my Uncle Ed hauled me out and burned my ass. Gave me one hell of a lecture about how a glassworks was no place for any self-respecting Sicilian. That's when he started teaching me about wood. Eh." The big man shrugged, his black suit jacket making a seismic shift above tonight's lapis blue dress shirt. "When God closes a door..."

"Yo, Mike!" Hugo Singer dipped past on his way to the bar, carrying a plate of baby pastries and a wad of napkins. "Hey, uh, Judy!"

"Hugo," she smiled, amused by the quick flash of relief that lit his face at remembering her name.

"Either you guys seen Edie? Lloyd was kind of asking about her."

"Ladies Room," Judy lied smoothly. After spending sufficient time with Kippy, Edie had slipped away. She'd wanted to protect the kids in Fulfillment, who would have been seen socializing with her if she'd stayed. "If I see her, I'll let her know you were asking."

Mike grinned hard and changed the subject. "Yeah, me too. Hey are those cannolis?"

Poised on the balls of his feet, Hugo frowned at his plate like an uncertain puppy. "I don't know what Milla likes, so I took a few of everything. They just put them out, over there." He pointed with his elbow and cleared his throat, too polite to leave, but impatient to make his delivery. His tuft of gelled hair quivered.

"We'd better grab some before they're gone." Mike kindly released him.

Relief again brushed Hugo's face as he moved to go. "There's coffee," he paused to call back. "But no lattes." He shook his head over such a sad omission and disappeared into the partiers.

"Isn't he well trained?" Judy hadn't noticed before. Since the TQM team had migrated their desks to the fourth floor, Hugo was rarely sitting at his. "I hope Milla wasn't waiting for a latte."

Δ

From: Scott Bell
To: All Pinnacle Associates
Subject: Client Relations

With the start of the new year, there will be some exciting changes to our client-facing division. I have spoken directly to those employees who are impacted by this information and wanted to share it with all of you as well.

To begin with, the department will now be known as Client Relations, a name that more accurately reflects the dynamics of the services performed by this team.

Moving forward, while continuing to look for opportunities to improve alignment with Sales, Client Relations will be positioned organizationally to work in tighter coordination with Fulfillment. In the refined organizational structure, Client Relations will report through Milla Kristol. Milla will continue to work closely with Kippy on all Operational matters, while teaming with me on Client Relations matters.

Milla will work collaboratively with Client Relations Management in defining future plans. Pinnacle has begun to explore options for the Vice President of Client Relations role. Ann Ling will continue to lead the group until that position is filled.

Scott Bell, President
Pinnacle Management Services

12 SCALABILITY

"Now that kind of thinking…" Lloyd Baptiste tipped his chair so far back that it grazed the frame of the Be the Geese poster on the conference room wall. He narrowed his eyes at George Waters. "That there is just *cooyon*." He shot a grin around the room, wagging a finger to telegraph that he was feeling mischievous. "Ahhh? Hmmm?"

Lately, the Director of TQM seemed to think almost everything was *cooyon*. which the Buzzard said meant something like silly. If that were so, Edie Brewer thought it was pretty damned *cooyon* of him to say this when so much was at stake. Mike Ventura agreed. She saw the red dot from his laser pointer scud across the projected workflow map before he blinked it out. Mike would lead the project, if it went through; a likelihood that was getting slimmer by the minute as their leader continued to loll, pushing his boots against the table's brushed aluminum pedestal, rocking his seat ever so slightly. For a man who made his living by clarification and streamlining, Baptiste's thought processes were perversely obscure, especially when he'd just come back from lunch. Edie wished this were a morning meeting. Right now, she wouldn't have bet a nickel on what Baptiste thought he was doing.

The proposal under discussion was using Boxer as the POC for a set of new workflows. TQM was presenting to the leaders of all teams that would be involved, most of whom reported to Milla Kristol. It was obvious where the final decision would rest. Milla sat stiffly across the table from Baptiste, her face telegraphing a mild impatience.

George Waters' impatience was not so mild. Above his tight collar, his ears, and what could be seen of his neck, had started to redden. "What the hell does that mean, Baptiste?"

"It means, Mr. Waters, that dog won't hunt. What you're saying doesn't fit. Remember all those lessons learned we gathered up from MSY, me and Mr. Ventura? That long *long* list of what not to do?" Lloyd popped the ever-present wad of nicotine gum in his cheek for emphasis. "And then, me and my team here, we dedicated the better part of two months working out how to do it right. We drilled down so deep into every process , it was like mining for magma. Mapping 'em down to the last decision point. Calling out the waste. Shining light on the gaps."

"Would you get to the damned point?"

"My damned point…" Lloyd leaned forward suddenly, his chair releasing with a loud snap. "My point is that we already showed you that the weak link is manual workflow. Papers get lost. There's too much room for human error. Now automation, done right, would prevent that. Without automation, things only get worse as your volume increases. Exponentially worse. The load we're fixing to heap on your people with Boxer and with who-all-ever-else our fine Sales organization signs up? You recall that little shut-down we had back in May? That's water off a duck's back compared to what'll happen if we don't make these changes."

"You're telling us to go for automation?! That whole mess in May was because OnRamp couldn't take it! You think I'm going to risk my work process on some blue-sky digital imaging and handwriting recognition crap when Peterson's team couldn't even keep a simple piece of software like OnRamp running?" Waters sneered.

So did Leon Shnapik. Edie caught the Russian developer bristling defensively, his lip curled enough for an ominous flash of gold tooth. Only Simran's cautioning hand on his forearm kept him from joining the argument. Simran was a wise man. This fight was between Milla's two favored gladiators. No one had to tell Edie to keep out of the arena. No one had to tell Mike either, or the perpetually harassed Ann Ling, here to represent Client Relations. As for the youngsters, Khosi and Hugo, they sat at attention against the far wall, eyes flickering from one face to another as they sucked up every word. Maybe it was all for the best that Edie had been benched to TQM. She was too tired to have to worry about the gears spinning around in those hungry young minds, or to deal with this pissing match for that matter. She didn't want to fight or play games; all she wanted was to keep her head down and do the work.

"That shouldn't be our basis for judgment, George," Milla smiled sweetly in the general direction of the two IT representatives. "I think we can all agree that Pinnacle has matured considerably since OnRamp. That particular infrastructure issue has since been addressed, and we understand how to forestall similar issues going forward."

Edie could feel everyone's shock as they digested this statement. Milla and Peterson had been chewing two ends of the same slipper almost since the day she'd arrived. For her to pass up an opportunity to disparage IT was not only surprising, but portentous.

"Whatever decision we make for this project," Milla concluded, this smile leaning more towards carnivorous; "I assure you that we won't proceed without sufficient budget to deliver successfully.

"With all due respect," George huffed, making it clear that he had no respect for any opinion but his own, "any money we spend on automation, we might as well be throwing at bums on the street."

Lloyd spoke with exaggerated patience, slowly shaking his head. "It wasn't automation that lost us MSY, Mr. Waters. It was not having enough of it. Setting aside that bitty infrastructure situation, as it's been suggested..." Lloyd had one particular smile that was as close to a wink as a mouth could get. He turned it on Milla Kristol before beaming it around the room. "With all the power in the world behind it, OnRamp the way it is? That's not gonna alleviate your pain. It's all those manual tasks, that's what has your people snowed under." Lloyd pitched forward far enough to grab the laser pointer out of Mike's hand. He jabbed it toward the screen, punching red dots of excitement at the diagram. "Now look here at what this paperless process is going to save you! Can't have transcription errors if there's no transcription! As for papers falling on the floor or piling up on top of the copier? Not possible. No papers! And just think of what you're doing for her department." He flung out his free hand towards a trembling Ann Ling. "No more waiting on news from your folks, no rummaging through file cabinets. Everything's just a few keystrokes away."

A flicker of hope lit Ann's wan face. Lloyd continued to enthuse about blindingly quick turn-around-times, and extreme scalability, two of Milla's favorite buzz words. Milla's smile remained neutral, but the atmosphere in the room lightened. Mike was permitted to continue with a brief description of the technologies under consideration and the development timeline he'd put together with Simran and Leon. Edie was starting to feel cautiously optimistic, until Waters rose halfway out of his seat to loom across the table, leaning his substantial bulk on his meaty hands.

"So you're saying I have to wait four to six months for you to deliver this magic widget? A waste of valuable time and a waste of good money." Waters was as definite as a weather reporter standing in waist-high waters reporting a flood. "I don't even want to hear the price tag. I could throw 20 more people in India on Fulfillment for pennies. Tomorrow. Now that's scalability! And that's what I'm going to say in my report to Feldman."

The Pune Fulfillment team was an open secret. One of Len Strauss's connections had recommended an ambitious young man. Ashok had been willing to train as a floater, in hopes of someday finding himself wearing a management hat. He'd spent a few weeks in the New York office, then returned to a cube sub-leased from a Pune call center farm. That was this summer. Since then, he'd hired four clerks to work with him, ostensibly to help Data Entry and Payroll catch up with backlog. Waters was confirming what the kids in Fulfillment had been whispering about since Ashok's arrival, that the LC had big plans for offshore.

"Feldman says we can get qualified people in Pune, college graduates with work experience, for less than half of what we have to pay in New York," Hugo piped up. "And that's without considering the savings in office space, even if we could afford all those extra bodies here."

Edie noticed Lloyd's flicker of surprise. Apparently Hugo had been spending more time with Gary Feldman than he'd realized.

Lloyd sighed with exaggerated sadness. "Sure you can staff up. You can staff up from here 'til Doomsday. But you can't keep throwing more people on a broken process and think that's going to fix things. You break an arm, does it help to keep slapping on band-aids? No, you got to get in there and reset the bone; stabilize things so it heals up good."

Waters snorted disparagingly. "Agree to disagree, Baptiste. "

Lloyd shrugged. "My job was to shine some light. I've done that. You want to ignore the facts? Up to you."

For an uncomfortable few seconds, the two men stared each other straight in the eye, neither backing down. Milla looked from one to the other. There was nothing more for anyone else to say.

Finally, Milla stood and smiled brightly around the table. "Well, that was extremely informative. thank you everyone." She gathered up her folders and her Blackberry and marched out of the room. Waters strode quickly after her.

Edie looked at Mike. He sank, deflated, into the nearest chair. "Tick tick tick" he said, under his breath. It had become their grim little private joke. Time was running out.

Δ

Judy Schneider logged in and took her first swig of Monday morning coffee. Today was her day to go through last month's emails, delete the pointless and redundant, and archive all the CYAs.

There was something strange in the air. Usually there was a buzz in the office. Mostly that generic morning buzz of people saying hello and making comments on last night's television. Sometimes it was the cynical buzz that accompanied the visit of a client or a prospect or an auditor, a event often preceded by an email, sent after most everyone had left for the day, saying "no jeans tomorrow, remember the business in business casual". And there was the frantic buzz of a deploy gone wrong or a large client taking a hike: the kind of things for which someone was bound to be thrown under the bus and, if not fired outright, marginalized and made miserable enough that they would walk if they possibly could. What was strange today was that there wasn't any kind of buzz. It was oddly quiet today; stormy day everyone's-having-transport-problems quiet. People sidled in, put away their things and hunched over their terminals in uneasy silence. Only it wasn't actually stormy, even if the sky was the color of an old tin cup you wouldn't want to drink out of. Whatever it was, it was rising in waves off the tweedy butter-bean carpet tiles.

Judy shrugged it off. There was too much to do. If we stopped work at Pinnacle every time there was tension in the air, nothing would ever get done. She scrolled determinedly through her inbox, reading the subject lines and clicking. Delete, delete, delete, move....Every now and then, someone on the floor would cough and her head would jerk to the side like a chicken's to see what might have happened. The task too quickly completed, Judy could no longer avoid prioritizing the mountain of work on her desk. Being old school, she kept a manual "to do" list pinned to her cube wall, annotated with levels of urgency. Highest priority, of course, was anything that someone on the LC had personally requested and had described, reasonably or not, as "ASAP." Next came anything that was a bug up the ass of anybody just below C-level. Then there were the truly urgent things, which should have been top priority except for being bumped by executive fiat. At the bottom of the list were things that only Judy seemed to understand needed doing. Occasionally, but not often enough, one of these would be acknowledged and migrate over to a higher priority before it was too late.

As always, Judy started with the latest LC demand, a new email from Marla, with the subject "Super Urgent for Scott." She noted the time stamp—8:46 p.m.—and was grateful they'd never hooked her to a Blackberry. Some unspecified person in Sales (with Scott requesting, it didn't matter who) needed a standard presentation rebranded for a specific prospect by EOD, logo enclosed. Based on the identity of the prospect, the appointment must have been scheduled at least a week ago, but naturally Sales would leave the presentation to the last minute. Judy wondered why it had landed on her desk. Usually making things pretty went to Graham, the art student who worked as a cold caller in Sales. Graham must be on vacation this week. She retrieved a copy of the standard presentation, hoping that Sales had updated the share drive for once. Marla's logo was obviously, inadequately snagged from the internet. If Judy tried to scale it up to the size needed, it would be a raggedy blur of pixels. She'd have to Google for one with higher resolution. She was so absorbed in the search that her cell phone ring startled her like an alarm clock. She grabbed at it in much the same way. The answer-back said "Mike." Why was he calling her cell and not her extension? "Yeah, hi."

"Hey."

She could hear from the background that Mike wasn't in the office. Her eyes went to her status bar; 10:30 already. Must be another cock up on the trains.

"What's up?"

"I'm downstairs."

"Huh?"

"I told you I was running out of time."

"Oh my God! You're kidding!" She whispered fiercely, looking from side to side and protecting the phone with her hand.

"Nope." The sound was something between a cough and a hoarse chuckle. "What's the prize for being right, huh? They grabbed me when I walked in. I didn't even have time to take off my coat."

"What do you need?" In a company that routinely let people go without a word of warning, we all had arrangements with friends.

"If you can get to my desk, take the picture of Kitty and my tablet and meet me on the corner. That's all. I took home most of the personal stuff back when Peterson threw me under. If you can't get them, come down anyway and wish me luck."

With brisk nonchalance, Judy crossed the floor to the TQM aisle. No one was anywhere near Mike's desk. She quickly unplugged the drawing tablet from the computer, slid the honeymoon photo against it and held it to her chest like a legal pad, tucking the cords and stylus invisibly between them. Mike hadn't mentioned his blueprints mug, but she wasn't about to leave it sitting there. If anyone saw her, they'd assume she was picking up some coffee on the way to a meeting. She grabbed it in her free hand and took the fire stairs down to the lobby.

The cold air felt hard against her thin silk shirt. Judy headed for the alley where the smokers hung out. It was empty now except for Mike, leaning against the damp bricks in his leather jacket, blowing puffs of foggy breath.

The sight of the mug brought out the ghost of a grin. "Thanks. They tell you they'll box up your stuff and mail it to you. I don't care about the books and stuff. But I shelled out almost 400 of my own bucks for this puppy." She watched him stow the tablet carefully in the satchel he used as a briefcase. "The assholes were too cheap to buy me one. Why take a chance they wouldn't be so cheap they'd, uh, forget to pack it."

Her anger kept her warm. "I don't believe this. They don't even let you go back to your desk? I mean, it's horrible the way they stand over you and watch, but at least they used to let you get your stuff..."

"They didn't let any of us. HR has a lot on their plate right now."

"Any of you?"

Mike stopped reorganizing his bag, surprised. "You mean you haven't heard? They didn't say anything?"

"When you called me, did I sound like I'd heard? They never say anything. I'm sure you'll be on that Leaders email on Friday, but I don't get it remember? I only ever know because you tell me..."

Mike started to laugh, not a nervous laugh but a round tickled expression of amusement. "Oh, damn, this is going to be good. It's not just me. There's a whole pack. I don't even know how many. Enough so they had to keep us in separate rooms. Damn, I have to hear how they spin this one. You're going to have to let me know."

Judy shook her head. "I'm being stupid. I don't get it."

"Downsizing," Mike said. "Our positions are being eliminated for the greater good. Have to trim the bottom line to keep the company going through hard times. Scale back. Cut all the unnecessary roles."

"Again? At the last monthly, Kippy said sales were good."

"So he did," Mike agreed. "But the economy is in the crapper. Which makes for a great excuse to cull the herd. More than last time. All the people they want to get rid of."

"You were MVP," Judy objected.

"Two years ago. And that was probably the only reason they didn't cut me lose when Peterson threw me under the bus last year. Kippy doesn't talk to me anymore, but he picks the MVP and you know how he hates to admit he was wrong."

"I never make a bad decision," Judy quoted.

"Exactly."

"But you said TQM was turning out to be a good thing."

"Trim/Delta was, yeah. I'm going to run with that. But you know how it goes. It's all about the love, and Milla never took to me. She likes them nervous or ambitious enough to be trained to fetch and roll over."

"Hugo."

Mike made one of those cryptic Brooklyn Italian gestures. "Not naming names. And it doesn't matter. Just saying, when the dust settles it's going to be really interesting to see who else got chopped. I was in Josefina's office. We had five of us in there. Adam.... Didn't you notice he wasn't at his desk?"

Judy thought. She'd passed Adam's desk on her way to Mike's. "That sweater of his was over the chair. I figured he was in a meeting."

"Oh, he was in a meeting alright. Getting educated about the generous severance package."

"At least there's severance."

He raised his eyebrows. "Two weeks' salary and some links to free websites that host job boards and resume tools. Oh, and compensation for unused vacation, but they have no choice about that. Actually, this is good for you to know. Because we accrue vacation over the year? It counts as earned compensation. If you don't use it and you leave, they legally have to pay you for that time. New York State law. That got me eight days right there. I'm almost sorry about that trip to Italy."

"No you're not. But two weeks? I once got two weeks for being let go early from a summer job. What cheap pricks! I think every dime he saves ends up in Gary Feldman's pocket."

"Well, he saved a lot of dimes today. Me, Adam...and isn't that an unnecessary role, by the way? Why would a company that lives and dies on banks of critical data need a Data Base Administrator? Not to mention how handy he is with the duct tape. I guess they think Freddie can keep this place going all by himself. Or maybe Clif's finally going to get his hands dirty. So, yeah, the two of us, Lily from Client and that strange kid from Switchboard, the one who wears the yellow glasses...okay those aren't big salaries, but I'll bet it adds up. Oh, and Donna. Shawn too, Donna thinks. He wasn't with us. I don't know who they had in the other rooms."

"Wait. Donna?" Judy was dumbfounded. "They fired the office manager? That's an unnecessary role?"

"Strauss treats her like she's an idiot and Feldman hates when she asks for things like new toilet seats. Oh, she's got some good Gary Feldman stories."

Judy shook her head. It was too much to absorb.

"Hey," Mike pulled her into a bear hug. "You'd better go upstairs. You've still got a job. We don't want you losing it until you have to."

She hugged him back tight. Without Mike as her champion, she wouldn't have outlasted Nick Andreas. "I'm going to miss you like hell. Are you going to be alright?"

He nodded. "I'm not worried. In a weird way, I'm kind of relieved. At least the waiting is over. It's probably the best thing that could happen to me. You know how hard it is to start looking unless you have to. Now I'll get out there and find something real, find a place with a future. I got a good deal when I sold the bachelor pad. I should be able to pick up some consulting work to tide me over. And we've got Kitty's health coverage, so we're fine."

"Call me, okay?"

"Promise. Maybe someday one of us will find a good place and bring the gang back together."

"So many good people."

"Misfits and broken toys, and thoroughly excellent," Mike agreed. "We who have been set free salute you." He gave her a mock salute.

Blinking furiously, she watched him disappear in the direction of the subway.

On the way to her desk, Judy craned her neck to see who else was gone. She was usually glad of the extra-high cube walls on four, but not right now. She was too short to be able to see much, except for the bristly shadow of Craig Parnes' close-shaven skull. So Craig was okay. But where Cal Jiang's shiny black thatch should have surfaced behind it, there was nothing. Cal was even taller than Craig; she tended to forget how tall except when she was standing next to him. There was a gap where his head should have been.

Turning down her own aisle, she was comforted by a scant inch of Simran's turban nodding in the cube behind hers. It was dark red today. That meant he was wearing his little girl's favorite, the grey striped shirt with the dark red tie. It was suddenly important to Judy to remember things like that. Slipping behind her desk, she heard a low cough from the cube opposite hers. Danny Zill caught her eye and nodded significantly at his monitor. The sticky note she found on hers said "Lunch @12:30, Diner."

For the next couple of hours, she kept trying to focus on the updates to the Bridge user manual. It was futile. The fourth floor vibrated with suppressed emotions: fear, confusion, anger. She waited for a blast email, for someone to call a meeting; but there was nothing except the cloud of trepidation shimmering in the air, a layer of heat below the fiberglass ceiling tiles. At 12:25, a deliberate five minutes behind Danny, Judy headed out. Peterson's door was still closed and the TQM aisle was still deserted.

Δ

A small group of survivors huddled together in the big booth. Each offered a bit of paper, notes scratched down from whispers passed in the kitchens or toilets. Other than Ann Ling's team meeting, there had been total silence from Management and HR. The assorted group around this table represented most teams, and a nearly complete list of names was patched together over the thick white plates of salty, sweet and always fatty comfort.

Before the day had a chance to become history we'd started calling it Black Monday. Twenty-five people: 18 percent of total staff; twice the amount of the Thanksgiving Massacre. And, as Mike had implied, nearly every person who'd been let go already had a target on his back. A few, like him, had been thrown under the bus for someone else's mistakes. Others had the habit of asking uncomfortable questions. Bonita, the second assistant bookkeeper, was a quiet, diligent girl and universally liked, but she'd been forced by doctor's orders to—horrors!—work from home during the last two months of her difficult pregnancy.

"That's not legal," Dawn objected. "They can't fire someone on maternity leave."

Alex made an interesting face. "Oh, she's not being fired. Her position is being eliminated. The same way they get away with cutting Bertha, who's in a protected category. That's how they do it." Bertha had a slight developmental disability, not to mention being close to sixty, which put her in two protected categories.

Orla couldn't resist. "Guess Kippy's going to be getting his own egg whites from now on."

"Or he'll make Gretchen do it," Freddie Vega suggested. "Want to start a pool?"

No one bit. It was too depressing for a pool.

"Are we sure they didn't dump Gretchen?"

Gabe del Monte's question was roundly dismissed. Kippy relied on Gretchen as much as his Blackberry; indeed we often thought he confused the two of them. Anyway, his congratulations call after the baby's birth had included a plea for her to hurry back sooner than planned, promising her some extra time off when he went away with his family in August. Danny had this straight from Khosi, who was covering Gretchen's desk while she was on leave and had overheard the call.

"Can you imagine him asking Khosi to get his breakfast?" Orla tried to impersonate Khosi's manner of inclining her head, as if from great height and topped with a crown.

"If he did, she'd have him in front of the ACLU before he knew what hit him. That girl is one fierce be-atch." Alex's voice held a note of admiration.

"I don't know. I think she just has a good sense of her own worth. She ought to be in Peanut Butter and Kippy." Hank Iversson had developed something of a crush on her. "We could all learn from her."

"Like all you hand-picked leaders of tomorrow learned from Kippy. Look where PB fucking K got Diego." Alex couldn't stop repeating that name, like worrying a sore tooth. "Hand-picked out on his fucking ass."

"Maybe he shouldn't have told Kippy he'd rather be grilling fish on the beach. Maybe the only reason I'm still here is because I'd take the Iversson account with me."

"You never got that referral bonus, did you?" Judy was often a few beats behind on the gossip.

Hank made a rude noise through his straw. "And I don't think I'm gonna see it any time soon."

"Yeah. But Diego?" Stabbing a fry into a puddle of ketchup, Alex regarded it like a bloody dagger. "Who doesn't like Diego?"

"Who doesn't like any of them? We lost a lot of good people today." Gabe dumped the tiny jelly tubs out of their rack and started building a fort. Both the del Montes were safe, but with Client down to bare bones, lunch scheduling had gone out the window and Martha wouldn't get her break until 2.

"Great people," Danny Zill agreed. "And smart. We're losing a lot of talent."

"All those speeches about how everything's booming, then they make these cuts. Second time makes a habit." Judy pushed a couple of packets of raw sugar towards Gabe. "Sandbags," she said. "Am I the only one who finds it especially troubling that they fired the office manager? Does that mean there's not going to be an office to manage?"

Dawn shook her head. "Just that they don't think it's a real job."

"They will once everything starts falling apart. Who's going to make the call when the copiers break down tomorrow?" Gabe was famous for his bad luck with the copiers.

"I'd say Finance, except the only one who wouldn't think it was beneath her is Bonita. Fucking Feldman." Alex stabbed another fry.

"They'll make Gretchen do that, too."

"HR maybe?" Danny suggested.

"HR will have their hands full processing the unemployment claims and all that. You know how long it took them to turn Tully's stuff around, and he wasn't part of a crowd."

"Maybe they'll hire someone in India," Alex cracked. All he got were puzzled faces. "What? They're putting together an office there. Ann's interviewing Client candidates, only last week. Don't you guys already have some people there?"

Dawn hadn't considered it before. "That floater guy's already turned into four people."

"Wait, Silva, so you think this is a first round? That they're trying to outsource the company to India?" With two incomes at stake, Gabe was twice as nervous as anyone else.

Hank was dismissive. "It'll never happen. Maybe Data Entry and Payroll someday. But nothing else. Think about it. We already *are* the outsource. And the whole premise of Pinnacle is that we're invisible. Can you imagine if Dr. Van Eyssen's evening receptionist suddenly had a Bollywood accent?"

"Who knows what's in their heads? Sheer selfishness, the way they play with people's lives." Judy started twisting her straw into a Mobius strip; her fingers needed something to do. "At my last company, Management lied like crazy. To us, to the press. Everything was a big giant 'misunderstanding.' Then, pow! One morning there was tape across the door and marshals, uniformed Federal marshals, walked us in to retrieve our personal belongings. They searched us, to be sure we weren't taking anything that wasn't absolutely our own." She still shuddered. "They handed us envelopes with two week's pay and that was it. We were out on our ears. And then we got to hear the worst of it on the evening news. All our pension funds, all the savings and portfolios they insisted we keep in house, were gone. We were wiped out. Damn, I hate liars and hypocrites, more than anything." She felt a surge of anger and banged her fist on the table, shocking everybody, including herself. "I hate this! I hate walking around scared that I'm going to come back after lunch and get shown the door."

In the subsequent hush, people politely took extra sips of water or did unnecessary things with flatware.

Dawn reached over and patted Judy's hand. "At least this time all you'll lose is a paycheck."

It was one of those times when the tension is so great that a mildly amusing comment sends a group of people into hysterics. They were wracked with giggles that didn't end. Gabe tried to choke back a laugh and it turned into hiccups, making the others laugh harder.

The waiter rather pointedly brought them their check. It was time to get back, anyway. Assuming, that is, that they still had jobs.

"Fuck them," Freddie said comfortably, counting out the change, "if they're going to fire more of us, I wish they'd just get it over with and let us know."

"We should all just walk out right now!" Orla's eyes shone with audacity.

"We can't afford to," Dawn reminded her.

Δ

On Thursday at 10 a.m., except for one Switchboard associate, and Martha and Alex who were holding the fort for Client, the full staff of Pinnacle Management Services filed silently into the Pit. For once, no one lagged at the rear. Drawing closer to the people with whom we shared the deepest bond, we stayed front and center, as if daring him to look us in the eyes. The only bodies shadowed by the columns were those of Senior Management, every one of them present and accounted for.

From the windowsill, Kippy looked down into a sea of staring faces. He was known to be pretty nearsighted. Maybe all he saw were blurred disks surrounded by aureoles of fuzz. Or maybe he was focusing beyond us, addressing his speech to the video display where Sales wins were flashed to inspire competition among the troops. Arranging his face into its most serious lines, Kippy cleared his throat. Mr. Microphone turned the sound into truck tires on gravel.

"I'm told there's been some confusion about what happened a couple of days ago." He shot a quick glance at Jo Vargas, hugging herself by the water cooler. We couldn't tell what Jo was thinking, her face was that buttoned up.

Kippy cleared his throat again and made a show of plunging into the fray. "Okay, you know how much I believe in keeping things transparent. We can't always be proactive about this, as I'm sure you can understand. But rest assured that I'm standing here now to bring you up to speed. First, I want to clear up a major misconception. Someone asked me, if sales have been so strong these last two quarters, why are we downsizing? The answer is simple. We did not downsize. We *right-sized*. As you know, better than anybody, Pinnacle Management Systems is a strong and vibrant company. Thanks to our All-Star Sales team under Scott Bell, we've experienced an unbroken trajectory of growth every quarter for eight consecutive years. You know what kind of record that is, every single quarter? Amazing growth. And this remains the case, right up to now. Now you also know that when we draw up our annual staffing budgets, everything is based on sales projections and the related increase we anticipate in Fulfillment and support volume. It's all calculated using several years' worth of same-day-comparison data. Isn't that correct, Mr. Channing?"

From his front row spot, Eric Channing gave a satisfied smirk over his shoulder. His eternal pinstriped suit jacket looked as he'd slept in it.

"We were projecting growth. And we scaled up to match the volume of that projection. But we were wrong. Now this is no negative reflection on our terrific Sales team. What they manage to do in this economy is nothing short of incredible. These guys are super heroes! But the economy is in a downturn. The smaller companies that are our bread and butter, they're all cutting costs. We're staying in the picture by reminding them how much money our services save them, but there are some companies that are panicking. And we see it on the news every day, how companies with names we all know are trimming down or going out of business. I'm not going to lie to you. It's hard out there and I would say it's going to be a solid year, maybe as long as eighteen months, before we see any positive change. Meanwhile, we're not going to bring in the volume of work we originally projected. As difficult as it was for me to do, I had no choice but to decide to bring our staff back down to a size more appropriate to the new reality. To the right size. This wasn't easy for any of us. We made sacrifices in every single department, across the board. The people we had to let go, I feel bad about them. They're all fine people. But it was a choice between right-sizing us, or risking it all. We made the cuts we had to make and now we're exactly where we should be. To stay alive in this economy, you gotta make the hard choices. And I assure you that I will always make whatever decisions are necessary, no matter how tough, to keep this company healthy!"

Kippy struck his best motivational speaker stance and held it while that statement rang out across the otherwise silent floor. Perhaps he expected applause. His hands came back to earth and something close to a thoughtful frown twitched at his mouth. He tapped a finger on the side of Mr. Microphone. "Okay, I understand everyone's feeling a little unsettled right now. And I know…You think I don't hear you, but I know. You're concerned this might not be the last adjustment we have to make. Look, I don't have a crystal ball, but right now there is nothing for any of you to worry about."

Those of us who thought to look at Jo saw a brief spasm of pain wash across her face. Kippy didn't notice. Arms spread wide to embrace the room, he barreled on.

"Look around at this great team! Everyone who is standing here now has been hand-picked. You are the best and the brightest, and together we're

227

going to weather this economy and come out stronger than ever. We have to double the customer base, and then we'll be fine. And if we double again, we'll be extraordinary. We'll come up with new products and sell them as effectively as the old products. I'm not saying it's gonna be easy, not for any of us, but we have the talent, and we're prepared to do the job. If we all do a better job, if we overachieve and outperform the level of talent we are blessed with, we will accomplish amazing things. I know it's going to be hard on all of us to make this adjustment. But I believe in all of you and I know that Pinnacle is gonna keep doing great things. We are so much better than our competition! We're not perfect, but we're driving up the ramp. None of our competitors are growing as fast as we do. We will prosper during these difficult times and we will win this race!"

Δ

Milla leaned forward on her pointy elbows, resting her chin in her clasped hands. She smiled the tight little smile she reserved for other women and any man she wasn't trying to win over. "Close the door."

It usually stayed open until Lloyd's predictably late arrival. They resisted exchanging glances while Khosi, being closest, took the cue. Milla hardly waited.

"I'm sure you know that Lloyd Baptiste was hired on a one year contract." It wasn't so very long ago that Milla relished saying Lloyd's name. Now she practically spat it out. "We're not renewing that contract. Lloyd will be working out his remaining weeks from home, in an advisory capacity. 'Quality Management Through Continuous Improvement' will remain a key part of our mission statement, but I'm convinced that the expense of maintaining a dedicated team far outweighs the benefits. The TQM team is being disbanded."

Despite the sudden fireworks in her cranium, Edie kept her face bland. She noticed Khosi's eyes shift in a flicker of calculation. Hugo's grin showed a complete lack of surprise.

"I will be meeting one on one with each of you to discuss your new roles in detail, but I see no reason to keep you in suspense." Milla seemed almost annoyed to have to deal with such pesky trivialities. "Hugo will be leading the new Pinnacle Special Projects team."

Hugo's grin only got broader as he shot a two-finger salute of acknowledgement.

Milla rewarded him with her own broad grin. "Scott and I agree that we need a Quality Manager to help bridge the gap between contract and implementation. Khosi, when Gretchen returns from leave next month, you'll assume that role, reporting to the new VP of Client Relations and, until that position is filled, directly to me."

There was an element of reserve in Khosi's cool smile. The young woman must have expected more. Hugo's bump certainly sounded grander.

"And Edie..."

Milla paused, thoughtfully. There was no particular expression on her face. Edie fought the hysterical desire to say "I don't think there's anything in that black bag for me." Anyway, it couldn't be true. Even at Pinnacle, they didn't terminate you in public. Edie forced herself to appear calm and unconcerned.

"You will be playing a similar role in Fulfillment. You will continue to report directly to me."

Edie nodded, showing pleasure that wasn't far from the genuine relief she felt. She still had a job and, thank heavens, hadn't been put in the intolerable position of reporting to George Waters. Eventually her TQM skills would lead her to a steadier situation, but not in this economy. She was seeing how rough it was for Mike out there, and he had his PMI certification. She had to tread water as long as she could. She had no idea what Milla expected her to do in this role, but she would take it on with all her heart.

Δ

Gabe del Monte thought there were two curious things about this year's PBK. One was that, in the wake of Black Monday, Kippy had decided to have it at all. Alex Silva said *au contraire*; that it was almost comically in character that, convincing himself that cutting nearly a fifth of his workforce was a minor corporate tweak, Kippy would naturally move on as if it had never happened.

The other was that Gabe was in it. It was hard to believe he'd been at Pinnacle for two and a half years. When had it stopped feeling like stop-gap? Certainly work engaged him since he'd moved into Training, had become something he wanted to do well. He knew most of this had to do with Martha. Instead of pushing him away from his real life, work blended into it now. When they filed their first joint tax statement, just the other week, for the first time ever he didn't write "artist" as his occupation. Gabe Formosa del Monte would never stop being an artist, but he accepted that this was something he'd always have to do in his spare time. There was no point in putting the rest of life on hold in hopes of something that would probably never happen. Once this was clear in his head, Gabe met his work queue with fresh energy and drew great satisfaction from doing it well. He might not have expected the PBK nomination, but he was willing to believe he might deserve it.

At the first meeting, trying not to feel self-conscious about being in the room, Gabe quietly absorbed the composition of the participants. Marla and Leon, the creator of Bridge, represented the bedrock of Pinnacle. There was the ubiquitous Buzzard, plus a pair of what Alex referred to as "Dependables": Roger and Gene's assistant, Bennet Liu. Balancing this were the company's rising stars: Khosi and Hugo, of course; and Pilar Camacho from Client. Pilar was fairly new on board, new enough that there had been some rumbles about her surviving Black Monday; but she was formidable. According to Martha, Pilar spoke four useful languages and made time to work on a suicide hotline two nights a week.

It wasn't until Kippy lead a round robin of introductions that the other attendee was revealed on speaker phone.

"Ashok here!" The line wasn't very good, but the voice was strong and perky—perkier than anyone should sound at midnight. Though if you were living your days upside down, your midnight was late afternoon and you were having a second wind.

When Len Strauss had brought Ashok to New York to shadow Fulfillment, Gabe had trained him on Data Entry procedures. Tully Mulhern had done the Payroll training. They'd all spent a good chunk of time together. Ashok was a good guy. On Black Monday, Gabe had wondered about him and his associates in Pune. Obviously they were still in place, which was more than you could say for Tully. And with Ashok now showing up at PBK, it seemed pretty likely that the rumors were correct about George Waters building an offshore team.

Maybe only Gabe found it remarkable that PBK was going on this year at all; but we all agreed with him about the second curious thing, about the presence of Ashok Fernandez.

Δ

Dave Broussard didn't expect to learn much from being in PBK. The big lessons were the ones he'd already learned, the ones that had got him here. Life had taught the Buzzard that if you want to make a living in this world, you need to know how to deal with people. More important even than job skills. It's people who hire you on and who decide whether or not you're worth keeping.

When Wesley Peterson first came on board, he seemed like another guy who got this. Peterson arrived on the scene with more Hallelujah's than a tent-circuit healer. Everyone got caught up in the excitement. Even Leon was seen to crack a few smiles. Kippy practically led the band.

The first big thing to understand about Kippy was that, for all his talk about leadership and excellence in management, he was fundamentally a Sales guy himself. Getting hired on must have been a piece of cake for fast-talking, always-smiling Peterson. From the tribe of hard-core CTOs, he would have stuck out like a brother from another mother.

The tricky bit was hanging on for the long haul. That's where you had to understand the other critical thing, that Kippy was worse than a Sorority girl when it came to chasing the latest trend. If he read that Buffett or one of his other heroes had done or said x or y, Kippy had to run and do likewise. And he had the attention span of a flea. If whatever he'd lit on didn't automagically turn him into a star, he jumped fast to try something new.

As long as Kippy was all about building an IT department, Peterson was in high cotton. Once Len Strauss spread the word that the big boys were all dealing with contractors instead, Peterson started taking too many risks. He misjudged his hand. Or maybe he was just so arrogant he thought he could bluff it. Wherever Peterson was raised up, he must have had it a whole lot softer than Dave or a hell of a lot rougher. Whichever, he didn't see himself as having any limits, so he never understood when to stop upping the ante.

If there was one thing the Buzzard had learned from a boy, it was how to sniff the air and see which way the wind was blowing. What his nose had been telling him for months was that Peterson was road kill, with only one play left in his hand. Stupidest of all, he'd left himself vulnerable to the other players at the table. Kristol and Feldman and Strauss seemed to be living in each other's pockets these days. Dave had seen just enough of Milla Kristol in action to keep himself politely, respectfully, out of her game. He could. He had Sales in his corner, in Kippy's head the only team that counted.

Okay, so he wasn't rising as hot and fast as, say, this Hugo kid. Three years and he still wasn't Director of anything. His brand new business card described him as "Product Evangelist." The title was Angie's idea; not specifying the "product" was his own, once again listening to that little voice inside his head that showed him how to survive. And he had his own direct reports now. Okay, with Peterson giving Simran Bhalla the boot out of the clear blue sky, it was only Judy Schreiber and little Danny Zill, but that was still two.

And now he was in Phi Beta Kippy. Just like the offsite, it was thanks to Scott Bell, not Dave's nominal boss. Peterson's candidate for PBK was Leon. Peterson must have thought he was being cagey: everyone knew how sentimental the CEO was about Bridge and the man who'd built it.

Dave knew for a fact Leon didn't even want to be there. "Waste of time," he'd grunted in response to Dave's congratulations. "I code. This is what I want to do, code. If I want to be leader, I make my own company. This I already know without Kippy teach me." He mostly sat and glowered. Kippy was used to this, and accepted it as a sign of Leon's innate genius, but the attitude wasn't doing Peterson any favors.

That wasn't Dave's problem. Peterson could kiss Kippy's ass 24/7 or not. As long as he kept up the balancing act with Sales, Dave's own ass was covered. The Buzzard didn't like to jinx himself, but some days it was hard to not feel like he was sitting the catbird seat.

Δ

From: Wesley Peterson
To: IT
Subject: Major Happenings!

Hello, IT!

More exciting news!

Sometime within this year we will be opening a "branch office" of Pinnacle IT at an off-shore site in Pune India. This will increase our ability to staff up for special projects, by providing a core group of talented individuals who will be employees of Pinnacle, NOT CONSULTANTS, and who serve as on-the-ground supervisors at such times that it does become necessary to hire extra guns. Our offshore team will be educated in our domain knowledge and, even more critical to maintaining the LEVEL OF EXCELLENCE we expect, trained in the SDLC we use here in New York.

To kick off this initiative, I'd like to welcome Vijay Jani as our FIRST Pune IT employee! Through his contract work on OnRamp and Denali, Vijay has already displayed the HIGH QUALITY skills and strong work ethic that make him a perfect fit for our team. With the extensive domain knowledge he accrued on these projects, he can "hit the ground running" as an OFFICIAL member of the Pinnacle family!

Vijay returns to New York this weekend and will be working in the office with us for the next three months, at great sacrifice to his home life! So please be sure to say "hello" and make him feel welcome.

WJP

THURSDAY

13 OWNERSHIP

Thursday. Zooming by in double-time, everyone pushing to get things done before the week is over. Working off the to-do list. Meeting deadlines. A one-day marathon ending in a treat: the false weekend. With shops open late, you can get through your errands early and leave the real weekend clear to relax. And Thursday Happy Hour gives you a jump-start on having fun. Best day of the week.

You can smell the weekend from here, like the iodine in the air when you get just close enough to the beach. Remember that clambake Angie took you to out in the Hamptons? Three busses to drive everyone there, and some famous chef's assistant, digging pits in the sand. How the banking class lives.

Seems like a million years ago that you sold your artistic soul for safety and thought you were set for life. But you were wrong then, and you were wrong when you thought this new world would be any safer. It's like working in a blender all day, clinging to the walls of the jar, trying not to get sucked down into the blades. And all night, you stare up at the ceiling wide awake, worrying about the work piling up, worried about getting canned, worried about ending up old and on the streets.

You're starved for sleep. You daydream about dreamless sleep. Maybe this weekend you'll say" fuck it" to all the things you need to do around the house. Pay no attention to the clock. Feed the baby and turn over and go back to sleep. Send Rory out for hot and sour soup and dumplings. Take a nap and watch old movies until dawn, then doze your way through Sunday with carbohydrates and the *Times*. Sounds like Heaven.

You only have to make it through one more day. Piece of cake! So tonight you're going out. Going down to the Pier to catch a concert. Maybe meet some like-minded people and hook up. What's the point of working all week if you can't bust out and have some fun. Isn't that what all this grunt work is supposed to be paying for? Stay out all night, what the hell! It's Thursday!

You only know it's Thursday because you have the reminder in Outlook to call your parents. You call them every Thursday. You hope it makes them think that means you're too busy on the weekends doing something wild and crazy. It's a pathetic way of trying to get back at them. Not that they ever say it, but it's pretty clear what they think. They blame you for Jason. His family was so well respected. You must have done something shameful to set him off like that. If not, it was still your fault. That meant it was there in him before and you chose not to see it. You made a bad choice. They didn't raise you to make bad choices. They didn't raise you to choose. They raised you to be dutiful, to do what was asked. What you're doing now. On the other side of the continent, your hair grown long enough to cover the scar, you listen carefully and do as you're told. You hardly ever have a real day off, or even just a night, especially now with people in Pune to train. But now you're officially a Manager. You wouldn't tell them until you had the written proof, but Chris gave you the business cards yesterday. Maybe you'll call them from the office. Then you can surprise the others by joining them at Whine Bar, like they're always asking. Why not?

It's the night for going out with the gang from the office. As opposed to the occasional evening out alone with your friends, or when she goes out alone with hers; or Friday, which is always Date Night. No Date Night this week. Tomorrow you're heading straight from work to the new apartment, to slap on a coat of paint. Martha made a joke about how she couldn't remember the last time she saw you with a brush in your hand. Funny how it almost doesn't matter that this is what life turned out to be. To think you'd have never have met her if you hadn't walked through that door. You can't even imagine. You'd be half a person without her. You'll paint again, when the time is right. For, now two coats by Saturday night. You should be able to borrow Tully's van and move on Sunday. Gonna be a crazy busy weekend. You'd better have a good time tonight!

Better enjoy the next couple of weeks. Soon it's summer session, and from there it's straight into fall. And after that, you will finally have that MBA. That deserves a pat on the back, even if you have to give it to yourself. Smartest bargain you ever made. 50/50 on the expenses adds up to a lot more than the salary bumps and bonuses you volunteered to do without. Made Kippy feel important. And Feldman, well once you showed him the tax benefit, he was so excited he would have adopted you. Talk about gaming the system. And soon...goal! Once you have that piece of paper, you only have to work here one more year to keep your end of the deal. Thursday? Hell, every day feels like Thursday now. The day before the end.

#RWeThereYet

Δ

Ann Ling's pen, held in a white-knuckled grip, flew across the pages of her spiral notebook. Was she taking down every word that poured out of Milla Kristol's mouth? Alex thought that would be enormously sad. Except for the weekly "recommendations," which were inevitably the polar opposite of whatever strictures she'd laid down the week before, Kristol spouted nothing but buzz words. Since she'd taken over the meetings from Scotty, Alex had stopped playing CEO Bingo on his phone. There was no challenge to it anymore; his card was full before she finished her opening remarks. Instead, he kept himself awake by pretending he was watching a telenovela. A pretty boring telenovela, Orla asserted when he described this, but Alex disagreed. Once you tuned out the conversation and focused on the body language, there was a lot going on.

Kristol was always enormously entertaining to watch. She had that lollypop shape, that big head on a little body thing that a casting agent once told him was movie-star gold. Like an aspiring actress in commercials for the family car dealership, all of her gestures were over-rehearsed and empty. That wardrobe was definitely a costume. Dolores Umbridge Jr. (as he currently thought of her) had more pastel suits than a politician's wife; though by now she realized no one was competing with her and had started pairing the jackets with perfectly creased trousers. If Dolores ever turned up in black, he planned to run for the hills; he refused to contemplate what it might signal.

Right now, she was talking very vividly at a printout of some chart. Lots of grimaces and pointing. He couldn't make out what the chart said. Frankly, it didn't matter. It was just one of her many cherished Metrics. Ding! If he was still playing the CEO bingo, he probably would have just scored. The paperwork in Client had easily doubled since she'd elbowed Scotty out of the mix. To Alex's thinking, the only significance to all her metrics was that she printed them out on our one color printer, the printer that belonged to Sales and was otherwise supposed to only be used for State occasions like Board meetings. He would almost admire Kristol's balls, except that all these charts and reports were an egregious waste of dead trees. Any fool knew a chart could say whatever you wanted. Any fool, but apparently not every.

Not everyone agreed with Alex about the EVP Fulfillment Services. There were some perfectly intelligent people—not only ass-licking ladder-climbers like Channing and Hugo Singer, but people whose opinion he usually respected—who thought Kristol was impressive. Take Martha Moon. Alex could never bring himself to call her Martha del Monte. Martha Moon was such a cute name, suited her so well. Something had lit a fire under Martha's ass. She was all kinds of ambitious all of the sudden, and whatever Kristol was serving, she was eating it with a spoon. Alex didn't get it. All he heard from Kristol was a lot of noise and fuss; nothing solid. Maybe it was a chemical thing with him. He just didn't like her. She'd put Spurious George on a throne and locked Edie in the dungeon. Either she was a blind idiot, or she was afraid of having any real competition. And he was supposed to respect this?

Ah, she'd stopped talking and was waiting for Ann Ling to respond. Talk about a non-event. His puppet manager hid behind a glossy curtain of dark hair that trembled when she did, which was often. Was she terrified of everything, or maybe just of something that was everywhere, like maybe her own shadow? Alex could never quite decide if Ling was smarter than she appeared to be; it was scary to think she was stupider. She seemed to be countering one of Kristol's points, handing her another chart.

Kristol didn't even look at Ann's chart. But she was looking at Alex. Shit. She must have noticed him zoning out. He hoped he hadn't missed anything important. Wisely keeping his mouth shut, he cocked his head inquisitively.

"Now that we're growing the night shift, I'll be expecting this from you, Alex. Starting next week."

"Absolutely," he replied smoothly.

Yeah, they were growing the night shift. In Pune. Already three people remoting in to beef up the day team. Alex could remember back to the transit strike, when the guy brave enough to suggest they work remotely was practically booted out the door. But now the LC were wetting themselves with excitement at the concept. By last count there were as many as six on the Fulfillment "backup" team in India. And Danny Zill said Peterson had already hired three developers there—not contractors but direct hires—and was talking about more, like he had a blank check. Oh, yes; you loooved remote workers when you realized you could get them at half price. Kristol must be asking him to put together some kind of metrics to back up the amazing value. He'd find out later which ones. Ann would tell him. Shit, he'd have to ask Dawn to show him how they do those charts in Excel.

Δ

There had been a time when Wesley Peterson's IT all-hands packed the eighth floor collaboration space and people would scoot their desk chairs down to that end of the floor so that they'd be sure to have a seat. It was a lot emptier now. Counting heads, Judy made it 16 to the 25 here at Christmas.

Not all the missing faces had been cut. Once upon a time IT had experienced the least attrition of any Pinnacle department, but now the bloom was off the rose. As tight as the market was, there were opportunities for developers and engineers. Only a week after being right-sized, Corey Smither landed a well-paid six-month contract with Time-Warner. Larry Winkel left voluntarily, jumping to a startup in Brooklyn of all places; apparently, Brooklyn was becoming a city again. Chances were the job wouldn't last a year, but at the rate Pinnacle was going, Larry thought he'd probably be out in a year anyway; and at least at a startup he'd get to really build something cutting edge, not just talk about doing it.

Eliot Tseng, the VP of Development, was also gone. He'd never been all that effective when he was here. The final straw had something to do with the older clients who wanted to keep some custom reports that weren't compatible with more modern operating systems. The details were too techie for anyone outside IT. Leon had written an elaborate patch that would dump the data out of Bridge and do the needful to make it work with the older system. The patch and the reports had to be run every Tuesday and Friday, between midnight and dawn, on an old file server kept especially for this. After Smither was gone, it surfaced that Eliot had let him take that server home to work. The data included Social Security numbers. Eliot's leaving was presented as one of those "by mutual decision" separations, but it seemed probable that Peterson had saved face for both of them by giving his erstwhile protégé the option of quitting.

There were no grey areas to Sid Reilly's exit. He'd handed in his two weeks this Monday, with a big grin. He was joining the MTA. It was a lateral move, and he'd have to wear a tie, but the benefits had us drooling: guaranteed annual pay hikes; sick days, separate from European amounts of vacation time; even tuition reimbursement for professional development.

In the early days, Peterson had announced having a budget for skills improvement. Judy Schreiber remembered asking for advice on areas to explore. Peterson had laughed. Not a mean laugh; only a little patronizing. She was doing such a fine job, he said; she didn't need any training. The budget was small and was reserved for classes the engineers might need to learn the new technology he was buying. He did everything but pat her on the head and tell her to run along.

Developers had it good. If Judy were even ten years younger, she'd definitely be learning to code. But by the time she could learn enough for an entry level role, she'd be competing against people who could, on a biological technicality, be her grandchildren. And in an economy that had shrunk like a wool sweater in a hot dryer. With companies falling into death spirals every day, if she did miraculously find something, there was a real risk of finding herself last hired first fired. It only made sense to sit tight as long as they would have her or until the economy turned around. Pinnacle wasn't a picnic, but there were still a lot of good people here and she was making herself useful. Accept it: she was frozen in place, with a heavy dose of better-the-devil-you-know.

"So I have a few exciting announcements!" Wesley Peterson played to this sparse crowd with as much energy as if he'd been facing a full house. "First, Vijay's team in Pune! These guys have been plugging away at the new travel product and they are making tremendous progress. Kippy and Len couldn't be more pleased. Are you hearing this, Vijay?"

"Am hearing that, Wesley." Vijay's voice came through the speaker with minimal distortion. "We are very pleased, yes guys?" We could almost hear the others in the background.

"Excellent! Then let's have a round of applause for these guys! And for the good news that we're adding three assistant developers to that team!"

Under cover of the spatter of applause, Judy whispered to Danny Zill, "what's an assistant developer?"

"Strauss has them recruiting kids right out of school. They pay practically nothing. You can get three for the price of one qualified junior developer here."

"Yes, Pinnacle has been through of rough patch. And I'm not going to pretend we haven't had a few blips of our own. But it's all behind us now and We Are Growing Again!! And I don't want to forget: kudos to Danny Zill here, for putting together a GREAT set of requirements!"

The applause, being for one of our own, was heartier this time. Red-faced, Danny ducked his head in acknowledgement,

"Kudos, Danny Zill," Judy whispered out of the side of her mouth.

"Simran did all the work," he whispered back. "All I did was walk Scott and Glenn through it and make the changes after."

"Simran's gone. If they want to give you the credit, be smart and smile."

"Some more excellent news," Wesley continued in his jovial way. "The Leadership Council has finalized the lease for a new failover data center. Finally. In Chennai.

"India?!" It was Freddie who said it, but we were all thinking it.

The current failover site was in Delaware. With the lease expiring and the rent increase big enough to choke Feldman, the LC had spent months debating relocation. Peterson's first choice was Omaha, but we knew he'd decided it was too far flung and had pushed for a facility in Pittsburgh. Chennai was half a world away from Nebraska. Peterson should have been steaming, but all we saw was a bland smile.

"Len Strauss has found space at a really great technology park. State of the art. 50 percent more footage than we have here. And by placing a data store almost local to our teams in Pune, we have tremendous latency reduction."

"For Pune," Craig Parnes objected. "But what about the latency here? You see what happens when we transfer packets from Vijay to us. Slow motion. Sloooooow mooooootion," he repeated, in case someone didn't get the point.

"We need to address those issues anyway, Craig." Peterson was still smiling, but his eyes glinted with calculation. "We need to be thinking BIG. And big means international. Consider what it says about the scope of this company, that we've got an international technology infrastructure! I'm not saying this is where we're headed, but if we ever get to the point of making an IPO, this is going to be a critical part of the package."

"What about security?" Sid Reilly asked. "Aren't there compliance issues around this, with the sensitive personal data we store? Do government regulations even allow storing payroll and medical records overseas?"

Peterson made an open-handed gesture; so-be-it. "Feldman and Strauss are satisfied that they've covered all the bases. That's good enough for me."

"Feldman and Strauss?!" Sid spoke up with the unrestrained vehemence of the freshly resigned. "Shouldn't IT be making technology decisions?"

"As you've chosen to abandon ship, I would say you shouldn't concern yourself, Sid." Peterson spoke with steely mildness. "Or is that Mr. Biro?"

"What about monsoons?" Judy didn't only want to break the nervous vacuum that greeted Peterson's odd coda; she honestly wanted to know. Her limited understanding of a failover site was that it be up and functioning if something happened here in New York. Cost aside, it had been another problem with Delaware that our hurricanes were their hurricanes.

Peterson laughed heartily, as if she'd scored a very funny joke. "Okay, okay. That's enough on that subject. Let's move on, IT. We have a lot more business to discuss."

Even though half the floor was empty now, Peterson continued to bring in the same number of donuts. Dave Broussard brought one of the untouched boxes to the PMO meeting that directly followed the all-hands.

"No reason to let them go to waste. Whatever we don't eat, I'll walk downstairs and put in the break room." He extracted a donut from the box and took a bite. A squirt of raspberry jelly landed on his shirt. "By the way, I'm hearing some buzz about moving us all back down there and sub-leasing this space, if the landlord'll okay it."

Danny and Judy leaned forward to listen. Having Dave for a manager didn't mean much insofar as being managed, but you did get to learn a lot about what was happening at Pinnacle.

"Numbers are down enough they think we'll fit, even if it's a little tight. I've already seen some floor plans."

"What happens when we have to staff up again?" Danny asked. At the last Monthly, Kippy had made big deal about all the impressive additions to the client list. "Where are they going to put people then?"

"Pune," Judy suggested. "Am I right?"

Dave made the lip-buttoning gesture; they weren't going to hear it from him. "Okay, more important right now. I'm going to cut to the chase. We're having another re-org."

Judy stopped breathing. Her eyes met Danny's across the table. He wasn't taking it much better. Dave looked from one to the other, confusion turning into consternation. He slapped his hand against his cheek. "Damn, I can be such an asshole! No, no one is fired!"

Danny gave a relieved laugh. "You really scared us Dave."

Judy smiled weakly and let her heart resume beating.

"Sorry. No, just that Milla Kristol wants anything to do with analysis to be under Hugo. That means you, Dan. And Channing. As soon as they shuffle some people around, you'll have the cube next to him.

"Channing's not going to be happy about leaving Finance," Danny noted. He wasn't all that thrilled himself about his new manager. They were contemporaries, with similar degrees in Business and, as far as he knew, Hugo had no more work experience then he did.

"He's not leaving. He'll be a dotted line. Like I'm a dotted line to Scott. They're moving him so it'll be easier for you to work on things together."

"What about me?"

"You're still with me, kiddo." After all this time working together, Dave had gotten genuinely fond of Judy. "You stay where you are and you keep doing what you do. The kiosks, the walk-throughs, all that. The newsletter. Kippy was pretty insistent on that. But you'll be 50 percent with Len Strauss."

Judy had already worked more than enough with Strauss. It wasn't merely that he was mean-spirited, it was his condescension. Even if he were as brilliant as Kippy claimed—and Judy had yet to see any evidence that he was—it was no excuse for treating people like idiots. "Editing content for the website? Len Strauss doesn't need half my time for that."

"He says he does. And he'll have other stuff rolling out. They've put him in charge of growth."

This was curious. New clients? New products? "Growth how? Everything comes from Scott."

Dave shrugged. "No idea what they mean by it, but they say growth. Hey, growth is a good thing, right? The way I see it, you supporting him is guaranteed employment."

Δ

```
From:        Josefina Vargas
To:          Pinnacle Leaders; All Operations Teams
Subject:     Employee Departure
----------------------------------
George Waters is no longer an employee of Pinnacle.


Josefina Vargas, Dir. Human Capital Management
Pinnacle Management Services
```

Δ

Most of us had fantasized about him leaving, and few if any were sad about it, but absolutely everyone was stunned. Completely shocked. "Gob-smacked," said Alex Silva, who'd just started dating a Brit. Danny Zill tried, but couldn't summon up a single one of Lloyd Baptiste's wacky analogies to cover the situation. Only termites, like us, got dumped instantaneously. Managers had some warning. If they had contracts, they sensed when they'd outgrown their usefulness and wouldn't be renewed. The others, as Mike Ventura used to put it, felt their desks being moved closer to the door or knew in some other way that they'd been marked to take the fall for something outside their control. George Waters' employment history with Pinnacle was one big upward trajectory. His neck had never been on the block. Things that would have been the kiss of death for anyone else, like the legendary Jeff Curry incident, were waved away.

As far as anyone knew, at close of business yesterday, the LC thought the sun shone out his ass. The email was time-stamped around 9 p.m., after the last of the late shifts would have left the building. We read about it in the morning.

Three days later, it was still all we knew for certain.

Alex, who could hear dandruff fall, swore there hadn't been so much as a whisper of a whisper. Confounded by his inability to ferret out anything of substance, he slumped against the bricks and, on a stream of smoke, counted off what little we did know:

On the day in question, Will Compton claimed to have heard shouting from Kristol's office, soon after lunch.

But Raney and Fritz reported an absolutely normal Switchboard team meeting at 2:30.

Waters must have gone out to a client after, because Kim at the front desk saw him return around 5. She's sure, because that's when the UPS guy comes for pick-ups. Did Waters seem angry? Does he ever not? He walked right by Jo Vargas and neither reacted, so it couldn't have happened yet.

"It could be almost anything," Alex mused. "Did I ever tell you about this guy, when I first started? Sat maybe three cubes away from me, only it was desks then, not cubes. Kippy took a major hate to him. I don't know why; he was nothing much, Darryl. Or was it Dale? You'd think I'd remember. Shit, I'm getting old. So anyway, he heads out for lunch one day and I hear this bang. There's Kippy, throwing...no, make that hurling...hurling this guy's things into a box, like they were grenades. Well, the guy comes back from lunch a couple of minutes late. We all were, usually. We only got a half hour, so what do you expect? But he was the one Kippy couldn't stand. He gets to his desk and Kippy's waiting for him with the box. Pushes it at him and marches him out the door, yelling all the way about how lateness showed a lack of respect for the business. Then Kippy comes back, powers down the guy's computer and looks around at the rest of us with this weird pride like he's just won a round with Mike Tyson. And what he says is: 'there is no place in this company for that kind of irresponsible attitude. You can't have a winning company unless every person in it is a winner.' Seriously. I'm not shitting you."

Whatever had happened with Waters must have been equally spontaneous. His stuff was still all over his office. We looked.

His work was ending up on Edie's desk. Dawn had already begged and had a meeting with her, requesting a transfer to Training. "Striking while the iron is hot," she noted wisely. "Edie says she can't make promises. She doesn't know if she's back in place or just a stop-gap until they bring in someone over her head...okay, she didn't exactly say that, but you know. Anyway, if a slot comes up, she'll definitely recommend me. She said she was surprised I hadn't made the move already."

Dawn paused to acknowledge the ripple of dark laughter. Spurious George had twice turned her down for a transfer, with no explanation except that it was his call to make and she had no right to question him. Always with that smug imitation of a grin, his mouth turning up at the corners, but the rest of his face never getting involved. Diego, always too nice for his own good, used to say it showed Waters was trying to be human. We missed Diego. We only got to see him for a couple of minutes a week, the day the tamale truck parked near us at lunch. His hours were insane and it paid shit, but at least it was more relevant to his future than Phi Beta Kippy.

"Edie wouldn't say any more, and I didn't want to force it."

"No point in messing up your chances," Danny noted wisely.

"Yeah. But also, well...you know. Edie. I got the feeling she was maybe even a little sorry for Spurious George." Dawn herself felt as if she'd found a twenty dollar bill on the pavement and pocketed it without stopping to look for a rightful owner. Gleeful, but a little guilty.

Even the bitchiest among us couldn't exactly feel *schadenfreude* at Waters' fall. We were too shaken. In the firmament of people who'd been thrown under the bus or mysteriously disappeared without a trace, George Waters was just one more shooting star; but, unlike any of the others, Waters had been chosen and raised up by the Leadership Council. He'd played by the nonsensical rules of the LC, and had been applauded and rewarded every step of the way. What could he possibly have done in the course of a single afternoon to make them turn on him?

"He called Milla Kristol a stupid cunt!" Skidding into the ally, Archie Ghosh was so breathless that we weren't certain we'd heard her correctly.

"Hello?" Alex put a hand out to catch her.

She grabbed onto him. "Del Monte heard it," she gasped.

It seemed Gabe was doing a late training session for a West Coast client. Taking off his headphones for a five-minute break, he heard what sounded like an argument, coming from the conference room. Martha'd said she wasn't going to wait for him, but for some reason he was worried she might be in the room.

"They've both been showing a lot of initiative lately," Alex noted. "And he's got that new haircut. If we had a corporate ladder, I'd think the del Montes had ideas of movin' on up."

We ignored him and urged Archie to continue.

"So he walked the long way to the men's room, to look. Martha wasn't in there. Only Kristol, Scott, Ann Ling and Waters."

"Ann!" Hank was shocked. "She hasn't said a word!"

"Ann wouldn't." Danny had a little crush on Ann. We couldn't tell if he admired her reticence or pitied it.

"He couldn't tell what they'd been arguing about, but Waters was all red and slobbery, like when Data Entry walked out. And then he said it! Gabe was only about a foot away. He heard it, clear as a bell."

"I wonder which bothered Dolores more, 'stupid' or 'cunt.' What did she do?"

Archie shrugged. "Gabe said it got really quiet. And next thing he knew, George was stomping out, with Scotty hot on his heels. He didn't see the rest. He said he was afraid to move in case anyone saw him. But he thinks they went to George's office. Then he heard the front door slam. Said he thought the glass would break. Scott came back to the conference room. While they were all talking, Gabe ran back to his desk and stuck his headphones back on."

Spent, Archie collapsed against the bricks and pulled out a cigarette. Her hands were shaking so much that Hank had to light it for her.

"Did you hear?!" A wildly grinning Orla bounced around the corner.

"About Spurious calling Dolores a cunt?" Alex said. "Archie just told us."

Orla's grin turned into a large O of surprise. "Fuck! Seriously?!"

Archie blew a feeble puff and waved for Alex to tell it; which he did with gusto, playing all the parts for a most appreciative audience.

"Wow!" Orla released a solid chain of smoke rings. "So that's what it was. Crime of passion, huh?"

Dawn had nodded slowly all throughout Alex's retelling, the chips falling into place. "And now they'll pretend he never happened. Like they always do. Kippy's not the only one on the LC who never made a bad decision,"

"Leaves the way clear for my new boss," Danny noted.

Alex raised his eyebrows, considering. "Hmmm. It does seem Golden Boy is on the rise. Maybe we should start a pool. Shit, I have to go back up."

Archie and Orla leaned against the wall in companionable silence for a while, until Archie took one last puff and ground the stub into the brick. Fixing her lipgloss, she caught Orla's eye in the mirror. "So wait. What was your news?"

"Huh?"

"When you came down, you said you had news."

"Oh that. Nothing as good as yours. They're renaming HR again is all."

"You mean Talent Management"

"No. I mean Human Capital. Tah-dah!"

Archie made a terrible grimace. "Ugh! Makes me feel like...I don't know. Yes I do. A slave, that's what. Chattel."

"They think it sounds like we're an investment."

"Yeah. Exactly. Like they bought and own us. Disgusting!"

"The email's going out later. Chris told Liz, and Liz told me. HC. I was hoping for once I'd beat Silva to the punch. You know he's going to call it Hopeless Causes."

Δ

```
From:        Josefina Vargas
To:          All Pinnacle Associates
Subject:     The Peak Experience
----------------------------------
Hello Pinnacle!
```

The latest version of *The Peak Experience* is now available on the Intranet. Topics include:

- Introducing Trekker, our exciting new Travel product!
- 40 Years and Counting! A celebration of Pinnacle's History
- Pinnacle Builds a House! Chris Keane's photo essay of our Habitat for Humanity Team

The Peak Experience is looking for new contributors! To learn more, please contact Judy Schreiber.

Josefina Vargas, Dir. Human Capital Management
Pinnacle Management Services

14 CHERRYPICKING

Judy had finally learned to do her flinching behind a mask. She was here to get a steady paycheck, that was all. If people were assholes, that was their problem, not hers. She tried to ignore it and do her job to the best of her ability. Sometimes she couldn't. Like now.

Right now, she was furious on behalf of the younger woman beside her. The last time she'd seen anything that flat-out vicious in the workplace, she'd been 25 herself and working for a film producer who made a thing out of hiring the guys he'd grown up with in a rough neighborhood in Naples. His friend Gino, a washed-up actor, was a functional alcoholic who drank his lunch every day at a hotel around the corner, coming back around 3:00 to hide out in his office. No one disturbed Gino in the afternoon unless it was absolutely necessary. One day, it was necessary and she was the one bearing the message. He'd lobbed a marble ashtray across the room, missing her elbow by inches and denting drywall. She'd marched up to his desk, picked up the stapler and punched it into his forearm, before storming out. But that was show business and everyone except Judy was Italian. You couldn't do that in a normal American office.

And also, except when the drink was speaking, she'd adored Gino. The man had been absolutely charming and delightful every day until 2. If Len Strauss had a charming time of day, she'd never seen it. With his perpetual scowl and a voice like a machete, he could make a baby cry at 20 paces. She might have been willing to cut him some slack if he'd only ever done or said anything worthwhile. They said he was a brilliant businessman, but supposed you had to consider the source of who said it. Maybe that was why Strauss, getting too old for his overseas exertions, had selected Pinnacle as a State-side berth. Some minor talent likes to boost itself up by latching onto a better, brighter crowd. Strauss was the other kind, preferring to generate the illusion of excellence by lording it over his inferiors. He'd be happy here as long as he kept his eyes above C-level; compared to the other geniuses on the LC, he looked impressive. On the other hand, Judy could name a slew of cube-dwellers who had better brains and equal or better educations. Will Compton for example, or herself, damn it! Or Pilar Camacho.

Subjected to a double-barreled sexist and racial slur, Pilar Camacho reacted visibly, hands flinching to grab the armrests, a pair of dull red blotches blooming in her cheeks. She was as embarrassed as Strauss had no doubt intended and also, Judy was pleased to see, pretty damned angry. Anger was much better than shock. The girl was no victim. Judy hadn't worked with Client Relations' rising star before today. She was very impressed with her poise.

"We're done then?" Judy phrased it as a question, but stood and opened the door.

Pilar glared silently at Len and followed. "I don't need this shit," she said, once the door had closed behind them. "I'm going to Josefina. Right now."

"Don't be disappointed if there's nothing she can do. This may look like a big company, but it's really just a mom and pop."

Judy was right. There was nothing Jo Vargas could do. A couple of days later, however, she called Judy into her office.

The Director of Human Capital was grim. "I wouldn't be talking with you, except you're part of this. You were a witness."

"I was."

"And it may come to that. If she finds a lawyer who considers it actionable. But the LC doesn't want to see it. Scott Bell thinks it's a joke."

"He would, considering what he gets away with."

Jo opened her mouth, clearly wanting to comment but prevented by her role. "No one complains about him," is all she could say.

"Khosi isn't about to. She's making good use of him. And Marla and the others...I think they gave up long ago. They know nothing's going to be done. Scott's too valuable to Kippy. Also, there's something inherently goofy about Scott, even at his most offensive. It's easy to shrug off. You might even take it as a warped kind of compliment. What Len Strauss did, that was flat out ugly."

Jo nodded. "Kippy doesn't get it. He's oblivious. Says Leonard Strauss is...what did he call him? A 'top flight professional'. And that Pilar must have misinterpreted."

"There aren't a lot of ways to interpret that." Judy still winced to remember the words, and the delighted malice in Strauss's face as he said them.

"She's going to walk," Jo sighed. "Once I tell her nothing's going to happen. I wouldn't be surprised if she takes it all the way. You'd better prepare yourself. She might depose you. That's what I wanted to tell you."

Judy's stomach clenched. Terrific. So she hadn't been right-sized; there were other ways to lose a job.

Jo sighed again. "I'm so tired of having my hands tied. Sometimes I wonder why they bother having anyone in this role at all."

Δ

```
From:          Josefina Vargas
To:            All Pinnacle Associates
Subject:       Moving On
------------------------------------
```

As many of you know, I will be departing Pinnacle, effective July 31, to pursue other opportunities. Over the next couple of days, I will be introducing each of you to Don Bryson who will be assuming directorship of Human Capital Management.

It's been an honor to work with such a fine group of professionals and I wish each of you the best in your future endeavors.

Jo

Josefina Vargas, Dir. Human Capital Management
Pinnacle Management Services

Δ

In theory, a monthly joint meeting between Sales and Client was a good idea. It was the reality that was a farce. First of all, try getting enough Sales in the room to make it worth the effort. As far as those guys were concerned, they were hemorrhaging money any time they weren't on the phones or in the field. The meat puppets could never get it through their heads that knowing more about their product and the customers might help them land more sales. Alex remembered Donny Rohmer telling him, back in the day when Rohmer was still around and lusting after his buff Portuguese ass, that the product and the customers didn't matter. If you were any good, you could sell anything to anybody, without knowing a damned thing. Okay, in the end Rohmer didn't sell enough stay on, but Alex was willing to bet these other yo-yos thought the same way. Which explained why they were always selling features we didn't have and leaving Client Relations to mop up after them.

Which was why (circular train of thought) this monthly meeting actually was a good idea. Except, second issue: the meeting was conducted by Dolores Umbridge Jr. herself and her new best friend Scotty Bell. Look at them, perched side-by-side on the credenza. Damn, they were a chirpy pair. All giant plastic grins, and sentences that went on and on and said nothing. Someone ought to get them a morning show. Scotty's slitty eyes were showing a little extra white these days, like something was holding them open. He'd just come back from another vacation in his favorite place in Mexico. Did he have an eye job while he was down there? Alex made a mental note to ask Gretchen what she thought.

248

That wasn't all he wanted to ask Gretchen. He needed her advice. He'd let himself get too comfortable here; he was well past his sell-by date. It was probably good, the way Dolores always turned away when she met his eye. It made him feel powerful at first, gave him a charge. It took a while to figure out that she hated not knowing how to play him, that gay men frightened her. So yeah, it was time for him to move on. Gretchen's friend who'd got him the coaching gigs said she could set him up with a casting agent, as an assistant. Alex wanted to bounce the idea off Gretch, see if she thought it was a real thing or just noise. A casting agent. Alex wasn't sure how he felt about that. He still wanted to direct. Could he do both? Maybe. Maybe he just needed to shake things up.

He stared at Milla Kristol, hoping she'd meet his eye and look away. Even better, she turned without looking. Almost like she felt him and didn't want to take a chance. 'Don't worry, Dolores,' he thought; 'I'll leave before you have to find a way to push me out.' Lowering his eyes to his doodle pad, he was arrested by the sudden awareness that something was different. Her chest. He narrowed his eyes. He could swear her tits were bigger. Was she wearing one of those magical mystical push-up bras that were so hot right now? He knew more about those things than he wanted to. Some day he would understand why all his female friends thought they had to have his opinion on their underwear. Excuse me, *lingerie*. Yeah, there was a definite, uh, blossoming in the area. The longer he looked, the more substantial it seemed. She hadn't had a boob job, had she? Didn't really go with the whole Lady Executive persona. Hmm. Something else to bounce off Gretchen.

Δ

After reeling off a list of new clients and telling us about last night's Yankee game (a guy two rows in front of him caught a ball, and Jeter was terrific), Kippy opened the floor to questions. "This being Don's first Monthly Meeting, I thought we should let him see the exchange of ideas we have here at Pinnacle."

Everyone's head swiveled wildly, looking for the newish Director of Hopeless Causes. We'd each met Don Bryson and shaken his hand, but he hadn't made much of an impression. He was one of those middle-height, middle-aged guys who blend into any background. If he was sharp enough behind the bland mask, and for all we knew he was, he might have made a great secret weapon for the FBI.

"I know you have a lot of questions. Anybody?" Kippy pointed a finger into the crowd, knowing one of us would think we'd been picked and would say something.

"I have one," Hank Iversson raised his hand. "It's actually kind of an HR thing. Human Capital, I mean. With all the, um, adjustments to staff size, teams are kind of stretched thin and a lot of us aren't able to take any time off. I mean, we're glad to do it, to help the team. But about the days...We're only allowed to roll over five unused PTO days to the next year, and we can't roll over unused floating holidays at all. Is this going to change?"

"Great question!" Kippy enthused, holding out Mr. Microphone to Bryson.

Bryson shrugged his sloped shoulders. "Very interesting. I don't have an answer right now, but I promise I'll look into it and get back to you."

"Great! Who else has a question?"

We all did, plenty of them; but we didn't think it was worth the breath or the risk of calling attention to ourselves.

Someone cleared her throat. We craned our necks, surprised to find ourselves looking at Kim, our receptionist. Chris Keane covered the front desk every month so that she could attend the meeting. Kim had been up front for more than a year now. She was an incredibly pleasant young woman, willing to pitch in whenever a team needed extra help. Her hope was to transfer into Client Relations at some point, but she would have taken any internal move. Thanks to overtime, even Switchboard paid more than our own front desk, and Kim had two young kids to support.

"I wanted to ask something about the health insurance plan," she whispered.

"Can't hear you, Kim!" Kippy beckoned to her to move up front. When she was standing almost at his feet, he bent to hand her the microphone.

"My question is about health coverage," she repeated. She startled at hearing her voice suddenly sound so loud and we laughed a little.

"You go girl!" Someone in the back cheered her on.

She straightened her shoulders. "Okay," she said. She sounded determined. "The Pinnacle insurance...the family coverage is very expensive." There was a murmur of support. Except for those of us fortunate enough to have spouses who worked for more generous companies, the cost of our healthcare contribution was a long-standing issue. It was especially punishing for single parents, like Kim. "I wanted to know if maybe with Don coming onboard, he maybe had some prior experience with a more affordable plan. Or if maybe with the company smaller now, maybe there was a possibility that Pinnacle's contribution could be a little more."

Kippy practically snatched Mr. Microphone from her hand. He seemed about to pace, but realized he was on a windowsill and caught himself. He took a deep breath. "You know, everybody has choices in life. I would kill for my kids. I'd cut off my right arm. I'm sure you would, too. Being a parent is the greatest thing in the world. But...and this may sound harsh, but I'm being honest here...you chose to bring children into the world. That was a choice you made, and by making it, you have to expect to make sacrifices. The person you should have questions for is you. Questions about fiscal responsibility. How much do you spend on things you don't need? Going to a movie, buying an extra pair of shoes? Have you educated yourself to increase your earning capability? Do you have a part-time job? You choose and prioritize what's important. Maybe health insurance isn't even the wisest choice. Doctors' bills could cost less than the insurance. And you know, the State has programs for uninsured children."

It was the kind of silence that follows a car crash or a gunshot. Kim froze. We all froze, except Don Bryson who gestured wildly at Kippy to shut up before he said something actionable. Kippy had a puzzled furrow between his eyes. He had no idea why Bryson was reacting like that.

Clifton Speck jumped to the rescue. "So Kippy," he asked, pumping up a facsimile of his usual joking manner; "what are you reading?"

Kippy turned away from Bryson, his habitual enthusiasm replacing his confusion. "I've got a really terrific book. *Zag: The Number One Strategy of High Performance Brands*. By who, Gretchen?"

Either Gretchen was still in shock, or her mind was on her own baby who, we'd heard, was going through a colicky phase that kept her up most of the night. Caught off guard, she started fumbling through her notepad.

"Neumeier," Khosi Shumbalala piped up. "Marty Neumeier."

Scott beamed as if he'd grown her from a bean. He never let anyone forget that he'd been the one to spot Khosi's golden potential. We all wondered what would happen if she and Hugo Singer ever went head-to-head against each other. It would be like Scott playing Milla at Rock 'Em Sock 'Em Robots. The pool would be interesting.

"Ha! Good thing you know that, because it's going to be the next assignment for Phi Beta Kippy! The rest of you got that?"

"Aye aye Skipper!" Eric Channing returned smartly.

Our silent groans broke what remained of the spell. Kim melted back into the crowd.

Kippy had already forgotten. He gave his usual manic grin. "Right! Now you all know how I feel about marketing."

We did. He'd told us often enough that "organic growth," the only kind he valued, happened one face-to-face sale at a time. Sure Scott had to take a few guys to some of the bigger conventions, or people might get the idea Kippy couldn't afford to make a showing. Other than that, since he couldn't see the immediate ROI, Kippy thought marketing was worthless and would therefore only agree to the kind that was free or nearly free.

"We've got the best managed office services company in the world. I'll be modest. In North America. Right? Give yourselves a round of applause."

He waited until we did. The sluggish claps made him as happy as if they'd been loud and spontaneous.

"We don't need to waste a pile of money on advertising or fancy branding. Which is why I'm the only Chief Marketing Officer Pinnacle will ever need. Ha! Now this Neidermeier...I tell you, the man's a genius. Because what he says...You see, the secret, is to figure out how you're different and run with it. Everyone else zigs, you go zag. Get it? Zag! Ha! Differentiation! Let all the other companies waste their resources rolling out the same kinds of ads, giving away the same...I don't know, the same mugs and calendars. What we do is differentiate ourself from the pack. That's what Scott's guys here, that's what they run with. How we're excellent. How Pinnacle does what nobody else can do. Word of mouth means everything, and with our 94 percent retention rate, we've got the greatest word of mouth in the world! We do! This is why Len has been reaching out to Client Relations for testimonials we can post up on our website. That's a great thing, right? I love the website. This is the kind of marketing that makes sense to me. Not some flashy slogan, but a chance for prospects to get to know us, to know who we are. See, when it comes down to real sales, the kind that build a business, you can only get those *mano a mano*. As soon as a prospect agrees to talk to one of our guys here, ha! The sale's made! What's our closing rate, Scott? I want some metrics on that for next month."

Scott bobbled his head. He was probably hoping Kippy would forget about it once the meeting was over.

"The tough part is getting a foot in the door, whetting someone's appetite. And that's where all these branding guys drop the ball, because if you're all doing the same thing, no one stands out. How Pinnacle stands out...this is how I zag..." Still holding Mr. Microphone, he made air quotes, leering by way of a double underline. "By using our reputation, and *only* our reputation, to get through that door. Word of mouth, like I said. And referrals. Probably a good time to remind you about our referral bonus program. Everyone knows about this? A thousand dollars on signing, then a percentage of the first year's business. Don here'll send out an email with the details. Okay? Terrific program. Everybody wins. Most of all, Pinnacle wins. So before we go, one more round of applause for yourselves, the best managed office services company...I'm sticking by what I said. Ha! The best in the world!"

Δ

Apparently word of mouth wasn't powerful enough. Pinnacle still wasn't exactly the right size. Six more people were laid off in July. This time, they got a month's notice. Rumor had it that a few of the troops from Black Monday had filed a lawsuit. Someone's uncle at the Department of Labor said that while New York was a "no-cause" state—meaning people can be fired or quit at will, with no cause required on either side—there were regulations about layoffs. The governing assumption was that, before eliminating large numbers of positions, a company would have to have a plan and therefore notice was required, especially if you laid off more than the particular percentage of your workforce that Black Monday had topped. It was interesting that the crack labor attorneys we used for Compliance hadn't alerted the LC back in February. Maybe Feldman wouldn't consult them unless he could bill it out to a client. Well, the LC was treading more carefully now. With Pilar Novas' harassment suit pending, plus a damages suit from a well-funded former client, Pinnacle could ill afford to risk another legal action.

We doubted this would be the last round of cuts. Significantly, while we were trimming down in New York, the LC was gradually growing the "failover" teams in India. There were already as many Data Entry people over there as in New York. Raney and Fritz, the two longest-tenured, had been asked to start training the Pune team on atypical situations. They were certain they were training their own replacements. Payroll Services was getting nervous, too. Ashok only had a few Payroll people so far, but there seemed to be no reason why the work couldn't be done over there.

Despite the still-soft economy, there was a growing conviction that we had to jump before we were pushed. Trying not to be too smug about his new job, Alex Silva let his friends vent.

"Hank could leave any time." Gretchen was smoking again now that she'd stopped nursing. She'd tried hard not to, but the combination of the baby, Rory's sudden neediness and this place was driving her nuts.

"No way they're getting rid of me that easy." Hank Iversson laughed darkly. "I used to just be annoyed. But since he made that new announcement, I'm angrier than Jeff Curry on a bad day. I'm not leaving 'til they give me that referral bonus, damn it!"

"I dunno." Squatting on the pavement, Orla was filling in the chips in her nails. Her nails were purple this week, but the only polish in her desk was black, which made the results more interesting. "Sometimes Carl and I say we'll jump a plane for Austin. Or maybe Germany. There's a big Metal scene in Berlin. Carl has some kind of cousin who'd put us up until we found something."

"Don't you need papers to work overseas?" Dawn still tended to cling to the rules.

Orla shrugged. "I can wait tables, I guess. There's always someplace. And Carl can get a passport in a heartbeat, because of his grandfather; you know, Right of Return."

"Well I can't quit until I find something. Tully and I can't both be unemployed."

"What happened with the Y?" Danny Zill asked. Some friend of Freddie's, or maybe it was his cousin, had hooked Tully up with a job back in June, teaching music.

"They lost their funding for next year. The private funding I mean. For the extras. It was all invested in the market and..." Twirling her finger in a spiral, Dawn made a sound like a slide whistle: down the drain. "It was in the news. Yeah. One of the Knicks kicked in to keep the basketball court open every night, but the music and art programs won't run past May."

"Which one of the Knicks?" Alex went pop-eyed with curiosity.

Orla stood up slowly, her hands spread wide. "You are such a star fucker, Silva. Can't believe they're handing you a casting couch. What does it matter, which one?"

"Lucky he was keeping up his shifts at the café. The barista salary isn't any more than unemployment, but it comes with a 50/50 pay for health coverage. On the flip side, it means more rehearsal time for Stail Fiáin."

Orla brightened. She was a fan of Tully and Lily's band. "That's right. I mean they're both still free."

"Free," Alex pointed out, "implies choice."

"Okay, so you're free." She wiggled her fingers close to his face. "You're free, and we're fucked."

"Speaking of fucked," Archie said, "what did you guys think of Martha's Facebook post?"

Alex dodged Orla's wet nails. "Well, she's totally pregnant."

"Absolutely," Orla agreed. "I was wondering why she looks so horrible every morning. I asked last week if she was okay, and she gave me some story about seasonal allergies. Made absolutely no sense until the post."

Gretchen was confused. "What am I missing?"

"Aren't you Friends on Facebook?" Archie assumed we all were. Everyone was friends, why wouldn't we be Friends?

"I don't belong to Facebook. Should I? How much does it cost?"

"Yes, how else are you going to keep up with my impressive new career. And it's free."

"For now," Hank predicted.

"Damn, Iversson, you've been hanging around me too long. When did you get so cynical?"

"I've been hanging around you too long, Silva."

"No," he reconsidered. "Much as I like the compliment, it's just that you've been at Pinnacle too long."

"Thing is, Gretch," Orla tried to steer them back. "Martha put up this post about needing a drink and not being able to have one."

"Missing Alex already but glad for tonight's party. Sure could use a drink. Too bad I can't have one." Dawn recited, emphasizing the last bit.

Gretchen nodded. "That does sound pregnant."

"She doesn't look it," Danny said.

"Probably three months. You don't show yet, but it feels certain enough that you can tell people. I only waited longer because I didn't know what Kippy would say."

"Another maternity leave," Alex noted. "No wonder the LC doesn't want fraternization."

"Cost of doing business," Hank shrugged. "At Iversson Brothers, we have three or four a year."

"I was an Iversson baby."

"You know, Gretch, I bet Dad and Uncle Ray would always find a place for you. If you ever want."

"I don't think I could ever drag Rory out of New York, but thanks. It's good to have a Plan B." She checked the time on her phone and groaned. With a quick flick of the wrist, she stubbed out her cigarette against the wall. "I won't be able to stay long but I'll pop in tonight to wish you good luck." She gave Alex a quick hug before heading back.

It sounded like the first goodbye. Stroking his soul patch, Alex watched her disappear around the corner. He coughed gently. "So. A Pinnacle Baby. And I'm going to miss it!" His jocularity rang a little hollow. "All the years I worked here, this is only, the...what? Marla's first was before I started, but I was here when Amber was born. Then that woman who worked for Gene Siriano for a while. Her husband was CIA or something and they got stationed in South America, I think. Then Gretchen. And now Baby del Monte. Okay, some of the guys have had kids, but really this is only the fourth pregnancy in all that time."

Danny was surprised. "Considering the average age around here, it's surprising we don't have more."

"In New York, on these salaries?" Archie raised her eyebrows.

"True that," Dawn nodded. "I wonder how Martha and Gabe can afford it. They'd better start lighting candles that next time heads roll neither one of them gets chopped."

Hank's eyes widened with a flash of insight. "This explains why they've been acting different. Silva, you called it."

"You mean when I said they were turning into little Channings?"

Orla objected. "I like them!"

"So do I. But come on. Haven't you noticed the change?"

"Martha has always worked hard."

"Hey, I love Martha. And the boy is a doll, and they're adorable together. But they've gotten so serious about it. Look how she handles Dolores. Like she wants her approval."

"Her approval means a lot," Danny pointed out. "Hers and Scott's. Hugo and Khosi and I started around the same time and we all have almost the same degree." There was no need for Danny to complete that thought.

Alex broke the brooding silence. What would we do when he was gone? "Dolores and Scotty. Scott and Milla." His eyes glittered. "You do realize, Scott plus Milla is Scilla. Wasn't that a mythical monster or something?"

"Like Cthulhu!" Dawn's taste in reading material made Orla's ink look like Disney. "Well, the octopus part. Scylla had a bunch of heads with three rows of sharp giant teeth. She used to grab sailors off of ships with her tentacles."

"Her," Orla said, approvingly. "I like that."

"In *The Odyssey*, the ship had to pass between her and Charybdis, the whirlpool that would suck the boats down."

"Suck the boats down." Alex sighed with deep satisfaction. "So, Scilla it is. On that golden note, I leave you, my Munchkins."

"Not so fast!" Archie wiggled her forefinger in mock reprimand. "We have your send off tonight."

"And we are definitely starting that alumni association this time," Dawn reminded us. "Bohemian Beer Garden in Astoria. First Thursday of every month. Unless Stail Fiáin is playing somewhere, in which case we're all going to show up there anyway."

"That's right. You can't get rid of us that easy." Orla decided her fingers were dry enough. She punched him fondly on the arm.

He massaged it gingerly. "That I won't miss."

Δ

Boasting such refinements as marinated house-made mozzarella balls and clean restrooms, Cin Cin was nothing like Whine Bar. Nor could the modest gathering here compare with the boisterous crowd that had jammed Pinnacle's favored local not 24-hours before.

Judy Schreiber loved the unofficial Pinnacle after-work parties: the post-deployment carousing, the birthdays, the send-offs. It was wild to walk into a bar and find so many familiar faces. It reminded her of her college days, and of those wonderful, painful years when every bar in the East Village was packed with people whose secrets she knew. She'd missed that feeling of being part of an extended family. With fewer of the key people remaining, people like Noble Landrum and Alex Silva who brought everyone together, the Pinnacle family was starting to drift apart. The alumni, as we were apparently calling them, had turned out in full force for Alex, but how many more of these gatherings would call them in? That's why she'd stuck around as late as she had yesterday, even if she was getting too old to be out at midnight on a school night. It was worth the next day's exhaustion, to feel like herself again.

Well, she'd better grab that feeling while it lasted. When you weren't doing what you loved, which Judy hadn't done in a good twenty years, work was work. You tried to find something that wasn't too distasteful and paid enough to live on. If you were lucky, it might have an element of fun, or at least enough challenge to keep your mind clicking. But what really got you through the day were the people. At Trowbridge, determined to blend in, she'd buried her old life far enough to forget it. Here, with so many of...what was Mike Ventura's phrase? Misfits and broken toys. Even with the usual stream of comings and goings, the flavor stayed the same. Among her own people, she'd started to expand again. However, the last six months had unsettled the family. There was a sniper on the roof, and people were either running or hiding.

Feeling prematurely drenched in nostalgia, Judy caught the bartender's eye to signal for a refill of the over-appraised house red. Through the ironic reproduction Cinzano mirror, watching what was left of his troops bid a perfunctory goodbye to Wesley Peterson, she remembered his arrival, back when the Pinnacle party line was about how we carried a bright future on our collective shoulders, and leadership made pretty statements about professional development and team building. In reality, people came out with nothing more than they'd brought with them, and the biggest team building exercise was the perpetual state of siege. But so long as Pinnacle had paid lip service to these admirable goals, Wesley Peterson had been the poster boy. With Wesley gone, there'd be none of that hypocritical cheer. And without the others who were gone, without the family, Pinnacle was a balder, uglier world.

Holding her wine before her like a lantern, Judy picked her way across the glassy black floor, to the back corner IT had claimed for the evening. "Lot's of luck, Wesley," she said, making her raised glass into the gesture of a toast. "It won't be the same without you."

Wesley shook her other hand and smiled at her with apparent fondness. "Lots of luck to you, too, Judy. I always thought you were one of the good ones."

15 SMES

```
From:        Scott Bell
To:          All Pinnacle Associates
Subject:     Organizational News
------------------------------------
```

As part of our continued efforts to increase Operational
Excellence and provide the best possible service to our
clients, effective immediately, Client Relations will be
relocated under the Fulfillment Operations umbrella. Over
time, we have come to understand that the needs of Client
Relations are more similar to those of our Fulfillment teams
than to our Sales division.

In conjunction with this reorganization, we are extremely
pleased to announce that, in recognition of her extraordinary
achievements, Milla Kristol has been promoted to Chief
Operating Officer of Pinnacle Management Services.

Scott Bell, President
Pinnacle Management Services

Δ

```
From:        Kippy Melcher
To:          All Pinnacle Associates
Subject:     Our New CTO
------------------------------------
```

Please join me in welcoming Jim Matticchio, our new Chief
Technology Officer.

Kippy

Kippy Melcher, CEO
Pinnacle Management Services

Δ

This had been Kippy's third trip to India this year. The first two were with
Leonard Strauss. This time, Gary Feldman accompanied him. They must
have come in straight from Newark. A clean suit not withstanding, Feldman

looked as crumpled as a used tissue. Kippy, on the other hand, was all pink and freshly-showered, probably from a pit stop at the health club. He paced along the windowsill, bouncing dangerously on the balls of his feet.

"Come on, come on! Let's get going. You guys should be raring to go!"

We made a show of looking perky and eager from the neck up, but we were dragging worse than Feldman and without the excuse of an 18-hour flight. Morale was still hovering around basement level. In the old days, Kay Kuperman or Jo Vargas would have done something to try and bring it up. The usual Hallowe'en celebration would have been a good move, but it was mid-October and there hadn't been a peep out of HC. Not that we were in the mood; but sometimes if you have a reason to pretend to feel better, you actually do.

"Well, Gary and I had a terrific time in Pune. Absolutely terrific! Right Gary?"

Feldman barely coughed up his almost-a-smile. Kippy didn't notice. He was wired with adrenaline, marble eyes popping, words gushing out. It was like a PSA warning about speed. When he got especially crazy like this, Noble Landrum used to put it all in perspective by remembering that, unlike Miriam Melcher, rest her soul, at least we never had to live through Kippy's Terrible Twos.

"The people we have over there!" He was visibly trembling with excitement. "Terrific people! Ashok, Vijay, Sharmilla... Well, I still say I've never made a bad decision, even if I don't always get the results I expected. But I'm also never ashamed to say maybe it's time to revisit a decision I made a long time ago. Or I'd still be driving a Chevy Malibu. Ha! Things can change. And the big change now about India is that now we've got our own branch office over there. Which is why I'm putting an official stick in the ground for Denali II!"

There was dead silence while we tried to absorb the news. The remnants of the IT Development Dream team, Leon, Ina and Craig, were as shocked as the rest of us.

Chortling into Mr. Microphone, Kippy cast a maniacal grin from one end of the Pit to the other. "Okay, okay. When we took on Denali, I'm not ashamed to say we maybe bit off more than we could chew. Never be ashamed to aim high, you got that? But you know what held us back, what kept us from success? It was that we gave over the power to the contractors. Okay, they came to us with top drawer, absolutely top of the line recommendations. And they talked a good talk. But in the end, they were hired guns, they weren't invested in the outcome. Now we're building our own team in Pune. Not contractors, but people who have a stake in the future of Pinnacle. We're bringing on bright kids, hungry for experience, and training them the way we want them trained. And it's not just Vijay's developers. Everyone we've brought on in Pune, all of them sharp, enthusiastic, best kind...From now on, nobody better argue with me when I say that Pinnacle is the best managed office services company IN THE WORLD! And that's the bottom line. Because with these folks, with the teams we're building out, nothing can stop us. I see endless potential for us in Pune. We can staff up to match our volume, take some of the pressure off all of you. Not that you aren't all doing a terrific job. Ha! Terrific! But I know we've been challenged to scale up our services to match what Scott's guys are pulling in. Well, this is our...what's that thing that keeps New Orleans from flooding over? Our..." he snapped his fingers rapidly, trying to summon up the word.

"Levee?" Dave Broussard suggested.

"That's it. Our levee. Pune is gonna hold the flood waters back so we can just surf that wave to success!"

"Okay, so one more thing and I'll let you all get back to work. Now, when we took the space up on eight...well, anyone who was here back then can remember, we were practically sitting on each other's laps. Am I right? Martha?"

"One hundred percent, Kippy. I wouldn't want to be doing that right now." Martha del Monte patted her stomach. The adorable rounding was emphasized by the high-waisted tunics she'd begun to wear as soon as autumn hit.

"Ha! Well, the way things were going then, I told the landlords I wanted first refusal on any space that came up in the building. And when that PR group on eight decided to move out to Jersey City...You know that saying about hesitation, right? And you know I don't hesitate. No, I snapped it up. And I will never be sorry I did. But that was then, and things are different now. Some of you may already have a hunch about where I'm going with this. We've trimmed down, and now that we're building the team in Pune we can stay lean here at the home office. I walk around this floor and I see plenty of empty desks. So we've got permission from the landlord to sublease the eighth floor. At the price we got it, I don't think it'll take long for us to find a tenant. The LC already has ideas about reorganizing space here. Milla and Don are finalizing the plans, and we may be able to start shifting around the fourth floor by end of next week. Our goal is to get everyone moved down from eight by November 1. Okay then. Lots of exciting plans, Pinnacle! Give yourselves a round of applause and have a great day!"

Δ

Dawn waved. She'd spotted Judy Schreiber coming from the wrong side of the alley, carrying a large shopping bag. "Excuse me!? If you won a lottery, why are you even here?"

Hank looked up from his phone to stare. "Who won a lottery?"

Dawn pointed to the logo on Judy's bag, then up at the wall behind the overhang of the posh Japanese-Italian boutique. They matched.

"Moving sale," Judy explained. "Their lease ran out and the landlord's doubling it. The guy there said they're reopening in Brooklyn in the spring, but they're clearing out what they have in stock. It's still more than I should spend, but $350 for an $1800 Yamamoto jacket is kind of irresistible."

"What kind of jacket costs more than a laptop?" Hank wanted to know.

"The kind I dream about," Archie said. "Can I see?"

Judy smiled and handed over the bag. "I managed to find a couple of shirts, too. You should go over after work. You're so tiny, there's a ton you could choose from."

Orla regarded a simple white blouse with some disappointment. "I thought Japanese was edgier."

"It's not meant to be in your face. It's unexpected, in a subtle way. Look at the hem."

"Good investment pieces," was Danny Zill's surprising comment. "Hey, my grandfather was in the rag trade. We're not allowed to buy crap. That's why I have to be careful now, sitting so close to the Pit. My suits are better than Scott's."

"How is it over there?" Judy asked. "I miss you since the move."

"Okay enough. A little strange being shut in with Hugo and Channing. The company, not the room. The room's plenty big enough."

"Well, yeah," Hank agreed. "I never understood why they let Strauss use it as an office."

"I still think of it as the Training Room," Dawn said, a little wistfully.

Danny laughed. "Strauss was so pissed he had to move. He made a big show out of waiting until we were standing around to pull his stuff out."

"He was a king, all alone in that big room. The way he put his desk at the far end from the door, so you had to walk all the way across with him staring at you." Judy's face twisted with distaste. "Believe me, Pilar Novas had a harassment suit before he even opened his asshole mouth. Sorry. Don't get me started on Leonard Strauss. And now they've put me right outside his door, so I can hop to whenever he needs me. Him and Jim Matticchio."

Dawn drew a blank. "Where's that?"

"Energy. Remember, when we started, that room that was IT? All the developers sitting on top of each other? Now they put a wall up and made two offices."

"Wait, who's Jim Matticchio?" Orla asked.

"The new Wesley. Didn't you see the email?"

"Almost a non-email," Archie noted. "Should we read anything into that?"

Judy shrugged. "Craig looked him up on LinkedIn. He's had three jobs in four years, and left the last one seven months ago. Craig thinks he's a...is there a name for this? For someone who comes in to close things down? Craig's pretty positive they hired him to shut down dev. Except for Leon and Ina, of course. Kippy would never get rid of them."

"Kippy's not getting rid of dev so fast," Danny said. "He just announced Denali II."

"With India!" Hank and Dawn and Archie were practically a chorus.

"They're already pushing Data Entry over as fast as they can staff up. Fritz and Raney keep waiting for the..." Making a clicking sound, Hank drew a finger across his neck. "I'm predicting the rest is right behind."

Danny looked uncomfortable. "I'm not saying I know anything, but we've been doing market research, about how our clients feel about Indian accents on the phone."

"Which reminds me," Dawn said, pulling her eyebrows into a ironic furrow. "Tully had a call from Jeff Curry. Who is now working...can I have a drumroll or something?"

"Seriously? This is what happens when you live with a musician. Tell us already. I miss Curry!" Orla gave Dawn a playful shove. She was missing Alex Silva, too.

"Ow, okay! So Jeff is working with Kay."

"Kuperman?" Judy asked. "What's she up to?"

"If you were updating your LinkedIn, which is something we all should be doing by the way," Archie shook her head sadly. Sometimes she thought she was the only one who thought of Pinnacle as more than a very prolonged summer job. "You'd know she started a training consultancy."

"Not just training." Now Dawn was bursting to tell her gossip. "She's training trainers. Specifically to send overseas to train call center teams for American companies. She's got contracts already in Belarus, the Philippines...India. Yah??"

"Let me get this straight." Orla couldn't tell if Dawn were joking or telling the truth. "Kay Kuperman is training offshore call centers in India?"

"I didn't think Kay was that sharp," Hank admitted.

"Tully said he didn't know which would be funnier—if all the competition hired them, or if Kippy had to hire them himself."

The playwright in Judy Schreiber couldn't resist. "Chekhov said you don't put a loaded gun on stage unless someone's going to use it." She smiled at the cluster of confused faces. "Kay took a leaf out of Kippy's second favorite book 'Infiltration of the enemy.' Right out of The Art of War."

Δ

Advancement, the large glass conference room and the only dedicated conference room left at Pinnacle, was filled with people who didn't actually know why they were there. The meeting request had been issued jointly by Scott Bell and Milla Kristol, who sat to either side of the slab of blonde wood. At its head stood Hugo Singer, radiating enthusiasm from the very bristles of his buzz-cut. Behind him, the projector showed a yellow presentation slide, glaring with deliberate blankness. Danny Zill and Eric Channing leaned against the credenza, apparently guarding a stack of yellow ring binders. Around the table and requiring a few extra chairs to be brought in, were representatives of every department: Finance, HR, Sales, Client Relations, Fulfillment, and Dave Broussard. We eyed one another with curiosity, but no one showed any indication of knowledge. Hugo toyed with his laser pointer. Milla Kristol frowned impatiently at the wall clock.

Gary Feldman flew in on a gust of self-important urgency, Bennett Liu trailing discreetly behind him. Feldman closed the door.

At this signal, Hugo took a deep breath and began in a voice too loud for the room: "Welcome to Project Lemonade!"

Despite the presence of three members of the Leadership Council, this meeting was in Hugo's large, untried hands.

"Before we begin, we're going to pass around some Confidentiality Agreements. I ask that everyone take a few minutes to go over these and sign." His two lieutenants handed out the surprisingly slim documents. "They're boilerplate," Hugo assured us. "Nothing to concern you. This is for the benefit of some other members of the team, who you're going to meet in a little while, to assure them that nothing we say today will leave this room. I mean, that it won't leave the people in the room."

There was a subdued rustle as people read at their various paces. It was an innocuous document, implying we would be privy to confidential information that was not to be disclosed. It probably *was* boilerplate. Feldman would never pay a lawyer for something he could download off the internet. We signed and passed them back, Channing checking off a list as each copy was received.

At Channing's nod, Hugo split his face with a grin. "Great! Now can someone get the lights?"

Judy Schreiber, utterly confused at having been invited, got up and hit the dimmers. With considerable light spilling in through the glass walls, it made little difference except as a cue for us all to focus on the screen.

Over the next 20 minutes, we learned that, because of our special skills we had been selected for a secret mission. An exciting one, of course, and

Hugo Singer had been appointed to lead us. We were about to embark on the takeover of Raskub Secretarial Services in Minneapolis, Minnesota.

Kippy's appetite for empire wasn't going to be limited to having his own colony in India. Now, despite having always championed organic growth through sales, he was determined to acquire kingdoms beyond his own. Raskub was only the first, Hugo said it flat out; the first of what would be an ongoing series of acquisitions. The vetting had already been done. What remained were the mechanics of merger, including the functional merger that we were all here to facilitate. Each of us would be partnered with an opposite number at Raskub. We weren't to worry about cooperation. The Raskub family, having fallen on hard times, actively courted a takeover.

"We're taking their lemons and turning them into our lemonade." Hugo was thrilled with his own zinger. Milla Kristol awarded him an icy tinkle. Hugo swiveled his head to bask briefly in the approval before returning to Slide 4: Synergies.

Raskub Secretarial had begun 70 years ago as a temporary placement agency. Over time, just as Kippy had expanded Sid Melcher's bookkeeping and answering service company, Raskub had developed a specialty in HR administration, integrating with other companies to provide payroll and background checking services.

"So we have a lot of services they don't, which means we can upsell to their list. And our guys can start selling background checking services through the Raskub portal. But there's a lot of overlap. The plan is to leverage their core competencies to expand Compliance," Hugo explained. "So Will, your role will be key."

Will Compton's smile was genuine. Pinnacle wasn't where he wanted to end his life, but it was nice to finally feel he'd made some impact. Maybe he'd even get a raise. At least a bonus. His former classmates who'd gone Wall Street were always getting bonuses for M&A. Then he could reapply to Columbia.

"We see an excellent opportunity to expand Training, too. On both sides. The big challenges of course will be pulling the cultures together. And the technology, of course. That's a big one. Dave, you saw their user portal during the vetting process."

The Buzzard nodded. He was relieved he wouldn't have to keep this secret any more. Well, he would, but at least there'd be a bunch of people in on it instead of just the LC and Edie. "Only the public-facing user portal. I won't get to see any of the back end until we get started, but I know it's mostly Java..." He belatedly realized there were no developers in the room. "Basically, it seems likely that when we're ready to bring it over to Denali, we'll be able to work with the code as it is. We won't have to rip it out and start from scratch. But in the short term, we'll probably be maintaining them on their own technology. Just replace the payroll integration with a patch to hook it up to Bridge. We want their client base to have the look and feel they're used to, at least during the transition."

Martha del Monte, hands resting complacently on her considerable bump, nodded her agreement with that point. "How much are they going to know about the takeover? The clients, I mean."

"We're calling it a merger," Hugo said smoothly. "But yeah, of course. We have to tell them. We want to tell everybody! This is big news! That's why we have Judy here. Communications. A whole big rollout. But for the Raskub client list, we're going to keep the announcement soft, you know, reassure them.

Absorbing her purpose, Judy started thinking aloud. "So in addition to a press release, we'll need two sets of client mailings..."

Chuckling, Hugo held up a traffic-cop hand. "Hey, hold on a minute! We'll get to everyone's deliverables at another meeting. But before we open the conference bridge to bring in Raskub, Judy, you don't have an opposite number. You're going to be working directly with me and the LC. On all the communications, whatever we need for the project."

"I have a matrix from the last merger I worked on at Octans-Bellums," Milla said sweetly. "And a packet of templates. I'll forward them to you."

The three C's disappeared as soon as they'd given a gracious conference-bridge welcome to the Raskub group. An hour later, our sunny leader dismissed us and our new comrades in Minneapolis. We staggered away from Advancement, numbed by contemplation of the scope of the job ahead. We were being asked to assemble a company out of two boxes of parts, to find all the places where we could, or should, fit Tab A into Slot B. There was not a lot of time. The takeover, merger, whatever it was would be signed, sealed and delivered by the end of the year—as the Buzzard said, "the good Lord willing and the creek don't rise."

Will Compton's initial excitement had dimmed a little when he realized how much he had to do, and how there wasn't really anyone else in Compliance to whom he could delegate his regular tasks; the team was already spread too thin.

Archie Ghosh was in the same position. All of us were. Rightsizing hadn't left enough wiggle room for two people in any group to catch the same flu. Losing coverage for more than two months was going to hit us hard.

When Judy returned to her desk, Milla Kristol's email was already in her inbox. She opened the famous matrix and winced. The spreadsheet had over 100 rows. Mailings, presentations, checklists; a wide range of communications materials. It also included all the paperwork for supporting what looked like every deliverable for the merger team. Communications were one thing; in fact, it was a role for which she arguably brought some experience to the table. This looked more like they were making her the Admin for everyone working on this project. Nice. Well, that's what you get for doing whatever work got thrown at you. The Buzzard always joked that he'd held the same job for five years, but they kept changing his title. Judy's title hadn't changed since she'd first walked through the door, but the work on her plate shifted constantly. Her reward was more work, and surviving rounds of layoffs, even when her managers didn't. She wandered over to her current manager's desk with a hard copy of the matrix.

"Hey." Dave scooped a plastic bag and a coil of Ethernet cabling off his second chair, so she could sit down. "Pretty intense stuff. I'm not gonna lie. It's a ton of work, but it'll look great on the resume, being part of something like this."

"I guess." She handed him the printout. "Look at this list. This is a full time job. I notice Len Strauss wasn't in this meeting. He's got half my time. Has anyone spoken with him about this?"

Dave gave his hair a brisk rub. It didn't help his thinking any. "Don't worry about it," he advised. "Milla and Scott want you on this, and they outrank him. They'll work things out."

"What about you? 'IT Project Liaison' sounds pretty important. Architecting another new technology? How are you going to juggle all your RFPs with that?"

He settling back in his chair, with a contented groan. "Not gonna worry. For now, we're leaving them alone except for the payroll integration. Raskub has an offshore team supporting their portal. In Belarus. Leon'll be happy as a clam for once. I'll only have to sit in on the occasional meeting and explain it all to the LC."

"So I guess they're going to hold back on Denali II for a while, until we see how Raskub is going to fit in down the road. I mean, it only makes sense, doesn't it?"

"Matticchio didn't say."

"He never says much, does he? Sometimes I wonder if he's even in there."

Dave opened his hands and looked skyward. What could he say? "Don't let it get to you," he advised. "Just do the best you can. That's what I do."

Δ

```
From:       Milla Kristol
To:         All Pinnacle Associates
Subject:    Welcome Bruce Korn
```

We are so excited to welcome Bruce Korn as the new Director
of Client Relations (for more about Bruce, <u>follow this link</u>
to his LinkedIn profile). Bruce will be ably assisted by Ann
Ling, who has done a tremendous job of covering in these
challenging times.

In addition to a wealth of impressive Client Relations
management experiences, Bruce is a certified Trim/Delta
Sensei. We plan to leverage all of these talents! Bruce will
be working closely with both Edie Brewer and Hugo Singer to
establish a cross-functional Pinnacle Center of Excellence.

At this time, I would also like to congratulate Edie and Hugo
on their respective promotions to Senior Director of
Fulfillment and Director of Process Improvement.

Milla Kristol, COO
Pinnacle Management Services

Δ

"And so, by applying Trim/Delta analysis in the design of the application,
we've got a tool that will cover nine of the top ten pain points identified by
our client survey." Bruce Korn surveyed the room with confident satisfaction.
His whole track record, the reason Kippy Melcher had been in such a
flattering hurry to have him onboard, was about applying Total Quality
Management to the supporting service products with technology. This
project, his first, would showcase all of that and prove he'd been an inspired
hire. "It's been a rewarding experience, working so closely with Edie and
Hugo and Dave over here, and with Ann's SMEs in Client Relations. This
project is a perfect proving ground for our new Center of Excellence."

"Can we go back to..." Gary Feldman rifled through the handout. "Slide 7."

Dave Brussard felt bad watching Korn reverse to the budget slide. Poor
guy. This was his first presentation to the LC. He didn't know that Feldman
smiled the way a crocodile did, just before snapping you up in his jaws.

"Why two consultants? For a company of our size, we have a substantial,
some might say too large, in-house development team. And what is..."
Feldman adjusted his glasses as if it were difficult to read a six-inch font on
the smart board. "How do you even pronounce this? Derailer?" He smirked
over his shoulder in Kippy's direction. "Sounds to me like something that's
going to take us off track. Why do we need that? It's a large capital
expenditure that depreciates to zero the minute you take it out of the box."

"Derailleur. It doesn't actually come out of the box; it's a cloud
application." Seeing his little joke had tanked, Korn hurried an explanation.

267

"It's a BPMS; a suite for Business Process Management automation. I used it at B of A. It's a very powerful tool."

"How intimidating," Milla Kristol said, with a wide-eyed little laugh. Dave had noticed she did this with any acronym she hadn't coined herself. Unless it was Kippy's or Feldman's, in which case she jumped on it and ran.

"Oh, not at all! You just sketch out your workflow, the way you would with Visio or with a pen and paper. But because you have a database mapped to all the widgets...I mean the symbols. The squares, the diamonds for decision points, even arrows, all of those...when all of those have meaning coded to the application, and by that, I mean our own custom business meaning, it's as easy as, um, baking a cake with a mix."

Until that last metaphor, Korn had been doing a good job of showing he was eager to make things clear, without being patronizing. The Buzzard would be giving him high marks, except for the chill in Kristol's nod of comprehension. Interesting. Does she have a thing against cake mix? What could the poor guy have already done in two weeks to piss her off? Maybe it was just that he'd done too much. Like anyone else when they first got here, Korn was a ball of fire. Thing is, he was used to places where they expected you to try and upset the applecart, where that marked you as someone with a big future. At Pinnacle, it just painted a target on your back.

Listen to the poor jerk going on and on. The first project meeting where he'd talked about Derailleur, Korn said that when he'd seen it demoed, it had absolutely knocked his socks off; that for someone like himself who didn't have a coding background, a tool like this opened up thrilling possibilities. Dave, who could code, understood how this was pretty cool stuff. But the way Korn was presenting it to the LC, he was shooting himself in the foot. He was owning it too much; he talked about that application with as much pride as if he'd invented it himself.

"For example..." Korn was straining now. "Symbols to represent the time lag we want to impose to keep the work flowing out to the Fulfillment teams at a measured pace...once it's set up like that, you won't need to turn to a programmer every time you want to make a tweak to a work process or set up a new procedure. Anyone can modify the flow chart in Derailleur. And the application automatically updates to match it."

The LC was doing their brick wall impersonation. Thing is, the only way to sell to them is to make them think it's their own idea. Yup, now Milla Kristol's doing that thing where she cocks her head to one side. Here it comes.

"I don't think our people have that level of skill," she tinkled gaily. "And we don't really have the bandwidth to be training them up. It sounds unnecessarily complicated."

"It's very simple." Korn was sincere as a Country ballad. "Edie was able to map a simple process after just walking through the demo."

Uh-oh. Making it worse for himself, poor fool; thinking just because Edie was damned good at what she did that she must be a star. Dave wouldn't turn in her direction, but he would have bet money she was looking down at a piece of paper and trying to turn invisible.

"We could have this all set up in five months, tops," Korn concluded.

"I don't know," Scott said. "Gary raises some legitimate concerns."

"What are our other options here?" Kippy polled his Leaders.

Milla shrugged her pale green silk shoulders. Were her tits always that big? "I wouldn't say that automation has exactly been our friend, now has it?" Laughter on the rocks. Some of the socialites he met at Angie's work events made that sound when they wanted to show they knew you thought you were being funny. "Pune has been performing extremely well. I suggest we escalate the build-out of Client Relations and institute additional manual processes to solve the pain points."

"Here, here!" Feldman chimed in.

"There are a lot of negatives to a manual solution," Korn said carefully.

Again, Dave felt for the guy. When Korn had showed them Derailleur, he'd been so excited about Pinnacle being so eager to use cutting edge tools to move forward into the 21st Century. Kippy must have sold him hard on that to pull him away from Bank of America.

Korn made a stand. "From a quality standpoint, manual means more room for user error, which is pain point number one on the survey matrix. More chances for tasks to get dropped..." He pulled up the related slide, apparently on the premise that sometimes executives believed it more if they saw in in PowerPoint. "And what about the cost of all those salaries? With my plan, the expense is all in the setup, just one-time."

"Salaries are Op Ex, not CapEx," Feldman shrugged.

Milla nodded. "And Pune costs practically nothing."

"But in the long term..." It was weird to see that happen, to watch someone realize he'd been had. Korn stopped flopping around, and his eyes glazed over. "Thank you all for your time this morning," he said.

Dave liked the idea of TQM plus technology helping Client Relations. Hell, he'd liked it when Lloyd Baptiste had tried it on Fulfillment. Too bad no one had told Bruce Korn about Lloyd Baptiste. Or Renee Ochs and Abby Witherspoon, for that matter. The only way to survive Pinnacle was to not make waves. Dave was kind of the expert on this. Edie Brewer wasn't doing too bad either, he thought. He knew Korn's wife was still out West, waiting until after the baby was born. Either Korn was going to have to find his own cave to hide in, or hope he hadn't sold his house yet.

Δ

It was the first time in a long time that we felt excited. The email said that Bruce Korn, the new Director of Client Relations, was offering a 3-part course leading to a Trim/Delta Kyudousha certificate. As a certified Sensei, he was credentialed to offer training. "Kyudousha" was only a semi-legitimate degree, not like the Minarai level he was mentoring Hugo, Khosi and Edie through. But Trim/Delta was hot right now and the certificate would prove we'd had exposure to the concepts and techniques. Pinnacle was finally offering something that would look good on a resume. The first class filled up instantly. Don Bryson shot out a follow-up email assuring us that if we'd missed out, we'd have other opportunities; Bruce planned on offering the course once each quarter.

Will Compton reached a triumphant fist straight up toward the ceiling. "Yes!" he hissed, making Gabe del Monte turn his head in question.

Compton had kind of a wacky smile. Gabe's mind's eye, which continued to want to draw, couldn't resist sketching a pair of connecting curves between Will's eyebrows, which got almost triangular, and the U of his thin lips; it was the profile of a cartoon cat.

"I got in," Will said. "To the Trim/Delta."

Gabe tabled the cat and sighed philosophically. "Guess I didn't. Maybe I'll have better luck next time."

"If there is a next time," Will said darkly.

"What are you saying?"

"Like Alex always used to say, people come and go so quickly here." So there were already rumors about Korn. Gabe made a mental note to tell Martha later. Lately they'd been getting a little out of the loop on the gossip. Martha said it was because the others were only biding their time here, while they were trying to build a life. Maybe so, and with a baby on the way, Gabe wanted to do the grown up thing. Still, he kind of missed some of the silliness.

Still holding Will's eye, he jerked his head in the direction of Milla Kristol's office. "Yeah? So where's a falling house when you need one?" he whispered.

Will smiled again. "Too true, my fellow Munchkin, too true." Even without the cat face, it was a crazy smile.

Gabe smiled back as the thought struck him: "Oh no, not Munchkin. We're so definitely Winkies, my friend. The ones with the tall black hats, you know, marching in front of the castle."

"The Oreo guys? Yes!"

Δ

From: Judy Schreiber
To: All Pinnacle Associates
Subject: The Peak Experience

Hello Pinnacle!

So much to read this month!

- A "no holds barred" interview with Pinnacle COO Milla
  Kristol
- Pinnacle offers clients "Follow the Sun" service!
- Trim/Delta Sensei Bruce Korn explains how Methodology
  + Technology = Success!
- Phi Beta Kippy: Eric Channing reflects on Lessons
  Learned

Judy

16 OFFSHORE

As far as Martha del Monte was concerned, the best thing about Pune was how it changed the LC's attitude towards working remote. If she and Gabe could each work from home one day a week, that would mean only three days of having to leave the baby with some stranger. And if his cousin Celia was serious about being willing to babysit for room and board, it wouldn't really be a stranger and they'd have the first year taken care of. Maybe more of Gabe's cousins wanted to try living in New York; they could have hot and cold running au pairs until the baby started kindergarten.

She shifted, trying to find a comfortable way to balance on Gretchen's donut cushion. Pregnancy sure did interesting things to your body. "Interesting" like in the old curse about living in in interesting times. No, she didn't mean that. She'd been lucky. Only a few weeks of morning sickness, and always gone before lunch. Her sister Dottie had it a lot worse, total narcolepsy both times, and practically living with her face in a bucket. All Martha really had was discomfort. She felt wobbly when she walked, a unique sensation for someone who'd practically been born with sea legs. Though she was elevating them whenever she could, her feet were too puffy to wear any of her cute shoes. And there was her butt, of course. She shifted again, moving her weight a little forward. How come they never tell you about that?

She was already tired of feeling fat, which was silly. She wasn't that big, really. And Gabe thought she was beautiful. The other night, right in the middle of rubbing in the coco butter his Mom sent, he'd put down the jar and told her not to move. She'd felt weird lying naked on the couch, while he'd sketched her with the first pen and paper he could find. He hadn't painted for ages, hadn't even unpacked his art supplies since they moved, and he hardly ever used to paint figures, but he wanted to paint her now. Like this. She blushed to think about it, a combination of embarrassment, and her joy at being so loved. "You're inspiring Daddy," she whispered to her bump. And me, she thought. You're inspiring me.

Even when she was tiny, Martha had always been a good worker, scrambling under Dad's feet to help with whatever would let her stay near him in the garden, in the shed, on the boat. She liked work. She liked seeing the results of her work. That was one of the nice things about Client Relations. Sure there was a lot of stress. But who would want to spend all day doing something that didn't matter? She loved solving problems, finding out what was wrong and figuring out how to fix it, or at least who could fix it. When you could tell the client everything was resolved, it was satisfying—it was an accomplishment. Martha was content with her work. And now Gabe was a Trainer and had turned out to have a knack for it.

She thought they were safe for the immediate future. Kippy was fond of her, which was a blessing. Of course, he'd forever see her as that little girl from Maine who knew how to type and answer a phone. That was good for keeping her and Gabe employed, but not for moving up the ladder. Not that there was a real ladder at Pinnacle, one you could count on. Look at Ann Ling. It was the same thing they'd done to Viv Karlow, dumping everything on her for so long, then bringing someone in over her head. Now Ann had to train this Bruce Korn, as well as manage the department until he was ready, and meanwhile she had all that work on Project Lemonade. How could you not throw a line to someone who was obviously drowning? It was natural for Martha to help Ann out whenever she could. Good for her, too. It was Renee Ochs who'd made her understand that she had a marketable skill. Ladder or no ladder, as long as she was here, she would learn as much as she could. From Kippy, from Ann, from Milla—because, difficult as she was, Milla did have a lot of experience and if you paid attention you could learn things, even if it sometimes took listening carefully to what wasn't said. When Milla picked her as Ann's backup on Project Lemonade, Martha was thrilled, both for what she expected to learn and for the confirmation that Milla, like Kippy, considered her someone worth having around. Now that Milla was on equal footing with Scott and Feldman, this was extremely important. What if Kippy got hit by a bus? You had to think about things like that when you worked for a company that was mostly one man.

Another reason she couldn't stay at Pinnacle forever. It was good to feel safe for now. But someday, well…if Baby was going to go to college, and if she and Gabe were someday going to retire where he could paint, they'd have to move on. Pinnacle would never pay them enough. It wasn't only the money or the safety. If she was being honest, she had to admit she wanted something more from her job. Maybe if Ann left…if maybe she did, Martha would ask Milla if she could be Bruce Korn's assistant. The thought had never crossed her mind before. Is it Baby, she wondered or have I always been ambitious but just didn't know? Maybe she'd even go for an MBA someday. Try for a career like Renee's. She'd reached out to Renee on LinkedIn. Renee had a big job now, with one of the airlines. Maybe someday she'd be brave enough to give Renee a call and ask her advice. Someday. When Baby wasn't a baby any more.

Δ

```
From:       Milla Kristol
To:         All Pinnacle Associates
Subject:    Expanding Our Horizons
```

I am excited to announce a major business milestone! As of
end of business today, Friday, October 17, 2008, Pinnacle's
Data Entry service has completed migration, in its entirety,
to our offices in Pune.

I would like to thank everyone involved for the smoothness of
the transition. Particular thanks are due to our Process
Improvement team, under the direction of Hugo Singer, for
their analysis of the migration process and for optimizing
Fulfillment workflows around this new paradigm.
Congratulations are due to our Pune Fulfillment Manager,
Ashok Fernandez, who bears responsibility for staffing and
training our Pune Fulfillment associates, as well as for the
ongoing management of that department.

I have recently returned from a tour of our Pune facility,
where I was extremely impressed by the quality and enthusiasm
of our staff. We can all feel confident that our new Data
Entry team meets our highest standards of excellence and will
continue to do so, as we continue to grow.

Milla Kristol, COO
Pinnacle Management Services

Δ

The Leadership Council was loving their visits to Pune. Len Strauss had of
course spent so much time on the subcontinent, well before joining
Pinnacle, that he referred to it as his second home. Even Feldman liked being
there; what he hated was getting there and back. Feldman preferred not to
travel much beyond Cape May. Gretchen told us they'd had to jump through
a bunch of hoops to get him a passport in time for his August trip; expensive
hoops, which must have galled him no end.

Kippy couldn't have been more delighted with his discovery. To celebrate
the complete migration of Data Entry to Pune, he took another trip over, this
time bringing Scott Bell and Milla Kristol. Kippy was always pumped when
he returned, but no one had anticipated the effect on Scilla. They floated
through the office wrapped in a benevolent glow that took the rest of the
week to subside. When Marla couldn't get a last-minute table at the new
Batali restaurant for lunch with the COO of Lutz & Lutz, Scott was heard to
tell her not to worry. During the weekly Project Lemonade status meeting,
Milla reacted to one of Dave Broussard's jokes with a genuine laugh.

Those of us who had never travelled anywhere more exotic than Epcot
fantasized about what it was that so charmed this insensible crew. Had they
been overwhelmed by vibrant colors, by exotic smells and flavors? Was it the

profound beauty of an unfamiliar temple that shook them awake or, perhaps, the vigorous clash of the modern and the traditional? From what we could gather from our friendly coworkers over there, it was nothing of the sort. To Ashok's chagrin, for he was something of a one-man Tourism Board, Kippy and companions never took so much as a quick peek at Mumbai. They didn't leave Pune, where they lost their days sleeping in the hotel, resting from the nights they spent in an office that was synched to the New York day half a world away.

For all the Cs knew, they could have been in Lisbon or Kalamazoo. But they adored being in India. The hotel staff coddled them with sweets and flowers, with silent perfect service and with extravagant thanks for tips that would slip unacknowledged into an American pocket. In the office, they were greeted with admiration and treated with a brand of non-cynical courtesy hardly known Stateside since before the Age of Aquarius; everything they did was wonderful.

To illustrate an article that he was writing for *The Peak Experience*, Ashok shared some pictures from the most recent trip. Our first sight of the Pune offices showed us a clean, modern space that was prophetically roomy for the 40 or so current employees. The desks were study carrels, with creamy two-foot dividers. They were shown unoccupied and shot from a marketing-savvy angle that made them seem endless in number. There were men's and women's locker rooms, which triggered the envious wonder that there might be a gym until one of the IT guys told the Buzzard that this was a standard office security measure: employees were required to leave all bags and outerwear off the work floor. Speaking of IT, their designated area was as large as the vanished eight floor and had obvious room for expansion.

The centerpiece of Ashok's album was photos of a pot-luck banquet held to celebrate the Data Entry milestone. The large room they used for meetings and training newcomers was festooned with lengths of spangled fabric, and with *Visit Incredible India!* travel posters showing all the sights the Cs never went to see. Clustered around long flower-decked tables were the Pune associates, wearing festive traditional garb, and our own Big Three. Here was a shot of Kippy, who lived on egg whites and tuna salad, gamely biting into a crisp, fried samosa, an embroidered hat plopped incongruously on his head. Here was a grinning Scott Bell, surrounded by attentive sari-draped young women, his hands providentially occupied with a beverage and something on a skewer. Here was Kippy again, deep in conversation with a self-important white-tunicked Vijay, a crescent of observers standing a respectful distance apart. In the final shot, Milla Kristol looked positively chummy with a pretty woman who wore an aqua salwar kameez. Milla's nautical blue jacket was accessorized with a beaded scarf in the same soft greenish blue and a discordant armful of glass bangles. Ashok's email identified the woman as Sharmilla, the Pune Client Relations lead. The baubles had been her welcome gift to her boss. Scott asked Judy to print the photos, with the Sales printer, using the photo-grade paper Sales used for proposals, and have Chris Keane mount them on the break room bulletin board. Every time we went for a cup of coffee we were freshly depressed. The Pinnacle Raj. Glamor and adoration at bargain basement prices. How could we compete with that?

Δ

The people who were on Facebook told the people who weren't on Facebook, so within an hour of his discreet knock on Don Bryson's door, everyone knew: the State Department had at last come to its senses about the value of a fluent Arabic-speaker slash Islamist scholar and, overlooking his mother's collegiate extramural activities, had offered Will Compton a post.

Gabe del Monte and Archie Ghosh reached over their desk divider for a smacking high-five. A laughing Judy Schreiber, tears shining in her eyes, ran across the floor to hug him so hard that she managed to lift him an inch off his chair. Eric Channing heard about it from Danny Zill and walked over to extend a stiff-armed handshake. Danny said Channing spent the rest of the day sulking.

Will didn't have the kind of face that could ordinarily be described as radiant, but today he was glowing like a bride. His goofy smile never ebbed. Not even when a pissed-off Milla Kristol marched him into Gary Feldman's office. Feldman tried to sway Will by offering him the meaningless title of Compliance Manager, plus a 10 percent raise that would leave him 20 K short of his new starting salary (not including the benefits package). The Cs were dumbfounded when, explaining the opportunity as the fulfillment of a lifelong dream, he graciously declined their generous offer. At which point, Kristol said cooly that two weeks was insufficient time for them to bring someone up to speed on Project Lemonade. Will politely explained that he couldn't negotiate with the State Department. He had to report in two weeks' time. Having not had a vacation in 14 months, he would much rather have taken the time off—and could have, New York being, as Pinnacle well knew, a no-cause state—but he felt a responsibility to his team and wanted to help them transition. We were awed that he hadn't either laughed or spit in their faces.

Milla Kristol decided that Gabe would replace Will on Project Lemonade. He was ordered to immediately hand over his Training appointments and begin work on the knowledge transfer. Early on in his Pinnacle career, Gabe had put in a brief spell in Compliance. It was an indication of how thin Compliance was, that Milla preferred to move Gabe across the board for this project, and reserve Jamia Malik, the newly senior Compliance associate, to lead her team. Archie Ghosh was tearing her hair out. Training had no more surplus bodies than Compliance, and unlike Compliance, they didn't have two "back-ups" in Pune.

Gripping the ladies' room sink, Archie leaned into her reflection. The cool water she'd splashed on her face was still running down. "I don't have to put up with this," she assured herself.

"You okay?"

Archie jumped, the cheap metal sink bouncing from the sudden release of weight.

Martha held up both her hands. "It's only me."

"Where did you come from?" Archie hadn't made a sound, but she was gasping as if she'd screamed.

Martha's cheeks felt hot. She jerked her head to indicate one of the stalls. "I was fixing my bra. I keep having to buy new ones, because they keep, you know, growing...I can't believe I wasted my whole life wishing for big boobs. They hurt!"

Archie shrugged. She snatched a paper towel off the roller and dabbed at her face, being careful not to smudge her eye makeup.

"Cool news about Will, don't you think?"

Archie balled up the paper. "Brilliant." She aimed for the trash can and slammed it down. The paper rebounded off the rim and ricocheted off the wall towards the stalls.

Martha waited while she stomped over to retrieve it and placed it, with great deliberation, into the trash. Archie was one of the most self-composed people she'd never met. Martha wasn't leaving her alone until she'd pulled herself back together. "Okay, so vent. Tell me."

"Did you speak to Gabe?"

"Since when?"

"Since Kristol made him the Compliance lead for Lemonade."

"But Gabe was only in Compliance for a couple of months. And that was ages ago." Which meant Milla Kristol must really be impressed by him. Martha couldn't suppress a happy little laugh.

"Oh, he'll be great. But Lemonade takes up almost all my time and now I'm down a body. You know how stretched we are. We've had everyone working at 120 percent and we're hardly keeping out of the weeds. With Gabe and me both off the roster...Look, it can't be done. I'm out of ideas. I give up." Her voice choked. She was almost crying.

Martha followed the impulse to hug her. It was either the best or the worst thing to have done. Archie began to cry in earnest. Martha patted her back and made soothing sounds until the tears stopped.

"I'm okay," Archie said. Her voice wobbled, but she was pulling herself straight. She turned to the mirror and shuddered. "Ew! I can't walk into Bryson's office looking like this." She dampened the edge of another piece of towel and began to address the damage.

"Walk into Bryson's office now? For what?"

"To quit, obviously. I've got enough in the bank to cover three months. I'll find something before then. Worse come to worse, I can always run the fry station at a KFC."

"Don't," Martha advised. "Not while you're this upset. Go over to Whine Bar tonight. Have a mojito. Play a few games of darts."

"Pretend the target is Kristol?" Archie forced a laugh.

"If that helps, sure. Burn off some steam. And sleep on it. See how you feel in the morning."

Archie shook her head. "Martha, sweetie, I appreciate what you're trying to do. But I'm only going to feel the same tomorrow. Nothing I do is going to make this work."

"What if you could get another person?"

"It takes three months before a new person is worth anything as a trainer."

Martha had been thinking. "Not a new person. What about Marla?"

"Sure. Of course. Piece of cake. I'll just tell Kristol we need Scott to give us Marla until Lemonade is over."

"No. You tell Edie. Edie'll figure out how to make Milla think it's her own idea."

Archie looked into the mirror at Martha. There was a flicker of hope in her eyes. "You think she can?" The flicker dimmed as quickly as it had appeared. "Scott'll never give us Marla."

"He will if Milla asks." Martha felt certain of this. Milla and Scott were thick as thieves these days.

"Maybe Milla'll lend him 50 percent of Khosi."

"What about Khosi's work?"

"Pinnacle managed for years without it. Anyway, since Bruce Korn's a Trim/Delta Sensei, he can do her job better than she can." Martha squinted into the mirror. "You have this one speck of mascara on your right cheek. Here."

Archie scrubbed it off. She ran the palms of her hands over her front hair to smooth it. She sighed. "Respectable. Not brilliant, but respectable."

"You look fine," Martha said, giving her another hug. "Now go see Edie."

"Thanks, Martha. You know, I think you're going to be an awesome mother." Archie hugged her back and, with a little salute, marched herself out the door.

Martha felt her cheeks get warm again, this time with pleasure. She smiled at herself in the mirror. "You think?" she whispered.

Δ

"...and another round of applause, this time for Pete Weiss. I tell you, this guy is gonna be an All Star! Only...when did you start Pete?" Kippy's head snapped; he knew the exact location of his subject in the Pit.

The voice that spoke up, flat and brisk, was unfamiliar to most of us outside Sales. "Right after Matsui scored that Grand Slam off Blanton. I was visiting my brother in Oakland. Last vacation before starting a new job."

"Ha!" Kippy chortled with delight. "You were there?!"

"I was." There was a definite trace of smugness.

Kippy could never resist a competition. "Hell of a game! I was at the final day at Yankee Stadium. Took my son, Alex. Nobody wanted to leave. I'm telling you, I sat in that parking lot and cried. Actual tears. Never forget it as long as I live." He blinked vigorously at the memory. "So, where was I? Oh yeah. Pete here only started with us back in June. He's been pulling in a solid bunch of contracts. Very solid, for someone not even five months, that's what I thought. And yesterday...Ha! He sealed a deal with Micklewhite & Pearce!!!" Kippy's wild grin was not inappropriate; with branches in virtually every mall in America, this was, indeed a name to be reckoned with. "I think that deserves a round of applause, don't you?"

We did. We were also restless after standing still for a fifteen minute laundry list of Great Accomplishments. Applause gave us a chance to let the blood circulate.

"Alright, one more announcement and then I'll take a couple of questions. So, our Charity of the Month, as we always do in November, is the Food Bank. Chris, give them the details"

Chris Keane brandished Mr. Microphone with the cheery aplomb of a street reporter measuring a snow drift. "Hi everyone. Yeah, we'll be putting out the boxes tomorrow, one by Maci in Reception, one outside Advancement and another inside the break room. All donations appreciated, but try and keep it healthy. Not just the Girl Scout cookies you want to get out of the house! Yeah, now you know my dirty little secret. Seriously, keep in mind that a lot of the people who get their food there have limited access to kitchens, so think about things that can literally be eaten cold or warmed up with just a microwave. Canned food is great. Not just soup and veggies. People need protein, so beans and maybe tuna or something would be really appreciated. The other thing we got a ton of last year was mac and cheese, so maybe we should dial that down. Poverty is depressing. Can we at least help cheer people up with a little variety? Oh!" She was about to had the mike back to Kippy when she remembered something. "They could also use Parmalat and jarred baby food. Powdered milk, too. There are a lot of homeless families out there with little kids."

"The volunteers!" Liz Dorn had a penetrating stage whisper.

"Right!" Chris tipped Mr. Microphone in salute to her partner. "Sorry. All the shelters can use volunteers to help cook and serve dinner on Thanksgiving. We did it last year, down at the Center and we're definitely doing it again. It's a pretty amazing experience." Even Kippy probably knew, on some level, that the purposefully vague "we" meant Chris and Liz, but we doubted any of the LC understood the cryptic "Center" to be the LGBT Center down on West 13th Street. "So if anyone would like to join in, just let me know. Also, if anyone who wants to make a cash contribution, Kippy's agreed to match it 100 percent! So we can really do a lot of good this season."

Kippy observed our applause with his most paternal face. "That's right, Chris. I expect to see those boxes so full we have to add more! And, like Chris just said, I will match any cash donation at 100 percent. Dollar for dollar! Remember. Don't wait until you're rich. Ha! You have the power to help someone, even if you only give a coupla dollars. I'm proud of how much we give, as a group, to charities all year and especially at this time of year. Okay. One more thing. I've been hearing there's a lot of concern about jobs migrating to Pune and I want to say one thing. Not to worry! Yes, in the short term we have to let people go. I'm not gonna pretend we don't. But these are jobs we can't afford to pay living wages for people in New York living to perform. By filling these positions in Pune, we can afford to grow the company and we'll have better jobs here. Okay, any questions?

"Kippy, I think this is really exciting stuff. All the growth and all." Hank Iversson's dad had told him to always open with a positive statement before asking the hard questions. "So, can you share your thoughts on what other departments, besides Data Entry, you'd like to move completely off-shore? And is there a balance you have in mind, in growing the two offices? I guess what I'm asking is, how many positions do you plan to have here a year from now, versus in Pune?"

We held our collective breath. We doubted Kippy would balk. Part of the dark fun of these sessions was that he'd often forge ahead and say something that was simultaneously hilarious and horrific.

He nodded with the ponderous gravity of Dr. Zaius. "Interesting questions, Hank. You're asking me to look a year down the road, and I don't know that I can do it. Sure, we've got a terrific formula for making projections based on year-to-year trending, but there are too many factors that play into it for me to put a stake in the ground. How many employees we'll have anywhere a year for now is impossible for me to answer, particularly in this economic climate. Certainly we have plans to continue to expand Pune, but how and when will ultimately depend on the success of the movement of jobs on a process-by-process basis."

It was obfuscation, but it was reasonable. It was even refreshing to hear him say the LC didn't know something, but we were a little disappointed and Hank Iversson wanted an answer. Before Kippy could ask for another question from the floor, Hank piped up again: "Understood. But could you give us a broad stroke picture, maybe just an idea of what processes you're looking to move? I mean potentially."

Our heads swiveled back from Hank to Kippy. We expected him to give Clif the sign to ask the usual "what are you reading?" question. Instead, he tipped his head back to gaze at a vision somewhere beyond the ceiling tiles. "We have to work together to find our way to the proper balance, which will work efficiently and be effective for both the business and our client base. We need both onshore and offshore strategy to support what I see, which is Pinnacle as a company with unlimited opportunities for growth. Growth for the business, which means for all of you, because every one of you is a Leader. Look at the person on your left. Now look at the person on your right. If you're standing here now, after all the changes we've had, then you've been hand-picked. Every one of you is bright and talented, the best at what you do. We've already done great things, and my one prediction for next year is that we're going to do even more!"

Δ

The last time Judy Schreiber knocked on this door, Nick Andreas was on the other side. It felt more like a decade ago than a mere three years. How odd that she hadn't had to work with Milla Kristol before. They'd been in meetings together, of course, but Milla was the only one of the Cs who'd never directly assigned her any work. Even Feldman, who turned his head to face the other way if they had to share an elevator, annexed her when there was work to be done for Board meetings or to polish the high-level Org charts for RFPs.

Though Hugo was nominally in charge of Project Lemonade, Milla micromanaged every aspect. This one-on-one "deep dive into Communications requirements," for example. Having dispatched the sample communications matrix and templates, the COO's job should have been done. Judy gave the packet a thorough review and made her own matrix of things that seemed legally-mandated or made basic good sense, adding items that were implied during the many meetings she was required to sit in on and record. She'd adapted the templates to fit Pinnacle, which had far fewer management layers than Octans-Bellums and no numbered artifact library to reference in memo headers or process documents. To accomplish all this while continuing to churn out her allotted quota for Len Strauss, who had decided this would be an ideal time to rework all the website content for search engine optimization, Judy put in two consecutive 70-hour weeks. Unlike Len, who scowled at everything she did, Hugo seemed pleased enough. Milla Kristol apparently was not.

The "come!" that followed Judy's rap on the door was cheerful enough. Widening her mouth to show her teeth, Milla pointed a finger at her headset to indicate "just a minute," while her ring hand gestured to the chair on the petitioner's side of her desk.

Judy closed the door as quietly as she could and slipped into the seat.

"I can see it through your lens but, not to put too fine a point on it, Ed, if the legacy system had been serving you that well, you wouldn't have been looking for suitors. I think our 94 percent retention rate speaks for itself, don't you?" Milla's steely positivity allowed for no contradiction. "Well, I suggest we pulse your client list...No, I'll have Ann put something together for you. Then Ronny Busch can rebrand it for Raskub...Consider it a trial balloon, Ed. I think you'll be surprised...Fine. Let's circle back on this after Ann's sent something off to Ronny...Great!"

Not everything was sunny in the garden of Raskub. The individual functional pairs were making warm connections, but Judy'd picked up a tang of fear from Minnesota pervading the process and making for adversarial encounters.

Milla punched a button and pulled off her headset. She leaned forward on one elbow, hand beneath her chin, inviting Judy into her confidence. "Ed Reinas is displaying some resistance to our plans for Client Relations. We can't afford to have him poisoning the well after we transition. Oh, he'll come around." 'He has to' remained unsaid. Milla twitched the corners of her mouth into an on-off smile. "Enough of that. That's not why I called you in." Pulling her head erect, she placed both palms flat on her desktop. "We need to discuss this matrix."

Was that a sigh of disappointment? Judy didn't know how to respond. The only intelligent thing was to sit still and wait.

The wait was longer than it should have been. Milla was accustomed to immediate response. She blinked. "Well, then. Let's go over it. I've got two hard copies here." She slid two stapled packets across the desk. One had Judy's matrix, the other was the original from Octans-Bellums. Milla flickered another pseudo-smile. "I don't understand what you've done here Judy."

"I thought you wanted this adapted for Project Lemonade."

"Yes. To rebrand the matrix and the templates for Pinnacle and Raskub. What I see here are changes to the deliverables."

Judy cleared her throat. They'd said she was the Communications Lead, and she'd tried to put her experience to work. "Some of the items on the matrix didn't make sense. Octans is a much larger organization than Pinnacle. We don't have that kind of corporate structure..."

"This is a proven matrix. I would like to keep it intact."

"International press release?" Judy had to ask. Octans-Bellums was a multi-national corporation, with offices in Switzerland, Singapore and Dubai.

"This acquisition makes Pinnacle the ninth-largest office services company in the US, and the sixth that focuses exclusively on managed services. I would say this makes for a significant announcement for all press outlets."

Judy nodded, hoping her acquiescence covered her incredulity. "I'll add them all back in. Everything. And if...uh, if you decide something isn't needed, down the road, how should Hugo and I handle it? Would you prefer we keep it on the matrix and mark it off as not applicable? Or remove it?" She knew about a third of the items on this list would never get created, but it seemed prudent to let Milla make the call.

Milla thought it over with the gravity of making a major decision. She nodded once. "I'll circle back with you on that. For now, just replace all the items you eliminated. Please."

"What about the items I added?" Judy took a final stab at being the Communications Lead. "Based on what's been said at the status meetings, it seemed maybe we should add a few things. Like the 'Getting to Know You' deck."

Milla dismissed the idea. "We have an Employee overview that will be shown at the all-hands meetings on Day One. You have the template."

"Yes, but it only has slides to announce the merger, and for the mission statement, the values and the org chart. At our first meeting with the Raskub people, you stressed the importance of winning hearts and minds. I thought it was an excellent point." She wasn't kissing up. Judy had been a pleasantly surprised that the Cs were sensitive to this. "That's why I thought we might want something, uh...friendlier than just the bare bones. Photos of the offices, for example. We could have a side-by-size of New York and Minneapolis with the things people talk about. Local sports teams, favorite food...I don't know. How much it snows? For the Pinnacle-facing deck as well as in the one for Raskub. It would break the tension, get a conversation going so we feel a little less like strangers to one another. I used to do this kind of thing for inter-office events at Trowbridge."

Milla frowned and thought again. "I'm not convinced we need it. If you think you have the cycles to take this on, you can put something together and run it by me. Now let's move on to the templates before we run out of time..."

A dispirited Judy left Milla Kristol's office and headed for the vending machine in the break room. Milla had undone every single one of her improvements. Only the 'Getting to Know You' deck had the breath of a chance, probably because she'd invoked Trowbridge. What was the point of her experience if all they wanted were a couple of logos and a search and replace for company names? Obviously Milla Kristol considered herself to be the Communications Lead; she just thought it was beneath her pay grade to execute the keystrokes.

Slipping a KitKat into her cardigan pocket, Judy hurried to her next meeting. Len Strauss snapped at her the minute she walked through the door. She was exactly on time. He preferred for people to be a minute or two early, so that he could pretend they were interrupting some critical task.

"I came directly from Milla's office," Judy explained. As COO, Milla Kristol out-ranked EVP Leonard Strauss.

"No excuse," he squawked. It hadn't taken much ingenuity on Alex Silva's part to nickname Strauss when he arrived at Pinnacle.

"It was about Project Lemonade."

"Which is, as you just stated, a project." The Penguin curled his upper lip toward his nose and made an undefinable sound. "Temporary. Passing through. Whereas our work impacts the long-term positioning of this company for internet visibility."

"I understand the importance of what we're doing, Len..."

"I don't think you do. For a supposedly well-educated woman, you seem unable to grasp the magnitude of our task. You do understand what SEO is? Certainly by now..."

"Yes, Len. I do." When the project began, Judy hadn't a clue as to what it was about, but she did know how to do research. Search engine optimization: the art of embedding tasty redundancies in your web content to lure the attention of the search engine spider. It hadn't taken long to come up to speed enough for conversations with Len and the Mumbai consultants he'd hired. Along the way, she'd also learned that the entire concept was already on the wane as being more expensive and less effective than paid advertisements. She'd made one tentative comment in that direction and had been castigated for it. Silly her; of course Pinnacle would rather squander the time of two salaried employees to try and achieve internet visibility "for free" than spend a fraction of what that time was worth on paid advertising.

"Then let me see you stepping up to deliver. You were supposed to have three pages for me today; I only see two." Before she could open her mouth, she was looking into an upraised palm. "And no excuses. Whatever minor tasks Milla Kristol may be throwing you, I have 50 percent of your time."

"Project Lemonade isn't a minor task," she protested. "The communications package is enormous. It's more than full time work all by itself."

"That's of no relevance to me," he said coldly.

Up until now she'd thought he was just being his usual ball-breaking self, but she began to wonder if maybe Len had been shut out of the merger in some way. She made one last attempt at getting him to see reason. "It's only for another five weeks. Once the deal is done and announced, I can work extra hours for you and make up the lost time."

He looked down his pointed nose at her and grimaced. "This is not a negotiation. I require 50 percent of your time on a regular basis. Here are my corrections to your pages. I expect to see this turned around, as well as the missing page, by end of day tomorrow." He shooed her away, in that delightful way he had.

Judy made a dignified exit and did not slam the door.

She took a step towards her own desk, then turned around. There was no point talking to Dave; he didn't have the clout to do anything. In theory, as CTO, Jim Matticchio did. The week he'd arrived, at the only all-IT meeting that he'd ever held, he'd made a sweeping gesture and proclaimed "my door is always open."

She turned on her heel. The door, next to Len's, was closed. Next time she was doing research, she'd have to look up the definition of "always."

Δ

Still zipping their jackets against the first cold day, Dawn and Archie came brrring through the alley. Danny raised a glove hand in greeting. Beside him, Orla leaned against the bricks, staring into the grey November nothingness, her soot-rimmed lashes unblinking. She seemed to feel, rather than see, her friends nearby.

"You'd think Feldman would cough up the money to print out real pink slips, just to be able to watch us cringe." The smoke around her came as much from her condensed breath as from the cigarette poking through her pale lips.

Dawn gave a shriek of outrage. "What the fuck!! What about those 'better jobs' Kippy was going on about? They can't be transferring Switchboard to India. The clients'll know the minute they pick up the phone. They won't stand for it!"

"Yup. You said it. But I'm out, January 15. Me and Laz...all of us except Wei, but she speaks Mandarin. Plus two in Client, I think. You'd have thought since they don't give raises or bonuses anymore, this end of year housecleaning shit would have stopped but I guess we can't compete with Incredible India."

Archie and Danny hadn't screamed; they'd only mumbled. Orla's gooseberry eyes, always so startling against the charcoal swipes of shadow, fixed on them in accusation. "You knew! Both of you! This isn't about Pune, is it? It's something to do with that company Kippy's buying." No one on Project Lemonade had breathed a word, but of course we all knew what it was.

"I didn't know it was you!" blurted Archie. "I only knew that there were going to be cuts."

"And it is mostly going to India, really," muttered Danny. Extending his lighter to Dawn, he averted his eyes from her face.

"You going to walk now?" Dawn asked curiously. Orla wasn't the kind to take it on the chin.

Orla blew one of her famous smoke-ring chains. They all watched the last loop wobble in the air and dissolve. "Nope. They offered me a thousand dollar retention bonus if I stay. And there'll probably be overtime, too. I plan on wringing every last cent I can out of Gary Feldman's pocket."

"And you'll get Unemployment," Archie reminded her. "Which is probably not so much less than you take home."

"Except for overtime," Orla agreed. "Yeah, the benefits of being underemployed. You don't have far to fall. And there's a few places I can pick up some cash. Bartending. Carl's studio maybe."

"You think you and Carl would actually go to Germany?" Dawn, who had a brother working in Iceland and a cousin opening a coffee shop in Lima, had always been curious how much Orla meant her usual threat.

She shrugged. "In the spring maybe. Who knows?"

"Pune isn't going to be the magic bullet they think." Danny was still fixated on India. The analysis work he was doing under Hugo was a whole different world from application development.

"How do you mean?" Archie asked.

"The whole work-life thing is so different. Like people actually expect to leave on time, to see their friends and families. And sick days—people don't think twice about taking sick days. Which is great. I mean, it's the way it should be. But can you imagine if we actually did that here?"

"We wouldn't, because of how they're lumped in with our vacation time. I'm sure as hell not taking a day off to nurse a cold when I can put it towards a week at Disney or a Friday on the beach." It wasn't only Dawn who thought that. Other than planned vacation, if someone at Pinnacle took a PTO day it meant either the flu or a job interview.

"Which is why we're all dragging our asses half the winter," noted Orla. "Bright thought: maybe I won't get January plague this year."

"Then there's the weddings and all. You know," Danny jerked his head at Archie.

Archie nodded. "Someone gets married in your family, everyone gets together for at least a week, maybe two. Other family celebrations, too. Attendance is mandatory. Wherever it is." Her face darkened. "When it's a close enough relative, Amma usually goes over to represent us. The advantage of being a caterer; you can plan your time off. But the rest of us are in such deep shit with my grandmother, you can't imagine."

"That's a little unreasonable," Dawn thought. "It's not your fault that's how vacation time works here."

"Reasonable is not a word I'd use to describe Nani. She says 'it's impossible that a civilized country can be so barbaric.' " A nasal musicality replaced Archie's usual faint Carolina tones.

"But it's more than all that," Danny continued. "It's the way it's all structured. The workplace I mean. All those grades and metrics. They're positively addicted to metrics!"

"I knew it wasn't the food Kristol loved over there," Orla cracked.

"But she's not seeing the dark side," observed Danny. "They don't do metrics just because. They expect them to mean something. If they make their milestones, they rise through the ranks. Raises and titles, both." He was finding the subject of comparative workplace cultures so fascinating that he was thinking seriously of going for an MBA/PhD in Global Business so that he could write a dissertation on it. "Meaning there have to be ranks. When was the last time you had a change in title, I mean except from transferring departments."

"I'm leaving with the same title I walked in with. Switchboard Operator."

"Uh-huh. After…how many years?"

"Almost six."

"In Pune, Orla would have started as Switchboard Operator Trainee and made it to Senior Switchboard Operator by the end of year two. You should see the stuff Hugo and Feldman are making up. That's assuming your metrics were acceptable and you'd taken the professional development classes. Because yeah, before you ask. They just hired someone to lead them."

"I can't believe they're doing all this over there," marveled Dawn. "We're the poor relations."

"Damn, maybe instead of cutting me they'd let me transfer to Pune." Orla wasn't joking. "I bet Carl would go for it. Have needle will travel."

"Are you insane?! Maybe it's a good thing they're forcing you out."

"They have to do all this stuff," Danny explained. "It's how things work over there."

Archie summed it up succinctly: "it's the Empire."

"How so?"

"How it worked under the British. The whole civil-service mentality. Ergo the whole obsession with pay-grades and rising through the ranks. And credentials. Don't ask! People collect them like trading cards. Last time I was in Kerala my cousins thought I was pitiful because I only have one Master's and no certifications."

"Wait, so what's your 'dark side', Danny?" Dawn wanted to know.

"Turn-over," he replied. "First full year in Pune, we had a bigger turnover rate, percentage-wise, than any year here ever. And you know what our turnover rate is. I mean people who walk away on their own."

"Pretty high, considering the shit job market," noted Orla.

"Because sometimes it's your wallet or your sanity. If I didn't have such a high threshold for angst, I would have quit on Waters a dozen times."

"Over there, the job situation is amazing," Danny pointed out. "If people don't get their annual bump, they just move on and start looking around for something with more potential. And they know they'll find it. So there's constant turnover. And because we always under-hire...yeah, even over there where there's no excuse about cost containment. Amazing isn't it? So there's never enough going to be enough coverage to make up the gaps while onboarding new people. The bigger the Pune office gets, the more of an issue this is going to be."

"All the LC cares is that it's cheap."

"For now. But Pinnacle is already getting a bad rep in Pune for low-balling and lack of career path. That's why Ayesha...the Aprotek QA lead? That's why she turned down an offer to hire, said she'd do better staying a consultant. She actually gave Peterson the choice of keeping her that way or replacing her. She said she was okay with either call." Danny grinned. That was his favorite part of the story. Ayesha saying she didn't care. "He decided to stick with her. But with all the people Vijay's bringing on, Feldman may not let it stay that way."

"Isn't that for what's-his-name to decide?" Archie honestly couldn't remember the new CTO's name.

"Matticchio?" Danny laughed. "I swear I've only seen him maybe four times since he started. Judy says the only decision he makes is whether to come in every day."

"In the old days we would have started a pool," Orla noted wistfully.

"Where is Judy?" Dawn asked. "I feel like I haven't seen her in forever."

"Chained to her desk. No one asked Len Strauss about putting her on Lemonade and he's taking it out on her. Plus, Kippy still expects that newsletter to come out every month. I picked up a sandwich for her yesterday at lunch. When I left at seven, she was first eating it."

"Fuck it." Dawn ground out her cigarette and shoved her hands in her pockets. The weather report said it was supposed to be warmer today. "I'm going for that Masters in Library Science. Will's idea, actually," she elaborated, in case people didn't know. "Like a year ago, but I was too lazy to move my ass. Not anymore. I've got to get out of here."

"Everyone has to get out of here," Archie agreed. "It only gets worse and worse. This Lemonade thing is crushing me."

"Everyone except Hugo. Milla's butt boy. Who wants to bet he gets MVP this year?"

Dawn grinned at Orla. "If they gave you until January, you get to come to the party and see for yourself."

17 PROOF OF CONCEPT

The Buzzard had intended to find those Minneapolis schematics yesterday and clean them up before showing them to Jim Matticchio. Best laid plans and all that. Anabelle came home from nursery school all stuffy-nosed and coughing. Usually he and Angela would take shifts, but with Angie presenting to her board tomorrow, the last thing she needed was some bug. So Jake slept in their bed with Angie, and he slipped in a couple of cat naps on the rug in the kids' room whenever Anabelle dozed off. She took after him, bless her heart, the way she burned up with the least little thing. Tossing and turning, tangling herself up in her pink-flowered sheets and making those kitten kind of whimpers. It was a heart-breaker. He kept soaking towels in cold water and wrapping her in them to cool her down. It was what his mama used to do for him. Poor dolly was cooler by the time Angela poked her head in to say she was leaving. The sitter came on time for a change, and said she'd be happy to keep Jake indoors so she could keep an eye on Anabelle, but Dave couldn't leave his dolly, not looking all wrung out like that.

So he'd worked from home yesterday, getting Scott to okay it, then telling Matticchio he was finishing up some work for Scott. Anabelle slept a lot. When she woke up, he fed her soup and animal crackers, droppered in the baby meds and read stories. In between, he did get a fair amount of work accomplished. A couple of RFPs. A long meeting with Leon, Cooper Fradkin in Minneapolis and the Raskub team in Minsk. A lot. Just not those damned schematics, because he hadn't brought them home.

He wished to hell he didn't have to work. They joked about it sometimes, that if Angela kept getting these promotions, he'd be able to quit this job in a few more years and stay home full time with the kids. Anabelle would be in school by then, but Jake would still need him. Maybe they'd even squeeze out a third, if Angie thought she could handle another maternity leave. Though he couldn't imagine his heart holding any more love than it did now. Love. That's what he had to hold on to. While he held on to this job, because there wasn't a lot out there right now, especially for someone with lots of less than impressive false starts in his resume.

"Dave?"

The voice was so uncertain, he had to look up to be sure it was Judy's. She looked like hell. She'd been looking like hell for a couple of weeks, actually. He made his voice as warm as could be. "Hey! What's up?"

"I don't know what I'm going to do" she said. Her face was as crumpled as Anabelle's had been the other night, only white instead of feverishly pink.

He cleared a mess of papers from his visitor's chair. She sat, briefly bending to scoop up a rag that had fallen half under it. So that's where his Yacht Club tie had gone to. He hoped the cleaners could take care of it.

"What's wrong?"

"I was just in Milla Kristol's office. A little thing. To tell her we have to have the press release ready a week before we release it, so that Len's webmaster in Pune has time to upload it to our public website."

"A week? That seems a lot."

There was enough uplift at the corners of her mouth for her expression to qualify as a smile. "Oh, it's ridiculous. But that's how it works. Because Len and Vijay hired the webmaster and Clif doesn't trust him. So for anything to go on the website, Sarang has to prep it, then I have to okay content, then he puts it up in the DMZ for Freddie to okay the code. Finally Len has to sign off as a CYA for Clif..." She rolled her eyes and shook her head. It was a ludicrous procedure. "Oh, and he works Pune days, which means I have a window of absolutely zilch to communicate with him in real time."

"Can't we do anything about that?"

"What 'we' is that?" She let the question lie there for a moment, then squeezed her eyes closed to continue. "So that's the drill. Milla and Scott don't want to finalize the press release until the final papers are signed. Which is reasonable. But then they want it on the website immediately. Which, for reasons just explained, is not. Either I send the press release to Sarang a week early, or we put it through on Milla's schedule and it appears, absolute best case scenario, within four days. She didn't like those choices. So she did that thing she does. She leaned her face this close..." Judy held her palm about four inches from her nose. "And said 'I don't accept that!' and threw me out."

"Can't you talk to Len? Get him to make an exception, expedite this?"

"Are you kidding? Len thinks the whole merger project is a personal affront. He's in some kind of war with Milla and Scott. Maybe with Feldman, too, for all I know. The worst thing I could do is ask him to speed things up for her. If anything, it would make him drag it out even longer. It's like that show...the one with all the women penned up on some island, fighting to date this guy..."

"*The Bachelor?*"

"Is that it? I don't watch it, but you can't avoid seeing the promos everywhere. I don't know. Back when I started here, there weren't any politics. I liked that. Now it's practically Shakespearean. And I have about as much control over what's happening to me as Rosencrantz and

Guildenstern. I'm working 12 hour days, weekends. If it weren't for people dropping food on my desk, I'd never eat. But I swear, the thing that's going to make me crack is that I do everything all of them ask, and none of them are ever happy."

The tears finally came. Judy did nothing to stop them, staring at him with tears trickling down her cheek and dropping off her chin. This wasn't just typical Pinnacle bitching and moaning. The woman had reached the end of her rope.

"I'm about to drop, Dave. This press release is only one thing, but it's unresolvable, and I swear...I just know I'm going to say something I shouldn't to someone, or maybe to all of them, and I'm going to run screaming out the door." She sniffed and tried to straighten up. Brushing her hair from her forehead, she fixed him with a steady, if overly bright, eye. "You know how everyone keeps calling everything ironic? Whether it is or not? Well, here's ironic for you: Pinnacle was supposed to be my safe place."

The Buzzard hated getting involved. It opened him to risk, and he hated risk. Maybe thinking of Anabelle, had him in protective mode. Against his better judgment, he said he'd talk to Jim Matticchio and see if there was anything that could be done to help, at least about the press release.

With a weak smile, Judy gave him thanks that were way over the top for what he'd agreed to do. She crept back down the aisle to her desk, and he started once again to search for the damned Minneapolis schematics.

"Hey, Buzzard!" As usual, Roger Didilian was announcing himself from halfway across the floor.

He'd get here soon enough. Dave didn't even lift his head from the piles he was trying to sort through. "Beats me where all this comes from," he mumbled. It was supposed to be a paperless office and this accumulation would have been too much for Scrooge's guy....what's-his-name, Bob Cratchit. Which reminded him, he needed to go through the house and find that old copy of *Mr. Magoo's Christmas Carol*. Anabelle loved it last year. He wondered if it was too soon to try it on Jake. He looked through the stack he'd moved off the chair. Something new was thrown at him every day. He didn't have time to finish any of it, no less stow things neatly away. Oh, face it, if he had all the time in the world his desk would still look like a trashcan had exploded. It wasn't his fault. He was the kind of guy who ought to have an admin. If only Pinnacle hired admins. Not they'd give him one if they did. Imagine having a real office, with walls and a door; maybe a window with some kind of view. And an admin. His desk would be as clear as the deck of a boat in drydock. He wondered if it would be any easier to find things then. Like those schematics, for example. They had to be here somewhere.

In theory, there was some chronological stratification of the pile. Dig down to the right layer and presto. The schematics should have been about two-thirds of the way down, but so far the Buzzard was coming up empty. The clutter seemed to have gotten worse of late. It wasn't only files and folders. There was a mess of computer detritus too: extra keyboards; coils of green and yellow cable. And here was the Nerf basketball hoop from back when they were up on eight and Peterson liked having those team-building activities. Anything that didn't have a place to go made its way to his corner, wherever his corner happened to be that month. Every time they changed his desk, he thought it would finally be the perfect time to throw things out and do some filing. They changed his desk semi-regularly. They changed his title nearly as often. His string of business cards was almost as long as Anabelle was tall. He should bring them home and let her measure herself against them. Then they could maybe measure her height on the wall, count the number of cards and divide to see how big a card should be. Anabelle was too young to be taught division, but she'd get the concept. The kid sparkled like a firecracker when you exposed her to a new idea.

Dave smiled at the thought.

Roger thought the smile was for him and took it as a cue to sit. The back of the chair creaked almost to breaking. "So, Buzzard," he announced, "we've got a face-to-face in Atlanta next Thursday." He looked for a spot to set his coffee down.

Dave shifted what was left of the gourmet food pyramid TerrifiCar had sent for the holidays. It was only spiced nuts and fake-butter cookies, but it was nice of them to send it; companies were doing that less and less these days.

"It's a big one." Roger swiped the last cookie with his sausage-like fingers. He stuffed it into his mouth and talked through the crumbs. "Scott's coming down. They're going to have a lot of Fulfillment questions. He wants you there to talk about the technology."

Angie wouldn't be happy. The following Sunday she'd be taking off for her quarterly two-weeks on the Coast. Thursday was meant to be their date night, to leave the weekend clear for being all about family. Well, there was nothing Dave could do about it. Angie's job was more the important one, but they still needed his. He'd worked hard to make sure he'd kept it as long as they did, slowly but surely, through all the craziness and re-orgs, carving himself a narrow niche and wedging himself tight.

Waving Roger off, Dave swiveled around to tackle the pile on the other arm of the L and barked his toe on the belt-driven turntable he'd bought from Conrad Beale's garage sale. Damn! That box was sitting her since... more than two years ago. Had to be; Conrad had been gone a while now. Dave kept meaning to bring it home, but there wasn't a decent place to set it up. Either he'd figure out a place, or when they got around to firing him someday he'd have to squeeze the box in the hall closet, under his duffle bag full of college stuff. It was inevitable. He'd made himself as indispensable as anyone ever was at Pinnacle, but everyone got fired eventually.

Aha! There were the schematics! He waved them through the air a few times, to freshen them up, and strode down the aisle to knock on Matticchio's door.

On the way out, Dave made himself stop by Judy's desk. Her eyes had that hopeful look of dogs you see in the shelters, the one that makes your stomach ache when you have to pass it by. He gestured for her to follow him back to his cube. Only when they were sitting down did he tell her.

"Nothing," he said, shaking his head. "I'm really sorry, Judy, but he won't do anything."

"What did he say?" Her face was closing down, but her voice was strong.

Dave shifted uncomfortably. Matticchio's words had taken him aback. He hated to have to repeat them.

"Please, Dave. I need to know."

"He said..." Dave felt his face redden, an echo of the anger he'd felt and swallowed. "He said, 'that's her job. If she doesn't like it, she knows what she can do about it.'"

Δ

```
From:          Kippy Melcher
To:            All Pinnacle Associates
Subject:       Our MVPs
-----------------------------------

This year's Pinnacle Holiday Party was, as always, a great
success. The LC would like to commend everyone on their
professional behavior at this event.

Congratulations to Hugo Singer, Director of Process
Improvement and our MVP for 2008! As Pinnacle has continued
to expand and mature, Hugo has taken on greater
responsibilities and risen to every challenge. We expect
Hugo's role to continue to grow as our organization does.

We're also proud to announce our first ever Pune MVP, Senior
Fulfillment Team Manager Ashok Fernandez. Ashok was one of
our first Pune employees and has been a key member of that
team from day one. Congratulations, Ashok!

Kippy
```

Kippy Melcher, CEO
Pinnacle Management Services

Δ

"I love you, too," Judy was saying.

Edie Brewer waited a bit, hoping she'd hear the door slam, but all she heard was quiet. It was going to be awkward, but she had no choice. She had a meeting to get to. She flushed and waited another minute to give Judy time to make a quick getaway. She'd know she'd been overheard but not by whom, which was something. This was the problem of everyone having to use the bathrooms as phone booths. Unless the call was planned, you still were likely to be overheard. Still, what happened in the bathrooms stayed in the bathrooms, so it was still better than staying at your desk and having the whole office listening in.

Judy was standing by the left-hand sink, staring at the mirror.

"Are you okay?" Edie asked. Everyone knew Judy was having a time. She wouldn't have even gone to the holiday party last week, except Kippy asked where she was and sent Clif Speck back to the office to drag her over.

"Not work, for a change." Judy cleared her throat and dabbed at her tear ducts with a paper towel. "My cousin's husband's in a comma and it looks bad."

Edie dried her hands and gave Judy a hug. "I'm sorry."

"They were high school sweethearts. He's the dearest man. Everybody loves him." Judy needed to talk it out and Edie was a comforting presence. "He had a bypass in the spring. They only gave him a 30 percent chance of making it, but there was no other option so he went ahead with it. He fooled them all, just refused to not get well. I saw them last month and he looked...oh! Ten years younger. Amazing. Everyone stopped worrying. Then my cousin woke up in the middle of the night. She heard a noise in the bathroom. She thought he maybe tripped and hit his head on the floor. He was breathing, but she couldn't wake him. When they heard his history, the EMS team said it might have been a stroke, but maybe it was an aneurism. They still don't know for certain."

"Where is he?"

"LIJ. He's got the best care. But it's been eight days. The doctors have stopped making positive noises."

Judy slipped downstairs and made a brisk, coatless circuit of the block to steel her resolve. Back upstairs, she gave her hair a quick brush and fixed her lipstick.

She knocked sharply on Len's door.

"Come," he quacked, giving her what passed for his smile. He did that now and then, since he'd won his little battle for her time. At the holiday party, with her standing uncomfortably in her work clothes, showing her tired face to Kippy, Len had actually walked by and said "Good work. Thank you." She'd nearly spilled her Scotch. She'd wanted to throw it in his face. In the end, she just drank it and left as soon as possible.

"A quick word," she said now. "I just want to give you a heads up. I have a family member in what's looking like an irreversible comma. If he doesn't make it…well, the funeral will be almost immediate. I may have to call in on a moment's notice for a personal day."

He looked at her coldly. "And why do I need to know this?"

She was flummoxed. "We're in the middle of an acquisition. In addition to our SEO work, I've got lots of related changes to prepare for the website. I thought it was only fair to put you, and Milla and Scott in the loop about a day off that I can't really plan."

He wrinkled his nose and gave that backhand shoo-shoo gesture that always made her think of that WC Fields line: "Go away little girl, you bother me. Go pick yourself some poison ivy."

The hairs bristled on the nape of her neck. She hated being dismissed as an annoyance. And this thing of his…all the Cs had, that way of treating the rest of us as though we were children. It was bad enough to be treated like crap. Somehow it was doubly hurtful to be patronized. She was older than most of them, for crap's sake, certainly about as close a contemporary as Len and Kippy had on the staff, and a damned sight more professional than any member of the LC.

The thought of that dear man lying in that bed, vacant except for the life that could be provided by a machine, changed the look of everything around her. Judy couldn't afford to quit, but she was damned if she was going to do anything to stop them from firing her. She had a better network now than she'd had five years ago. This time she should be able to find something before unemployment ran out. Even if they didn't fire her, which she almost wished they would, she had to start polishing the resume. As soon as there was a whiff of change in the economy, she'd start pushing it out.

She stared back at Len, with coldness matching his own and for just long enough that he had no choice but to meet her eye. 'Do it,' she thought; 'just fucking see if I care.' She said nothing.

She whirled to leave, closing the door quietly but firmly behind her.

Δ

From: Milla Kristol

```
To:             Pinnacle Leaders; Client Relations
Subject:        Bruce Korn
```

Bruce Korn is no longer with the company. Please direct any issues or projects to Ann Ling

Milla Kristol, COO
Pinnacle Management Services

Δ

```
From:           Don Bryson
To:             All Pinnacle Associates
Subject:        A New Addition!
```

Congratulations to Martha and Gabe del Monte on the birth of their daughter. Luna Elizabeth del Monte was born at 6 AM this morning, weighing in at 7 pounds 9 ounces, and 18" long. Each parent insists she looks more like the other one. Martha is doing well. Photos from Gabe's phone have been posted on the Intranet.

If you'd like to sign the card that will accompany the Pinnacle gift, please stop by the HC offices before end of work today.

Don

Don Bryson, Dir. HC
Pinnacle Management Services

Δ

"Oh, look at those cheeks!" Gretchen held her cigarette away from Archie's phone as if it were the actual baby. "And her hair! She's got a full head of hair!"

"She's got Gabe's hair." Archie made the obvious comment.

"Ya think?" Dawn had already seen the latest pictures of week-old Luna and her thatch of black fluff. "Martha must be ecstatic. She hates her hair."

"Why? Martha has lovely hair." The wind blew some of Gretchen's tawny locks into her eyes. She tucked them more firmly under her knitted tuque.

Dawn shrugged. "Nobody likes their own hair. Orla's really a blonde, you know. Dirty blonde, like me, under all that dye. Damn, I miss her already."

"I miss Gabe," Archie confessed. "I can't wait for Lemonade to be over so we get him back."

"Can't argue there, as much as I like the overtime. Tully's up at five to get to the Bronx, so if I'm not home for dinner, we hardly see each other." Dawn blew chagrin through her front teeth, pausing in mid puff. "So, wait! If Gabe's using his PTO days for the baby, who's covering for him on the Great Work?"

"He's working from home."

"They're okay with that?"

"It was Kippy's idea." Gretchen checked the time on her Crackberry and took one last lungful.

"Amazing." Dawn rolled her eyes. "You guys have no idea. When we had the transit strike? Before your time. You should have heard them, when people asked about working from home. Kippy and Scott acted like we were attacking them with pitchforks."

"Well, Lemonade is time-sensitive. What Gabe is doing is pretty key."

"More key than..." Dawn extended both arms and performed a minor obeisance. "...Sales? Come on, Archie. You know how they are with the Boys of Summer? Well, during the strike...I can never forget this. Glenn Levine asked to work from home and they wouldn't let him. Glenn Freaking Levine!"

"Times change," Gretchen called over her shoulder, causing a near collision with Hank Iversson who was coming the other way.

"Careful, Gretch!" He made a show of flattening himself against the wall until she'd disappeared.

"I thought you weren't coming," Archie said shyly, when he finally reached them.

"Only got five minutes, but I wasn't going to miss you." Hank winked and gave her mitten a quick grab.

Dawn did a double take. She hadn't seen that one coming. She was going to have to email Orla. And Alex. Will, maybe...

"Ann is having an absolute cow today. This Lemonade thing."

"It's pretty crazy. I'm only out here because nothing happens in my silo for a few more weeks. Most of the others are in the weeds."

"Danny's been sneaking into the stairwell and smoking out the window. I went to make a phone call and caught him." Dawn grinned. It seemed a very long time since the days when she was the girl who followed all the rules.

"Well, we're down to the wire now. Ann's got some major deliverables landing and she's on her own. You guys should cut her some slack," Archie teased. Hank grinned down at her.

"She's on her own again," corrected Dawn. "You'd think by now they'd give in and make her the official Director."

"They don't have to. She does it anyway."

"All she does is take orders from Scilla," Hank observed.

Dawn peered quizzically into his face. "And your point is...? Anyway, more important...do we know yet what happened with Bruce Korn? Walked or pushed?"

Hank tapped his temple with his forefinger. "I say walked. More like ran. I have it from a secret source that he's gone back to the West Coast. Seattle, I think. The company's called ProLine. Automated managed services for purchasing and a few other things. I checked their website. The purchasing was the only piece that made sense to me," he admitted.

"Secret source? What secret source?" Archie was curious.

"He sent me an invitation on LinkedIn."

Archie gave his collar a gentle tug. "Smart ass."

"Do you know, Edie's not on LinkedIn? She wrote me a great letter for the MLS program, so I asked if she'd post a recommendation on LinkedIn. She said she doesn't do social media, that it's too much exposure."

"She has a point." Archie asked, "did you hear what happened to Jamia?" She'd met the Compliance lead in the ladies' room soon after the incident. "You know the bonus..."

That was something we all knew. The "Recovery Bonus," Kippy'd called it, in honor of our extraordinary efforts to keep Pinnacle healthy through hard times. It had been the highlight of his January Monthly address and a major morale booster. The boost was short-lived. Our individual meetings with upper management revealed we were getting a flat $250 across the board, a pleasant Christmas present, but not enough to make a difference in our lives and negative reinforcement for those "'extraordinary efforts."

"Don called her in yesterday. He told her that her bonus would be forfeit because she quote unquote posted a negative comment about Pinnacle on social media. You know how Scotty's Angels are running Pinnacle accounts on Twitter and Foursquare and asked us all to follow, to build the numbers? They're monitoring us." Hank and Dawn looked as stunned as Archie had been when Jamia told her the story. "It gets better. Jamia couldn't figure out what the hell Don was talking about. She's pretty careful about social media, because she wants to work at the Fed someday and they do incredibly thorough background checks. Anyway, she asked Don for details and he showed her. A few months back, she checked into the office on Foursquare and later she posted something like, um, 'week from hell, TGIF.'"

The corporate-heir-apparent look came over Hank's face. "No," he objected. "Even if we'd signed a contract with a no-disparagement clause, which we haven't, they wouldn't have a legal leg to stand on. That's not a comment about the company. It's an expression of her state of mind."

"I'm not disagreeing. But so what? That was their decision. Because she was checked in at work when she said it. There wasn't even a discussion. I've already updated my privacy settings."

"Mind. Blown." Dawn fumbled for another cigarette. The rubber bands on the pack reminded her she only had four more left for today, so she stowed it away.

"Stupid," was Hank's judgment. "She's their senior Compliance person now and they've basically shown her the door. I'd start a pool, if there were enough of us left to bet."

Δ

"Can you hear me now?"

The last connection had so much static, Kippy didn't understand that we couldn't make out a word he was saying, because he couldn't hear us either. Gretchen had finally hung up, forcing him to call again. She leaned toward the speaker. "Much better this time."

"Terrific! Good morning , Pinnacle!!!"

Following long habit, our eyes fastened on the windowsill, even though the only person there was Gretchen, who leaned against it balancing an office phone on the knee of her plaid tights.

"I have some exciting news for all of us! I am pleased to say something I couldn't have said until two hours ago, which is that Pinnacle now owns Raskub Secretarial Services, a 70-year-old office services and temporary placement agency in Minneapolis!"

No one was surprised at anything but the name of the company. Project Lemonade was an open secret. When the blast email requested our presence for "a very special All Pinnacle meeting," we'd pretty much known what to expect. We were all so blasé that Clif Speck had to raise his hands over his head to cue our applause.

"That's right! As difficult as these times are, I am a buyer not a seller! Ha! As well as significant fulfillment synergies, this acquisition gives us a big footprint in the Midwestern markets, as well as tremendous opportunity for greater penetration into the West. But no matter what, I wouldn't have bought it if I didn't think it was a perfect match for Pinnacle. Raskub is a terrific company. Scott'll tell you all about it when I hand this meeting over to him. Got a remarkable pedigree and some very impressive talent."

It was disconcerting to hear Kippy's familiar enthusiasm emanating from a plastic appliance. Divorced from the physical energy of his body, it had a hollow quality. Kippy often said things we didn't believe but, at the time he

300

said them, we knew that he believed. The speaker phone made everything somehow dubious.

"So I'm in Newark right now with Milla, about to board the plane to Minneapolis to announce the news and welcome our new team members into the fold. But before I take off, I wanted to make the announcement to you in my own words and say it again: We are all winners here!"

Clif didn't need to cue us again. We applauded until Gretchen showed that she'd hung up the phone. Scott Bell, brandishing Mr. Microphone, stepped in front of the windowsill. Only Kippy ever stood on top of it.

Scott flashed his porcelain veneers at our assembled ranks. "Thanks, Kippy! So, fantastic news, isn't it? We've been working on this deal for months, and there's a lot to say to bring you up to speed, but I'll try and keep it brief."

He glanced down to the page in his other hand. Sixth from last of the Project Lemonade artifacts on Judy' Schreiber's matrix, not that she was counting. Scott's talking points: What is Raskub Secretarial Services? Why Now? What Does This Mean to Us? Next Steps.

And finally, the laundry list of Thank Yous. "A lot of hard work and talent on both sides went into making this merger possible and paving the way for a smooth transition. I'd like to thank the entire Project Lemonade Team at Pinnacle, starting with Hugo Singer, who did such a great job of stepping up and leading this initiative. Hugo was ably assisted by Danny Zill, Eric Channing and Swati Prasad, our first Pune-based Quality Manager. Next our Operations leads, Bennet Liu and Dan Bryson. Ann Ling..."

Judy had reviewed that list twenty times, at least, to make sure she hadn't missed a single name. Despite Hugo's optimistic October announcement, this was probably the only thanks any of them would get. It had felt like self-promotion to put her own name on the list, but when Hugo insisted, she tacked it modestly onto the end. "And finally, last but certainly not least..." Scott folded the paper in half and made another broad display of dentistry. "For all the extra work she's been doing, keeping Kippy's crazy schedule and all those flights between here and Pune and Minneapolis, a big thanks to Gretchen! Okay, let's have a round of applause for everyone and get back to work. We're going to be busier than ever now!"

Judy strolled back to her desk and hit "Send" on the Press Release job ticket. She'd made her own arrangements with Sarang and Clif, and this ticket was going straight to Freddie Vega, to be turned around the moment it arrived. It had been a hell of a negotiation. She'd been sure to cc the entire Leadership Council on the final memo, so that Len would have no choice but to sign off. If Len had been reading the Thank You list, it wouldn't have been a surprise. Every single name had been read out except hers. She checked the time on her monitor. It was a little early for lunch, but maybe a walk to that new coffee house was in order. She'd heard they had some kind of 12 thousand dollar coffee maker that only brewed individual cups, so you have to wait five minutes for even a basic black coffee. Right now, that sounded like just the kind of coffee she needed.

18 CENTER OF EXCELLENCE

Reprinted in *The Peak Experience*

PMS Acquires Raskob Secretarial Services
New York, NY and Minneapolis, MN – February 1, 2009

Pinnacle Management Systems Inc. announces its acquisition of Raskub Secretarial Services, Inc., the oldest continually-operating provider of clerical and administrative services and personnel in the Midwestern United States.

"This acquisition expands Pinnacle's presence in the managed office services industry," said Clifford J. Melcher, CEO and founder of Pinnacle Management Services, Inc. "Through Raskub, we're able to introduce Pinnacle's best-in-breed technology and quality methodologies to a new market, while benefiting from their amazing track record in service excellence."

Edward W. Reinas, President of Raskub Secretarial Services and great-nephew of founder John Raskub, joined with Mr. Melcher in affirming that the combination of the two firms capabilities will enhance the client experience and create a formidable competitor in this growing service sector. "PMS and Raskub are a natural fit," said Reinas…

Δ

Kippy's contribution to blending the corporate family was to make a regular royal progress from New York to Minneapolis to Pune and back around again. From a man who'd once been so involved in the day-to-day that he'd known when people took too long a lunch break, he'd became a transient presence. Scott had, of course, always travelled a lot. With Milla spending so much time in Minneapolis, dealing with the transition, the office had become a quieter place.

Edie Brewer enjoyed the quiet. Thoroughly. She wallowed in it, stretching her legs under her desk, wiggling her toes, occasionally lifting her face to the warm caress of the overhead energy-inefficient fluorescent strips that Feldman was replacing only as quickly as tax credits required. Without managerial interference, she settled into her cube each morning and, in that precious bubble of peace that lasted until the daily run of emergencies began, she got things done. With Hugo glued to Milla's side, entirely absorbed in the nuts and bolts of the merger, she was free to exercise her own Trim/Delta skills and common sense: not to build an empire, but to make things work. Edie kept her solutions surgical and subtle. A slight shuffle of personnel in the fledgling Travel Services department. A minor change in the Data Entry workflow that Milla and Hugo would likely overlook, registering only that the metrics for that team were looking up. Nor would they notice the effort she'd put into mentoring Ashok.

Ashok was young, ambitious and gaining in confidence. His team was growing. Now that he had two complete services under his aegis, he reported directly to Milla. He had quite a good head on his shoulders when he wasn't expected to automatically agree with whichever important person had last spoken. It had been Ashok's idea that Edie vet the "American" names the Switchboard team had adopted as part of their "cultural training," a practice that began just in time to prevent one "Randy Stallion" from picking up the overnight Switchboard line for the Engelbury Pediatric Clinic. Whenever Edie needed to laugh, she thought about Randy Stallion. It had been a good laugh for Phil, too. They were enjoying a lot more laughs together since the squeaky wheels had headed out on the road.

Even when all the LC was on site, Edie felt less friction than she had in ages. Milla Kristol finally understood that Edie wasn't competing for her crown, and they were almost collaborating. Feldman had found bigger fish to fry. Edie was content these days, except for the bug in her ear that kept warning her it couldn't last. Data Entry and Switchboard were already fully migrated to Pune, with Gary and Milla declaring victory after each round. Payroll Services was being beefed up to support the incoming Raskub business; once that was stable, complete migration wouldn't be far behind. It was inevitable that all of Fulfillment would eventually end up in Pune. Until some day when Pune got as expensive as the U.S. and companies like Pinnacle started moving to Ghana or Nigeria. Edie hoped to be out of the workforce by that time. What she had to focus on was the immediate future.

According to the LC's road map, all Edie would have left by the end of this year (if not sooner) were Training, Travel and Compliance. Phil said she was silly to worry; they couldn't move these three off shore any time soon. There was too much client contact for these services, and clients expected to hear American voices when they picked up the line. But that was just as true of Switchboard. Clients expected their answering service to sound as if the phones were being answered right next door, and yet the LC had brushed aside Edie's concerns, reminding her how little clients were willing to pay for the service and how difficult it was to find people in New York to fulfill it. They were right, but so was Edie. She knew in her heart that someday the decision was going to rise up and bite them on the nose, that one day a Randy Stallion was going to slip through the cracks and the shit would hit the fan.

No, Edie wasn't living in a fool's paradise. She was using the current calm to prepare for the storm ahead. Once she completed that Trim/Delta Minarai certification she'd started with Lloyd and continued, ever so briefly, with Bruce Korn, she'd move on to the next level. The agency Mike Ventura was working through said there was a lot of Trim/Delta work once you had Shokunin certification. Mike was looking into a school in Brooklyn that supposedly had classes on the weekend. If it panned out, it would be worth driving down to join him there.

Edie worried more about what would happen to her kids. So many bright, talented kids had passed through Fulfillment. She was delighted for those who'd left for something bigger and better, even as she continued to miss many of them. What bothered her were the ones Pinnacle had short-sightedly lost or set adrift. She still had a handful of the best and brightest on her team. She didn't want to see another round of poor decisions cutting loose people like Archie or Gabe or Dawn. Experience and intellectual capital weren't so much as a blip on any of the dozens of metrics Gary and Milla had instituted. The LC had two major measures: saving money and making money. Keeping a body count in New York was never going to be saving money, so it had to be about making money. If these kids were going to stay in the house, there had to be a way to spin what they had to offer and tie it to Sales.

Δ

Dave had never been on an away trip with both Scott and Milla. He expected the deal must be huge to warrant both of them going, but not according to the cheat sheet he was reading. Oh, it was big enough to be a good win for Glenn Levine, a couple of hundred grand a year if the prospect signed on for the whole bundle. To get four people on a flight, it should have been more. Pinnacle always kept an eye on the bottom line.

With airlines cutting flights and charging for everything you weren't wearing, there was no such thing as a cheap ticket anymore. Technically, Pinnacle travelled Coach; and since Gretchen was never allowed to book until the last minute, they almost always got middle seats. Levine, lucky bastard, had somehow landed an aisle up front near the toilets. The Buzzard, on the other hand, was lined up bang over the wings, smashed between a nervous flyer and a big guy who sweated garlic. Scott and Milla were nowhere to be seen because, like always, Scott claimed to be using his personal miles to upgrade. What could you say? Maybe they were his personal miles, or maybe he paid the difference out of his pocket. Or maybe it was just that, no matter what, the guy was President of the company. Dave popped an Ambien as soon as they were high enough in the air for the cabin attendants to hand out water. His seatmates notwithstanding, once he'd finished his prep, he was going to grab a snooze.

He was still groggy when they piled into the rental car. Scott drove, as always and not well. Milla sparkled beside him. Like Ventura used to say, before they squeezed him out, the woman effervesced like a Polident commercial. She smiled like one too, all about the teeth and nothing behind the eyes.

When the GPS put them a quarter of a mile from the last turn, Milla passed around a tin of strong peppermints. It was a good idea, something to wake everybody up and get that dozy stink out of their mouths.

"Curves ahead," Scott cracked. "Gotta keep both hands on the wheel." He opened his mouth like a bird. Milla popped in a mint. He pretended to bite her finger and they laughed, his a snort, hers a cackle.

Dave opted to be impervious to rumors. He hadn't heard this one, but Glenn had and poked him to attend.

There was no real reason for Dave to be in Chicago. Once Glenn had impressed the hell out of the prospect team by introducing the President of Pinnacle, Scott did most of the pitch himself. At one point, he threw the ball to Milla, who'd prepared a complete slide deck branded with the prospect's logo and custom graphics. Judy's work, he guessed. Instead of the claims on her time ending with the Raskub assignment, they'd morphed into a regular flow of what she called "make nice" jobs. Dave never understood why they'd rightsized that Graham who used to do the artwork for Sales; kid couldn't have cost much.

Milla flashed the deck like semaphore flags. She whipped through the presentation so fast there wasn't a way in hell their hosts had caught more than a blur of color and the word "leverage", which she used eleven times that he counted. "Synergies" wasn't far behind, together with "excellence" and "deep dive." The rhythm of it brought him back to when he was a kid in a little black suit telling people to give their troubles up to Jesus. The catch-phrases were different, but patter was patter, he supposed; and a mark was a mark.

The EVP of Operations advised them that the wind had changed. Tomorrow's snow had jumped the gun, and it looked like it was going to be a good-sized storm, too. A March Surprise. They admitted they'd been a little surprised that Pinnacle hadn't wanted to reschedule. They were very grateful to everyone for coming all this way and giving them such an informative presentation, but they strongly urged getting to the airport early.

"So why didn't we know there was a storm in the forecast" Dave waited until they were safely away from the prospect, and made sure to keep his tone lightly curious rather than pissed off. Scott made that dismissive "harumph" noise. He'd known, Dave understood. That dick had known but he'd dragged them all to Chicago anyway. It was all part and parcel. With the one whole question he'd had to field, there was certainly no reason why Dave couldn't have participated in this meeting via phone. But that wasn't how Scott Bell rolled. Scott and Kippy were both like that: the only way they knew make a point was in your face.

"Well, let's hope we're lucky," Dave said. "It's Parent Visiting Day tomorrow."

"Come on! I made reservations at Morton's. It'll be fine. You know how the weather likes to exaggerate." Scott fiddled with the wipers and the defogger, trying to get the windshield clear. "They have to create drama, that's how they get viewers." He jerked his head in a way that would have tossed his hair if he'd been a woman. Hell, it was tossing his hair. Scott's hair fetish was mired in 70's when real men had manes. Like Dave's dad, who still wore what was left of his in a neat pony tail. Scott's hair was shorter, Senator length, but plentiful and moussed full. A lot of people thought Scott's was a piece but, at a long-ago convention, Dave had seen him get splashed in a jacuzzi by an affronted chick. Scott's tan had turned out to be bronzer, but the hair that streamed over his face definitely grew out of his scalp.

Despite Scott's pooh-pooing, they dismissed the idea of dinner and headed straight to O'Hare. The roads were already getting slick and the shoulders were collecting a coating of white.

The minutes they saved with Scott's car rental VIP drop-off didn't make a dent on the airline check-in line. Both arrival and departure boards were flashing delays. When he finally reached the Globtrotter's Club counter, Scott learned that not only was their 9 p.m. flight cancelled outright, but that all the unbooked seats on any flight had been snapped up half an hour before. Not even paying for First Class could get them seats. The best that could be done was one of the first flights out in the morning, the 6:30 to Newark—assuming the wind didn't take another detour and blow the storm East during the night.

Glenn Levine never let anything faze him. Completely out of character, Scott and Milla shrugged it off as something that couldn't be helped. Dave could do nothing but fume internally. While the others looked for a hotel, he made his way to a corner for some privacy for his call home.

"Hannah, is everything okay over there?"

"Dave? Anabelle already had her grilled cheese and we read *Fancy Nancy*? The stars one again? I think she's asleep?"

The sitter was a sweet girl, and she was great with the kids. Usually her speech patterns made his nerve endings throb, but right now that nasal soprano thrilled him like a lost Coltrane recording. "Don't wake her," he said quickly, knowing she was probably halfway to the bedroom now. "I'm stuck in Chicago. There's an effing snowstorm. All the flights are cancelled. We're booked for first thing in the morning, but who knows. Fingers crossed. Will you be able to stay until Angie gets home from the Met? I know it's going to be really late."

"Oh, poor Dave! Don't worry, okay? All I have is tomorrow is Abnormal Psych? I can miss it?"

"You are a total angel! I'll pay you double. You know where we keep the bedding for the sofa. And would you leave a note, in case you're asleep when Angie gets in."

"No problem. You take care, okay?"

The trio he rejoined was a little less blasé than the one he'd left. All they'd been able to find near the airport was one room with two double beds. They'd snapped it up. It was either that or sleeping upright in the terminal. At least the hotel would have a shower.

"We'll pick up a bottle or two on the way," Glenn suggested, putting a bright Sales-style shine on the situation. "Have a real guys night out. No offense Milla."

"None taken. I'm just one of the guys!" The room was on a smoking floor. All of Milla's flouncing at the desk couldn't change that. It smelled of stale cigarettes, old fiberglass and pine sanitizer. On the plus size, the beds were King-sized and the bathroom was the kind where the toilet lodged behind its own sliding door.

It was assumed that Glenn and Dave would share a bed. Scott made a show of offering to sleep in a chair, so that Milla could have the other to herself.

"Don't be ridiculous," she said, with a sharp little laugh. "They're enormous beds and we're all adults here. Anyway, I'm one of the guys, remember. Now let's find the glasses and open a bottle of scotch." She ducked into the bathroom, returning with one paper-wrapped glass and a frown. "One glass. How many out here?"

"Two," Dave counted.

Glenn volunteered: "I can drink from the bottle."

"We need toothbrushes and more towels, too. And there's shampoo, but no conditioner."

Dave reached for the phone to call Housekeeping.

"Oh, don't bother," Milla said airily. "I used to stay in Homeaways all the time. They always keep a cart stocked with supplies near the ice machines on the odd number floors. I'll just run up and grab what we need. It'll be faster. Meanwhile, you boys do the needful so we can expedite sharing one bathroom between four people."

Glenn started to pour himself a drink, then stopped. "I guess it would be polite to wait," he said, hoping someone would contradict him. No one did. He picked up the remote and switched on ESPN. A few minutes later, Scott excused himself to go down to the newsstand in the lobby. "Maybe they'll have some air freshener," he said; "something not pine."

The door clicked shut behind him.

This time Glenn did pour the scotch. He poured two, passing one to Dave. "May as well. It's going to be a while."

Dave took off his jacket and tie. He sat on the edge of one of the beds and set the glass on the shelf between. What he really wanted to do was lie down and go to sleep, but when you're four in a room sleep pretty much has to be a mutual decision. "I think I'll wait for the ice."

"I wouldn't go near that 9th floor ice machine right now." Glenn sank into the armchair and loosened his tie. For Glenn, that was stripping down.

It took a minute for the penny to drop. Dave's eyes goggled. "Oh come on!"

Glenn raised his glass in salute before taking a swallow.

"No way! She's married, isn't she? Anyway, she's not at all his type. He likes them rounder, curvy."

"We used to think he liked them darker, too. Times change. Have you taken a look at Scotty's Angels lately?"

It was true. The current crop of Sales Assistants were a model of diversity. The newest addition, an ice princess named Diana Thorson, could not be more different from the long-suffering Marla.

"Wow." It was a lot to digest. Dave reached for his glass and knocked back the generous pour.

Glenn handed him the bottle. "I'll give them a half hour. Then I'm taking a shower and turning in."

"Do you think she'll actually dig up some toothpaste."

"No worries." Glenn bent down to hook the strap of his leather laptop bag and haul it onto his lap. Reaching in, he pulled out a fresh shirt, an energy bar, a roll of deodorant, a toothbrush and a tube of toothpaste.

"Who are you? Fucking Mary Poppins?"

"I like to be prepared to make a good impression. What if I'd ended up next to some kid on the plane and he spilled juice all over my shirt?" He tossed the toothpaste to Dave. "Here, knock yourself out."

"Thanks." It wouldn't be the first time the Buzzard brushed his teeth with his finger, and it probably wouldn't be the last. "I don't think I want to be awake when they get back. I don't know if I could keep a straight face."

"Sure you could. You're almost as good a bullshitter as Didilian." Coming from Levine, it was a compliment.

Dave nodded his appreciation. "Maybe one more slug."

Δ

It was so strange being back, like that first Thanksgiving in Freeport after she moved to New York. Her body navigated through the familiar floor plan on auto-pilot. Her eyes, sweeping left to right and back again, caught only tiny differences: a bright green octopus mug on Dawn Kollist's desk; a pink cardigan over the chair in the cube that was once Will Compton's. It wasn't the changes that bothered her. It was the gloss of claustrophobia. Everything had somehow shrunk while she was away. Martha del Monte's new world was so much larger than this one, she couldn't help but feel like an alien in her old skin.

Blinking away a vision of her tiny daughter, pale and translucent as a shell, she yearned to flee the office and hop the next train home. She could hardly wait for Wednesday. Gretchen had warned her about this, volunteering to be her…coach? Whatever the name was, for that person you're supposed to call when you're in a 12-step program and think you're about to fall off the wagon. It was nice of Gretchen. But she couldn't really understand. Her husband wrote novels and stayed home most of the time. Martha's husband couldn't even work from home for at least another month. It was because of his new role. "Implementation Specialist." Kind of halfway between Fulfillment and Sales. It sounded so impressive. She knew it was a good thing for them, for their family. She should be happy, but all she could think of was the baby being all alone except for Celia.

Celia was a nice girl. Really nice, and comfortably matter-of-fact about everything to do with babies. Cheerful, too, thank goodness; Martha could never have left Luna with someone who wasn't cheerful. Since she'd arrived last week, she'd never shown anything but the best of humors. The house felt a little cramped with three adults, but it was going to work. Martha couldn't help congratulating herself for convincing Gabe to take the two bedroom in Sunnyside when they moved in together, instead of the one bedroom in hipper, more expensive Astoria. Luna hadn't been so much planned as inevitable. The second bedroom was big enough for a box spring and mattress along with the crib. With the playpen, the baby swing and all of that in the living room, they'd be fine. Sure it would take some time to work out a bathroom schedule, and to get used to bumping into someone else every time she left her bedroom, but it was worth everything not to have to leave Luna in the hands of strangers. Luna swam into sight again. This time, Martha imagined the delicious whiff of brand new baby that curled from her head while she was nursing. Martha's breasts responded with a tingle. She flushed. It was too soon! She'd nursed right before leaving the house. She knew it was natural and all that, but she hated being such a bundle of emotions. With a quick glance around to ensure no one was looking, Martha peered down at her chest. No leakage. The breast pump, in its carrier bag, and the insulated case of plastic bottles, could continue to sit discreetly under her desk, waiting for 11:00, which was when she'd told Ann she'd need to take her break.

Poor Ann! These last few months had ground her into dust. When Bruce Korn left, Martha felt bad enough that the baby was due any minute and Ann would be left alone. But then the guy at Raskub left, too and the whole transition fell on Ann's shoulders. Looking at her now, Martha could see the toll it had taken. Running on yoghurt and nerves, Ann had always been enviably skinny. She was no skinnier now, but her energy had drained off. She was a shadow. She'd been working 12-14 hour days for months, besieged with calls and emails even over the weekend. Ann was too introverted to ever be a demonstrative type—Martha could sense the barrier, but had never been able to penetrate far enough to find out why—but this morning she'd hugged Martha like a long-lost sister.

"The only good thing, other than having you back..." Ann squeezed her hand, "is the Implementations team. Kippy loved when he heard how Raskub's Client Relations people were doing it. Such a great value-add. He insisted we had to pick it up on our end. Except Raskub had the bodies. Or they did, until we started making cuts there. We never even have enough to handle the everyday. There was no way I could manage it. It was Edie's idea to break it off as a separate team and use some of the Trainers for it. I love Edie," she added fervently.

"So how many do we have now? Bodies, I mean. On our team."

"We've got ten here and Sharm has thirteen in Pune."

"Thirteen? Wow! Renee would have died to have thirteen! Sorry, before your time."

"It sounds like a lot, but it's really not. Remember, we're transitioning the Raskub clients. And with the attrition, we lost more there than Feldman planned."

Gabe had told her lots of stories about the attrition. The day the acquisition was announced, 30 percent of the Raskub workforce had been immediately terminated on the grounds of redundancy, and the workload migrated to Pinnacle Pune. A further round of cuts had been planned, targeted for the end of May and meant to follow additional off-shore transition, but a lot of the Raskub folks had beat them to the punch. Half the Raskub workforce bled away before Pinnacle was prepared to absorb the work. We couldn't help but applaud them, even while it knocked us deeper into the weeds. The LC was hilariously furious about people they were ready to dump walking out on them first.

"What do we have left there?"

"Six," sighed Ann. "Four, really. The other two are moving to Implementation."

Martha did a quick calculation. "So 27 altogether? That sounds huge, even for covering both sets of clients."

"Except that half of it's in Pune. And we're already starting to get pushback from clients who don't like it. Clif's setting up a telephony system where each client has to punch in an id number when they call, and the one's we identify as at risk will be routed to a Stateside extension. You should take a look at our folder on the intranet sometime today; it's a pretty big list already."

Δ

At 3 a.m., a freak explosion in New Jersey brought down the data center, automatically triggering the failover to the new backup site in Chennai.

It was the kind of situation for which IT Disaster Recovery plans were intended. The problem was, Pinnacle's plan had been made by Feldman and Strauss, not by anyone with technology DR experience.

At the time, Clifton Speck had begged the LC to at least consider bringing back Mac Fraser for a few weeks on a consulting basis. They'd told him it was unnecessary. The Pune Help Desk lead came with a shiny new DR certification. Trishul had reviewed the plan with the equally new Pune DBA and both had blessed it.

"What about testing?" Clif had asked his then-CTO, Wesley Peterson.

Peterson, that infuriating pleasant expression on his face, had brushed away Cliff's concerns. "Oh, Feldman and Strauss assure me everything is great. Their certified DR expert ran a bunch of tests"

Expressing his concerns about the thoroughness of any testing that had left him out of the loop, Clif was criticized for displaying the knee-jerk xenophobia too many Americans feel in regard to their off-shore co-professionals. Strauss and Feldman further suggested that, if Clif were serious about his work, he should invest in a few more certifications himself.

On the day of reckoning, it seemed at first that Feldman and Strauss had been correct in placing their trust in Trishul, who'd since compounded their belief in his superior qualifications by leaving Pinnacle to run a Mumbai Helpdesk team for a major American banking institution. When Jersey went down at 3 a.m., Chennai indeed came up like a dream, and the Pune computers changed partners and started dancing nicely with their subcontinental neighbors. The data, however, stopped there.

The failover to Chennai failed; specifically, the connection to the US. The Pune teams were well occupied with data entry, payroll and procurement orders that had reached them before the outage, but new orders weren't getting through to them. New York was dead in the water, as was the Raskub Payroll Services integration. Only the Raskub services that hadn't made the transfer to our systems were fully up and running; that and the second backup email server that Clif had installed in Minneapolis as belt-and-suspenders. Clif didn't have time to say "I told you so," not that it was ever a smart business comeback anyway. He was too busy chugging sufficient coffee to spin the straws he was grasping at into gold. He hauled Cooper Fradkin out of bed to run to the office to flip the switch.

By the time the rest of us got in, Clif was juggling flaming balls with chainsaws, simultaneously trying to find a kluge and get to the root of the problem. Dave Broussard, called in so early that he had to bring his toddler to work, ran interference between IT and the rest of the world, bringing regular updates of a less-than-optimistic nature. Freddie was over in Jersey with Bart Maple, authorized by Kippy to consult and brought in at twice the going rate. Clif was running a conference bridge linking them, the current Pune Helpdesk lead and a hastily-hired Chennai consultant. It looked like it was going to take at least a day, maybe two, before we were back up and running. Fradkin, still in his moose-printed flannel pajama pants and Vikings sweatshirt, was monitoring the email load, and hooking up a new scanner to beef up the ability of the Minnesota team to manually send orders to Pune. The Buzzard, the Swiss Army Knife of Pinnacle, was trying to do something similar for us.

None of us understood the technical details, but we understood the talking points and knew we were in deep trouble. Our phones were ringing off the hook with calls from clients who, attempting to access the online Pinnacle or Raskub portals, were told by their browser that the site was down. Payroll and Procurement couldn't go through because the digital signatures weren't matching the security protocols of the US banks and suppliers. Ann's people started drafting communications, which Feldman and Strauss insisted on revising a dozen times before anyone was allowed to send anything out. It made the crash that had nearly lost us MSY the first time seem as petty an annoyance as an old phone battery. We all pitched in however we could, helping field those angry phone calls and emails, putting Edie's workarounds into effect to so that we could email work back and forth with Pune, brewing coffee, running after Jake Broussard, planning ahead for playing catchup when all this was over. Feldman and Strauss stalked the office with their noses held high in the air, as if the stink in the air had nothing to do with them. Kippy, Scott and Milla stayed behind closed doors.

Somewhere around noonish, Chris Keane was sent scurrying from desk to desk with the exciting news. As a thank you for all our efforts, there was pizza in the break room. With so much to do, it was suggested that we grab a slice or two and eat it at our desks.

Δ

It was too beautiful out to run back to the office. Beckoned by peals of laughter, Judy strolled down the alley towards the little knot of smokers.

"And then when he turns around...'I am not our father' seriously? Nimoy?!" It was hard to tell if Hank was happy because he'd liked the film, or happy because he had a bone to pick. That was Hank.

"Oh, come on." Dawn rolled her eyes. "That was great! However...Spock and Uhura?"

Judy put in her own two cents, grateful that she knew what they were talking about. "I bought it. With this cast? Why not?"

Danny was eyeballing the logo on her paper cup. "You went all the way to Grumpy?"

"All the slave drivers took Ashok and Vijay for lunch, so I took a walk for mine." She removed the cover and inhaled the aroma. "Mmmmm, lunch! Got a cookie, too." She produced a napkin from her jacket pocket.

"I can't believe they flew two people from India for an offsite." It wasn't the first time today that Dawn had said this.

"Some of the Raskub people are flying in tomorrow morning. I have to meet them at the airport and bring them to the country club."

Dawn made a strangled sound.

"They're not staying over," Gretchen assured her. "They'll take the last flight home."

"Of course they will." Judy took a careful sip. Her cappuccino was delectably creamy, but still too hot. "Typical. The LC trying to act like the big boys and just missing the mark. It fascinates me. I wonder what Mamet would do with them."

"I don't know." Archie disagreed. "They did just buy another company."

"And Kippy's looking for more." Danny could say that without breaking confidentiality. Kippy had said as much at the last Monthly.

Dawn rolled her eyes again. "Mind-blowing. He really thinks he's Warren Buffett."

Danny had the look of someone probing a cavity with his tongue. "I'm kind of surprised they didn't bring Swati over, too. You know she's got three TQM people over there now? Here it's just me and Channing."

"And Khosi, right?" Archie corrected him. "I still don't understand what Khosi's supposed to be doing with Client."

"Not much." We opened ourselves expectantly; Hank's grin implied more than Client Relations snarkiness. "Not official, but Khosi's gone."

"She gave her two weeks? Please don't tell me she actually got Google." It drove Danny crazy, Khosi's assertion that she would one day land a job there. It wasn't that he doubted her, only that he wished he had her confidence.

Hank nodded significantly at Gretchen.

"I don't know," she told him. "I really don't." She usually did.

"Okay. Well, to be fair, she had some ideas, but there was no one to give her buy in. She never clicked with Korn, and after he left…"

"I thought Scott was crazy about her," said Judy.

"That is so last year," Dawn informed her.

"Whatever. I heard she's moving on. How come you don't know this Dan? She reports to Hugo."

"Technically, sure. Dotted line. But he's been doing the buyout and…uh, you know…future projects. With us. Swati's got everything Fulfillment." There it was again, that wince that accompanied saying her name.

"It makes sense," Judy thought; "with so much of Fulfillment being over there."

Archie agreed. "It does, really. Swati must be doing a good job. Kristol said something about 'Center of Excellence' the other day. Yes, that again," she added.

Danny didn't try to control a bitter tinge of envy. "They've been sending her to school for Trim/Delta training. She's halfway to her Minarai certification."

"I take it you're not?" Judy was surprised. Last she'd heard, Hugo's whole team was supposed to be getting training. Maybe that was back when Korn was still around. She really was out of the loop. Danny shook his head rapidly. The subject was a sore point. "Hugo's not even talking about TQM these days. We're all about business development. Boring as hell."

"Yah, but good for the resume." Since her library science classes had her looking to the future, Dawn interpreted everything at work in those terms.

"If that's what I wanted to do, I'd be doing it at a bank for twice the money. Which reminds me. Hank? Where did you say Korn was working these days?"

"Making big money reminds you of me? Archie, honey, you were right about the haircut. My lady gives me class."

Archie lowered her lashes, as she always did when Hank gave her a compliment. It turned her smile into a secret. "No, I just made you stop running from who you are."

Hank's eyes softened and he pulled her close. "Yeah, you did that. No wonder my folks love you. My folks love her, did you guys know that?"

"Hey!" Dawn held up her arms in a rough anti-vampire cross. "Ew! Stop fraternizing, you guys! You want Gretchen to get in trouble for not reporting you?"

Judy chuckled. "You have to love the double standard. Only no fraternizing if you're below C level." At least she was in the loop on one piece of gossip.

Gretchen frowned. "People should stop spreading rumors. It's not true."

Hank was honestly surprised. "How can a girl who danced in Christmas tinsel at the Mirage possibly be so naïve?"

"You danced in Vegas?!" Judy was delighted. "I swear, Gretchen Keneally, you are probably the single most interesting person at Pinnacle. I might have start writing again, just to make you a character."

Gretchen cleared her throat and peeked at her Crackberry. "Damn! Kippy'll be back any minute. I've got to run and open the conference bridge for PBK. Fingers crossed it's not on the fritz again. Clif says he can't do anything if we won't pay for the latest upgrade."

"Feldman sure learned that lesson, didn't he?" Judy punctuated her comment with a decisive cookie crunch.

Archie lifted her head from Hank's chest to look Gretchen. "He's doing PBK again?"

"He is. And the scheduling is driving me crazy."

Dawn was peeved. "If I'd known, maybe I would have put in for it. For the resume."

"You couldn't have." Gretchen sounded apologetic. That something wasn't her doing didn't stop her from feeling bad about it. "It was all nominations this year. And only three people from here. The rest are Pune and Raskub."

Danny offered his own form of consolation. "Don't feel bad, Dawn. I ran the numbers once. Just because. Do you know that, historically, 17 percent of all PBK participants are canned while they're still in the program? 17 percent. So much for the value of face-time with Kippy."

Hank couldn't resist trying to guess. "I'm betting Peter Weiss, right? From here? Roger Didilian better start looking over his shoulder."

Gretchen nodded. "Yes. And Rachel Kramer."

Judy had no idea who that was.

"The redhead in Travel," Gretchen described.

Archie was more specific. "The high-maintenance one. She makes me feel like I'm wearing orthopedic shoes." Archie frowned at her own black patent kitten heels. "Last year's orthopedic shoes."

Dawn wasn't fashionista enough to be in competition with Rachel Kramer. There was another point that bothered her. "She practically just started and she's in PBK? I've been here four years. Almost exactly. Shit!"

"Her mother is Scott's cousin. See, when I know something is true, I say so." Gretchen wrinkled her nose in Hank's direction and took off.

"Great!" he called after her. "Who's number three? You said three."

"Lara Kovasova!"

"I should probably go up, too." Danny started walking, considerably slower than Gretchen's sprint. It had been a while. We all fell into step beside him.

"Lah-ra Kvah-sova," Dawn elaborated, doing her best Natasha Fatale. "Is from my team. Also pretty new. Maybe her mother is Milla's cousin."

Hank blinked in surprise. "Milla's Russian?"

We paused, our combined reaction enough to turn his face beet red.

"Anna Ludmilla Kristol? No, Hank, she's as Irish as Tully."

"Okay, I'm a moron. I mean, I thought her family probably was originally, but I never thought she was. She doesn't have an accent."

"I was born and raised on the Island and I don't sound like Ray Romano." Dawn sounded a little testy.

"I'm sure she worked very hard on that." Judy slipped into story-telling mode as we walked. "She always strikes me as the type who does. Works hard, I mean. FYI, she's Milla Kristol-Younger in some circles. An old friend invited me to a celebrity fundraising thing for Project ALS; I saw it on the donor list."

Hank was incredulous. "Wait, Milla Kristol is a Russian socialite?"

"Ish."

"Socialist?" Dawn smirked. "I don't think so."

"Socialite-ish. Project ALS is posh, but not so much society. A lot of big show business types, so you get the kinds of people who want to make them happy. Drexel Younger is something in Real Estate. I asked."

"No." Danny chopped the air with his hand. "There is no way anyone names a kid Drexel."

"Unless they have to," Hank reflected. "Mother's maiden name maybe? Can you say 'trust fund'?"

Archie wanted to get to the gossip. "Was she there? Did she say hello? What did you do?"

"Oh, she didn't notice me. I was dressed. You guys have never seen me dressed, have you?"

"My first Holiday party," Archie said promptly. "I went over to that sample sale the next day."

"That was Business Festive. I mean seriously dressed. Black tie. Full makeup." Judy waved her hand, implying a Cinderella transformation. "If you didn't know me, you wouldn't know me. And Kristol doesn't know me; she looks right through me. Couldn't even pick me out a yard away from her, talking with Julianna Margulies—who does know me, by the way, because when she was starting out in New York, she had a small part in my last play. That was before both of our careers changed direction. Guess whose went which way? If I even looked remotely familiar to Kristol, she probably assumed I was Somebody."

Dawn made a rude sound. "Can you imagine Kristol's husband? I bet he's old. Old and rich. Was she dragging him around by his tie, making him introduce him to all the famous people?"

"Older, but not old. And not bad looking. Not my type, but perfectly reasonable. And no, she was following him. Sticking pretty close. I don't think she was comfortable there, out of her natural habitat. She was surprisingly subdued. I bet I was the only one who noticed she was there."

Danny couldn't visualize it. "That must have been a very interesting experience for her."

"I wonder which one is the real Milla Kristol," Archie mused. "It's almost sad."

"Honey, I love you. But there's such a thing as too nice. You don't have to give everyone the benefit of the doubt."

Gabe del Monte was waiting for the elevator. On the days Martha worked from home, he treated himself to a burrito. "Damn, I didn't think. I should have gone looking for you guys. It feels like years since I hung out."

"How's Luna?" asked Judy. "I'm thinking of joining Facebook just so I can see the pictures."

Gabe's face lit with pleasure. He thumbed his phone to bring up the latest shot of his angel.

Archie peered over Judy's shoulder. "Oh, is that the sweater Martha knitted? It fits already!"

"She's so beautiful!" Judy gave him a quick hug. "You guys did good."

"We're lucky. That's why I'm extra glad they picked a children's charity this month."

"Oh, great!" Dawn had run two of the charity-of-the-month projects herself. Whatever Pinnacle was going to give, why shouldn't it go to something she believed in? "So what did they pick?"

"Didn't you see?" The announcement from HC must have been emailed while we were all out. "They give shoes to kids all over the world. The name is weird though. Beautiful Feet. That can't be right."

"Where have I heard that name?" Dawn screwed up her face, trying to remember why it sounded familiar.

Gabe shrugged. "They also help with Central American adoptions. I think Walt Sacco got his kids through them."

It was, indeed, Beautiful Feet. The website, linked to the email from HC, proclaimed "How beautiful are the feet of those who bring good news of good things!" So did the brochures Don Bryson left in the break room and with Maci at the front desk. Marla Cox, a minister's granddaughter, supplied the source: Romans 10:15.

Beautiful Feet not only facilitated adoptions and distributed brand new shoes to the deserving impoverished in 26 countries, they ensured that the communities they served were deserving by staffing the distribution chain with vigorous evangelists who spread the gospel along with the footwear. The Beautiful Feet missions were only one initiative of Chadband International, a faith-based philanthropic cephalopod whose many arms shared food, clothing and certain medicines around the world, as well as supplying millions to Congressional lobbyists to forward a Conservative social agenda. Chadband International opposed same-sex and single parent adoption, gambling, gay rights...even divorce. Of course, they weren't against everything. There were many things they enthusiastically supported, including a chain of behavioral modification "retreats" for gay teens.

With Dawn's mad library skills, it took a whole five minutes to ferret this out. Without them, it might have taken ten; but apparently no one had thought to look. Walt brought in a flyer and HC took it at face value.

Chris Keane's pale face exploded in red blotches when she heard.

Walt was surprised at how upset people were. The younger of the two long-awaited Sacco children had joined the family through the affiliated adoption agency. He thought the shoes project would be a great way to pay it forward. Sure, he'd known it was a Christian organization. Walt and Marie were Catholics themselves. It seemed only appropriate that a child would come from God. He didn't see why that was a problem.

Don Bryson, palms damp with nerves from the deluge of email objections and people knocking on his door, explained to Walt that it wasn't Chadband's spiritual component as such, but their political agenda that was causing the problem. In respect of the varied beliefs and lifestyles of its associates, Pinnacle needed to remain politically neutral. Walt didn't understand it, but he accepted it, an attitude that was the key to most of Walt's happiness and his long friendship with Kippy.

Δ

```
From:          Don Bryson
To:            All Pinnacle Associates
Subject:       Charity of the Month
------------------------------------
```

We would like to apologize for the confusion around the selection of this month's designated charity. Thanks to everyone who expressed concern. It is heart-warming to know invested everyone is in the causes we support.

I hope you will be as pleased as I am to know that the May Charity of the Month is St. Jude's Children's Hospital. As always, Pinnacle will match all donations dollar for dollar. I'm also very excited to announce that, as a special acknowledgement of your enthusiasm for our charitable giving, Kippy is kicking off this month's fund with a personal donation of $250.

Don

Don Bryson,Dir. HC
Pinnacle Management Services

FRIDAY

19 ROADMAP

Light at the end of the tunnel. Doesn't matter that it's a temporary light. Even if nothing happens over the weekend—no jammed client uploads demanding a fast manual workaround, no surprise security audits calling you back to the city—Monday is going to start the same old cycle again. But on Friday, you can draw a line under it and pretend to call it done. Tonight, for a change, maybe you can relax for a couple of hours. There's a laundry list of things to do tomorrow—including the laundry—but no one's going to be breathing down your neck. And that piece of the day when Phil's rested and alert, when he's almost like he used to be, there's time to be together. With that to look forward to, almost within reach, you can do anything with a smile. What was it the kids said now? "Sweet." Friday was one sweet day.

And it was almost done. "Just a few more hours, and Mommy'll be home too! And then we'll give you a bath! Both of us, together! What do you think of that!?" She's only giggling because you're tickling her tummy and making your voice go all squeaky. She's too young to understand the words. But she can understand that you're happy; you're sure she can. You kiss that sweet little tummy and set her down in the bouncy saucer thing, so she can see you while you're on the conference call with Dawn and Minneapolis about the Hy Steaks implementation. Imagine working from home all the time. Well, that's impossible, so remember how lucky you are to have the one day, luckier still that it's Friday. Martha says she likes breaking up the week, but you think spending Friday in sweats, doing business with the baby on your knee, is like having the weekend start early. You wish all days could be Friday.

It feels like it'll never end. Ssssllllloooowwww motion. Everyone dragging their feet, metaphorically speaking. And so many meetings, as if there's some kind of compulsion to round up everyone in a holding pen right before they have to let us out. You just want to get out of here already! You have plans! Okay, so it's not Mardi Gras, but they're still plans. Tully and Lily have a gig at Otto's tonight. And you're trying out the new slow-cooker tomorrow. Then Sunday, he has his project to finish for his Teaching Fellows class and you need to study for Tuesday's test. Two more semesters. When you get out of here, you are definitely quitting smoking. Tully was right about the money, but you can't stop, not as long as you're still here. As soon as you're not, then you are totally quitting and putting all that money into a vacation fund. A Disney honeymoon, that's what you're after. Not a Disney wedding. You want your princess moment as much as any girl, but that's way overboard.

You're much too sensible. A sensible librarian engaged to a social studies teacher. Who'd a thunk it? You are seriously turning into your parents. And you know what? That's not such a bad life. It's funny how it always hits you halfway through the day, and everything suddenly looks brighter. Even if the day goes on and on.

How great is this, the week almost over? You were so lucky to get away from engineering when you did. SysOps is a young guy's gig, all the 48-hour blitzes and weekend deployments. Not lucky; smart. Sure you have to hop on a plane whenever Scott or one of them says jump. And yeah, you have your share of late nights, dealing with yet another last minute RFP or whatever. But never on Friday. A smart sales guy knows to never set up a call on Friday; it gives the client a whole weekend to forget the pitch. Which means you can count on your weekends. Pile the family in a car and drive somewhere with more air. You miss having your own wheels, but it's easier to stumble on a Tibetan Lama in the streets of New York than an empty legal parking space, and the cost of garaging is obscene. No wonder TerrifiCar is booming. And since you busted your chops for them and they thanked you with that free membership, it only costs for the few hours and the gas. Tomorrow your kids are going to see that food grows on trees. You're heading out East to the pick-your-own market garden. Free as a bird.

Acres of time. Two entire days, plus tonight. Such a delicious feeling, that you can do absolutely anything tonight. You don't even have to go to sleep, though you probably will. It's not like when you were in school and had all that energy. Damn, how you used to laugh when people said those were the best years of your life. All that angst you had! You didn't grasp that it was the only time of life without repercussions. You could hardly wait to graduate, for real life to begin. Real life, where everything has to be weighed and assessed, the tradeoffs considered. A donut for a pound. Dinner and a movie once a week all year or a single week on a white sand beach. A headache tomorrow for a party tonight…except this night, Friday, when (with apologies to Kander and Ebb) tomorrow belongs to you. You can sleep all day tomorrow if you want. You can do anything you feel like doing, within reason. Reason being your bank account, which still leaves plenty of room for possibility.

You push against the door and walk out into the street. Even in the winter darkness, in an icy rain, you look up and feel soft kiss of the sun as you walk away, draped in the almost unfathomable luxury of it, of all those hours stretching ahead of you, and your lungs swell with the astonishing breath of freedom.

#tgif

Δ

From: Milla Kristol
To: All Pinnacle Associates
Subject: Fulfillment Changes Roadmap

In the aftermath of the explosive growth Pinnacle has realized over the past year, rumors are bound to circulate regarding the future plans of management. Let us put such rumors to rest.

As you all know, Pune Fulfillment was envisioned as an extension of the New York office. Over time, as procedures were adjusted or developed on an ad hoc basis, the two work flows diverged. The acquisition of Raskub, and the LC's decision to mitigate client disruption through a prolonged transition period, resulted in yet a third set of procedures.

Now that the dust has settled, we are developing a multi-pronged strategic plan to maximize Pinnacle's efficiency through work process alignment. Earlier this week, I met with managers and Fulfillment teams across Pinnacle to discuss the roadmap by which we will facilitate this alignment. In keeping with our published Core Values of Transparency and Innovation, I share the high-level goals of this roadmap here:

Compliance: Pivoting off the Raskub paradigm, the service previously known as Compliance is being re-envisioned to leverage the synergies of employee relations and benefits/compensation management. Following a major rebranding initiative that is already in progress, the new Pinnacle Sherpa service will be formally rolled out at the SHRM convention in San Diego at the end of this month. The tri-location Sherpa fulfillment team will be organized and managed out of Minneapolis by Mary Ann Stone.

Procurement: As of August 1, we will have completed the transition of all on-shore positions to Minneapolis. In conjunction with this, Peter Eichel has officially assumed the position of Procurement Lead.

Travel: I am excited to announce that our first International Travel resources will join the Pune office Monday. Like the Minneapolis team, International Travel will report through Rachel Kramer, our NY Travel Manager.

Training: The evolution of user-friendly application interfaces, combined with the influx of the first "digital generation" into the workplace has significantly changed the focus of Pinnacle's Training service. As you are all aware,

we have phased out our training services for MS Office
products and other third party applications, refocussing our
resources on training clients in the use of OnBoard, the
Denali User Portal and other Pinnacle enterprise
applications. The recent addition of Pune-based Trainers has
been a notable success, and we look forward to expanding this
area in the coming months.

Implementation: Under the leadership of Archandra Ghosh in
New York, the Account Implementation team is expected to
continue to grow significantly over the course of the next
year, as Sales begins to leverage this service as a
significant market differentiator.

Having completed an extremely successful transition to Pune,
Payroll, Data Entry and Switchboard services will continue to
be provided solely through that office.

Please join me in acknowledging the efforts of Swati Prasad
and her Center of Excellence team in analyzing and effecting
these changes.

Milla Kristol, COO
Pinnacle Management Services

Δ

From: Don Bryson
To: All Pinnacle Associates
Subject: Changes to Human Capital

In response to the challenges presented by Pinnacle's
tremendous expansion, we are adjusting our organizational
structure to better serve your needs. In this regard, I am
delighted to announce the following:

Surinder Bhatti has been promoted to Associate Director of
Human Capital, India, a title that more accurately reflects
the integral role he already plays in Pune Operations.

To align with this, as Tyler Robertson transfers to
Minneapolis this month to take over responsibilities from the
departing Sue Skuza, he will be assuming the title Associate
Director of Human Capital, US.

Please join me in congratulating both Surinder and Tyler.

Don Bryson, Director of Human Capital
Pinnacle Management Services

Δ

"It's not like Raskub," Hugo stated baldly, once the non-disclosures had been duly signed and collected. "They're not exactly welcoming us with open arms. ProFile was a start-up until Bamford snapped them up a couple of years ago. When Bamford decided to spin them off, the employees tried to pool their resources to buy themselves back, but they couldn't get financing. Now they're kind of pissed off."

Judy understood, but didn't see that it would make much difference in the end. Of all the enthusiastic Raskub employees who'd cheered the conquering heroes back in February (was it really only February?), maybe a quarter were left in Minneapolis. The headcount for voluntary attrition had been nearly as much as the LC's planned cuts. Of the managers she'd met during the merger project, only Cooper Fradkin and Mary Ann Stone were still in place, and she had a feeling Cooper was just marking time until something he really wanted came along. She didn't have much contact with regular associates, but she got the impression that people in smaller cities didn't take to well to being termites.

The way Dave was describing it, at least Raskub could breathe easy about Project Grapefruit. This West Coast company was mostly about data, so the main hit to Fulfillment would be in Pune. Judy got a kick out of listening to Dave. She'd put in enough time trying to tease information out of his head to know how tangled his thought processes were, but stand him in front of an audience and damn if he didn't sound as if he knew what he was talking about. She even thought she was starting to understand what "data mining" was. What she understood made her a little queasy. It was the kind of concept she could off shrug off if it showed up it in a Philip K. Dick story, but not when it was earnestly pitched by Pinnacle's freshly-dubbed Director of Product Development and Special Projects. ProFile must have great EBITDA for Kippy to want to take it on; it had only peripherally to do with any of our existing product lines and, being all about technology, it couldn't be that cheap to run.

She would have liked to have gauged Feldman's reaction, but none of the C's had shown for this meeting. Second time around, they apparently needed no one higher up than Hugo to shepherd the process. If she were one of the ProFile people, she'd feel a little snubbed. For her own part, Hugo was plenty. She'd learned how to deliver to expectation: no suggestions, no deviations. All she had to do was clone everything she'd done for Raskub. One giant copy and replace would get her well on the way, and with Len shepherding Jim Matticchio around India for the next couple of weeks, she had a big block of time to do it.

Even when Len got back, this project would be way easier to handle than the last. Not that she would dare to say "I told you so," but her contention that the SEO project was a waste of time had been well born out. All Len had gained was the fun of having someone to bully. Now he had her exploring cheap advertising, and even that was a half-hearted request. Like a lot of those my-way-or-the-highway types, Strauss didn't acknowledge defeat; he veered off at another angle, pretending it never happened. He was currently indifferent to the website, zeroing in on IT as the silo in which to promote the value of his sub-continental expertise.

If Matticchio hadn't been such an asshole to her, she'd feel sorry for him; with Len and Feldman pulling the strings, he was CTO in name only. Maybe that was all Matticchio wanted. She really didn't know anything about him. Nobody did, except he'd once asked Dave's opinion about some boat-related thing. Maybe he was tired of pushing his way up corporate ladders and only wanted to lie low and collect a paycheck. The same way that she did. She sensed that the always quiet Bennett Liu shared that wavelength. Someone said his wife wasn't well; some chronic thing, like MS. She hoped not; that would be a sad reason for his air of stoicism.

The rest of the team around this table wanted something more. Dave was another survivor, but he was more proactive about it. It probably had something to do with that weird childhood of his, little Brother David calling people home to Jesus. She grinned, imagining two-year-old Jake in a dark suit; the toddler was an absolute clone of his father. Hugo's hyperactivity, on the other hand, was frankly ambitious. It was in his booming laugh, his restless pacing of any space, the way he sat so nearly off his seat that he seemed about to spring. He probably didn't need gel to make his hair stand on end; the energy was bursting out of him. That he didn't trouble to disguise it gave it a kind of charm. Ashok, even as a disembodied voice, chomped just as greedily as Hugo at the bit. They were an exhausting pair.

The only other major player on the Grapefruit team, Ann Ling, was something of a cypher. They'd started within a few months of one another, but they'd never actually worked together until Raskub. Watching her hack away at that mountain of work, especially while Martha was on leave and there was no one to take up the slack on the day to day, Judy had acquired a level of respect for the girl. Hank Iversson's sarcastic comments weren't far wrong; Ann wasn't the sharpest knife in the drawer. But she was dogged and determined, she absorbed whatever Milla dished out and she didn't stop working for a second. Ann seemed more beleaguered than driven, but that might be an illusion. Maybe she ducked her head so that her glossy curtain of hair would hide the fact that she was as ruthless as Catherine de Medici, but Judy doubted it. She'd seen the girl flinch if someone slammed a desk drawer. There was something there. Whatever it was signaled "keep out" so clearly that even Craig Parnes kept his distance. Which made Judy more inclined to admire her perseverance and ignore the temptation to join in the Asian Blonde jokes.

"Judy?"

Damn! She'd been drifting down her own stream of consciousness again. She couldn't help it. The people here were so much more interesting than the work was. Hugo was looking directly at her. If she didn't say something quick, so would everyone else.

Flipping her notebook closed, she patted it as if it held copious and critical notes. "I'm good," she said brightly. It was a comment that could cover a lot of situations. This, fortunately, was one of them.

"Great!" He flashed his usual quotient of happy teeth. "Okay then. Just one more thing before I open the conference bridge and we meet the other side. Turns out there's someone over there in Portland we already know. Especially you, Ann."

Δ

Martha settled back in her seat, determined to enjoy the flight. She hadn't been on a plane since their trip to Vegas. This wasn't quite as much of a milestone, but it was her first business trip ever. She was still surprised that Milla and Scott had asked her, not Ann, to go on this exploratory mission. Hugo said it was because they were being discreet and keeping the crew small; she knew so much about Fulfillment from the old days that they'd wouldn't need anyone else. Her "'institutional memory," he called it, which kind of convinced her they weren't just trying to save on airfare. Yup. This was a big deal. So was being away from Luna overnight. That was also a first, but she was trying not to think about it. It was silly to worry. Tomorrow was Gabe's work from home day. Besides, Celia was perfectly competent. She was great, actually. Being the oldest of six certainly taught you a lot about babies. It would have been pretty demoralizing, except that Martha could teach her so much about living in New York. As it was, it was like having her own sister around except that, unlike Dottie, Celia didn't think 7:00 was too late for dinner—probably because she didn't go to bed at 9:30.

Which reminded Martha that she'd be landing in Portland at midnight, which was really 3 a.m. It would be smart to try and nap for a bit. Maybe she should have a glass of wine, now that she could again. She had mixed feelings about that. As long as she'd nursed, it was like Luna was a part of her. Sure it was nice not being a cow; but in a way weaning was Luna's first step away from her. Before she turned around, her daughter would be wearing lipstick and talking about boys. Wrapping her light cardigan around her shoulders, Martha hugged herself and tried to laugh. What was she going to start imagining after she had that wine? She'd have to find something to distract her until she got sleepy. She liked how Jet Blue put the screens in the seat backs, so short people could actually watch the movie. Better still, they had TV; if it was one of those Nicholas Cage conspiracy movies, she wouldn't even have to watch it. Maybe she could find a Friends rerun, something she'd seen a million times and could doze in front of. It was good Milla and Scott had flown ahead. She was traveling alone, so she could do whatever she felt like; two glasses of wine, if that's what it took. Tomorrow was going to be a long day. Bruce Korn was coming to pick her up at the hotel for breakfast and then take her to the ProFile office. Talk about weird!

"I have to ask," Bruce said, after they'd ordered, and the coffee was poured, and he'd seen the pictures of the baby. "How long as this been going on?"

"Huh?"

"People keep asking me if they're married. I don't know what to say."

Suddenly Martha knew what he was talking about. There were a lot of rumors about Milla and Scott. Martha didn't believe them. It wasn't that she was naive. She knew a giant diamond ring was no guarantee that people wouldn't cheat. Actually, in her experience, rich people cheated like crazy. She used to watch the summer people in Maine; in fact, she'd dodged a few herself. She assumed they'd either married for the wrong reasons, or that maybe having all that money made you bored. No, the reason she didn't buy the "Scilla" whispers was pragmatic: she'd known Scott far too long. It wasn't only his thing for Marla; that was almost misguided friendship and it was kind of sweet, except at the Holiday party. In general Scott had always had a thing for dark women with cute figures and girly taste in clothes. Milla Kristol was washed out and boney, and everything she put on looked like a suit. Kind of androgynous really, except for her boobs – and Martha didn't believe that rumor either; hadn't people ever heard of Wonderbra? She laughed. "They just get along well."

Bruce was skeptical. "When I worked for her, she wouldn't give me the time of day. That was the main reason I started looking elsewhere so soon. I knew I'd never get any buy-ins from her. It was a dead end for me."

Martha shrugged and started drizzling her pancakes with blueberry syrup; everyone knows that food you eat when you're traveling has no calories. "It's different. They're on the same level, so it's easier. Not everyone's good at connecting with their direct reports." She refrained from noting that Bruce was connecting with her more right now than he ever had when he was her nominal boss.

He stared at her intently, until she wondered if there was syrup on her chin and started dabbing with her napkin. His eyes cleared and he smiled. It was a friendly smile. "You're a straight arrow, Martha Moon. I always liked that about you."

He had? She smiled back. Bruce Korn was definitely much nicer in Portland.

After that, Martha couldn't help being hyper-aware of them. She'd be talking with the two Business Analysts in the conference room, hear a distinctive cackling laugh, and crane her neck to look across the room to where Milla and Scott were talking with Bruce or the ProFile President or the head of Sales. Lucky thing it wasn't a glass box like the one in New York, since most of the staff wasn't supposed to know why they were there. Milla would often lay a hand on Scott's shoulder; once, when she was laughing especially hard, it was her head. He winked a couple of times.

If you were looking for things to comment on, you could probably make something out of how attentive he was when she was speaking; but hey, Milla might not be a sweetheart, but she was smart. Scott knew he wasn't. He probably admired her for that. Martha still didn't believe the rumors, but she could see why people might think things.

The day was crazy long, as Martha had expected. She wasn't sure what they'd expected of her, but she felt she'd accomplished something. She felt good. At one point, someone called out for sandwiches. There was an extra one for her to take on the flight home, Scott said, since there wouldn't be time for her to go out to dinner with them before heading for the airport. That was really nice of him; thoughtful. He also gave her a five and said to buy a glass of wine on the plane. It wasn't until she was drinking it that she wondered whether he and Milla were going out for a fancy Friday night dinner...and when they were flying home.

Δ

```
From:        Milla Kristol
To:          All Pinnacle Associates
Subject:     Organizational Changes
------------------------------------
```

I am pleased to announce that Ann Ling will be assuming the Senior Management role of Director of Client Relations, responsible for Client teams across Pinnacle.

Please join me in congratulating Ann on this well-deserved promotion.

Milla Kristol, COO
Pinnacle Management Services

Δ

```
From:        Don Bryson
To:          Pinnacle Leadership
Subject:     Employee Departures
-----------------------------------
```

As a reminder, the following scheduled terminations will become effective as of end of business today, Friday, August 28:

In New York:

- Erin Cunningham — Client Relations
- Antonia Guitterez — Client Relations
- Randall Gordon — Compliance
- Veronica Andretta — Travel Services
- Ron Ingelton — Travel Services
- Craig Parnes — IT

In Minneapolis:

- Jeremy Phillips — Compliance
- Kathy Sackett — Compliance
- John Hoffman — Placement and Training
- Janet Thomas — Travel Services

Don Bryson, Director of Human Capital
Pinnacle Management Services

Δ

Time bled out in that endless year, the weeks marked only by who left when. The old Pinnacle, with so many entry-level jobs, had been a way station for people bankrolling a vocation or passing by on the way between college and a career. There had always been people coming and going. Lately it was mostly going. Entire teams had been migrated away from New York entirely or slimmed down to a synecdoche. Most who hadn't already left, either voluntarily or because of cuts, were lifers by temperament. Even we were beginning to leave on our own, afraid we'd otherwise soon be shown the door. There were more empty cubes now than at any time since Kippy had first leased the space. Only the Pit remained fully packed.

Since the Pune workforce were direct employees, not contracted, Sales continued to sell Pinnacle as an "American company," and the tax benefits continued to flow. There were, however, a few bumps in the road. Despite the presence of two cultural trainers, and a requirement that all "American" names be vetted by Edie, clients were expressing dissatisfaction with and even dropping the relocated Switchboard service. Many were specifying US-based Training or Client Relations in their contracts. Moreover, the LC had recently been advised by legal counsel that HHS regulations required a certain percentage of "Sherpa" positions to remain State-side, causing a sudden staffing frenzy in Minneapolis. When Hank Iversson told Don Bryson he would be leaving in a month to return to his home town, the LC made him an almost immediate counter offer: if he stayed with Pinnacle, they'd make him Director there and pay his moving expenses.

"It was hard to keep a straight face," Hank told us afterwards. "But I told them flat out, 'why would I move back to Minneapolis for a dead-end job like this?'"

"You didn't!" Danny Zill was simultaneously thrilled and horrified.

"Who was in the room?" Judy Schreiber wanted to know.

"Bryson, Kristol and Edie. I thought Edie was going to lose it. She did that thing where you pick up your mug and pretend to take a drink. So then I told them I was joining my family business, and that I start as EVP of Operations with a voting share on the Board. You should have seen Kristol's face."

Dawn Kollist hazarded a guess. "Purple."

"White. Corpse white, with red blotches on her cheeks, like poison ivy. It was sick. And before she could say a word, I threw the final punch. 'By the way,' I said, and I said it just this way, no anger or anything. 'You can tell Gary Feldman I'll be moving our account to ADP. Since that thousand dollar referral bonus never came through, I've got no conflict of interest.'"

"OMG!" Dawn extended her arms and kowtowed to him. "I am so not worthy!"

"It was worth the thousand dollars. Not that I was getting it anyway. It amazes me how this company keeps growing when they are absolutely clueless about running a business. Seriously, I had no idea how much I'd learned as a kid until I saw this train wreck."

"I never understood why you stuck around," Danny admitted. "If I had a family business to go into, I'd run. But the kind of shop my family had is all in China now. Or Lithuania; someplace like that. You can't make cheap coats in the US anymore."

"I was lazy," Hank admitted. "And I was enjoying being with you guys, and going to the clubs... the whole New York scene. I probably should have left three years ago, but I was having too much fun. But I'm ready now for the grown-up thing." He grabbed Archie Ghosh's hand, where a small ruby glinted on the fourth finger, and gave it a squeeze.

"So Archie, when do you give notice?" asked Dawn, making a scrupulous tally mark on the packet before lighting her cigarette. By the time she graduated, she wanted to be down to half a pack a day; it would make quitting that much easier.

"In about a year, I think." The expressions of dismay made Archie giggle. "I don't have to. As soon as Hank told me about the counter offer, I marched into Milla's office and asked for the spot. She was thrilled. Since it's me, she can skew the slot to cover Implementation as well. I'll be Mary Ann's assistant. A month from now, I'll be in Minneapolis, with a title bump and Pinnacle paying all my moving expenses. All ours, actually, except Hank's plane ticket. I think that non-fraternization thing worked out pretty well for us."

There was a series of high-fives.

"So you guys are good. And I'll have my degree before you know it. What are we going to do about Dan and Judy?"

"Hey, as soon as the year passes, you can come work for me," Hank offered magnanimously. The "year" was the amount of time an ex-employee had to wait before being able hire away a former Pinnacle coworker. It was in the agreement we all had to sign when we first started work, together with a basic non-compete clause. Judy's lawyer friend said the whole contract was boilerplate and wouldn't stand up to litigation, but it was the rare Pinnacle employee who had the discretionary income to risk a day in court.

"You know who took me to lunch yesterday?" Judy asked. "Eliot Tseng. Totally ignored me all the time he was here, but now he wants someone to put together a brochure for his new business."

"If he's willing to pay..." Hank said. He was making the mental adjustment from employee to entrepreneur.

Judy grimaced. "That's the kicker. He says he's still pulling together the capital so he can't pay me anything now, but if we keep working together there will eventually be some money. He says he figures I'd want to build my portfolio, 'seeing how uncertain things are' here."

"Piece of work." Dawn flicked her ash by way of punctuation.

Judy shook her head. "You want to know a real piece of work? Though actually I don't know whether it's Matticchio or Feldman."

"Feldman!" It was a nearly perfect chorus.

Judy laughed. "You're only saying that because no one knows anything about Matticchio. Including me. For all we know, he's the same as Feldman. Anyway, it was probably a unanimous LC decision to let Parnes go."

Craig's termination had been something of a shocker. He was the last developer with advanced skills in the technologies used for any of the recent applications. Now Pinnacle's only senior developer at all, in any office, was Leon. If something other than Bridge broke down, we'd be in deep shit.

"Well, one of the guys in Minsk reported some kind of glitch in how Trekker connects with the billing portion of the Raskub app. The clients can place orders and get their bookings and tickets and things, but only certain items generate invoice records."

"Oops, I did it again!" Dawn sang, in her best Britney Spears voice.

"Big oops," Archie agreed.

"It's something in the SOAP wrapper," Judy continued. "Leon can't track it down. He went in to Feldman and said we need to ask Craig back for a Knowledge Transfer."

"He isn't going to, is he?" Archie was incredulous.

"By 'he' do you mean Feldman or Parnes?" asked Danny. "Because I can definitely see Feldman having the chutzpah to ask, but I can't see Parnes saying yes."

Judy pointed to Danny. "Bingo! Give that young man a PTO day! They had Dave make the call. I was at his desk. Craig was laughing so hard, Dave had to put the receiver down and let him get over it. He finally got it together enough to basically say they should have thought of that before they fired him, and that now it was the LC's problem. Dave decided to tell them it made Craig uncomfortable to face his former coworkers after having been terminated, and that it also might mess with his Unemployment."

"Would it?" Hank wondered.

Judy shrugged. "I don't know, but it sounds good."

Dawn agreed. "I especially like the 'uncomfortable' part. One of my favorite HR words. There's no contesting 'uncomfortable.' It sounds like there's a possible legal action if they push you."

"Why didn't you ever point that out when I was up to my eyeballs with Len Strauss in December?" Judy demanded. "Instead of saying his demands were unreasonable, I should have said he was making me uncomfortable?"

"Yup. And you say it with a little pause, as if it's a euphemism."

"It makes me extremely...uncomfortable...to think that's the way things work."

Δ

The email was signed by Chris Keane and only said that the "Inspectors" were coming Friday at 6:00 and to be sure your desk was clear when you logged out for the day.

Running into her in the break room a few minutes later, Gabe asked Chris what kind of inspection it was. Friday was his work-from-home day. Was there anything special he should do? Was it a client audit or something about network security? He usually worked until 6:30 or 7, when Martha got home. Did he need to log off his VPN earlier?

Chris gave a vague wave of her hand. "Just don't leave any food around," she said with a smile. Chris always smiled. "You really shouldn't anyway."

Clifton Speck was on the conference bridge with Minneapolis and Pune when the email arrived. As soon as he got off, he strode over to Don Bryson's office and rapped on the door.

"Why wasn't I told about this?" he asked. "I'm supposed to be the Security officer."

Don chuckled. "Not a security issue, Clif. Don't sweat it. Just something we have to do from an HSS standpoint."

Clif frowned and coughed, but Don shrugged and turned back to his monitor. Clif, unsatisfied, had no choice but to leave.

Friday afternoon at around 5:30, from her seat at the Reception Desk, Maci Cole watched the elevators decant two men and a dog. The men wore navy blue work clothes, with some company's logo embroidered on the pocket. The dog was a beagle and wore a red harness. One of the men pressed the buzzer. The dog wagged its tail. Maci buzzed back.

"We're here to see Chris Keane," said the man who'd buzzed. He handed her a card.

Glancing at it, Maci made the call. "Chris," she said, a little breathlessly, her brown eyes glittering with suppressed hysterics. "Um, Roscoe, is here? The, um, the bug-sniffing…Yes of course. Right away." Maci came around the front of her desk. "Follow me," she said. She walked briskly to Don Bryson's office, the two men and Roscoe following behind.

They'd arrived early. No one was meant to see them on the floor. Only Gene Siriano and two or three people in Client Relations did, but that was enough. One look at the beagle was all it took. We all watched the news; if there was a beagle, everyone in New York knew what kind of inspection it was. Bed bugs.

As soon as they disappeared into Bryson's office, the people who'd seen them started spreading the word. Within minutes, we were jumping off our cushioned desk chairs. Stripping the extra plastic bags out of the trash cans, we stuffed in the cardigans and jackets that usually hung over the chair backs. We were afraid to sit down again. The more susceptible among us started to feel itchy, especially around the ankles, and along the length of the spine where it usually pressed against a chair. There were bed bugs at Pinnacle—or someone thought so, with enough basis that Feldman was springing for the beagle. But none of us had been told. HC hadn't said a word. For all we knew, we'd been carrying them back to our homes for weeks. Even the more stoic among us were furious. We went home scratching at phantom bites, jumping at the sight of a piece of dark lint or a stray poppy seed. We spent the weekend pacing our rooms, imagining which of our meager belongings would have to be tossed and which could be disinfected, and wondering how we were going to afford it.

Monday morning, we found a cheery email from Chris stating that Pinnacle had passed the still-unspecified "inspection" with flying colors and thanking us for our cooperation. We were relieved enough to shrug it off. Business as usual.

Milla Kristol happened to be in Pune that week, and Scott Bell was with his team in Minneapolis until Wednesday. Nothing was ever confirmed but, passing by their offices, several of us noted a slight chemical tang wafting through the closed doors.

20 TRANSPARENCY

"Can you see me in New York?"

We could, though the low resolution image wasn't all that great. Projected on the window shades in the Pit was a grainy vision of Kippy, waving wildly from the Pune conference room.

"You're coming in loud and clear, Kippy," Clifton Speck assured him.

"What?" Kippy leaned to one side, presumably the direction of the speaker at his end. The packet speed of the transmission gave his movements the jerkiness of flipbook animation.

Clif leaned closer to the hub and repeated himself.

"Terrific!" Even in the faded projection, we could tell that Kippy was beaming. "How about Minneapolis? You there, Cooper?"

"We're here, Kippy," Cooper Fradkin's voice was raspier than ever over the conference bridge.

"Terrific! Okay then. Happy Diwali, Pinnacle! I don't know if you can see behind me, but the conference room is all decorated from the bang-up celebration we had for lunch. A big hand to Dhaarna and Navjot for doing such a terrific job."

As Kippy pointed to people beyond the lens, more unseen people responded with enthusiastic applause.

"That's right. Terrific lunch. Except...well, you know that Diwali is the Festival of Lights, right? So I was asking Ashok, where's my latkes? Ha! Seriously, this week marks a major milestone for Pinnacle, the first office holiday since we shifted certain of our teams to Pune. This was a test to see if we have what it takes to run a truly international organization and we passed with flying colors! We were closed all day over here and not a single hitch."

We were grateful the video was a one way transmission. Faces were ferocious in New York, and presumably in Minneapolis. Because the conference bridge wasn't on mute, we had to swallow our groans. The only thing that had prevented a total meltdown yesterday was that the "big" day of the five-day holiday, the day Len Strauss had advised that the LC should close the office to show goodwill, fell on a Monday this year. With Pune mostly working New York business hours, that meant much of the downtime was on our Sunday and only Switchboard ran over the weekends. Still, yesterday had been a nightmare. The Center of Excellence had neglected to account for the fact that not a single member of Switchboard, Payroll or Data

Entry remained stateside. Once the gaff was spotted, Edie put a freeze on all new client implementation so that members of that team could cover Fulfillment until the Pune "PM" shift would report at what was, for them, 2 a.m. Tuesday. Enough of the Implementation team had started Pinnacle as Payroll or Data Entry that they were able to keep the squeaky wheels under control. Switchboard was a hot mess. The CoE had organized skeleton crews to clock in during the closure. They were sufficient to handle the light Sunday afternoon and overnight calls, but not the volume that kicked in on Monday morning. Those of us in New York who habitually came in before nine found ourselves fielding Switchboard calls, because the message boxes were already full. It was so bad that Edie drafted Chris Keane, Judy Schreiber and the Buzzard to cover phones. Client Relations had already spent all this morning making amends to angry clients. And it wasn't over yet. Many of the Pune staff had opted to use some PTO time to work half days today and tomorrow.

Blissfully unaware of the emotions of his remote audience, Kippy blathered on. "And there's not a doubt in my mind that the rest of the week will go equally well. So I want to applaud the efforts of Swati and her team at the Center of Excellence over here, for producing such a great set of Holiday Closing workflows!" There were enough cheers in Kippy's room that he didn't notice the lack of response from the US. Chuckling happily, he held up a hand. "Wait, one more thing! Everyone here in Pune wants to give a big shout out to all of you in New York and Minneapolis for making their holiday possible! Now you can give a big hand."

The cheers from Pune were joined with some ironic applause from our end.

Someone off camera handed Kippy a sheet of paper. He eyeballed it and nodded. "Okay, great! So Gretchen emailed me some questions. Thanks to everyone who sent one in. I'll just take a couple. Don't want to keep you here all day. Ha! And then I'll turn things over to Scott and Mary Ann for local announcements. Let's see. Ha! Here's an easy one. 'Who's going to win the ACLS? No question. That pennant belongs to the Yankees!"

The New York Sales team raised a hoot and holler so big it probably didn't need the conference bridge to reach Kippy.

"I can't believe I'm missing the playoffs! Shows you how much this," he made a sweeping gesture to embrace Pune; "how much all this means to me! But I'm going to be in my seats for the Series and, let me tell you, we're gonna take it!"

Sales roared again, enabling Kippy to glide neatly to the next question.

"'Does Pinnacle have more plans for inorganic growth, such as our expansion to Minneapolis?' Good question. I don't know who asked it, but I bet it's one of my Phi Beta Kippy guys. Ha! Well, all I can say is we've got a pretty full plate already."

Those of us who'd already put in a couple of months on Project Grapefruit scratched our heads.

"So I would say that at this point, we are not seeking any additional acquisitions. Our concentration will focus on the continued integration of Raskub Secretarial. However, if business can be acquired through earn-outs, we will continue to be interested in doing deals on that basis. And with that, I'm gonna turn you over to Scott and Mary Ann. Vijay and his wife have kindly invited me to their family celebration, but first some of the gang here is taking me out to see how Pune looks all lit up. Ha!"

Δ

From: Milla Kristol
To: All Pinnacle Associates
Subject: Exciting News

Pinnacle Management Services is excited to announce the creation of a new product: FrontDesk.

Housed in Minneapolis, FrontDesk offers Pinnacle clients a premium telephone answering experience. To lead this white gloves service, we are pleased to welcome Diego Guzman back to Pinnacle. Diego's deep experience in this vertical ensures that FrontDesk will hit the ground running!

Milla Kristol, COO
Pinnacle Management Services

Δ

Dave read the email over and over again, trying not to sweat. A meeting invite from Jim Matticchio. He usually met with Matticchio for half an hour on Monday, giving him a quick status report on what he and Judy, who was still nominally 50 percent his report, had done the previous week. Clif had a similar meeting. They assumed Vijay must as well, now that he was the official Development lead. It gave Matticchio enough to spout back to the LC at their regular meetings. Beyond that, the man's management was strictly of the hands-off style. Today was Thursday though and, out of nowhere, Matticchio called an 11 a.m. meeting. Dave thought hard. As far as he knew, things were okay with Judy. Strauss had other things on his plate and hardly used her any more. The rest of whatever she was doing, the documentation updates, the newsletter, even Project Grapefruit...he got confused sometimes about exactly what Judy did. It seemed like anytime something needed to be done, if no one knew who to give it to, it ended up on her desk. She was a lot like him that way. Maybe it made sense that he was her manager, even if he didn't really, well, manage anything. But she seemed to be doing okay. No, Judy wasn't making waves these days. And he was keeping Scott happy. Milla had stopped giving him the snake eye, so maybe she finally understood Dave wasn't the kind to go running his mouth. This was a lot of maybes. Amazing how a stupid meeting invite could make him worry that, even with all his efforts, his time may have run out.

It wasn't only Dave. If he hadn't been so nervous, he would have registered that it was a group invitation. He ran into Clif at Matticchio's door. They exchanged a little shrug and knocked.

"Okay!" Matticchio called. He was sitting back in his chair, with a coffee. Unlike the others on the LC, unlike Peterson, he never kept his jacket on in his office, and his sleeves were rolled up. If he ever kept the door open, it would make him seem approachable. "Sit down, sit down. We've got Vijay dialed in. This shouldn't take long."

Dave and Clif took the guest chairs across from Matticchio. You could never figure out what the man was thinking, not with that vague smile-ish expression that lived on his face no matter what came out of his mouth.

"Okay. So we've got a new project. Kippy does. The LC. We're going to be putting together a packet of information. Not sure exactly what we'll need, but expect to have to round up a lot of details. You know how we've been expanding. Kippy's pretty transparent about things, right? This one is maybe a little hush-hush. We're looking to get a big investment. Teclu Holdings. Private equity. Very big deal for all of us, you know? Anyway, I wanted to put you all in the picture. We should start getting specific early next week. We're expecting a bunch of due diligence questionnaires from them. IT'll be one of the biggest, because, you know, most of the cap ex and probably the highest op ex." He looked at Dave and Clif expectantly.

They made some non-committal sounds and tried to look eager.

"Vijay, you still with us?"

Vijay's voice crackled over the line. The cap ex had yet to extend to a sufficient telephony package to make calls with Pune sound anything other than very long distance. "Still here, Jim. Waiting to know how we can help."

"So yeah. Big thing is, anyone from Teclu asks anything, you tell them. No holds barred. Kippy's instructions are to treat them like an extension of him. When we get the questionnaires, there'll be a lot of data gathering. It's going to have to be top priority. Assume every deadline is ASAP. Clif, I'm gonna ask you to make us a secure folder on the share drive. For all of us, all the LC, and Hugo's team. That's all for now. Just wanted to put you in the picture. Meeting over. Bye, Vijay."

"Goodbye Jim. Dave, Clif." The lack of ambient sound confirmed Vijay had disconnected.

"Okay then." Jim made a sweeping gesture at the door and swiveled to face his monitor. "See you."

Still absorbing that the meeting was over, or indeed that it had occurred, Dave and Clif stood and nodded. Clif opened the door.

"Oh yeah. Broussard!" Jim called, not looking away from whatever was on his screen. "I'm gonna need someone to get this due diligence thing organized. Send Judy in here, okay?"

Δ

The door to Hugo's office was open when Judy arrived to go over the presentation. She was right on time, and Hugo was always a few minutes late. She took a seat and waited. Her mind still boggled that he had an office at all. She understood that extremely confidential information was passing through his desk and over his phone lines, but by that token she should have an office, too.

"I am so sorry," Hugo said with his usual boisterous grin. He left the door wide open. Hugo was so hyperactive that he was always hot. He never closed the door; another thing that made the office so ridiculous. "Milla's off to Pune tomorrow and suddenly grabbed me to do a brain dump. Like we'll crash and burn because she'll be out of communication for more than 12 hours. So what do you have for me?"

Gary Feldman appeared in the doorway. He looked past Judy, his eyes skipping right over her head, to catch Hugo's eye. "Just saw that email," he said. "Engelhart. What is he smoking, do you think?"

"I know, I know." Hugo laughed. "So Gary, you should see the excellent presentation Judy has for launch day. She has done such an amazing job. We're almost done already."

"Yeah, well. So we better start cutting Engelhart down to size before he gets in front of the Board."

"Hey, I'm sure you guys will figure it out. Seriously, Judy's been awesome. Saved me a week's work." Hugo pointed at Judy.

Gary had no choice but look at her. He quickly looked away again. "Uh, yeah," he said. He waved at Hugo and was gone.

Judy was resigned to it by now. "Thanks for trying, but you don't need to bother. He's not a fan of mine."

"I know. That's why I did it."

It was stunning to have her suspicions so baldly confirmed. "He doesn't see any value in what I do for this company. It amazed me I wasn't resized. Or since, to tell you the truth."

"Uh huh."

It hurt doubly to think it was that obvious. Who else knew? She waved the printout in her hands. "I know the org charts are just the tip of the iceberg. How many are we cutting when we get ProFile. I'm sorry; I know you can't say."

Hugo shrugged. "We're not doing a thing until after Christmas."

"Wow. That's, uh…very thoughtful."

"It's the smart way to go. We had a lot more attrition than we'd planned in Minneapolis. And that was a friendly buyout. This isn't. Plus all that pushback from the rightsizing, about not giving warning. You get burned a couple of times, you get a little more cautious. So we'll wait. And then we'll give a month's notice. Anyway, nothing for you to worry about. You're on 'the hands off list.' Because you're cheap," he explained, guilelessly. "And Kippy loves you for *Peak Experience*. Drives Feldman crazy!"

Even when what he was saying was mildly offensive, Hugo's boyish frankness had a kind of charm to it. Besides, she had the impression he enjoyed Feldman's discomfort as much as she did. Judy couldn't help but smile back.

Δ

"This is so nice." Edie was surprised at how happy it made her to look at the faces in the booth.

"Nice?" Judy threw up her hands. "It's effing miraculous! How many years have you been promising to have lunch with me? And I know you only did it because of them." Judy cast her own foolish smile at the other side of the table.

Mike Ventura stroked his beard. It was as neatly trimmed as ever. "Well, I'm impressed."

"You should be," Ginny Chicosky said. "It's definitely you, not me."

"I'm glad to see both of you," Edie insisted. "And thrilled about your timing."

"Seriously," Judy agreed. "The whole LC is out today. So we can have a real lunch for a change and not just eat and run." Since Ginny'd found a job nearby, the two women met every few weeks. Once in a while, Mike's schedule allowed him to join them.

"Another offsite?" Mike asked. "Is it that time again?"

Judy tapped her lips with her forefinger. "Something else. But I can't exactly say."

"Don't tell me Peterson's dream is coming true without him? Kippy's actually going public." Mike snorted ruefully.

Judy shook her head and picked up her sandwich. "Not that." She took a big bite, to show she wasn't going to say any more.

"Too bad he's not," Edie joked. "I actually have some of those famous options."

"So did I. Had," said Mike. "When they dumped me, they didn't even offer a buyout. They told me they were forfeit because I was leaving the company. As if I were leaving by choice. I always knew it was bogus."

"You mentioned Peterson..." Ginny broke in with her round, hearty chuckle. "Did I tell you about meeting him on the street last week? Right around here. I think he lives nearby. I used to sometimes see him in running clothes back in the day, when I was on a deployment."

"Did you spit at him?" asked Judy. "I could never look at him the same way after what he did to you."

"I should have. But no. I was so fucking thrown by it, I didn't do anything. I was doing some errands at lunch. Stuff I had to pick up at Modell's for the twins. Can you believe Tim's signed them up for preschool ice hockey this year? It's only about getting a feel for the ice and learning the rules, but still." She grimaced and ran a hand through her yellow crop. "I sometimes wonder if I'll live through getting them through high school. Anyway, I've got all these packages, so I'm not really paying attention to anything except not banging into people. And this voice comes at me. Down at me. 'Ginny!' it says, loud enough that I couldn't pretend not to hear. And I look up and there he is. Smiling like a...what? I'm not going to say cat with canary."

"One of those politicians in a debate," Edie suggested. "The ones who say exactly what they want to say, even if the moderator's asked a different question."

"Oh, that's good!" Judy's eyes gleamed appreciatively.

Ginny nodded her approval. "Yeah, that's Peterson. Always following his own agenda. I tried to acknowledge him and move on without saying anything, but he wouldn't let me. 'Aren't you looking well?' he says. 'What are you up to these days?' Can you believe this? I swear he would have tried to shake my hand if I hadn't had those packages. By that point, the shock was over and I could think again. It was too late to drop everything and smack him. Anyway, why give him the satisfaction of doing it in public and embarrassing myself. I just said, 'I'm running late. I have to go,' and pretty much floored it."

"So what does he need from you?" Mike wondered.

"Exactly!" Ginny laughed again. "I keep waiting for the phone to ring. I'm so glad I like where I am now so I wouldn't be tempted, whatever it is."

"He sent me a LinkedIn invitation last month," Judy noted. "I left it sitting there. I didn't know what to do."

"Oh, accept it," Ginny advised. "I did. It's about building a network, not friendship."

"Speaking of networks." Mike wiped the burger grease off his hands and grinned. "I bet I know something you don't know. And I mean none of you."

Edie and Judy leaned forward expectantly.

"Did you know that Leon gave notice?"

Edie, always straight as a popsicle stick, went so rigid she bounced off the vinyl seat. Ginny almost did a spit take. Judy was glad she'd swallowed the last of her coleslaw. Mike paused, enjoying the reaction.

"Mike?" Edie prodded him to continue.

"He's not leaving." Three faces suddenly fell, making Mike laugh. "Not yet, okay? Not yet. He's got a piece of a startup. I know because when they were negotiating the lease, he asked me to be a personal reference."

"They've got office space?" Ginny was impressed. She knew lots of people with startups, but most of them were working out of their living rooms or garages.

"Oh yeah. Since June. He's been grooming the company for almost two years now. I almost did a consulting thing for them when I first left Pinnacle, but it fell through and then I got the airline. Timing. So about two weeks ago, he called to let me know he's going to start working there full time and that I should call him when the airline gig is up because he thinks he'll have something for me. Then the other day he called again to say he's staying on until probably through January. Kippy has some big mysterious project." Mike narrowed his eyes meaningfully at the two women across the table. Judy started to giggle. "Riiiiight. Whatever it is, Kippy practically begged him...no, not practically. Kippy did beg him to stay on until it's done. Promised him a fat retention bonus, plus a two-year retainer for Bridge maintenance. Did you know they tried to patent Bridge?"

Judy nodded. "Who do you think edits Feldman and Strauss's illiterate prose and cleans up all the diagrams? I think they're still trying."

Ginny blinked. "What is there to patent? Copyright maybe, but Leon probably owns that automatically. For a patent, you have to prove something unique about the functionality."

Mike's face rippled with a combination of amusement and disgust. "Isn't the arrogance mind-blowing? That the LC thinks they're going to bring Bridge to market? That other people are going to buy it? Doesn't matter. Whatever they do, Leon owns a piece of it. As well he should."

"What about Ina?" Edie mused. "Is he taking Ina? I can't see her hanging on without him."

"I asked. Ina wants to stay. Leon said it: she hates change. You can't argue."

"There's hardly any IT department to stay in," Judy pointed out. "Almost everything is in Pune now."

"It doesn't matter," Edie thought. "With Leon gone, she'll be Kippy's good luck charm."

"True," agreed Mike. "If Feldman tried to cut Ina, Kippy would give him hell."

"The hands off list. Hugo thinks I'm on it too."

Ginny and Mike exchanged looks of hard-won experience.

"I wouldn't trust it," Mike advised Judy. "Other than Walt and Ina, I wouldn't say anyone is 'hands off.' Maybe Martha Moon, but at this point who knows."

Ginny agreed. "It's all 'what have you done for me lately.' And you know how good they are at throwing people under the bus. You should be looking." She nodded at Edie, including her. "Both of you should. It's much easier to find work while you're still employed."

"I keep my eyes open," Edie assured her. "There isn't much out there. And what there is, they want to get someone with only a couple of years' experience and no responsibilities, someone who'll do it for the title bump."

Judy frowned. "Everything I see is contract work."

"I'm doing very well out of contract work," Mike reminded Judy.

"That's how I got this job," Ginny reminded her. "Contract to perm. Jude, you should call the agencies I gave you, at least get your resume in front of them."

"I can't risk it," Edie said. "Not with Phil to think about. And Russell only just now managed to get a job."

Mike gave her a thumbs up. "Way to go Russell!"

"Working a register at Yankee Candles," she elaborated. "Now he's thinking of going for an MBA, so he can get an entry level office job. So, shall we say I continue to be risk averse for the foreseeable future?"

"I'm just scared," Judy confessed. "I only ever wanted security. Otherwise I'd still be working in theatre."

Mike reached across and patted her hand. "Security's a dying concept. All we can do is keep running."

Δ

Like most telecom systems, Pinnacle's had a broadcast speaker function. It was used once a month to call us to the Pit for Kippy's cheerleading sessions and otherwise only to announce fire drills. The exception had been the actual fire in our former fourth floor office, when Donna, the once-and-only office manager, had used it to inform everyone up on eight. When it went off this time, the distinctive burst of white noise had us jumping half out of our seats. The crackle was followed by Clif Speck instructing everyone that a network problem required IT to perform a forced logoff of all terminals. There was no need to panic. Members of his team would be coming around to individually reboot and restore service. We should remain near our desks to assist them. While we were still absorbing this, every single monitor in the place went black. There was a collective gasp, followed by an escalation of chatter as members of client-facing teams manufactured rapid apologies to the people on the other ends of their calls. The rest of us muttered to ourselves or our neighbors.

Delegating the Buzzard to reboot Senior Management, Clif, Freddie and Bern Diaz started with Client Relations. Each machine took a good six or seven minutes, a process requiring the owner to log in, the technician to run some program off a USB key, and the owner to reset her password before logging back in and resuming work. As lean as we were, it would take hours to reboot every single machine. The coffee urn almost immediately needed to be refilled. Edie and Ann sent people for early lunch. Once Scott was back in, he logged into Sales Force with his master password and sat Marla in his office to print out call sheets for each of his guys.

The general assumption was that it was some sort of virus. We whispered; we tried to tease information from Freddie. We took guilty inventory of the personal emails we'd opened that had funny videos or animated gifs, of the schoolwork uploaded from our own USB keys because our home printers were broken or non-existent. By end of day, service had been restored and we were none the wiser. A stern email was issued in Scott's name, reminding us that our workstations were for business use only and subject to inspection at all times, that only business-related files were to be uploaded or downloaded to either the network or our local drives, and that violations were punishable by immediate dismissal.

It wasn't until the following week that the answer was revealed to a group at Whine Bar by a pissed-off Freddie. Someone had been streaming pirated films from a Chinese website. Picking up a feed, an SEC spider traced it back to the Pinnacle network. There was a significant fine, along with a tough warning that any further such transgression would be met by a much more sizable reaction. The EC went ballistic. Clif began a backdoor search of the network to find the culprit, but Feldman and Strauss insisted he stop and immediately check every terminal in the office; they always were always sniffing out proof of how the New York team's sense of entitlement was stealing the company blind. Only after every terminal had come up clean was Clif allowed to proceed with the network scan.

The issue was traced to a pair of work stations in Pune that were used by off-shore members of the Travel team. For months, they'd entertained themselves during the often-quiet swing shift by streaming the latest films, sometimes even burning them to DVD to share with friends. They reacted to their dismissal with puzzlement: everyone bought pirated videos, they said; it was movies, it wasn't as if it was hurting anybody.

Theft of intellectual capital didn't bother Feldman and Strauss; they only cared about stealing if it was out of their own pockets. Occurring at night, this film caper didn't interfere with work and it kept the low-paid Pune employees happy. They would probably have let it pass, except for the SEC fine. Instead, they severed the participants and had Kamal remove dvd burners from any Pune workstation that had one. Then they lit into Clif Speck for not having installed the monitoring product that the LC had refused to pay for, and blamed his overworked team for not noticing the impact of streaming on the network during the hours they selfishly chose to sleep.

Dave Broussard felt bad for Clif Speck. The guy could be a bit of an asshole sometimes, but he was a likable one and he was up to his eyeballs in work. The network had been hard enough to support before it was spread across two continents and three metropolitan areas. Add to that the Project Grapefruit task roster and 115 questions (so far) from Teclu, and the last thing Clif needed was this whole SEC situation.

Now, on top of everything, Clif had to handle the biannual IT data security audit. He and his guys, in every city, had been hustling almost round the clock for a week to prepare.

The auditors showed up at 0900 hour, with military promptness. Actually, everything about them made Dave think ex-military: their plain white shirts and black suits, mirror-shined black shoes, the matching black-framed glasses on two of the three and the brush cuts all around. And the faces...Jake's teddy bear had more personality. Having lived in shore towns all his life, the Buzzard had seen a lot of MP patrols in his time. These guys followed Clif so close behind, it looked like they were dragging him off to the brig. Adding to the impression were Clif's eyes, darting all over the place. The unshakably cool Clif had been showing some frayed edges of late. Dave hoped the poor guy wouldn't have a heart attack before the three days were over.

Δ

```
From:          Eric Channing
To:            All Pinnacle Associates
Subject:       Goodbye and Best of Luck
--------------------------
```

Hello Fellow Mountaineers,

As some of you know, today is my last day at Pinnacle.

I have really enjoyed my time here. To my thinking, Pinnacle
is a microcosm of the most positive aspects of Capitalism,
the economic system I steadfastly support. You can be
whatever you want to be at Pinnacle if you apply yourself
with drive and perseverance. My experience proves this. I
started in Data Entry, moved on to Payroll (my ID still stays
I work there, but it also says it expires in 2008) and
started taking evening classes at the Zicklin School of
Business at Baruch College, always keeping my eye on the
prize of working in Finance. I worked hard, studied hard and
dressed for the position I wanted. Less than four years
later, I have an MBA, work on 9 figure deals and have had the
great opportunity to consider the entire LC as mentors and
friends. I'm proof positive that you are free to choose your
own destiny.

That said, please come and join me at Whine Bar for a goodbye
drink tomorrow after office hours. Even if our interactions
have been limited, you should come. We can get to know each
other before I leave and build our network!

Thanks for being part of my journey. Best of luck to all of
you, and to Pinnacle, in your future endeavors.

Eric

Δ

"Yo, Archie!" Apparently returning from a lunch run, Freddie Vega reached her and Dawn just as they were leaving the building and followed them into the alley. "Spoke to my boy, Diego before. He says to tell you he found a good Indian place not far from the office, in case you get homesick."

She laughed. "If I want Indian, I'll make it myself. What I'm going to be homesick for is the Belgian waffle truck. I'll probably eat myself sick there between now and Christmas."

"That when you're going? No one sent me a work order yet to move you over."

"I don't fly out until the 29th."

Danny seemed puzzled. "The 29th? I thought it was around the holiday party. Didn't we say the after party was going to be your goodbye thing?"

"No, you're right. But then I'm taking a couple of weeks vacation. I have a ton of final packing. And I'd really like to see New York before I leave it. Everything I never did: the Christmas show at Radio City, ice skating in Central Park, maybe walk the Brooklyn Bridge if the weather holds."

Her message apparently finished, Gretchen pocketed her Crackberry and accepted a light from Danny. "You're missing the Iversson family Christmas? Too bad! It's legendary. Eva's cookies and Lars's eggnog..." In reminiscence, her eyes glowed to match the tip of her cigarette. "At least the lights will still be up when you get there."

Dawn was recalling the tightrope act that first holiday season that she and Tully split across the Irish and Polish celebrations, and that was with both of them being Catholic. "It's probably a good idea. Buys you a whole year to get used to each other, you and the 'rents."

"That was my thinking," Archie confessed. "They have a New Year's Day thing at the house too, but that's all about football. No religion involved."

Gretchen sputtered a laugh. "Don't be so sure about that!"

"Hey, don't go dissing football!" Despite his chuckle, it wasn't certain that Freddie was joking. He threw back his shoulders and puffed out his chest to give a little strut.

The action made his coat swing open.

"What the hell are you wearing?!" Dawn touched a hesitant finger to the pulsing green acetate ribbon on Freddie's chest and quickly retracted it, making the face usually associated with the syllable 'eeeewwww!'

"Excuse me!" said Freddie, indignantly. "This is my new power tie. I'm dressing for the position I want."

"Which is what? Chief leprechaun? Even Tully wouldn't wear that thing!"

"Sorry, Dawn," Archie contradicted. "I think Tully definitely would."

"Absolutely," Danny agreed.

Dawn rolled her eyes and turned decisively towards Freddie. "So. How the hell is Diego? I keep meaning to call. I still don't get why he's in Minneapolis. The tamale truck job seemed so great."

"Money sucked," Freddie said succinctly. "Even worse than answering phones at Pinnacle. Diego says it's the same with any of the interesting food gigs, and a lot of the ones that sound good are boring as shit. Before the truck he was at one of those fancy places in the Time Warner? They had him tearing lettuce into little pieces. All day. After a couple of weeks he said fuck it. It's not like he needs to build a resume to take over his uncle's place, right?" Thinking about food reminded Freddie about the bag in his hand. He pulled out a foil tube and peeled off enough to take a punctuating bite. A waft of West Indian curry mingled with the cigarette smoke. "So when Edie called, he figured what the hell. With the cost of living there, he's got a nice place in a condo complex with a gym and everything, for less than his studio in Sunnyside, and meanwhile he's putting together a bankroll for the DR."

Gretchen nodded. "If Rory wasn't so set against it, I'd move back in a heartbeat. I've had my time in New York."

"Would he like Portland?" Dawn asked. "Assuming they don't just shut it down..."

Danny put up his hand. "Not happening. They like the idea of having a home on the West coast."

"Too cold and damp," Freddie mumbled through his curry. "I'm waiting for Kippy to buy a place in Austin or Miami."

"Portland is supposed to be very cool." There was a wistful note in Archie's voice. Minneapolis seemed fine, the little she'd seen of it. But sometimes she wished she and Hank could have been free to look at other options. "I could see you and Tully there, D."

Dawn stared up at the sky and squinted. The sun was trying to push through what looked like a dirty gauze curtain. "Umm...actually I don't see us moving any time soon..."

Archie jumped up and squealed. With a loud "fuck me!" Freddie gave her a hard high five with his clean hand. Danny just looked depressed.

"What am I missing?" Gretchen asked.

"I got the library job." Dawn blushed happily.

"Which one?" Archie demanded. She smiled at Trudy. "Dawn is so good, the placement office had her out for three different spots."

"NYU." Dawn's grin broadened. "I don't officially get my degree until the end of January, but they want me to start at the beginning of the year. So I'm leaving the same day as Archie. I'm giving a month's notice on Monday. Only because of Edie really, so I can do a good knowledge transfer."

"Congratulations!" Gretchen hugged her.

"Yeah," Danny tried to smile. "Congratulations. I'm really happy for you, Dawn."

"Only now you really can't wait to get the hell out of here, right?" she gave him a little punch on the shoulder. "Start looking, Danny. The hard part is getting off your ass and starting to look."

Freddie swallowed another bite. "Yah, I may have to do that pretty soon myself. Without Clif, this whole place is going to shit."

"Clif's leaving, too?!" Danny kicked the dumpster. It made a satisfying crash.

"I thought Clif Speck was a lifer," Dawn observed.

Gretchen was suddenly occupied with putting away her cigarettes and fixing her lipstick.

"You didn't hear?" Freddie asked, unnecessarily. "They're gonna say it's one of those mutual decision things, but really the LC wants him out."

"Not because of those idiots in Pune?!" Archie exclaimed.

"Yeah, how was Clif supposed to know?" Dawn rolled her eyes again. "If anything, it should be Kamal's neck."

"Hey, I hear you. Anyway, that's not what did it. You remember we had that security audit? Well, the auditors found a buttload of unlicensed software. Scotty keeps putting more people on Salesforce than we have concurrent licenses. And you know how many people Kristol has using Visio, even though we only bought three copies? Clif keeps warning them, but Feldman doesn't want to pay for anything and people just load them up. Then there was that dev tool Jim Dagny insisted on using back then. When Feldman wouldn't okay the budget, the Centient guys hacked the expiration code in the demo."

"Why is any of this Clif's fault, if they keep overruling him?" Danny asked.

"That's the kicker," Freddie said with an ugly laugh. "The LC is blaming him for letting in the auditors!"

Archie stared at him. "I hate to sound stupid, but wasn't it mandatory? The audit?"

"Data security audit, fuck yeah," Freddie confirmed. "If they want to keep all those certifications that Scotty likes his guys waving in front of prospects. Safe Harbor and all that. So now they've got to pay this major fine..."

"On top of the ginormous fine for the streaming thing," Dawn smirked. "When do we get to see Feldman's head explode?"

Freddie was too angry to laugh. "Wish it fucking would. Clif's a good guy. He's kept this place running, no matter how they tied his hands. And he takes good care of the team. With him gone, the place is going to fall apart. I don't want to be picking up the pieces."

"What about your CTO?" Danny asked, guilelessly. "Where is he in all this?"

This time, Freddie did crinkle up his eyes and laugh.

Δ

There weren't a lot of us left any more. It had happened gradually, but this was the season when we made our reckoning. Tonight we couldn't pretend not to see how much had changed. Even Tavern on the Green had closed; we could still see Central Park from the holiday party, but it was through the windows of a new event space in the Time Warner Center. We huddled there in knots, invoking ghosts, feeling like remnants of a lost age. The watershed was generally agreed to have been the Right-Sizing. It felt like a decade ago, the age before Pune ate Pinnacle and when acquisitions were only an invisible twinkle in Kippy's eye.

Sure there were still plenty of Pinnacle employees, but more than half were in Pune and about a third of the Stateside roles were in Minneapolis. Of those left in New York, only a couple of dozen were "us." The others were either managers or people too new to know our history. The divide was strong enough that Roger and Glenn were actually socializing with the rest of us, rather than mixing with their more recently minted teammates. Ann, having made dutiful rounds of the LC, drifted away from Hugo and the out-of-town managers to slip beside Martha and Gabe at one end of our cluster of tiny tables.

The del Montes thought of the holiday party as their anniversary and had hired a sitter from the expensive agency, the one that only booked nurses and teachers, so that they could enjoy themselves without worrying about the baby or about Celia falling asleep in class tomorrow. They were in high spirits. Martha was heard to tell Freddie, not so laughingly, that if he drank himself sick he was going to have to find someone else to take care of him; this year they were going to the after party. Most of us were, because of Archie and Dawn.

The two girls were the center of everything this evening. It was their last Pinnacle party. Tomorrow, that always ridiculous post-festivities Friday-on-fumes, would be their last day in the office; for Dawn, her last day at Pinnacle period. They sparkled with excitement and, in Archie's case, a gold-embroidered net sari quite different from her workday minimalist blacks. She found it hilarious when someone pointed out Scott eyeballing her as if he'd never seen her before; in a way, he never had.

"Let him try," she said, tossing her glossy braid, heavier than ever with its burden of gold cord, over one shoulder. "Hank would love another lawsuit."

"Another?" Roger asked.

"I'm not at liberty to discuss, Rog," she said, her face remarkably placid. The rest of us, except for Glenn, tried not to snicker.

"I wish I had grounds for something," Dawn remarked. "I still can't believe what that asshole Feldman said to me." We all knew the story. Just like with Will, Dawn was told that she'd given insufficient notice. "A man who chopped 25 people without a moment's notice is telling me that an entire month is 'insufficient.' I only gave that month because of Edie. Like he's so fond of repeating, New York is a no-cause state. That means no cause for quitting as well as firing. I could have waited until tomorrow and walked out without saying a word!"

"The important thing is that you are walking out," Danny reminded her.

"True that. You know, the only thing I hate about leaving, other than missing you guys of course, is that I'll never get to see Feldman get his. It's got to happen someday, if there is even a drop of justice in the world."

"He's probably got so much socked away by now it doesn't matter," Freddie said morosely. He looked over his shoulder to the bar, where Clif Speck and the Buzzard were chatting with Cooper and the recently-arrived Vijay. There'd been nothing said officially, but everyone knew that Clif was leaving at the end of January.

"Maybe Orla can cast a spell on him," Danny suggested. "Alex says she's getting into some kind of South African witch doctor thing out in Austin."

"Alex is coming to the after party, you know," Dawn smiled happily. So was Tully, of course. And Lily and Crescenzo and Raney. A lot of people. There was a rumor that even Jeff Curry might turn up.

Tapping briskly towards the ladies' room, a vision in luminescent peach down to her stiletto heels, Marla veered closer as she passed. "Psst! Text from Noble." She wiggled her phone, the rhinestone case shooting stars across the tables. "What time is the after party?"

"Noble's coming?!" Freddie perked up.

"Tell him Tully's getting there at 9:30."

"If they woulda flown Diego in, it woulda been perfect," Freddie mourned.

Martha looked at him sharply. "Freddie, what did I tell you? I'm going to get you a coke, right now."

From a nearby table, Edie Brewer raised her wine glass in their direction. "To our baby birds flying the nest. I know; one's only moving to the other side of the tree. Still, you know what I mean."

Judy touched her glass to Edie's and took another swallow of bourbon. Straight. Not the best, but a better bet than the mixed drinks. The venue might be new, but the bar and the catering were playing by the same rules. "I know. It's hard not to miss them. I had the sweetest email from Will Compton. He's loving the State Department."

"It's nice how they keep in touch. Remember Mia? Mia Freeman? She still sends me the occasional postcard. Just this week in fact, wishing me a happy Christmas. The Thames, with that big Ferris wheel they built." Her sigh was uncharacteristically regretful. "It's been decades since I've been. I wouldn't recognize London today."

"Why did I think Mia was in Venice?"

"She was. At the Guggenheim. She did so well, she's in a doctoral program at the Courtauld now."

"All the youngsters moving off to start their lives. And here we are, clinging to the ice floe." The bourbon showed incremental signs of improvement.

"It's not so bad. These acquisitions are a nice challenge, and it looks to me like Kippy's just getting started."

Judy took a quick peek around, making sure no one was close enough to overhear. "Unless Teclu has other plans," she muttered.

Edie grinned. "If anything, they'll ramp things up. More work for us. Job security."

"For you, maybe. I hope. But for me...I don't know. I keep waiting for my Anne Boleyn moment."

"That's silly."

"No, it's not. They don't need me enough."

"I know Teclu's done, but they still need you for the acquisitions."

"No, they don't. Seriously. I'm just regurgitating the same artifacts. Now that the LC is used to this template, they could bring in some kid fresh out of college. Someone who'd work for practically nothing to get the experience. Feldman would love that."

"Feldman doesn't always get what he wants. Kippy has a lot of respect for you."

"He's the only one who does. Your boss thinks I'm there to take dictation and my boss doesn't even know what I do." Judy put down her glass and made her eyes level with Edie's. Her voice was as serious as her face. "Jim actually told me to stop working on training materials. Not for Denali or Trekker or any of it. He says we don't need them, because Vijay's team is making the user experience idiot-proof."

Edie was incredulous. "Starting when?"

"The magic of Pune. All Vijay had to do was hire a 'certified' UX analyst and a 'certified' UI designer and poof!"

"Not to say that Vijay's people can't make some improvements, but Denali is pretty complex. How can Jim think people won't need training?"

"He'd have to actually spend some time with his fingers on the keyboard. I don't know that he's ever seen any of our apps in action. He told Dave he 'wasn't a development guy.' I'm cringing to say it, but it was different when Peterson was around. He was a self-protecting shit, but at least he saw his paycheck as being tied to what we did here and made an effort to master it. And he thought there was value in the work I was doing. He encouraged it. Jim thinks I'm an overpaid junior admin."

The bourbon was loosening Judy's tongue a little too much. It was an office party. Music and multiple conversations made a reasonable din, but it was still possible to find yourself caught in one of those awkward moments when something hit 'pause' and it was your last sentence that floated up to fill the vacuum.

Before this could happen to Judy, Edie interrupted. "On the bright side, at least you're not being pulled in seven different directions. Think about last year at this time. Now it's only Len..."

Judy's lips twisted into a wry smile. "Len doesn't love me anymore. I talk back too much. Now that he's given up on the website, he's been offloading his grunt work to Scotty's Angels. So it's pretty much just the acquisitions and the newsletter. Which is the only thing that still uses my brain."

"Did I hear someone say she had a brain?" a harried Gretchen banged down her glass and her evening bag with such force that a few drops of red wine flew over the rim and landed on beaded surface. She yanked a chair from a nearby table and plopped down between them. The other two women watched, fascinated, as she pulled her device from the little purse and began to hammer away with her thumbs.

"Anything we can help with?" Edie offered.

Gretchen shook her head furiously, like a dog getting out of a bath, and briefly held up a forefinger. "Northwest," was all she said. They waited. Finally, she made a decisive stab that seemed to conclude the matter. She let the block of black plastic drop onto the table and slumped in her stool. One hand snaked out for her wine glass. She took a deep swallow before acknowledging their stares. "Flight changes," she told them. "Gary had me book everyone on the last flights out, because it's cheaper. But there's a storm watch over Chicago. Anyone going in that direction needs to leave earlier or they might not make it out. Brent was easy; there are plenty of LA flights. But the others....I have Mary Ann locked up, and I just got Chad and Stan on standby. So that leaves Cooper. Dave says he has a couch, if push comes to shove."

"Cooper probably hopes it does," Judy thought aloud. "They're all going to be dead, if they aren't already."

Scott's remotes had been flown in for their annual Sales conference and a few from Minneapolis selected to spend the day in "knowledge exchanges" with their bosses and counterparts. With Vijay and Ashok arriving for a two week stay, it made this an All-Pinnacle party. On paper, it sounded very grand. In reality, Pinnacle frowned on hotel bills so only the two Indians were here for more than a quick in and out. The others had all had arrived just after nine this morning, meaning they'd been up well before dawn to get here. Brent, traveling coach on the red-eye, probably hadn't slept at all. Unless they won the annual PTO lottery, none of them had tomorrow off.

"What time is the flight?"

"Minneapolis? It's a 9:20."

Edie had never stopped wearing the slim gold watch her parents had given her for graduation. "They're going to need to leave in about 20 minutes."

Gretchen pointed towards the middle of the room. Hugo was helping Marla, teetering on her peach satin heels, onto a chair next to the one where Scott had already balanced. "That's why they're doing the announcements now, instead of waiting for after dessert. Spoiler alert. The MVP isn't anyone in New York."

Δ

```
From:        Judy Schreiber
To:          All Pinnacle Associates
Subject:     The Peak Experience
-------------------------
```

Hello Pinnacle!

Lots of news for us to share in this first *Peak Experience* of the new year:

- Pinnacle Continues to Expand with the Acquisition of Seattle's ProFile
- Meet this year's two MVPs: Ingrid Magnusson (Team Minneapolis) and Sarang Kotwal (Team Pune)
- Pinnacle Pune: Excellence Across Two Continents

Judy

Δ

```
From:        Milla Kristol
To:          All Pinnacle Associates
Subject:     Organizational Changes
-------------------------
```

Pinnacle has undergone explosive growth over the last 12 months. Hugo Singer played, and continues to play, a leadership role in the special projects that drive this expansion.

In recognition of his achievements, I am very pleased to announce that Hugo will be assuming the new role of Vice President of Product Development.

Please join me in congratulating Hugo on this highly-merited promotion.

Milla Kristol, COO
Pinnacle Management Services

21 ENTERPRISE

Called by the speaker and herded by our managers, we all filed in. Hiding was no longer possible; there were too few of us. Some of us still managed to cling by the cubes of whatever Sales guys weren't on the phone but we mostly drifted down the aisles in clusters of our own choosing. It was preferable to what would happen if we tried to stand at the back: Kippy calling us down by name, and everyone staring as we slunk to whatever empty spot he pointed out. Arriving with us, Senior Management just below C-level took up their customary positions to either side of the window. The three C's always waited until most of us were in place to make their entrance; that was the point when Alex Silva used to whisper "pa-rum pum pum pum" to whoever was standing next to him.

The window sill, however, was oddly deserted. Where was Kippy? The tripod was in its usual spot, centered on where he ought to be standing. Gretchen was fiddling with the buttons, Clif doing some supervisory helicoptering back and forth between her and Freddie, who was hooking up the webcast. Kippy was certainly here; otherwise we'd be looking at a screen instead of at the three of them setting up.

We waited at the front of the Pit, restless and exposed. Feet shuffled, throats cleared. Feldman consulted his Crackberry and furrowed his brow. Edie Brewer sneaked a peak at her wristwatch. The swishing sound was Glenn, who'd cut short a follow-up call with an interesting prospect for this meeting and was now swinging his tiny Yankees' bat in time with his impatience.

A loud "Ha!" made us all turn. Kippy bustled towards us from his office, trailing Scott, a handful of suited strangers and, most intriguingly, a smartly groomed Mrs. Kippy. Marcy Melcher was in full helpmeet glory: a wrap dress in Pantone's color of the year, accessorized by a multi-colored necklace too conservative to be anything but real gemstones.

Kippy was grinning even wider than he usually grinned, cheeks glowing fiercely pink, blue marble eyes popping. He kept one hand raised, as if waving to the camera that Gretchen swung around to capture his entrance. Followed by his entourage, he made a beeline for the window sill. He stopped there, with a quick pause that we interpreted as regret for not standing on it, and picked up Mr. Microphone. The others split off to either side, the managers scooting over to accommodate them.

"Hello Pinnacle!" Kippy cheered. "We got the webcast working? Freddie?"

Freddie tossed a laconic two-fingered salute.

"Let's see then...Can you hear me, Pune?"

"We can hear you, yes, Kippy!" Ashok's crushingly enthusiastic tones rang out from the speakers.

"Ha! And over in Minneapolis?"

"All here, Kippy," came Cooper's more laconic reply.

"Portland present and accounted for, too," Bruce Korn volunteered. Our eyes flicked towards Milla Kristol; it was fun to watch her recoil when she heard his voice. Word was that he and Kippy had bonded out in Oregon over some ideas Korn had to monetize Trim/Delta analysis.

"Terrific! Good morning all of you out there in the West and Mid-West. And good afternoon New York!"

Something was up. We could tell, even if only a few of us had an inkling of what it might be. There was an awkward moment of silence until Roger called out "Yeah!"

Kippy said "Ha!" and some nervous laughter rippled over the Pit.

"Okay, now that I have everyone's attention. We had an exciting year last year. Tremendous growth. Thanks to our terrific Sales team..."

Someone whooped, probably Roger again.

"Ha! And...give me a minute here...and the terrific job of upselling from our Client Relations team..."

This time he was interrupted by loud applause from Pune. Kippy laughed again, but his eyes showed a flicker of impatience. "That's right, give yourselves a round of applause, now. Everyone. Now." He made a sweeping gesture at his extended audience. Unseen by either Kippy or the camera, Hugo raised his hands high over his head and put them elaborately together. We dutifully joined in, followed by a spatter from Minnesota and Portland, and a second ovation from Pune. Kippy seemed torn between basking in it and wanting to push on. Before the applause had completely died down, he jumped in. "So yes, a tremendous year. We broke all our own records for organic growth. And a major spike from inorganic growth with the addition of Raskub and ProFile to the family...that's two deals closed in ten months! Do you know how impressive that is?! In their year-end round-up, *Money* magazine put us as the sixth largest managed office services company in America, and the third largest privately owned. We can really say we've, ah, reached the pinnacle. HA!"

Pune started to applaud again, but Kippy held up a hand to stop them. "No more interruptions. Please. There'll be time at the end. Okay then. So pretty impressive stuff. And we've done all of this, had this tremendous success, with nothing more than my vision and all of our hard work and dedication to excellence. Now you know me. Number six isn't good enough. Neither is number three. I'm sure we can go further, keep growing until we're number one. Ha! We're already the best, right? Well, when you do something as impressive as what we've done, the world takes notice. Which is a good thing, because to go that extra mile to the top, we're gonna need some extra support. After a lot of soul-searching, I have accepted an equity partnership offer from Teclu Holdings. Teclu has an outstanding record of investing in only top quality companies and helping them on to the next level. In joining with Teclu, Pinnacle accesses not only capital, but the kind of business expertise usually only available to Fortune 500 companies. With Teclu behind us we can be number one in our area in five years tops and we're already working on the plan to see that it happens. And now I'd like to introduce Pinnacle's new Chairman of the Board, Mr. Douglas Lattimer, who'll tell you more about that plan."

The applause was polite but carefully loud. Douglas Lattimer bowed his head to acknowledge it as he stepped forward. A tall silver-haired man, a snow-capped cedar to Kippy's holly bush, he had to bend slightly to accept Mr. Microphone.

"Thank you, Kippy. And thank you all for that warm welcome." His smile was friendly, perhaps a little paternal. "I'll keep this brief. It's a great pleasure to be here today, to mark this new chapter in Pinnacle's history. You probably won't be seeing much of me. Teclu has a non-interventionist approach to partnership. If you're curious to learn more about who we are and about some of our other partnerships, I suggest you visit our website. For a company to attract the interest of Teclu, it must have already achieved substantial success. We're not here to upset the applecart. We're here to strengthen what you've already built; as Kippy so succinctly put it, strengthen it with investment capital and top flight business expertise. Our advisory team has already begun working with your Leadership Council to develop a five-year roadmap, combining market saturation, targeted acquisitions and product development, that will indeed put Pinnacle at the top of the managed office services sector. We envision great things for Pinnacle, and I am delighted to stand here in front of you and take these first steps into the future. Thank you."

We applauded again. There was something reassuring and likable about this Lattimer, even if he hadn't actually said anything.

Kippy stepped forward for a hearty handshake, and to retrieve Mr. Microphone. "Thank you, Doug! Okay, then, I'm sure you all have a lot of questions. Who wants to start?"

We were possessed by more than the usual panic. Sure we had questions, but none seemed safe to ask. What percentage of the company had Kippy sold? Who was really in charge at Pinnacle now? Was there going to be another right-sizing or, conversely, were there retention bonuses in our future? This was Clif's last Monthly meeting; he sure wasn't going to lead us out of this one by asking what Kippy was reading.

One of Scotty's Angels raised a tentative hand; the Valkyrie, Diana. "Kippy, what about...? I mean, I hope you'll still be leading us." It was the kind of thing Eric Channing would have been expected to say.

Kippy chuckled. "No need to worry about me, Diana. I'll be continuing on as CEO for the foreseeable future. I just won't be Chairman of the Board any more. That honor belongs to my new boss, Mr. Lattimer here. And that's a good thing, because with that off my plate, I'll have all my attention focused on what we need to do to keep building Pinnacle to the level of excellence we all want." He beamed at his audience and waited for another question. None came.

"Uh, Kippy?" Cooper spoke up from Minneapolis. "We've got someone out here with a question."

"Fire away, Coop!"

"The question was..." There was a tiny pause, as if Cooper had his hand over the speaker. "Sorry. The question was, have additional acquisition targets already been selected?"

"Afraid I can't share that information, Coop. We have a few candidates under consideration. We may have even begun to make some overtures." Kippy nodded in Lattimer's direction. "But we don't release a name until after its signed, sealed and delivered. Next question?"

Ashok spoke up. The connection from Pune was, as usual, full of static, but his excitement was tangible. "Kippy, Mr. Douglas Lattimer, the Pune team offers congratulations on this auspicious partnership. We are extremely excited about the bright potential for Pinnacle and for all of us."

"Thank you Ashok. Anyone else??"

"No questions on this end," Korn volunteered. "But we look forward to being part of this new chapter."

We stared at the pillars, down at our shoes, at anything that was nowhere near Kippy.

"Well then, I guess we should all get back to work and get starting making this the number one managed office services company in the USA! Congratulations, Pinnacle!"

Δ

```
From:        Jim Matticchio
To:          IT
Subject:     Welcome Bela Kovac
------------------------------------
```

As many of you know, Clifton Speck is leaving Pinnacle, effective March 1, to pursue other opportunities. To lead Systems Operations at all locations going forward, please welcome our new VP of System Services, Bela Kovac. Bela has many years of experience in the technology sector. He will be a great addition to the Pinnacle team.

Jim Matticchio, CTO
Pinnacle Management Services

Δ

"Oh, I'm not an engineer. Operations, that's my practice. In my experience, most companies only need some local desktop support people to maintain the technology. A few really solid guys. And maybe a network engineer. Other than that...let's be honest. An in-house infrastructure team is not only a luxury, it's a useless one. You only need top level infrastructure specialists when you're planning a new environment. And when you are, well...Technology changes like that!" He snapped his manicured fingers so loudly that half the staff turned towards their table.

Dave would have said Bela Kovacs was oblivious to the reaction, except for that little twist lurking in one corner of his mouth. It was an expression Dave had already caught popping up regularly on the new VP of Systems Services. It was one of the reasons he'd invited the man to lunch. Not just to extend a friendly hand and make a connection. There was something about this guy, an undercurrent the Buzzard needed to get a handle on.

Dave discreetly waved away two busboys and their waitress, while Bela continued his thought. "When you have that kind of project, you want to be sure you've got people onboard who have cutting-edge knowledge. The only way to do that is to hire the best consultants on the market. Which you can afford, because you've saved so much by keeping the in-house team lean and focused on support, yes?"

"I never thought of it that way before." Dave made sure to sound impressed. "On my end of things, I'm so used to relying on institutional memory. Now that you say it, though, it makes a lot of sense. Excellent sense."

"Operations," Bela shrugged. "Which is why my role reports through the COO."

It was one of those moments when Dave blessed everything he'd ever learned about not reacting. The new VP of Systems Services was reporting to Kristol instead of to Matticchio; no one had said a word about this. He nodded sagely. "Again, it just makes sense." A harried-looking busboy set down their plates, enabling him to hide behind the food. Dave raised his Thai tea in a mock toast. "Bon appetite."

"Salut."

"Ah!" Bela said, a moment or two later. "This was a fine choice. I haven't had a decent curry since my time in Bankok." He dipped his chopsticks for another bite of yellow curry. "This is quite authentic. Thank you David."

"Just Dave. Glad you like it. There's a Thai place on every block in this part of town, but this one is the one we all like best."

"I can see why. Quite a Pinnacle hangout, is it?"

"At one point. I think there are only a few of us left."

"Understood. The modern workforce, yes? We've lost the concept of loyalty, of a job for life." There was that almost-grin again. "How long did you say you'd been with Pinnacle?

"Uh, a few years. So, you were in Bankok? That must have been fascinating."

Passing the table, they gave the Buzzard a tiny wave. He acknowledged it with a subtle tip of the head. They noticed he was with the new Clif; probably didn't want him to realize there were other Pinnacle people in the house. Funny. It seemed like yesterday that you couldn't walk into this place without tripping over half the office. They usually saw Dave here with Roger, and Chris and Liz liked it, but these days it was mostly only them.

The del Montes always lunched here on Thursdays, unless one of them had a business trip. It was the day between their work-from-home days and Martha wouldn't be home for dinner because she had school at night. Martha was going for an MBA. Gabe wanted to start the Curatorial Studies program at NYU, but they'd agreed that her degree would be a better use of their limited resources. Martha had built up a lot of equity at Pinnacle. She still held some special meaning for Kippy, Scott was used to calling on her and Milla Kristol considered her an asset. In this new era, there would be new opportunities. But there would also be new decision makers, and the del Montes didn't want to miss out because they came up short on paper. It was getting so you couldn't cross the street without an MBA, so Martha was working at collecting one. Once she was done, Gabe could make his first steps back to the world of Art.

It was funny, how he'd drifted away so gradually he almost didn't notice. In the days when every overtime dollar was going to rent and food, paint became a luxury. Then he fell in love with Martha, and his world so filled with her that there wasn't room for anything else. Except for a brief flutter, while they were preparing for Luna, art faded into a dusty memory. These days he had a family he loved with all his heart and spent long days working at a job that actually held his interest. There was no room in life for more than the plenty he already had, and yet art had returned to him now, slyly seeping out of wherever it lay buried to strike him with unexpected bursts of longing.

He thought it must have started that Date Night when he and Martha ended up at a tiki bar for a Stail Fiáin gig. Listening to the room buzz from all the part-time performers and such, watching Tully and Lily fussing before their set and then transitioning to their playing rapture, flooded him with nostalgia. He was working a lot with Dawn then, on a major client implementation. She was almost through her studies and tended to ramble on about her future career. That night, she laughingly mentioned trying to convince Tully to take the same course "and maybe he could get work at Lincoln Center or ASCAP. It wouldn't be the same as playing for a living, but at least it has something to do with what he loves and it would be better than dealing with eighth-graders." Her look turned to one of sharp assessment. "Maybe you should too," she suggested to Gabe. "You used to paint, right? There are art libraries." It stung, that "used to." But it also set him thinking, that maybe there might be jobs out there that would allow him to live in his own world. He couldn't teach, even if schools were still hiring art teachers; he'd worked through his MFA that way and he was rotten at it. He also knew from experience that he didn't have the temperament for gallery sales. He couldn't see himself in a library, but maybe a museum…The idea hooked into his brain. Those nights it was his turn to stay up with the baby, he started poking around online.

Around the same time, Josh was in a show at a small coop space in DUMBO and Gabe's chest hurt so much he couldn't breathe. He blamed it on the converted factory causing his childhood asthma to flare, but it was all the painters glowing in front of their work, and words like "Bienniale" and "Tate Modern" floating out of the casual conversation. And then Celia won an award at FIT and they all had to go to the ceremony, where there were more proud artists, and some famous designer he'd never heard of offered his cousin an internship. He was proud of Celia, and happy for her, but felt a phantom pain where a part of him had been amputated. On Luna's first birthday, he took her to one of those pottery places where he'd coated her chubby feet and hands with bright paint and stamped them on mugs for the grandparents. He was in tears when he handed the pieces over to the girl for glazing. "I know," she'd said; "those tiny footprints kill me. They grow up so fast." He'd been too embarrassed to admit he wasn't being sentimental over his daughter's lost babyhood but over his own lost soul. He thought he was doing a good job of covering it, until Martha gave him the Utrecht's gift card for Christmas.

The curatorial program was the candle in the window that was going to help him find his way home. First they'd get Martha's MBA and decide whether or not they could handle another child. He agreed that these had to be their priorities. It helped, though, to think that there were still possibilities

for him. And on his work-from-home days, during his lunch break, he'd take
the notebook out of his underwear drawer and sketch for a little while.

Δ

```
From:        Kippy Melcher
To:          All Pinnacle Associates
Subject:     Exciting News
-----------------------------------
```

Some of you will be happy to learn that I am stepping down
from my position as Pinnacle's Chief Marketing Officer!
Please join me in welcoming Zachary Gelman, who will be
assuming this position. Zach is a very bright and talented
young man with some great ideas to help us to shape our image
for the 21st century.

Kippy

Δ

```
From:        Milla Kristol
To:          All Pinnacle Associates
Subject:     Organizational Changes
-----------------------------------
```

The LC is pleased to announce a fresh new beginning for the
Pinnacle Technology team (see attached revised organizational
chart).

Vijay Jani has been promoted to Vice President of Development
and, effective immediately, will assume full responsibility
for development teams on all shores. In view of the shared
ownership of development projects at Pinnacle, Vijay will
report directly to the LC.

Bela Kovac will continue to lead Systems Services which will
now be appropriately located within the Operations bucket.

Milla Kristol, COO
Pinnacle Management Services

Δ

The new Chief Marketing Officer hooked a chair from the empty cube across
the aisle and plunked himself down. Rather than the "ease and openness" he
probably meant to telegraph, his sprawl made Judy think he was waiting for

a pizza. "Hey! Zach Gelman! You must be Judy." He was still waiting to fill out and had a voice that was unconvinced of its change.

She minimized her screen and turned to face him. "Yes, hi. Nice to meet you."

"Yeah." His grin was so wide, it hurt to watch. "So Kip and Len tell me you're my go-to person for verbiage."

"I'm a writer, yes. Pretty much the writer around here. If it needs words, it generally ends up on my desk. Except the Sales brochures and tear sheets. I actually don't know who Scott uses for those; I've always assumed he must have an agency somewhere. And the LC does their own press releases for the most part. But I do the demo kiosks for conventions and the client-facing release notes for new products. And the newsletter, of course."

"Right. I have to circle back with you on that. And you run the website." It was a statement, not a question.

"No," she corrected. "There's a web-master in Pune, and Len Strauss makes all the decisions. I only worked with him while he was doing the SEO project. And I wrote a couple of white papers, but even then I mostly edit whatever Len buys."

"And the SEO? You guys do that yourselves?"

"There's a consulting company in Mumbai. They did the analysis and told us what keywords to use for what page. And gave us a formula. You know, how many times to use a word."

"Gotcha. You have to give me the contact info, so I can touch base. How often do they send results?"

"Len gets them every month. He used to forward them to me, but since we stopped making changes..."

His nod had more gravitas than the conversation warranted. "Send me the last ones you have, okay? I'd like to review them before I talk with those guys. So tell me, who designed the site? It's pretty old school."

She shrugged. "They hired a designer a couple of years ago. I wasn't part of the process. Len didn't pull me in until it had already been up for a while."

"Well, you know, any website only lasts about three years. The technology moves so fast. After that, it just looks old. Boring."

She agreed with him. "It would be great to see some changes there. I once suggested they switch some of the photos, the canned ones that look like they were taken in the 80's? They said it was a waste of money."

He actually winked. "No worries. I'm putting together a proposal that'll blow them away. A new look for the site is just part of the package. There's an agency I know. Right on the edge, super hot. I want them to pitch to us. I've got a call set up for tomorrow and I want you on it, okay?"

"Absolutely. Thanks!"

Flashing a cocked-finger salute, he jumped up and loped away with as little ceremony as he'd arrived. Bemused, and cautiously pleased, Judy pushed the extra chair back where it belonged.

Judy took her phone off mute for the third time. "I'm really sorry." She hated this. She and the agency rep had been logged into the web conference for almost ten minutes now, waiting for the boy. He hadn't responded to any of her messages; she had no idea where he was. "Zach must have gotten stuck in a meeting. I'm sure he'll be here soon."

At the other end of the line, Sophie laughed. "Oh, he'll show up. He always does, eventually."

"You've worked with him before?"

"I danced with him at his bar mitzvah. Our mothers are like best friends."

Judy wondered if she was supposed to know this. Not that half the business in the world wasn't done this way, but you usually didn't say it outright. "Well, I hope this isn't holding up the rest of your day."

"Oh, no. My day is over. The company's in Boston, but I'm in London, you know."

"Hey, ladies! Didn't mean to keep you waiting but...Reasons." Zach on the phone was as floppily confident as Zach in person.

"No problemo, Zacho. Gave me time to put dinner up."

"Cool. So, you and Jude get started?"

Judy startled. "On what? Sorry Zach, but you never said..."

"Right, right. Hey, no problemo. Sophie's group does design, SEO, the whole enchilada. She's been looking at the website, getting a feel for where we are. And I sent over those SEO reports for her to analyze. What did you think, Soph?"

"Totally agree with you on the design, Zacho. How old did you say?"

"Like three, four years, right Jude?"

"A little over two, I think."

"Right. So pretty old."

"It looks way older," Sophie said decisively. "Whoever did the work was like a generation behind. It's just so static. No engagement factor. And the Flash is totally ridiculous."

"I hear you, Soph. My thinking is we rip it all out and start over."

Zach and his friend went over a few specifics so that Sophie's designer could start working on a wireframe.

Judy could feel the dollars mounting up. "Rip it out" was a world away from the "new look" he'd previously mentioned. The LC was never going to go for this. "Maybe you should also work on a more conservative proposal," she suggested. "Maybe a phased approach? Start by targeting a few initial changes that would give a lot of bang for the bucks."

Zach laughed. "That's not how winners think, Jude. And Kip, he's a winner. Got to meet him on his own terms, show him how the big boys do it."

This was when Judy decided to keep her mouth shut. The boy wonder would have to learn for himself. Let him show the LC his proposal. And when the fireworks died down, he'd realize he had to seriously recalibrate his wish list.

Zach was still talking. "So, Soph, the SEO analysis. What's up with that?"

"It's pretty basic. They did all the usual research, ran a bunch of algorithms. The keywords aren't particularly creative, but they make sense. If you're still insisting on organic search, I mean. Which of course is so three years ago."

"No, you're not hearing me. What can you give me as a smoking gun, to show these guys aren't doing their job? I gotta get rid of these clowns first, clear the way for you."

"Gotcha. Okay, I can put together some stats. Especially on sound-alikes. That's always a good wedge. And then I'll add in our research on paid placement, you know, compare and contrast. They'll look super old and out of it."

"Cool. So ping me when you've got something, so we can go the next step."

"Right. Bye for now. Judy, nice meeting you."

"You too, Sophie." Judy disconnected and stared blankly at her monitor. "O brave new world that has such people in't," she thought, feeling super old and out of it.

Δ

```
From:        Zach Gelman
To:          All Pinnacle Associates
Subject:     Growing The Peak Experience
-------------------------
Hi to all my fellow Pinnacle associates!


Starting with this issue, I'll be taking the lead on "The
Peak Experience," aligning our newsletter with the dynamic
marketing initiatives we have in the pipeline
```

No surprise, but we're kicking things off by sharing mondo
intel about our new relationship with Teclu Holdings.

Zach Gelman
Chief Marketing Officer
Pinnacle Management Services

Δ

No one seemed to know what the meeting was about. Since the invite had
come from Milla Kristol, Edie knew her attendance was mandatory. There
were the usual suspects: Ann, the Buzzard and Judy; though Judy's inclusion
might indicate nothing more than a need for administration and note-taking.
Gabe del Monte had been specifically invited. So, more unusually, had Chris
Keane and Glenn Levine. And Bruce Korn had dialed in from Portland.

Edie discreetly checked her watch again. Almost ten minutes. Soon
someone was going to suggest they call a reschedule. Chris Keane, her round
eyes rolling without pretense to the clock on the one solid wall, seemed
about to do so when the glass door swung open. It had recently acquired a
kind of bouncing creak when someone pushed it too hard. Whenever this
happened, Edie had to fight the desire to hide under the table; she had
visions of sympathetic fissures spreading across the glass walls, the entire
conference room shattering into treacherous splinters. Instead, her hands
dropped to her lap, to protect her wrists, and she discreetly bent her neck so
that her eyes faced downward. A vagrant shard might still sever her carotid,
but at least it would be quick.

"Hey, sorry I'm late. Hope I didn't hold you up." It was a young male
voice that didn't sound sorry at all. The moment of resonance having passed
without event, she raised her eyes. The boy didn't look sorry, either.

As stepmother to a recently teen-aged boy, Edie knew that look. The
elaborately casual posture, the frank stare, the winning grin. She used to
think of it as Russell's "watch me try and get away with something" look.

"No problem, Zach. But I'm giving a heads up that I have a hard stop at
half-past." Bruce Korn kept it matter-of-fact.

"Me, too," Dave chimed in.

Zach. Of course. That's who it was, Kippy's new CMO. He was
accompanied by one of Scott's girls, the blonde one, Diana.

The boy draped himself across the chair at the head of the conference
table, pushing back with his feet. His oversized sports jacket fell open,
revealing what looked like a black Ramones t-shirt. When Edie was a
teenager, that would have been too subversive to wear to school, and now
you could apparently wear it to the office and be taken seriously. Very

seriously. Diana wouldn't be hovering so attentively if she didn't think there was some power there. She was an ambitious young woman, subtler than Khosi had been but equally formidable for all her chipper voice and dimpled smiles. Judy said she had Len Strauss wound around her finger, which was no small feat. Edie shot Judy a covert look and received a nod in return.

"No problemo. You guys drop off when you have to. So yeah. Hi everyone. For those I haven't met, I'm Zach Gelman and I've called this meeting...You know what? I hate to think of this as a meeting. What this is, is a visioning session. I've called this group together because everyone here has a unique perspective on what Pinnacle is. The company. Because what I want to do is toss around some thoughts about the Pinnacle brand. What I mean by that is, who are we? What makes us special? What makes us great? Cool? So Diana's passing out some paper. I'm going to ask a round of questions, and you'll write down your answers. Bruce, when we're ready to read them out loud, you'll go first and Diana'll write yours down. Because then we're going to stick them up on the wall and see what we've got. What I believe is that we'll start to see a picture, and that picture is where we're heading. Okay, so the first question is, write down three things... use three pieces of paper, okay? One for each...three differentiators. Three things that set Pinnacle apart from other companies in the same vertical. Don't worry if they're big or small. Or even if they're negative! No judgment here! The goal is to find the differentiators. After that, we see how to spin them? Okay, start writing now! And when you're done, raise your hand and Diana'll take the papers."

By the time Dave got back to his desk and dialed in to the other meeting, it was already in progress. When he confirmed he was on, Bruce said "well, that was interesting." So Dave thought maybe they had the same reaction to Zach's visioning session, but he wasn't about to ask and open up a can of worms. Bruce was Kippy's best buddy for now, but this kid Zach was kind of his protégé. Who knew which, if either, would last? No; if Dave wanted to voice his thoughts about the new Pinnacle brand, he'd wait and have lunch with good old safe Judy.

In any case, whatever Zach or whoever came up with wouldn't much concern him. He'd use whatever he was handed. This other project, however, would actively end up on his plate. At least a huge chunk of it would, if it came through. He'd be putting back on his analyst hat. With ProFile bringing so much technology into the company, Kippy was making new platform noises again. In one way, it made a hell of a lot of sense. With all Peterson's big plans, scope creep had left Bridge separate from Denali and OnBoard, and the links that connected them weren't scaling to current load. Trekker had been completely developed on the side, with more links. And after a year, there was still only a crazy patch linking the old Raskub platform with any of this. Kippy was convinced, on the basis of their seriously slick UI, that the ProFile package should become the core of a whole new platform, and he'd already committed to throwing a few dozen extra Pune Fulfillment bodies on manual workarounds until this could happen.

Dave was all for a new platform. He had enough chops to know how tenuous the current situation was. Thing was, Kippy and the LC didn't have any more patience than Jake waiting to get pushed on the swings. Peterson had played chicken with them and lost. Now they had twice as many systems to integrate, three times as many kinds of coding technology, and resources in five different time zones. Dave didn't honestly see it happening, but the Buzzard's job was to play out whatever hand he was dealt, put a positive face on things, and make sure that when the shit flew, as it had to, it didn't stick in his vicinity.

Δ

"But now that you see them first-hand." Freddie started pressing for an opinion the second they turned into the alley.

"I don't know." With a non-committal shrug, Diego accepted a light from Danny.

"You don't know what?" Danny asked.

"If they're spies. Bela Kovacs and the marketing guy."

"Well if not, what else are they?" Freddie demanded. "That Zach? What an asshole. Do you hear the kind of shit he's spouting?"

"More than you do," Judy said ruefully. "Hi, Diego. So good to see you! Is this just for the day? How's life in Minnesota?"

"Pretty good." He gave her a quick hug. "I asked if I could come on a Friday so I could see my family. So then they said I might as well come in Monday, too."

Danny snickered. "Cheaper than flying you back Sunday night. Since they don't have to put you up."

"Works for me," Diego grinned. "I get to hang at Whine Bar tonight, then a whole weekend in Hoboken with my new niece." He passed around his phone.

Freddie, who'd already seen the picture a dozen times, continued to fume. "No, he's got to be a spy. Either that, or he's a friend of one of Kippy's kids."

"He's not. I asked." Judy wafted the lid back and forth across her cup, trying to cool the cappuccino to a reasonable sipping temperature without dissolving the foam.

"Okay then. It's not like Feldman's gonna pay for marketing, so it's just an excuse for someone to walk around and ask everyone a lot of questions. Which is what he's really doing, right Jude?"

"Sweeping statements that don't mean anything," she agreed.

"Maybe the new guys, the Tech-whatever people. Maybe they really like marketing." Typical Diego, putting a positive frame around everything.

And typical Freddie, shooting it down. "Teclu," he corrected. "Then how do you explain Kovacs?"

Diego leaned against the wall, tapping the bricks affectionately. "Funny the things you miss. I don't. Explain Kovacs. I don't even get what he does."

"He's the new Clif," Judy supplied.

"Not," Freddie grumbled.

Judy ignored him, hoping to forestall the umpteenth Freddie rant about losing Clif. "Except he reports to Milla Kristol."

"Exactly!" Freddie wasn't about to quit. "You ever hear of anything like that? Desktop support reports through the same chain as Fulfillment? And Pinnacle's all about technology, and I'm all we've got as a Network Engineer? I'm not saying, I know a lot and I've been taking some courses online, but we need more. There's all kinds of knowledge we don't have any more. I mean, the passwords. What the fuck?!" From the blank stares, it was obvious that no one had a clue what he was talking about. Freddie cupped one palm and slapped his other fist into it, hard. "Oh man! You didn't hear? This was so cool! So you know that Clif gave us a heads up when he got his walking papers. A couple of days later, Feldman calls us in, one at a time."

"Why Feldman and not Matticchio?" asked Danny.

Freddie screwed up his face in a caricature of shock at this idiocy. "Because that would mean he would have to actually do something. Peterson was maybe a dick, but he ran a department. Matticchio is a total wipe."

"And history." Judy risked a sip. Almost ready for drinking. "Craig always said they hired him just to take the team apart, and now that that's done and his contract's running out…"

"Done with a fork in it," Freddie agreed. "People all over the place and no one in charge except one guy who says yes to everything and another who I still say is a spy, because he's got too much experience to take a job being middle man for Kristol."

"So what if he is?" Judy wanted to know. "A spy, I mean. What's he going to do? Say we all work too hard and care too much? Imagine the hilarity at that LC meeting."

"Just burns me is all."

Diego gave him a friendly cuff on the shoulder. "Chill, Freddie. Is what it is. Nothing's gonna change by making yourself crazy. Find something to laugh about."

Freddie brightened. "Right! Like I was saying. So you know Feldman gave Lynch and Rosko three months. But didn't offer any retention bonus, so they started looking like ASAP. Lynch got snapped up almost immediately by Bloomberg. Walked into Bryson's office on a Wednesday and told them Friday would be his last day. Feldman went ballistic!"

Danny grinned in reminiscence. "It was classic. I could hear him through the wall."

"I know!" Freddie was smiling now, too. "I never thought Ben Lynch could be that cool. He says he told Feldman, really calm, that since he knew he was being terminated he had an obligation to accept a new job when it was offered and 'unfortunately'...how can you not love this guy, 'unfortunately'? That 'unfortunately' he had to start right away or lose the position, and he just couldn't afford that."

"Was it true?" Diego was curious.

"Nah. He took two weeks and went to Thailand. He'd been planning it for the summer, but that wasn't gonna happen with the new job, so he figured he might as well squeeze it in. Anyway, you'd figure after that Feldman would offer Rosko a retention bonus, right?"

"Feldman?" the others said in unison.

"Exactly. So then when Rosko got that offer in Colorado, and figured he'd need time to find a place to live and everything, he also gave only about a week."

"Can't blame them," said Danny. "It's not as if either of them is ever going to work for Pinnacle again."

"And if they ever need a reference, it would be Clif in any case," Judy added. "There's no one here anymore who even understands what they do."

"Exactly, Jude! That's the laugh. Seriously, I'm getting to it. So anyway, they're both gone. And Clif. And last week, there was a problem with the failover site." Freddie paused for effect.

"Wait." Judy remembered something. "That's all outsourced."

"Yeah, it is. But we run the VPN tunnel through the firewall. Which they had to bring down. And bring back up, which is when they found out that they'd chopped the only three people who knew the passwords!" There was joy in his grim satisfaction as he watched them absorb this.

Diego finally spoke up. "So what did they do?"

"Feldman had Kovacs call Clif. Took Clif a couple of days to call back."

"I bet it did," Danny muttered. "Good for Clif!"

"Well, only because Feldman was too cheap to set up a consulting retainer with Clif, like they did with Leon."

"Would he have wanted it?" Judy asked. "I didn't think it was Clif's idea to leave."

"Yeah, but he would have done it. He's got two kids and money is money. But Feldman said no. I know this is true because Clif told us about it, just in case they ever asked one of us to call them. I bet when he called, he made them pay up front before he'd talk. By then they had to. They'd called Lynch and Rosko while they were waiting, but they didn't call back either. Anyway, Clif said of course he didn't know it of the top of his head and that it was a stored in an encrypted file on his home drive which, he reminded them, had been migrated over to Kovacs when he left. Amazing Feldman didn't have a heart attack, paying for that answer! So Kovacs takes a look and there's like hundreds of files in that folder, all encrypted including the names. Which is when they called me in to do a backdoor search, except I couldn't I don't have the permissions to get past the master security key, and the only workaround I had was hosed when Clif's login expired. So Kovacs had to do it all by hand. Took hours. We lost almost a week. All because of being so fucking cheap."

"And short-sighted," Danny observed. "They should have at least made sure to get a knowledge transfer while Ben and Sam were still here."

"That would mean admitting that what they knew was valuable." Judy had a strange fleeting vision of a tall pillar of what looked like guano. A termite tower, she realized. She was flashing back to her first Monthly meeting.

"They admitted I'm valuable," Diego reflected.

"After the fact. The same way they had to pay Clif when they needed him."

Danny summed it up. "Reactive, not proactive. I see a paper in this." He was finally about to start leveraging his experiences for that MBA. He hadn't been able to bargain for any financial support, Channing's departure having left some scorched earth in that area.

"Whatever it is, it's working for them." Judy sighed. "When I think of all they've gotten rid of over the years…institutional knowledge, skill sets…all the good people. And every time I think they're cutting of their nose to spite their face, the company just keeps raking in the money."

"You mean Kippy is," Freddie corrected her. "All the LC. Keeping it lean and mean."

"And in Pune," Diego added. "Mostly. Pune and technology."

Freddie coughed up a nasty laugh. "Yeah, technology. We don't have a CTO and our SysOps team is all ad hoc consultants. But we're all about technology."

"You know Dave's gathering requirements for another platform?" Judy knew because he'd told her, paving the way for her to walk behind him, picking up the pieces.

Freddie hadn't known. "Another platform?"

Judy nodded. "This makes...what? The fourth, I think, since I came on board." And the final nail in the coffin, as far as she was concerned. She'd been through this enough times to be certain of how it would spin out. She'd slog through endless piles of boring but necessary work, making up for everyone else's lost deadlines, while simultaneously running hamster wheels on the acquisition matrix whenever Kippy found a new company to buy. There'd be no raises, no bonuses and not even so much as a thank you in return. Certainly no promotion. And with Zach in possession of the newsletter and his new best friend Diana at his side in the Sales Pit to volunteer for anything new and interesting before Judy would even hear about it, the only road to something better was by leaving. She still didn't feel comfortable about the idea of going contractor, but it might be time for a leap of faith. Bracing herself against a possible burn, she took a big swallow of her cappuccino. Milky espresso; she'd let it wait too long.

Δ

She hadn't slept much the night before. Now she was trembling a little and her throat was dry. This was never going to do. Taking a deep breath, she snatched the sheet of paper from the printer and marched over to Chris Keane's cube. She rapped on the divider.

Chris looked up with her big round eyes. "Hi, Judy. What can I do for you?"

"Don not in?" She was stalling. Everyone knew Bryson was on vacation this week. He'd sent an email.

"Just me," Chris said, flashing her patented happy grin.

"Then I guess this is for you." It was embarrassingly childish, but she couldn't help giggling a little as she said it.

Chris scanned the page. It didn't take long. It was only a single paragraph. Three brief sentences. Her eyes popped. She jumped up, making a beeline for Don's office. Judy followed. When they were safely inside and the door closed behind them, Chris leaned against the desk and shook her head, like a dog coming out of the water. "Wow!" she said. "Congratulations!"

"Thanks. It goes to you. I mean to Human Capital, right?"

"Yeah. And with Don out, that's me. And we tell your manager, and that's it."

"Okay." Judy smiled with relief. That was it. "No paperwork?"

"Not until the last day. You want your exit interview before lunch, so you can leave then? Or after, for more time to say goodbye? It's okay either way."

"Oh. After. You know. So I don't have to wait around at Whine Bar as long, if people want to meet after work."

"Okay then. Great. I'll put it on the calendar." She smiled again. Judy had never been able to tell how much of that smile was real. No one could be as happy as Chris always seemed to be.

Judy also smiled again. There was nothing else to say. She started for the door.

Chris called after her. "Hey, Judy. Lots of luck. Really." Turned out that when Chris really smiled, her eyes didn't pop out half as much.

"Thanks." Judy put as much warmth into the words as she could. She and Chris had never had much to do with each other, but she felt oddly fond of her just now. "You, too."

Judy drifted back to her desk in a kind of fog. She pulled out one of those emotional blackmail notepads, stamped with her name and the logo of some charity she'd never supported. The first two items had already been crossed off the list: "take home personal papers" and "remove personal files from computer". Now she drew a line through the third: "hand in notice." It made her giddy. She stared at it the pad for almost a minute before tucking it back into her bag. She took a stabilizing sip of the coffee she'd poured when she'd first come in. Figure two cups a day on average, that meant maybe a couple of dozen more cups of Pinnacle coffee.

It was the riff that would play through her mind for the next two weeks. How many more…? How many more of these meetings? A little before 3:00, Judy Schreiber sat in one of the sprung-back chairs in the glass-walled conference room. As always, she waited with pen in hand, said hand resting on the blank legal pad in front of her. Her other hand surreptitiously stroked the thickly-resined blonde wood surface. How much of her life had been spent sitting at this table? Figure five hours a week on average, fifty weeks a year for five years…easily over a thousand hours. Was this the last one? Once word trickled down, would they drop her off the meeting distribution? Or would they keep her coming in, necessary or not, just to make sure they were using every one of her minutes that they had left. It could go either way.

Through the glass, her eyes wandered over a landscape that had become as familiar as her own apartment. From this distance, nothing had changed in five years. Close up, she knew that the walls, still the color of boiled butter beans, showed scuffs and the occasional scrape where someone had briefly taped up a chart or an inspirational poster. Like the chairs that had seen better days, the fabric covering the cubicle partitions was frayed around the edges and speckled with stains. Despite the increasing gaps along the way, the maze hadn't changed in so long that she could have followed it blindfolded, instinctively knowing when to lift her heel so that it wouldn't catch on the seams where newer bits had been set into older, darker stretches of industrial matting.

It wouldn't have taken much to brighten up the place. A lick of fresh paint would have done it, but Feldman didn't think it was worth the outlay. The lease expired next year, and Kippy was already in negotiation for space elsewhere in the city. As befitted the national headquarters of an ever-expanding Pinnacle Management Services, the new offices would be housed in a slick, ultra-modern building with amenities like security cameras and a rooftop garden. The Sales team was already getting excited. The space would also be smaller—too small for even our severely reduced numbers to fit, making for some interesting conjectures and proactive decisions like Judy's.

The door's distinctive jounce brought her back into the conference room. She blinked and nodded at Hugo and Danny. Ann Ling came next with Martha, who settled in the seat opposite and gave her a friendly smile. Hugo flipped the toggle to bring the screen down and logged onto the share drive. Ann began punching numbers into the conference bridge; people would be dialing in.

Heels clicking, elbows bristling, Milla Kristol strode in and assumed the table's head. Edie was right behind her, balancing a stack of folders on her laptop. Taking the seat to Milla's right, she took a second to shoot Judy a questioning glance. Edie and Mike had written her references, the ones that convinced the recruiter to put her up for the temp-to-perm slot instead of the six-month contract. Judy nodded once. Under cover of laying out folders, Edie gave her a quick wink.

Every few seconds, there would be a beep on the speaker and another caller would announce they'd signed into the conference. Milla eyeballed the room and frowned. "Is Dave Broussard ever on time?" she asked testily?

The door to Kippy's office flew open, making Milla whirl around.

"I'm so sorry I'm late," Diana the Valkyrie breezed through, her apologetic smile in counterpoint to her entrance. "Our call to the logo people ran over. And I'm afraid I have a hard stop at four. Scott wants me available when he lands." Tossing her golden hair over one shoulder, she folded neatly into the chair next to Hugo's.

Milla's pursed smile was noncommittal. Before she could ask again, Dave arrived, spilling papers as he hurried to the empty place at the opposite end of the table. Martha discreetly bent to retrieve the pages as Danny lowered the lights.

With occasional commentary by Swati in Pune, Hugo walked them through the Center of Excellence requirements for the proposed new platform. It was all window dressing. In the end, all that would matter was what Milla Kristol decided she wanted; and she'd decide that without anyone else's input.

Not that it mattered to Judy any more.

Judy's mind began to wander. Not the way it used to during Peterson's all-IT meetings, when she could grasp the general concepts but the details were so much white noise that she would zone out until something, like Craig Parnes falling off his chair to riotous laughter, brought her back. She wasn't really daydreaming now. She remained present in the conference room, watching but seeing something beyond the meeting.

Across the table, Martha's attention was firmly fixed on the presentation. What Judy saw was Martha Moon growing five years in time-lapse; little Martha, now a wife and mother, and fiercely keen to have a career. Judy's imagination whisked Gabe del Monte from his desk to hover at his wife's shoulder. Sweet, decent Gabe; Gabe, the artist. Judy conjured other artists from the shadows beyond the table: the gloriously tattooed Orla, with her kohl-rimmed green eyes; Alex Silva, throwing back his head and laughing; Tully of the crazy ties, accompanied by Dawn of course; the art historian, Mia Freeman; and gentle Kaimi Poole, who always made her think of Will. She could see Will Compton winking at her, his glasses popping up from his nose.

Archie Gosh's voice came over the speaker, some question Judy didn't hear. The sound was enough to place her at the table, with Hank, right next to Danny. Somewhere near Archie was Diego, physically in Minnesota of course but, in Judy's mind at this moment, here in the room. Sweet-natured Diego, and his polar opposite, Jeff Curry. Jeff, standing on his desk right outside the conference room door, yodeling his freedom.

She would have to email Jeff her news; he'd send her a giant thumbs up, which would help when she started to panic at making the change. She had to call Mike. Ginny, too. She sketched in both of them, Mike's sparkling black eyes and Ginny's fluff of yellow hair, nodding at her from either side of the Buzzard. Noble materialized, giving her his okay sign. And Craig, making wacky faces. And Sid and Mac and Adam and Malcolm, Cal and Lin-Fei. And Clif—which meant summoning Freddie's shade from wherever he was in the office right now, and then Ina's, to peek behind Leon. Once she'd gone that route, her mind's eye ranged the rest of the office to bring in Gretchen and Gene Siriano and, because why not, Roger and Glenn.

The conference room was filled with ghosts now, more than the banquet scene in The Scottish Play. Her imaginary Marla arrived in a drop-dead cocktail dress and holding a brass plaque that said "Pinnacle Graduates." Judy could read the names, some of which she hadn't thought about in ages. Renee Ochs and Alan Reisch, Abby Witherspoon and affable, too-clever-by-half Lloyd Baptiste emerged from shadows and wisps of memory. Art Russo, Kay Kuperman and Josefina Vargas. So many more crowding in. How long would she remember all these names and faces?

"It isn't a question of 'nice to have'!" Milla Kristol's voice, sharp as gunshot, jolted Judy out of her reverie. "These will be the first features we put in place, not midway down the list. The first, or we can't consider moving forward."

"I am understanding your thinking." Vijay always conceded the other speaker's point. It would be months before there was a day of reckoning, and by then any number of mitigating circumstances would have occurred. "Of course, we will do whatever is possible to accommodate you."

"These are extremely high priority features, Milla. Absolutely." Dave Broussard burned with zealous accord. "We would want them right at the top ourselves. But first we have to handle the dependencies in Bridge and the patches. We have to retrofit the system architecture before we can add any of the new features..."

Milla jumped up. Resting her palms on the edge of the table, she leaned as far forward as she could without falling flat on her face. "I don't accept that!" she hissed. Yards away, at the other end of the table, Dave flinched.

"Milla, my guys agree." Bruce Korn was so much smoother now than he'd been when he worked in New York. "They tell me it's a matter of putting in the scaffolding before we add the bricks. Not complicated, but it will take time..."

"Not my problem." Resuming her seat, Milla glared at the conference bridge, willing Bruce to see her from across the continent. "I expect delivery of my top twelve requirements for a January 1 deployment, not end of June."

"So, Vijay," Hugo asked, pumped and cheerful as always. "How do we facilitate this? I'm thinking we run the project through Trim/Delta analysis, we can probably cut the time in half."

"Ahhh," Vijay tried to buy some time before answering.

Milla laughed her tinkling little laugh. "I don't know why technology people make everything so complicated. I'm told how well-educated you all are. You might try and learn a few things from Fulfillment and Client Relations. What is our formula for success, Ann?"

"We trim unnecessary steps from the process," Ann Ling said promptly. "And we put in the hours."

"Exactly." Milla practically patted her on the head.

"With all respect," Vijay said apologetically, "we have kept the proposed deliverables as lean as possible."

"There isn't a lot of wiggle room," Dave agreed. "Maybe we could cut a couple of months if we could throw more people on it...."

Hugo checked his notes. "The LC approved a budget for two additional developers and one tester, if Vijay thinks it's necessary."

We could hear Vijay's hesitation. "Ah...with those resources I think perhaps we can deliver the core and those twelve requirements, perhaps by April 1."

"January 1." Only those in the room could see the dismissive flick of Milla's hand, but her voice made her attitude abundantly clear. "That's my deadline and I see no reason not to meet it. All you have to do is make the effort."

Judy couldn't help herself. Why should she, this time? She had nothing to lose. "I'm sure everyone is willing to put in the work," she said quietly. "But what if it's not humanly possible to make that deadline."

There was total silence, in the room and over the conference bridge.

"Don't be ridiculous!" Milla snapped. Her eyes narrowed to a glare. "Of course it's possible. If people are lazy, they don't belong at Pinnacle. We all do what has to be done. Success takes sacrifice. Those of us who will still be here in five years' time will see the benefit!"

Judy met the glare calmly. Five years. The nest had grown tall over the last five years. In another five, it probably would be taller. Would any of us be among the last termites standing, or would a new colony occupy the tower? "I'm sure you will," she said. And she smiled, because it didn't matter to her any more.

The elevator doors slide closed.

The iris shuts, eclipsing months, years. The office is no longer our own. Passing through the lobby with our cardboard box or shopping bags, we say goodbye to the people at the Security Desk (if there is one). "My last day....yes...Lots of luck to you, too."

The minute we exit, our passport to this world expires and the strangeness begins. The familiarity of the walk, to the subway to the bus to where we park the car, unravels with every step. Behind us, the building has already flattened into anonymity. Along the way, so do all the stops along our regular beat. We probably won't use that branch of the bank, of the post office, again. The place where we ate so often they knew our order by heart is just another restaurant or sandwich shop. In any case, it'll be replaced soon enough by a fast food place or a chain store, once the landlords triple the rent. If we make a special trip back to that little shop where we could pick up a great birthday present during lunch, like the café, it probably won't be there anymore, or else we strangely won't be able to find anything there that we like.

With the routine dissolved, the significance of everything fades and the city slowly takes back its own.

Even us.

ABOUT THE AUTHOR

Lori Berhon has never made Vice President. Over several decades and across many industries, she's seen companies start and fold. She's been merged, acquired, downsized and frequently reorganized. She has never received options, shares, retention or signing bonuses or, for that matter, promotions. Lori lives in her home town of New York City where, technically, she makes her living writing.

www.ingramcontent.com/pod-product-compliance
Lightning Source LLC
Chambersburg PA
CBHW072111250626
47159CB00007B/2393